THE
SNATCH

BY
DAVID CHAMPION

ALLEN A. KNOLL, PUBLISHERS

First Edition

Publisher's Cataloging in Publication

Champion, David.
        The snatch / David Champion.
        p. cm.
        Preassigned LCCN: 93-081067.
        ISBN 0-9627297-2-8

        1. Title.
        PS3553.C32S53 1994   813'.54
                                              QBI93-22667

For Elaine

With gratitude for her unstinting friendship and
extraordinary dedication to the details of storytelling

SNATCH

There are 49 definitions of the word "snatch" in the *Oxford English Dictionary*. Here is a representative sampling:

I

2.   A trap, snare, entanglement.

3c.   A sudden twitch or jerk.

6a.   A hasty meal or morsel; a snack.

9.   A quibble; a captious argument.

II

1b.   To make a sudden catch *at* a thing, in order to secure hold or possession of it.

2b.   With immaterial object: To take, obtain, acquire, etc., in a hasty or improper manner, or so as to take advantage of a momentary chance.

4a.   To devour hastily.

5.   To remove quickly *from* sight, etc.; to hide or conceal suddenly.

6.   To remove suddenly from this world or life.

7.   To save or rescue *from* or *out of* danger, etc., by prompt or vigorous action.

14.   *dial.* and *slang.* The female pudenda.

PROLOGUE

THE bridges of San Francisco framed the town like sleeping sentries: inert but implacable. On Harry's map the bridges seemed more like the horns of a dilemma. Today, he didn't have time for the niceties of map-reading. The dock was between the bridges, and he was out of time already.

Harry's dilemma was simple. Did he try to reason with the captain of the ship about releasing his prey, or did he just snatch the con? The first way was the correct procedure, of course, but the captain would probably insist on extradition from the first port, and Badeye Iler could by then make himself as scarce as the tooth fairy.

Just going for the snatch could wind the cop up incarcerated in the hold of the ship to Tahiti, but he would count on the surprise factor with a quick in and out.

Harry Schlacter was getting frustrated in his rented compact car. Traffic was building and things had not gone with perfect smoothness since he got the word. Rush hour was a stupid time to be on the streets of San Francisco, but what choice did he have? A helicopter would have been better, but they are a little harder to come by for an off-duty cop from out of town.

Off duty or not, Harry wore his police-blue uniform. He wasn't ashamed of it. And it still fit him, seven-plus years after he first put it on.

As the traffic slowed to a crawl he wondered if his informant was playing with him: giving him the word on Badeye when it would be just a few minutes too late to stop him.

In the engine room of the S.S. Yemen Castle, Earnest "Badeye" Iler was intent on leaving California and the clutches of a certain cop. Greatly exaggerating his experience and qualifications, Badeye signed on for a spot in the hellhole of the ship bound for Tahiti, where, he heard tell, a man could lose himself in a bevy of amorous babes without fear of extradition.

Harry Schlacter had other ideas. This time Whistler and his gang had gone too far. They had taken out the best friend of a friendless man. Charlie Rubenstein was murdered. And they did it in a way you'd keep from the women and children.

This time they got Harry's dander up, and when you got Harry's dander up, you'd better keep your back to the wall and your finger on the trigger.

Harry was approaching the marina, wishing for flashing red lights and a siren, when he spotted an opening off to the right of the grid-locked cars. Harry whipped the car into the space, accelerating suddenly without seeing the young lad in the Corvette lusting for the same space. Harry stomped harder on the gas and beat the lad to it, only to discover up ahead a car illegally parked in his lane.

Harry swerved the wheel. The car hopped the curb with aplomb, when a ragged pedestrian with a cardboard sign materialized. Harry hit the wheel and missed the homeless man by an inch but crashed through a bus bench painted with the slogan:

Where will you spend eternity?

He glided the car, with its new accordion fender, over the side-walk as though he were driving a hydroplane.

He hobbled down the sidewalk until he came to the phony facade storefront dock buildings and he turned sharply into the first area to show him a ship.

The street front of the dock buildings had facade arches and pilasters and all the architectural falderal provided by a benevolent government works project.

Inside, facing the ship, were low, warehousey dock buildings you wouldn't find in any books glorifying the architectural highlights of the Bay City. Low, dull and dirt-white, they hugged the ground as if afraid of being shaken loose by some notorious earthquake or other.

The big boat at the end of the dock was a prone skyscraper as it slid out to sea, pulled and pushed by a dwarfed tugboat. They were head-ing for the Golden Gate Bridge (open up your Golden Gate, California, here I come).

San Francisco from the deck afforded the passengers generous views of its dramatic bridges and hills. Fog was lying over the far end of the Golden Gate Bridge like a goose-down comforter. On the hill facing the departing passengers, over the top of the warehouses, stood San Francisco's concession to the nation's colonnade fetish: the Coit

Tower–white, thick, cylindrical, one end pointing (accusingly?) to heaven, the other (apologetically?) to hell. It was the Leaning Tower of Pisa without the lean.

The screech of Harry's brakes pierced the revelry of the vacationing cruisers aboard the hulking ship and the gaggle of bon voyage well-wishers on the dock, waving and shouting at their departing friends on deck–reveling in the paper streamers cascading upon them.

The opening in the side of the ship was like one of those mouths you walked through at the carnival to get into the fun house. Often as not, it would be adorned with painted teeth and maybe a couple of eyebrows. Above it would be the open balcony where compressed air would blow up the girls' skirts. Today, the teeth and eyebrows were missing from the mouth, but upstairs the girls were clutching their skirts against the wind, not the air compressors.

It wasn't the kind of ship you'd be traveling on if you had any kind of bucks. Nor was it one of those tubs they painted all the time to make it look spiffy clean. Oh, they kept the rust down wherever it made sense, but the owners, a couple of Greek cousins, were not big on squandering drachmas. It was a cruise ship for bargain hunters.

The trip was half passengers and half freight, and it was a tossup which had the better of it.

There was another screech of brakes and the cry of skidding tires as Officer Harry Schlacter came barreling around dockside in the rented car that wasn't going fast enough for him. For a moment he smelled burning rubber, then the pungent brine. The car screamed to a jarring stop, and he leapt out as though he were abandoning a toy he had outgrown.

It took Harry only a fraction of a second to realize the ship had left the dock. The opening was largely obscured by packing crates. Harry dove for the crates. Headlong. There were no half-measures with Harry. If he'd had time to reason, he might have aimed for the slender opening left beside the boxes. On the other hand, he might have reasoned the boxes would break his fall. But Harry didn't reason, he just jumped.

In the fun-house opening, the crew was still hustling boxes of provisions, which minutes before had ceased pouring through the deck-level door. When Harry crashed into the cardboard boxes there was a collective gasp from crew below, and passengers above whistled, "Jesus Christ."

The cartons contained eggs. Omelettes would appear less frequently on the menu.

3

So when the passengers saw this good-looking blond fella leap on board over what had to be a six-foot chasm of water (which chasm, of course, grew with the telling), why, they knew they were in for more excitement than promised in the package deal they went for.

But Harry Schlacter, a blond bazooka matinée idol, angel of mercy, sworn to protect and serve, didn't hold still for anyone to get really good pictures. His informant said the pigeon was in the engine room, and that's where he was headed. Woe betide the mortal who got in his way.

So they got out of his way, but there was the hum and titter of excitement that went with him, right down the corridors to the bilge level. And, my God, this great postcard fodder was being dumped right in their laps. And without any pictures they could tell everybody he looked just like Robert Redford.

One of the uniformed staff yelled after Harry, "Hey–what...? Wait a minute, you can't..."

"Police officer," Harry shouted without stopping his breakaway run.

It was the way Harry came at you that made you think he was big. "Like a Sherman tank," they said, or, "Grant through Richmond."

"But you can't...not here."

Harry kept going down until he found what he was looking for. The door had a sign over it:

ENGINE ROOM

How thoughtful, Harry thought. Then, underneath:

NO ADMITTANCE

Tsk, tsk, he thought. Not very friendly.

Harry never went into battle without seeing the fresh faces of the lads on the wall at the Southeast Division station house, in the dime-store black frames with the fifty-cent piece of glass. The lads who gave their lives for the L.A. Blue in the line of duty. One single misstep, Harry realized, could put him on that wall in the black dime-store frame with the crummy piece of glass. So when Harry hit the engine room, he took his fear with him. He may have looked the swashbuckling bushwhacker, but inside his gut gurgled with fear.

The swashbucklers were all in the movies. They could afford to be cool, for what was their risk, a stubbed toe on the camera dolly?

Harry reached for the lever on the engine-room door, sucking in the dank air for courage.

Inside the engine room, with its hissing and groaning of pipes and boilers, with its suffocating smell of humid diesel fuel, Badeye Iler was already getting used to the cacophony of valves and pistons and whatever the hell else made this tub go. His job watching a couple gauges did not totally engage his intellect, so he had time on his hands. Time he used to think.

Badeye was a slump-shouldered man of unimposing stature, with an annoying chip-on-the-shoulder way of carrying himself. He wouldn't win any beauty prizes, even with his eyes closed, but admittedly, the off-cast eye was the eeriest thing about him. It made him look like he was always keeping his eye on his back.

He had pasty tan skin, and the perspiration stood out on that gooey skin in marble-sized droplets.

How much of the sweat was from the heat, and how much was from his fear was moot.

Charlie Rubenstein. It was Charlie Rubenstein sent him on the lam.

Charlie Rubenstein! Charlie Rubenstein didn't know black from his asshole. Trying to suck up to the kids, teach 'em to be white. You don't make white out of black, no matter how hard you try. Nobody knows that better than Earnest Iler–a man with a white daddy and a black-as-coal mammy. And both black and white are suspicious of him, as though he picked this white-passing tan color just to aggravate everybody. Like he was trying to be Michael Jackson, for chrissakes. When you were half black you were *all* black, and no nose job and skin bleaching would put him on the angel's side of the street.

Though it hadn't been his idea, Earnest agreed Charlie had to bite it. What he hadn't reckoned with was how hard Horseshid Harry Schlacter took it. But word got to him real fast, and, just as fast, he wheedled his way into the engine room on this Tahiti-bound tub. He took this moment of luxury to congratulate himself on bringing it off–room, board and transportation to a safe haven, with amorous babes that he heard were exactly his color.

His gauges showed him they left the dock. Goodbye, Harry, wherever you are. And good riddance.

"Jesus Christ," he said aloud when he heard the door burst open on the iron-grate catwalk above. "I'll be goddamned," Badeye muttered, "if the sombitch isn't Batman or some goddamn Superman." Badeye reached for his piece. "God, I hate that sombitch." Deep down in his heart of black hearts he knew the sombitch would dog him to the bitter end.

"Okay, Badeye," Harry was hollering, trying to be heard above the friggin' engines, and embarrassing the shit out of Badeye in front of the engineers, "come on out with a smile–and you' hands up." The engineers kept low, with their backs to the wall and out of the line of fire.

Badeye knew most cops would not blow you away for no reason. But with Harry he was hedging his bets. So he squeezed that trigger, but even as he did so he realized it didn't feel as good as it should have. The steel of the piece didn't feel cold and reassuring to the touch. The hot ambiance of the black hole warmed the metal so Badeye felt like he had a handful of puke, and that piece just vomited bullets seventeen ways to Sunday without coming close to doing the job.

It was a spray of bullets that would have made even the National Rifle Association blanch. Then the gun fell silent.

Harry crouched on the catwalk, shielded by pipes as thick as the ranks of a pipe organ, listening to the ping of the bullets striking the iron. Here he was in this humongous steel cave with deafening engines pounding away to turn the propellers that were propelling Badeye Iler to the bitchen broads on the sandy shores of Tahiti, and the fear and the heat welled up inside him. The spent adrenaline had sucked the oxygen right out of him and he thought he would pass out.

"Too hasty, Badeye," Harry shouted over the roar of the engines. "You gotta take time, you want to hit anything."

"Bastard!" Badeye choked out. "You got no business here."

"Charlie Rubenstein's my business, Badeye. I'm taking you in. Throw down your piece. There's no other way outta here, and you aren't getting by me alive. So use your head."

Badeye licked his lips while rubbing the gun against his thigh, as if that would put bullets in it.

"Drop it," Harry commanded.

"It's empty."

"Super," Harry said. "Drop it." There was little option for Badeye. The damn thing *was* empty, and he knew nothing would give Harry more pleasure than to put a bullet in him for resisting arrest.

Run for it, Badeye's fuzzy brain told him, but there was no goddamn place to run. And Horseshid Harry be closin' in. Son of a bitch. Harry was such a pain in the ass. Badeye threw his gun at Harry. There was no kidding around, he tried to hit him one last shot–but the gun ricocheted off one of those organ pipes and fell at Harry's feet.

Harry stooped to pick up and pocket Badeye's gun, keeping his own pointed at his prisoner. Then he descended to the engine-room level and encouraged Badeye, at gunpoint, to lead the way up the ladder to the hatch.

The captain was on the bridge at the mercy of the tugboat pilot. He sent his second in command to handle the unpleasantness. The first mate confronted Harry, all right, and told him in no uncertain terms that the captain, and the captain alone, held exclusive jurisdiction over his ship at all times.

Harry said, "This is a capital crime–murder–call the LAPD if you have any problem with it. Now will you radio the tug so we can get a lift to shore?"

"Certainly *not*, sir. You're under arrest."

Harry pushed Badeye into the water below, then jumped in after him, nearly landing on top of him. The freezing water instantly iced their bones. It felt good to Harry after the stinking-hot boiler room, but Badeye was no swimmer and he panicked, flailing his arms until he got a choke hold on Harry and they both went under. Badeye's panic induced superhuman strength and made it impossible for Harry to free himself.

The passengers had congregated on the fun-house balcony to marvel at the spectacle in the water.

Harry cocked his arm and drove his elbow into Badeye's solar plexus. Badeye tightened his grip–Harry felt like he was about to pass out. In desperation, he bit Badeye's biceps and plunged his elbow into his solar plexus again. And the panicked man loosened his grip long enough for Harry to get his arm in as a wedge and surface for a gasp of air. While Badeye was sucking in the world's precious air, Harry got him in a cross-chest carry and yelled, "Keep kicking, Badeye, and I'll put you under."

Badeye couldn't stop thrashing, but Harry finally got him to shore, then handcuffed him, which he would have done on the ship if the first mate hadn't been so unfriendly.

The first mate realized later he should have radioed the harbor patrol, but there would be all that unpleasant publicity, and this second-class line was having enough trouble as it was.

⛊   ⛊   ⛊

When he strode into Parker Center, the Los Angeles downtown police headquarters, after booking Badeye, Harry was frankly expecting plaudits for a job well done–perhaps a citation or commendation.

Harry had been assigned to a special gang detail, headquartered downtown. It usually irked him when he had to report to the Parker Center. It smelled of administration to him; of guys who chauffeured their way to the top. He couldn't wait to get back to Watts and the Southeast. He had been assigned to the Southeast Division for most of his tour, and he loved the action. That was home to him.

Instead of the plaudits Harry thought he would get for collaring Badeye, the lieutenant read him the riot act. He had no jurisdiction aboard ship, and rather than being a hero he was an embarrassment. Harry had to endure yet another torrent of profanity lightly sprinkled with parables on the absolute necessity of going strictly by the book.

Heaping insult on this injury, the lieutenant told him the "Powers that be" had determined they could not hold Badeye.

Stunned, Harry tried to get the release time from the lieutenant.

The lieutenant looked at his star trooper. Hell, he thought, I can understand it. The frustration is always worse for the hot shots. Nobody's more gung ho than Harry Schlacter. Must be eating him alive.

"Schlacter, I don't know what time. That's not my department. But if I did know, you're sure as hell the last person on God's green earth I would tell."

"Thanks," Harry said with somewhat less respect than the lieutenant felt was his due.

"What you need, Schlacter, is the woman's touch. When's the last time you got laid?"

Harry stared at his lieutenant, who knew as well as the next guy that Harry was a prude. Talk like that not only made him uncomfortable, it disgusted him.

"You aren't queer, are you, Schlacter?" the lieutenant needled, as though the thought just occurred to him. "A gay boy?"

Harry saluted and left. There was no mistaking the contempt on his face.

So Harry telephoned the jail, impersonated an assistant district attorney, and got the time.

⛉ ⛉ ⛉

Not a bad night, Harry thought. A reasonable night to be alive in Los Angeles. There was a touch of moisture in the cool air and the smog seemed to be taking the night off.

Nearby, the lights on the Music Center stayed on to make things tougher on the vandals. The Water and Power building water fountains' timers had clicked off. Lights were off in the condos, and in the office buildings all but a few of the obsessive lawyers had gone home.

While he waited, in uniform, for Badeye, Harry's thoughts spun with questions.

Why was he out here at two in the morning?

Why did they want to release the con in the middle of the night, and secretly? Did they think someone might go after him? And if so, who but Harry Schlacter could that possibly be?

Sure, Harry preferred that the system take care of Badeye, but the system had broken down.

Oh, he knew all the arguments: that he couldn't be the judge, jury, prosecutor and executor. But he had signed on to protect and serve, and he would be doing neither by allowing Badeye Iler another entrée to society, where he would kill again, probably with impunity, and possibly Harry.

And Harry's final question to himself was why was he a policeman?

Harry was the second of two sons. In his brother reposed all their father's hopes and dreams for a brighter tomorrow. The kid, they said, would be a doctor. He had the brains for it. Never mind that implicit in that wearing reprise was the maxim that Harry's brain didn't measure up.

Harry looked up to his brother. Albert Schlacter was almost four years older and was just a nice kid. He treated Harry like a benevolent father would, which was fresh air next to the *modus operandi* of their real father.

When you consider the size of a bullet next to the size of the world, it seems almost impossible to be shot by mistake. And when you diagram how Harry's brother got it, it seems doubly impossible.

Albert was out front, playing kickball in the street. The car sped by in pursuit of some unseen goal. The semiautomatic popped out of the rear side window and began to spray bullets. Some speculated that the fusillade was aimed at a rival gang–but no one could remember seeing them. All that was known was that no gang member was hit in that rain of terror, just Albert Schlacter, fourteen-year-old honor student, president of his class, eagle scout and model student.

In her post-tragedy hysteria Mrs. Elmer Schlacter railed most uncommonly at her husband. "Now will you *finally* take us out of this godforsaken neighborhood?"

The answer was, of course, no. They owned the house, and it would be a cold day in hell before they could ever own another in *any* other neighborhood.

Harry's mother pulled the shades in mourning–and, she said, to shut out the evil of the neighborhood. She never pulled them up after that, and the small house was plunged into darkness, a pall befitting a tragedy that never lifted.

It was in the emotional chaos of the aftermath of the murder of Albert that Harry learned about the murder of his father's first wife.

Elmer Schlacter had spent four and a half years in the slammer for slicing his first wife beyond repair. He claimed the butcher knife had been wielded in a flash of anger, with no conscious attempt at harm, but the woman got hysterical, reached for the knife and somehow got her throat in the way of the blade.

The story just came out of his mother's mouth as she withstood yet another tirade of verbal abuse from her hubby. Elmer Schlacter (to have and to hold till death do us part) turned a deathly blue. "Goddamnit to hell, bitch, can't you keep your goddamn fukkin' mouth shut? I'll teach you to fukkin' tear me to shit in front of my last fukkin' son." And Elmer went for the knife. In a flash of survival, ten-year-old Harry swooped up a kitchen chair and swung it at his father's hand, knocking the knife across the floor. It was the first overt act in Harry's life.

Stunned, the man reached for the boy, grabbing his shirt and twisting his arm behind his back until Harry thought it would break off.

"Elmer!" his cowering wife exerted herself. "Let the boy alone!"

"Shove it up your ass, bitch!"

Elmer Schlacter felt the boy go limp in his hands. His first thought was he had killed his only son, but it was no great loss–not like losing Albert. But the goddamn sissy had just fainted from the pain, and when he awoke, the patriarch of the household said to him, "You goddamn pansy. Your brother never would have passed out like a goddamn queer."

Harry decided soon thereafter to look into police work. Guys like his father, he reasoned, should be restrained from doing harm to the weak and innocent.

The big doors opened on the stroke of two. As though they didn't want to keep Badeye a moment longer than was necessary.

Coming toward Harry, Badeye was the cock of the walk, a man who had faced down the gas chamber for killing a cop.

When Badeye reached the corner of the city park–elevated above the detritus of its everyday life–Harry fell in behind him. Badeye turned suddenly and exclaimed, "Horseshid," and started running up the steps to the park.

He was no match for Harry, who made a religion of keeping himself in shape–he easily tackled Badeye on the grass.

As the wily con's nose sank into the moist green grass, he decided he liked the smell. Where he came from, nothing smelled like damp grass.

Harry snapped a nice new pair of handcuffs on one wrist behind Badeye's back, then the other.

Badeye wanted to put up more of a fight, but there wasn't that much fight left in him.

Holding Badeye's arm, Harry directed him to his Volkswagen Bug, sat him inside, none too gently, on his cuffed hands–then shut the door as if on a date.

In the driver's seat, he smiled at Badeye and gave him a playful wink. Badeye spoke first as Harry started the engine.

"Fukkin' sewing machine," Badeye sneered. "Fuzz on the take like you oughtta have a big-assed car."

"Now, now, Badeye, mustn't judge others like they were you."

"So what do you want, hotshot? You gonna waste me, get it over with."

"Hey, would I do that? I'm a policeman."

Badeye snorted, but seemed to relax.

Harry shifted gears and climbed the on-ramp to the Harbor Freeway.

"This thing's a piece of shit," Badeye snorted.

"I notice you were walking," Harry said. "Let's just rap a little about the meaning of life and stuff like that. I'm speaking, of course, of the late Charlie Rubenstein–a prince, Badeye–and you will admit you are a punk–and next to Charlie your stature is something between a wart and a festering boil."

"Hey, get off my case, man, I wasn't even indicted," Badeye snorted. "Shitty police work." He seemed amused.

"Ah yes, my boy, the system." Traffic was light on the freeway. Harry was in the right lane, the speedometer needle frozen on fifty-five. "It's a system that lets a punk like you take the life of the prince of the police force and get away with it on some flimsy technicality. Now, Badeye–you boys don't seem to spend a lot of time worrying about the law of the land, and I'm just speculating on how you would handle the thing if you were in my shoes."

"Charlie was gettin' too close to the boys..."

"He was trying to show the ten- to twelve-year-olds there was more to life than killing each other. So where's the beef?"

"Not his business."

"Rather have cops on your case all the time? Better than trying to work with you–give you an alternative to the streets?"

"She-it, you don't know nothin' 'bout the street. We ain't gettin' outta here nohow. There ain't no opportunity out there for the brothers."

"Yeah? Tell that to the black mayor–tell that to the black police commissioner, tell that to all the blacks on the city council. Charlie Rubenstein wanted to help, so you killed him."

"Hey, man, I ain't had nothin' to do wid it. I mean, man, I incarcerated, or I free as a bird?"

Harry nodded vigorously, "You is free as a bird."

"Then get these goddamn cuffs offa me. They's killing me."

Harry headed the car down the Century Boulevard off-ramp. Badeye felt another twinge of relief. He was going home.

The car stopped outside an isolated deserted building that served as a warehouse in happier times. Before the brothers took it in their heads to burn the neighborhood back in '65. Though this building employed fourteen local men, the owners threw in the towel after it had been looted and burned.

"This is where we get out, Earnest," Harry said, waving his pistol in the direction of the burned-out warehouse.

"We? Hey, man, you a policeman, remember–you no execution-er." Badeye's good eye was starting to twitch. "You said you wasn't gonna waste me."

They were inside the charred building, with the blackened bricks and the steel beams still intact.

"Now you just stand there, Earnest, nice and quiet like, and give me the details of how you gave it to Charlie."

Badeye stared dumbly at Harry. "You *is* gonna waste me."

"No, no, I hope not. Certainly not if you cooperate."

"Cooperate? What I gotta do?"

"Tell me about Charlie, for starters–how did you get the brainstorm to pull out his fingernails? Was that your idea–Whistler says it was–or was he really the genius behind that?"

"Stop jerking me off, Horseshid–I know my rights backwards and forwards. You get me a lawyer, you wanna ax all these personal questions."

"A lawyer? Why, what a good idea! But, geez, lawyers go with indictments, and we wouldn't want that," Harry said. "And the teeth, Earnest, you broke all his teeth with a hammer. This was the best friend your boys ever had. He was a guy who cared about them. He wasn't a cop, he was an optimistic social worker. You cut him down before he had a chance to get jaded. Hey, you know I've had a little trouble keeping partners–I never had one like Charlie. Here was a guy more interested in his duty than a free lunch. And the cuts, Earnest–the cuts all over his body and the ants–if you are in that line of work, I suppose that would be considered artful."

"I don't know nothin'."

Harry sighed.

"Now I'm walkin' outta here, man. I ain't takin' no more a your shid."

"Ah, Earnest. You wouldn't want me to have to shoot you for resisting arrest."

"Hey, man, you said you wasn't gonna waste me."

Harry was beginning to smell the perspiration. "Satisfy my curiosity," Harry said. "How did Charlie take it? I mean, was he stoic–you know, brave–or did he cry like a baby?"

"Oh, man, you know it weren't pleasant–took it a hell of a lot better'n you woulda..."

"I appreciate that, Earnest..."

"Hey, but I had nothin' to do wid it. I was just watchin'."

"Yeah, watchin'." Harry drew a breath. "Okay, Earnest, here's what I'm offering you..." He backed away from Badeye, keeping the pistol pointed at his forehead. Harry reached into his back pocket for his handkerchief, then drew another pistol from the side pocket and wiped it clean of his fingerprints.

"Here," he said, "I brought your piece from Frisco. I even put a bullet in it." He laid it on the floor a few paces from Badeye. "I thought a long time about this, Earnest. My first choice was to give you the exact treatment you gave Charlie. An eye for an eye. Then I realized Charlie would never have gone for it–woulda said we gotta treat you better 'cause we had more advantages. I never, myself, bought into that philosophy, but in Charlie's memory–I'm going to make it easy on you."

"You said you wouldn't..."

"Earnest, you got three choices. One, you run for it like a coward." Harry smacked his hand against the gun. "History. Put your prints on the piece. Two, you take yourself out like a man. Eye for an eye sort of thing." Harry stopped.

"You said three."

"Very good, Earnest. You got a good memory, and on top of that you can count as high as three." Harry shook his head. "You'da made it in the real world, Earnest. What a terrible waste. But, hey, I thought your third option was obvious. You try to get that bullet in me before I get one in you."

"How I gonna do that? You already got the piece pointed at me."

Harry smiled. "Won't be easy."

"Man, you said you wouldn't..."

Harry unlocked Badeye's cuffs, then walked around to face him, keeping his gun pointed at Badeye's gut.

Badeye looked at the gun down near his feet. The lazy mind was working, calculating his chances.

"Where's the bullet?" he asked.

"First chamber."

"How I know?"

"Pick it up an' look at it, stupid."

"You'll shoot."

"Yes, unless you shoot yourself, that's the plan."

Badeye Iler licked his lips. He had to admit he enjoyed more giving Charlie his.

Slowly, Badeye picked up the gun and gently turned it to look in the chamber. Harry told the truth, there was one bullet in the first chamber, ready to go off.

Badeye whipped the gun around, but Harry got him–Badeye's went off, but he was already on his way down.

Harry looked down at his adversary in the last throes of life. What a rip-off, he thought. An unfair trade, a sacrifice of a punk for a prince.

Badeye's eyes were open. The last thing he saw was Officer Harry Schlacter, LAPD, looking down at him. The huge, blond, lily-white policeman was crying.

POLICE stations always seemed they could benefit from the woman's touch. But though women began to proliferate on the force, they weren't allowed to touch the decor. A matter of economics. The taxpayers were always crying uncle.

After an unusual day of rest, Officer Harry Schlacter found himself downtown in the lieutenant's quarters seated again across the desk from the man he disdained as a passionless paper-pushing policeman.

The small room was as neat and orderly as a boot-camp barracks. There was no clutter in the lieutenant's surroundings or in his mind.

"So how was your day off, Schlacter?" the lieutenant asked, patting the tufts of dark hair they had plugged into his bald head in a neat row across the front.

"Not bad, Lieutenant–went deep-sea fishing."

"Deep-sea fishing? I didn't know you were a fisherman."

"I'm not–but with you accusing me of being a pansy, I thought I should do some of that macho stuff."

"How did you like it?"

"It's okay."

"Not a bad way to ditch a gun."

"Hadn't thought about it. I got no intentions of ditching mine."

"Cut the crap, Schlacter," the lieutenant said. "They found Badeye with a bullet through his pea-brain."

"Badeye? *My* Badeye?"

"How many you think there are?"

"They popped him in the slammer?"

"No, dingbat, he was out of the slammer."

"Oh."

"Schlacter, you don't look too broken up over the news. Not too surprised either, you ask me."

"Well, Badeye and I were not what you call close. I wish I could tell you I was sorry, but you won't catch me crying over him."

The lieutenant fixed Harry in his sights, then dropped his bomb.

"Transferring you to West L.A.," he said.

Harry stared at him, slack-jawed. "You're kidding."

The lieutenant shook his head.

"That's a graveyard out there. That's where you send the dead-end cops."

"And that's where we're sending you."

"Why?"

"Why? We don't question orders around here."

Harry opened his mouth to protest. The lieutenant waved him off. "You can't be that thick, Schlacter. You think there's a guy in this department doesn't know you blew away Earnest Iler, better known as Badeye?"

"These guys are killing each other every day. This is no..."

"Save it, Schlacter. We got nothing but surmise, but that surmise's strong enough to move you to West L.A. Just between us, gung ho, it's the last step before you're out on you' ass altogether."

"Wait a minute–you can't railroad me like this–you got some kind of evidence? *Any* kind of evidence?"

The lieutenant shook his bald head. "Don't need any. We aren't indicting you, Schlacter, we're transferring you. Look at it this way if you want. Let's say you didn't do it. You think Whistler and his gang are going to buy into your innocence?"

"Maybe they did it."

"Nice try, Schlacter. The brass figure otherwise. They figure you stay in the neighborhood ten more minutes and poof!" The lieutenant snapped his fingers.

Harry groaned. "The brass. We got so much brass weighing us down we can hardly move."

"Sometimes, Schlacter, you're so goddamn naive it astonishes me. You think you can win a war like this with the gangs? Human life's cheap out there. They'll keep coming at you till they get you. How many can you waste? Forty? Fifty? There's another fifty where they came from."

"So we should be intimidated?"

"Oh, goddamnit, have it *your* way. Jack us around like the Lone Ranger. I'll come to your funeral. I'll call you a cop's cop, but the old tear ducts'll be dry's a bone. And even as I'm paying tribute to you before the assembled troops–a full eighty percent who had a go at being your partner but thought staying alive would be more fun–even when I'm

16

bullshitting them about what a stud you were, I'll be thinking the dumb sombitch asked for it from the day they pinned on his shield. Protect and serve? In spades–but the stupid asshole didn't know how to protect *himself*."

Harry left the lieutenant's office feeling he had just reached the low point of his career.

In the corridor he paused to control his temper. He saw at the end of the hall what he, at first glance, thought was an apparition. He pinched his eyes suddenly tightly shut, then opened them to see a startlingly beautiful girl coming toward him.

She wasn't wearing jeans with holes in them–or exaggerated cowboy boots with three-mile heels. She wasn't drowning under a carload of makeup. She wore a dress! A lime-green thing, smooth-looking, the right size for her perfect frame–not hugging her cheaply, but cut with tailored good sense.

Her skin was almost milky in its purity. Her lips were full, her eyes were sparklingly alert, like a pair of diamonds when the sun was just right. Her hair was blond but not brassy, a darker, more genuine shade. And when she walked it was so disarmingly sensuous it took his breath away. She was getting close enough for Harry to touch her, and she was smiling at him–showing teeth of alarming perfection.

His mind was too clogged with her beauty to supply him with any clever greeting or any introductory words that he thought might set him apart from the run-of-the-mill flirt.

He did manage a sickly smile and an inadvertent jerk of his hand to smooth his already smooth hair.

"Hi," he said, immediately embarrassed at the cliché.

"Hello, Officer," she smiled at him, giving him another glimpse of her knock-'em-dead white teeth.

Harry found himself again short of breath. He was rooted to the floor, but this dream woman floated past him. She was a sleek speedboat, he a cruiser in dry dock.

His mind whirled. How could he stop her? He fell into step behind her and searched his brain for some way to get her attention again without appearing foolish.

She floated through the main floor, smiling at, it seemed, everyone. Harry thought, she knows everyone, I don't have a chance. And yet it was her air of unspoiled innocence that took hold of him. He followed her outside, where he panicked at the thought of losing her forever. "Could I drop you someplace?"

She turned and smiled again, the smile of a person who should be shielded from the mean streets of Los Angeles. "Oh, no thanks, I have a car." She lingered on his eyes just an extra moment before she turned.

Harry blurted, "Could you drop me someplace?"

She turned toward him and laughed light, musical notes that drifted on the air, engulfing him in her unspoiled charm.

"Where did you want to go?"

Harry stared at her, realizing how foolish he must have sounded. "Anywhere," he said.

She examined him from head to toe. She seemed to be considering the danger. "Okay," she said, and Harry dissolved into helpless happiness.

"You want to go change out of your uniform?" she asked.

"I have nothing to change to."

"Oh."

"Do you mind?"

"No."

"I'm not ashamed of my uniform. I guess I'm a little odd."

"No, that's fine–just I heard everybody else changes to go home."

"Yeah, they do. You sure you don't mind being seen with me in uniform?"

"No, no, I think that's admirable."

"Do you really?"

"Yes. Really."

They both laughed for a reason neither could understand.

"Come on then," she said, and they walked to her car, three and a half blocks down the street. Harry walked beside her, yet a half step behind. He was racking his brain for something clever to say. Nothing came.

Lela considered herself out of step with her times. She couldn't keep up with the easy morals of her day. She thought she was born about a century too late and could rather see herself on a farm at the turn of the century setting her cap for one of the neighboring boys. She wouldn't have minded at all devoting her life to raising children, milking cows, planting and harvesting crops, canning and preserving for the winter. Her mother was such an old-fashioned woman. Lela wondered if her mother had lived, would she be holding a job outside the home just to keep up?

Lela, just like her mother, would be uncomfortable with a lot of partners. Just one was her dream. Just one. She only wished her father had not been so set against that one being a policeman, because this handsome hunk of cop walking beside her, looking so ill-at-ease, was starting to do things to her no one had ever done before. Was it because he looked so helpless? This physical specimen who surely could have tamed the lions and lifted her to the ceiling with one hand.

Harry didn't look as nervous as he felt. He was angry, he was trembling. What would she think? He was some kind of sissy? He just couldn't help it; her incredible wholesome beauty just made him tremble.

Harry, for his part, burned with lust, but was restrained by a strange near-reverence for women. His loving mother, and father who abused her, caused him to become protective of the entire sex. Most cops didn't care for policing domestic arguments, but Harry enjoyed it. He liked being the protector of beleaguered women everywhere. He was not as adroit at handling a domestic case where the woman had the upper hand. In these rare cases he turned to his partner, who generally had no trouble subduing an unruly female.

They arrived at Lela's car with ten minutes left on the meter. It was a compact domestic product, bullet-silver in hue. They got in the car.

"I'm Harry," he said.

"I'm Lela," she said, and they fell into silence again. Then simultaneously burst into laughing. They were caught up in a laughing fit and couldn't stop.

"What's so funny?" he choked out of his laughter.

"I don't know," she said, gasping for relief. "Nothing, I guess. That's what's so funny," and she exploded with laughter again.

"Where to?" Lela asked after they brought their hysteria under control.

"Could we go somewhere to just talk?"

She looked across the seat at the big teddy-bear lug. "We haven't done too well talking so far," she said.

"Yeah," he agreed. "It can only get better."

She drove to a modest coffee shop on the edge of the hubbub. She didn't know Harry didn't drink coffee. She apologized when she found out. He waved his hand. "I'll eat something, don't worry," and he ordered a hamburger, rare.

It was one of those postwar structures where the use of glass *was* the design–all glass on the street for the customers to watch the cars go by. The solid walls in back kept the building up and kept the help's minds on their work.

Inside, the booths were red Naugahyde and the tables woodgrain plastic. The waitresses wore short brown dresses with tiny white aprons which Harry thought of as navel shields because that's about all they were good for.

The waitresses were a generation beyond the optimum for parading in those skimpy outfits, but not the least self-conscious about their ridiculous predicament.

"So," Harry at last found what he thought might pass for a bright line, "what's a nice girl like you doing at the police station?"

She smiled, and relieved Harry's sudden anxiety that the line, instead of being bright, might be insulting instead.

"Slumming," she said.

"Oh?" Now Harry wasn't sure–but she laughed again.

"I just got a job, and I was so excited I went to tell my father."

"Your father's a cop?"

She nodded.

"Oh, wow. Probably wouldn't approve–you being with a cop."

"That's right."

Harry blushed, then shuffled in his seat as the waitress set the hamburger in front of him and the coffee in front of Lela. "Guess I can't blame him," Harry said. "I'd probably feel the same about my daughter."

Lela's face fell. "You have a daughter?" she asked.

"No, no," Harry threw up both hands in surrender. "Never been married, honest–I just meant *if* I had one."

She seemed relieved.

"So what job did you get?"

"I was substitute teaching–I just got my degree in June. The regular teacher decided to retire. She was sick a lot and I guess it was getting to her."

"Yeah, I guess it could. But that's great. Where's the school?"

"A Hundred Eighth and Central."

Harry set down his hamburger and stared at Lela. "Watts! That's in Watts!"

She laughed. "Well, I know where it is," she said. "After all, I've been subbing there for three months."

"Yeah, but you can't teach in Watts."

"Well, it would be nice to get an offer somewhere like West L.A., but it doesn't happen that way in the city."

"West L.A.?" he said. "I'm going to West L.A."

"Lucky you."

Harry shook his head. "I'll trade with you."

"That's a deal," she said. "Why don't you want to go to West L.A.? It's the nicest area in the city."

"That's the problem for a cop, nice is no action. There are more law abiders per square mile than anyplace else in the city."

"You mean you'd prefer Watts?"

"It's where I've been. You want to do some good, you go where the trouble is."

"Well, couldn't you say the same about teaching?"

"Well, geez, for a husky man, maybe–not for a young girl." Harry paused to reflect. "What does your father say?"

She smiled that killer smile. "Just what you said," then she looked away and shrugged her shoulders. "What do you expect?–he's a cop."

"Sure, and nobody knows better how dangerous it is out there. It's a jungle."

She laughed. "Maybe I can make a difference, and instead of going out to be part of the jungle, they can join the real world. Wouldn't that be worthwhile?"

Harry stared at this vision of loveliness–unspoiled, innocent loveliness–and thought of his dead partner, Charlie Rubenstein, who wanted to make something out of the kids. Though he couldn't bring himself to tell Lela about it. But the terrible thing was he couldn't erase the thought from his mind that the same thing would happen to her.

"Hey, no–really, no kidding. It's not too late to turn it down, is it? I mean, when do you start?"

"I already started. I told you I've been substituting–I'm just on permanently now."

"Oh, but, Lela, no, really, no! It's just too dangerous. They kill people out there. No place for a gentle, beautiful woman like you."

"White, you mean?"

Harry was startled. He hadn't meant anything racist. "No, no. Any color. Probably *more* dangerous for blacks–but dangerous enough."

"Oh, Harry, really. How many third-grade teachers get killed? Probably no more than in Milwaukee."

"Tell you what," Harry said with a sudden brainstorm, "I'll take you to school and pick you up."

"That's really nice, Harry. You are a wonderful guy–but I'm not afraid, really. There are many more good people in Watts than bad people. Besides, my hours aren't going to be regular. I'm setting up programs for after school, some days before school, others to bring those slower ones up to speed, to counsel those families I think would be receptive. I'm really excited about it–I'm starting to agree with you."

"You mean, that it's dangerous?"

"No, that it's more exciting working in Watts than in West L.A."

Harry groaned.

While they drove back to the Parker Police Center for Harry's car, he worked up the nerve to ask her, "Would you let me take you to the movies tonight?"

"Oh, I'd love that," she said.

"Great!"

"But, could we make it tomorrow night? I've got to do my lessons, correct some papers. When I heard the news I was just so ecstatic I ran out of there to tell my dad. Besides, I just moved into a new apartment and I'm not too well-organized, yet."

"Where do you live?"

When she told him, Harry almost fainted. In a city of four hundred eighty-five square miles, it was less than two blocks from his apartment.

THE three mother fuckers were hanging out. Nobody was better at hanging out than Whistler, Bull and Moose. Badeye had been all right at it too, but Badeye was gone.

They were out in front of the projects–named the Oak Terrace, as though there was an oak tree somewhere. Seven hundred apartment units and not one goddamn tree, and they had the nerve to name the place after a goddamn tree. Whistler felt the irony to the tips of his toes. Whistler was intrigued by irony. Whistler wasn't stupid. His ma always said he could amount to something if he'd just find a legitimate job and stop hanging out by the chain-link.

But hanging out they were; three specimens of prime manhood, all three with their backs to the chain-link that purportedly protected the Oak Terrace from the streets. But, in reality, the streets lived inside the chain-link. And when an off-premises gang took it in their heads to invade their turf, the chain-link was as effective at keeping them out as cream cheese.

They were smoking cigarettes. They thought it made them look tough, but it only made them look like they were trying to look tough.

Whistler had one foot bent back against the chain-link. Bull and Moose were not about to screw with their precarious centers of gravity in that fashion. Stolid, they were. Solidly stolid, they looked like it was their duty to stand firm on the sidewalk, to lend their respectable weight to keep the sidewalk from jumping up and hitting them in the face.

Whistler's lips were always puckered, like he was ready to whistle. His mother, at one time in her life a fearful woman, found enormous solace one day quite by accident in the song "I whistle a happy tune whenever I'm afraid. The happiness in that tune convinces me that I'm not afraid." Someone had accidentally flipped the radio dial to the wrong station. And when her son was born in the back of a police car, not the same car in which he was conceived, she thought she heard a whistling noise from him. It was actually just the wind and the sirens, but no one could talk her out of nicknaming him Whistler. "I knows what I knows," she

23

said. Of course, his *real* name was Jason. The one they called him by in church, while she could still drag him to church.

At his birth, Whistler's mother was a strikingly attractive woman in her fourteenth year. Whistler took after his father. Whistler's mother often told him she would have married his father in a minute if she knew which one he was. It was, the best she could remember, a particularly busy night, but she had been able to narrow the paternity to two parties, but no further. So she named him Jason, employing the first two letters of "Jack" and the first three of "Sonny." "Jason's double daddies," she called them.

And with those sirens blasting away and the red lights flashing (those were her roses, she always said) and the rookie cop sweating like a pig and driving like a madman to get her to the hospital (he didn't want any mess in his car), she felt like a celebrity.

When he was born she thought he was special. After all, he had two daddies, and that was special enough right there. She didn't care what any doctor said; if you could mix the stuff of two menfolk's seed, it stood to reason that you would get some of each of them in the child. If the encounters had been further apart, she might have let the doctor talk her out of it, but being they were so close, you couldn't convince her for love nor money. Why, if a twin was half an egg, why not two eggs for one child? There were a lot of mysteries in life and nobody had all the answers: so she expected him to be special, all right, until he was old enough to form his personality and exhibit his damned independence.

It wasn't the physical resemblance that caused Johnny Walker to be called Moose. Though Harry Schlacter said he wouldn't want to have to pick him out of a herd in a hurry. Maybe he was built like a moose, and maybe he moved like a moose, but in fairness he didn't really look all that much like a moose in the face–except for the beard. He was more a bison than a moose.

Bull was a different matter entirely. There was no mistaking him for anything other than a bull.

Whistler was a bare bones kind of guy, the brains of the outfit, who packed sufficient heat in case his reasoning was not sufficiently understood. What *was* sufficiently understood was that Whistler had no hesitation about putting a bullet where it could keep you from annoying him.

It took courage to break the silence at the chain-link in front of the Oak Terrace. Moose spoke first. His voice was not altogether feminine, it was just surprisingly high for a guy of his build.

"I say we waste the mother fucker."

24

Whistler made a whistling sound, during which smoke poured forth from the funnel of his puckered lips, creating a momentary neat column of grayness which finally broke and oozed toward the maker. "Tolt ya. Too good for 'im."

"Livin's too good for Horseshid Harry."

"No argument."

"So what we waitin' fo'? Ain't no doubt he wasted Badeye."

Whistler shook his head in agreement. Bull's eyes never left the streets. He wasn't going to be the victim of a surprise attack. From time to time he grunted his agreement with his pal Moose, but he didn't see no sense in forming no words.

"Puttin' Harry's lights out, easiest thing in da world," Whistler allowed. Behind them the two-story pastel-green stucco structure blocked the setting sun. Here and there the skeleton of the building showed through its rotting two-by-fours. It was a testament to the shoddy construction funded by a benevolent government agency, haphazard maintenance and the mindless vandalism of friend and foe.

Whistler whistled. "Lotta shit when a cop eats it."

"You lettin' him off?" Moose was red with outrage at the thought. "You a pussy or somethin'?"

"Poppin' him, too good fo' him. Over too quick. Nothin'."

"So what you gonna do?"

"I'm thinkin'. It gonna come to me somehow."

"Yeah, meantime whiles you usin' dat head o' your'n, they's gonna send fuckin' Harry out to West L.A. or someplace."

"No sweat, Moose. He's fucked, no sweat," Whistler said. "Just gotta do it right."

From within the chain-link came the tittering of the female, followed by two young representatives in the post-puberty stage, tripping out to the sidewalk for some relief in the daily grind. One was especially notable for the large protrusions she sported in the area of the thoracic cavity.

"Oh, man, look at the set," Bull said. He could usually be called upon to break his silence at the sight of pleasantly formed young women. The boys turned to look.

"Man she be nursin', dat baby ain't never fuckin' go hungry. You ever seen anything like that set, Whistler?"

"Hm? Fuck yeah...lots of times." Whistler seemed distracted. "Hey, Moose."

"Mmm?"

"You ever think of Miss Wills?"

"The history teacher? Nah. You?"

"Sometimes."

"Wouldn't, I was you. She long gone."

"Yeah."

"'Sides, it do no good to think on unpleasantness."

Whistler considered this. "Weren't no unpleasantness far as I'm concerned."

Moose rolled his eyes.

Whistler caught the eye of a dark-complexioned, smooth-faced young boy heading toward him. When he arrived in front of Whistler, he stopped in his tracks and turned to look up at the tall sentry.

"I'm looking for a Whistler," the boy said, his high-pitched voice unchanged since his first word.

"Why's that?" Whistler said, looking coolly down at the lad without shifting his stance, which sent the message to the world that he was one laid-back dude.

"They tell me he's the guy to see 'bout joining a gang."

"They did, huh?"

"You Whistler?"

"That could be."

"What I gotta do to join up?"

"What you want to join a gang for?"

"Want to belong, man," the lad spoke in earnest.

"Look like you about the right age for the Boy Scouts. Hear they got a good troop over by the Baptist church."

"She-it. Don't want no Boy *Scouts*. I wanna be a *man*!"

"Wanna be killin' people, stud?"

"If I hafta. I ain't afraid."

"Killers can be killed, you know. How you feel 'bout that?"

The boy shrugged his brave shoulders. "Gotta be somebody. You wear the colors, you be somebody."

"Maybe be somebody dead?"

"Not much worse off I am now."

"What your mamma think?"

"Shit, she don't think nothin' 'bout me."

"Lemme tell you something, stud. This ain't the life for anybody's got another choice. Kids you' age shouldn't be giving up so young. You look like a kid who could make it out there."

"Say, boy, where you live?" Moose asked.

The boy threw his head to indicate down the street–"Over by Avalon."

"You a nice-lookin' boy," Moose eyed him with an appraising hoist of his eyebrow. "You want I should show you the ropes?"

The boy swallowed the enormous flattery he felt. "Sure," he exclaimed, eyes swelling.

"Hey, just a damn minute, Moose–you stay away from the kids. Kid, you stay away from this fag, you hear me? You don't, you liable to be twice dead to the world. Once for being black–that you can handle. But you be black and queer, you a dead duck. Now run on home and amount to sompin'."

The boy was not that easily dissuaded. "Hey, well, what about you? I don't see you out there workin' in the market."

Whistler smiled at the lad's perspicacity. "Yeah, stud, but I got twenty years on you. Things gonna be lookin' up for your generation..."

"Shee-it."

"Yeah–but you gonna have to participate. You pull yourself up, you can be mayor someday too. Stay away from this gang shit. It's a merry-go-round that never stops; so once you on it, you never get off. Go join the Boy Scouts."

The young boy looked at him in unbelief. "Don't shit me, man."

"Lotta guys lots tougher'n you in the cemetery. Now get lost."

The kid turned, then, as though he had forgotten something, turned back to shoot a hateful stare at Whistler and spit at his feet.

Like lightning, Whistler's hand shot out and caught the boy under the chin, the force of the blow lifting the boy off his feet and setting him down again a decent distance from where he formerly stood.

"Boss," Moose admonished Whistler with a frown. "Why you be go doin' that to such a sweet-lookin' boy?"

"Oh, can it, Moose. This fag shit gettin' to be a drag."

Lela's apartment was built into the hills of Mount Washington, between downtown Los Angeles and Pasadena. It reminded Harry of Pueblo caves. The garages housing the Pueblo cars were under the buildings–so Harry had a respectable climb to reach Lela's lair.

The landlord had painted the doors with Standard Brands

mahogany to complement the desert sand of the stucco. Each new move-in got a freshly painted door. But the painter was a young Rumanian who prided himself in setting world-speed records for door painting. Often the paint didn't stick on the door any longer than it took him to paint it.

Harry was confronted with such a door, where the paint was only three weeks old–what was left of it. Fortunately, the last twelve paintings had been the same color, so, given the allowance for sun bleaching, the spots were more or less the same shade.

Harry pressed his fingers to the doorbell unit in the center of the door at eye level. The door opened instantly.

"Hello," she said in her musically cheerful voice.

"Gee, you sure opened the door fast."

Lela hung her head. "I know I should be playing more demure, but, well, I was just anxious to see you, I guess."

"Really?" Harry couldn't believe his ears. "You too?"

She hung her head again. "Is that too forward, do you suppose? You better understand right now, Harry Schlacter, I'm no good at playing games! My dad always said, 'With Lela, what you see is what you get.' I hope that's okay with you?"

Harry was put momentarily off his track by her candor. "Well, no. Gosh, no. I like that. Should be more people that way. Personal relations be much simpler."

"Oh, I don't know. Sometimes it could be better not to blurt out your true feelings. Could get you in trouble."

Down on the street Harry opened the door of his Volkswagen Bug for Lela. "How nice," she said, sliding gracefully into the seat.

When he got behind the wheel he just stared at Lela.

"Well?" she said.

"Oh, I'm just so stunned at how beautiful you look," he said. "Speaking of blurting out your true feelings." And they both laughed.

Harry started the car and drove to Westwood Village.

At every stop Harry gazed over at Lela and let her loveliness engulf him.

"When we met yesterday I was too tongue-tied to ask what your father's name was."

"Frank Eberhart."

"Don't know him."

An awkward silence followed.

"He knows you," Lela said softly.

"Really?"

"And he's not too happy I'm going out with you."

"You mean I *do* know him?"

"No–but apparently everybody knows you, Harry. You're what they call a high-profile cop."

"That's not good," Harry said. "What department's your father in?"

Lela hesitated, checking Harry's face as if to see how he could accept the answer. "Internal Affairs," she said, barely audible.

"Oh," Harry grunted. "That's why I don't know him. Don't want to, either," he added.

Lela let a small laugh escape.

"Not a job I'd want."

"Why not?" she asked.

"Investigating cops."

"But if you haven't done anything wrong..."

"Yeah," he said. "Still, it's not a pleasant idea."

"You don't think there are bad cops?"

"Oh, sure there are. I know more than a couple. I just don't want to be the one poking around to hang something on them."

"My dad sees it differently. He sees his job as protecting cops from overzealous prosecutors; as helping guys who might have gone wrong. Sometimes it's only a short-lived slip."

"Yeah, I guess. I just don't schmooze with Internal Affairs."

"May you never need them," she said.

"Amen."

Harry pulled into a lot in Westwood and complained about the price of parking.

"We could have gone somewhere around home and parked free," Lela said.

"Yeah, but the car might not have been there after the movie."

Lela noticed Harry swallow when he took his insignificant change from his twenty-dollar bill for the tickets. Inside she declined his offer of popcorn.

As soon as the movie was over and Harry and Lela were standing in the aisle to leave, Harry began apologizing. "Oh, Lela, I'm sorry to put you through that."

"Through what, Harry?"

"The movie."

"I liked it."

"Oh, but the rotten language; I don't see any justification for that.

It's just another sign of the moral breakdown of society." Harry and Lela were out on the street, walking to the parking lot. "I should have picked a better movie. I'll never understand why these movie people find it necessary to have everybody talk like that."

"Why, Harry, how charming you are. Most of my third-graders use all those words we heard tonight."

"Really?" Harry shook his head at the wonder of it. "Well, don't let them."

"I try not to." She let a small laugh escape. "But they hear it at home–everywhere. That is a battle. I tell them they are in school not only to learn to read and write, skills that will make them useful citizens, but also to learn manners and social responsibility that will help them improve society."

"A little sophisticated for third-graders, don't you think?" Harry asked her as he held the car door open for her again.

When he got in she said, "Not the third-graders who use that language. You'd be surprised at the kind of sophistication they have. These kids have grown up with a TV set for a babysitter. They learn language they wouldn't get at home or on the streets, so that is good. But, they also see about two hundred thousand acts of violence by the time they are eighteen–and about twenty-five thousand killings."

"Yeah," Harry said. "No wonder we got problems."

"You think seeing it so often makes people *do* it?"

"It sure makes them hardened to it. Seems as commonplace as eating. You see more violence on TV than you see eating. These ghetto kids don't have anything else to balance it. No role models. Daddy's long gone. Don't read. You got to realize TV is probably their biggest influence."

"Think they'd be better off without it?"

"I think so. Do you?"

"I'm not that sure," Lela said. "I think they'd be lots better off without the violence–and some of the soap-opera behavior–but they do hear more intelligent language than they ordinarily get."

"Don't any of them have normal homes?"

"Too few, if you ask me. Some have a man in the house–but only in two cases is it the child's biological father."

"Did you have both parents in your house?"

"Till my mother died."

"How did that happen?"

"A car accident. Dad was driving and a drunk hit us."

"Us? You too?"

"I was in the car, but so young I barely remember Mother or the accident. Dad, I think, sort of blamed himself, but I don't know what he could have done to avoid this drunk who came at us out of the blue."

"So, your dad brought you up?"

"Yes he did. Single-handed. I love him very much. I don't know what I'd do if I fell in love with someone he didn't approve of."

"Like me?" Harry didn't look at her.

"Oh, I think if he really knew you, he'd like you," Lela said, turning up her nose in that way that drove Harry crazy for her. "All he knows is your reputation."

"Oh–and what's that?"

"Let's talk about it later," she said.

"Why?"

"'Cause I don't want to talk such heavy stuff now. Okay?"

She was so adorable, Harry couldn't deny her anything. "Sure," he said.

When Harry parked the car and walked Lela to her door, she surprised him. "Want to come in for a few minutes?"

"Oh, gee. I'd like that–if it's all right with your roommate."

"I don't have a roommate."

"Oh."

"You look surprised. Do *you* have a roommate?"

"Well, no," Harry stumbled. "But...I thought...well, a woman...this neighborhood and all."

"*You* live in this neighborhood," she teased him with her smile, "and *you* don't have a roommate."

"You have me there," Harry said. "I'll tell you what, I'll not only come in, I'll go in first and case the place."

"Oh, Harry–you're so old-fashioned."

"Yeah. That used to be a compliment."

"Still is," she said, taking out her key and opening the door.

There wasn't much in the way of furnishings in Lela's single apartment.

"There aren't a lot of seats, are there?" she asked rhetorically, wrinkling her nose. "Most of what you see are Dad's castoffs. I'm going to start getting a piece at a time now that I'll be getting a regular paycheck."

"How does your dad feel about you being here alone?"

She nodded her head. "Scared."

Lela sat in the straight-backed kitchen chair, leaving the careworn stuffed chair with the apartment-house stripes for Harry. He quickly sat, as though any hesitation on his part might cause Lela to change her mind about extending her hospitality.

"So, what did your father say?"

"My, you're a persistent one, aren't you?"

"If he said that, I guess I'm okay. Is that what he said?"

"Well, yes and no–not exactly."

Harry laughed–but with an uncomfortable edge. "What does that mean?"

"Oh, it's all just rumors, far as I can see."

"Lela–" Harry coaxed, "what rumors?"

"Oh, Dad says there is talk you might have–well, I don't know–they call you 'Happy-trigger Harry.' Said you might have killed a cop killer–taking the law in your own hands kind of thing."

Lela watched Harry. Harry said nothing.

"Did you?" she asked, not looking at him, as if to give him a polite escape.

Harry decided he didn't like her father. What was he doing feeding her rumors? Trying to forestall a relationship? "Did I? Did I what? What were you told I did?"

"Dad said you made a spectacular but irregular collar of a man suspected of killing your partner. Because of some jurisdictional technicality they let him go. But they found him dead–with a bullet hole through his head."

"Did they tell you they found a gun on him? Been fired?"

"No," she said slowly. "How do you know all the details? Like the fired gun?"

"It's what got me exiled to West L.A.–their suspicions. Nothing else."

"The maverick cop," she said with a beguiling smile. "You don't go much by the book, Dad says."

"Dad always square with you?"

"Always."

"Then I guess I'm in big trouble," he said, searching her flawless face for a sign of disagreement.

She gazed at him, steadily, mystically.

"I don't know," she said with a seductive twist to her words. "Maybe I'm a rebel. Maybe maverick cops appeal to me."

"Maybe I've been overglamourized," Harry offered.

The look she gave him tantalized him. Was she meaning she really liked him? She looked almost brazen. Nobody had ever looked at him like that before. It paralyzed him.

"Would you like to kiss me, Harry?"

"Oh..." Harry swallowed hard. "Oh...oh...would I!"

Why was she so much more sophisticated than he was? he wondered. He had so little experience with women. Could she have had much more with men? She was just out of college, but these days you never knew.

But, Lord, where did she learn to kiss like that? She was, he felt, part of him in those moments of intense exhilaration. Not only had he never experienced a kiss so delicious, he had never imagined one.

3 WEST L.A. was different from the Southeast Divison, all right. Trendy little boutiques and eating places where you were liable to sit down and use knives and forks. More trees, more lawns and people dressed off the pages of chic magazines. The jeans they wore had a designer's name sewed to the back. The babes were blond and tanned. Malcolm X was right when he noted black was the better skin color and as proof cited all the whites who baked in the sun to make their skin darker. And some paid big bucks to get their hair braided or kinked into an Afro. It was as though passing was the goal. Passing for black. Amen, Malcolm.

The cars too were tonier BMWs, Mercedeses and Range Rovers, Jaguars and Volvos. The whole place was class. Upper, upper, upper. And even the crime was genteel. Unless you were a lightning-rod cop like Harry Schlacter.

It was Harry's constant memories of Lela and his time with her that got him through the boredom of being a policeman in a low-crime neighborhood.

As his relationship with Lela deepened, Harry was screwing up his courage to meet her father. It would have been much easier for Harry had not Lela's old man wielded such a loving influence over his daughter.

All Harry had to do was drop into Internal Affairs downtown and introduce himself to Frank Eberhart. But something held him back. Did he fear making a poor impression? Fear the competition for Lela's affection?

Lela encouraged the meeting at first, then seemed to back off as she came to understand Harry's quiet terror. She finally decided the matter would take care of itself sooner or later.

The call came while they eating. Harry Schlacter and his partner, Billy Bartholomew, were just beginning to wolf down the pizza at the tiny round table on the patio of Mario's Italian Delicatessen in Brentwood. Harry always parked the LAPD black and white where he could hear the radio because Harry liked nothing better than answering calls. His partner liked nothing better than eating.

Billy was a good old boy–very likable. He'd joined the police force for financial security. His father was a bounder, and they never knew where their next burger and fries were coming from.

"Way I see it," he told Harry their first day in the car together, "I put in my twenty and I'm outta here with a cushy pension, no worries. All I gotta do is stay the hell alive."

"Yeah," Harry said, "and watch your language. No man is made bigger by letting his vocabulary slip down into the gutter."

"What's that?" Billy Bartholomew asked, as though his hearing mechanisms were out of whack. "Hell? You're talking about *hell* being a bad word? Jesus Christ, where the fuck you been all your life? They talk like fukkin' girl scouts out in Watts?"

"No, the criminals talk pretty much like you. Our side's supposed to set an example."

"I mean, Jeezuz Chreeist," Billy said in abject wonderment. "I never heard so goddamn much shit in my life. Son of a bitch!"

"Finished?" Harry asked. "You got any more in your repertoire you want to impress me with, Billy? You sure know a lot of the big ones."

"Holy shit."

Billy Bartholomew, amiable as he was, embodied for Harry all the worst traits of policemen. He liked to malinger; he liked to eat popped meals. He was in no hurry to answer a call. "Maybe someone else'll get it," was his favorite.

"Come on, Billy," Harry would say, pounding him on his shoulder (Harry was already on his feet, Billy was still chewing), "earn your keep."

Usually Billy would hoist himself, with a show of martyrdom to be sure, and make a pass at earning his keep.

Not tonight.

The car radio crackled at the curb. Harry perked to the call.

"Let's go," Harry said, taking a last bite and getting up.

Billy kept his seat. "Go where?" he asked, chewing intently on a wad of mozzarella.

"The call, didn't you hear it? We're only three blocks. It's a domestic."

"Aw," Billy waved a slice of pizza at Harry in dismissal. "If half the dames called in their husbands were killing them got theirs, there wouldn't be room in the cemeteries..."

"You coming?" Harry asked, his mouth a twisted challenge.

"Let someone else buy the call," Billy said, shifting uncomfortably in his chair now. "Even cops are entitled to eat."

Harry took a couple of bills from his pocket and threw them on the table. "Take care of the check, partner," he said.

Billy smiled a smile of relief. He would wait until Harry was around the corner to put the money in his pocket. Of course, when he finished eating he would ask the clerk as always, "What do I owe you?" but they would always smile and say, "It's on the house." He was glad Harry was gone. Always embarrassed him to have Harry insist on paying his. A real pain in the ass.

Harry jumped into the car, the pulse racing in his large, muscular tailback's body, his full head of dirty-blond hair flapping in the cool breeze. His hair was cut much the same as it was when he got his first haircut: full on top, shorter on the sides, and it sat on a large, menacing head that seemed pushed too close to his body by all the linebackers who stopped it with their guts.

He picked up the car mike and called in he was buying the call. He drove through the tiny commercial core of the area, a reluctant concession to the necessity of commerce, and went straight up Barrington, feeling the exhilaration he always felt when he answered an "armed and dangerous" call.

He never could get too excited about eating so close to midnight anyway. There was plenty of time to eat while he was off duty; why waste time that could be spent productively?

The night was cool and the stars were blanked out by the low clouds as Harry raced without his siren to the appointed address. The street was lined with hotel-sized houses and football-field lawns.

Harry was grateful for the call. He'd begun worrying about spending so much time thinking about Lela. There was just so little competition for his thoughts in this graveyard. West L.A. was a lousy part of town for action, and Harry felt like a taxi driver cruising the streets for a fare. A domestic was a big deal here–at the Southeast he'd handle one every night. He thought of the one he was called on when he had gotten out of the car and heard the shot and dove for the ground. His partner, not as quick, took a bullet in the leg before Harry shot in the dark and brought the sniper down.

But he couldn't imagine a sniper in West L.A. He missed the Southeast. Cops may be hated out in Watts, but they weren't looked down on. The worst thing about the new assignment was the way the citizens seemed to patronize him.

The police weren't called to referee family squabbles here. Rich couples had a way of fighting it out in the same manner they worked and played: exclusively. No need to sully a good fight with a dirty policeman.

Well, they called the cops this time, and here he was.

Harry saw the elephantine figure first as he stopped the car at the curb and jumped out, his gun dangling, and darted to the lawn, behind a yellow hibiscus.

The house was a pastiche palazzo, like a pregnant Pizza Hut, with columns and arches, stucco and red tile.

The light from the house was warm and cheery, as though the loving couple who inhabited this palace, the size of Harry's twenty-unit apartment building, were cuddling by the fire instead of shouting at each other–he from the second-story balcony just over the heavy oak carved entry door, she from inside the bedroom.

The palazzo seemed to have an identity crisis–half Italian, half Spanish and all glitz.

The fiery tempers were legitimate Latin, though Harry was too far away to make out any features. All he saw was a seriously overweight man naked on his balcony, waving his shotgun like a drunken sailor.

Harry caught a quick glimpse of the outline of a woman through the French doors. He instantly thought of his girlfriend and the terror he would feel if she were on the wrong end of a shotgun.

"Drop it," Harry yelled.

The dancing elephant looked down his nose, across the wrought-iron railing, into the yard below, at the uniformed apparition.

"Up yours, fuzz," he said, and turned back to the business at hand.

Harry tightened his grip on the 9 mm in his hand.

The man on the balcony turned his back on Harry as though he didn't exist.

"Whore!" he shouted with a saliva assist into the room.

Harry advanced to cover himself behind a clump of bushes closer to the house. Harry judged the man to be in his late fifties, paunchy, certainly in no shape to be displaying himself naked.

Here through the balcony doors Harry got a better look at the woman. She seemed to be pleading with the naked man. She was blond with a drop-dead figure, inadequately wrapped in a flimsy peach negligee. She was a good twenty-five years younger than the man. Harry yelled again, "Police! Freeze!" The man ignored him.

A scene from the past flashed across Harry's mind. Another naked man: in a cheap motel room with a tittering black girl. Suddenly, he felt again the sickness and the shame.

On the balcony ahead of him now, the man shouted, "Whore," at the woman, while the woman was shrieking hysterically..."Go ahead; you don't have the nerve!" Then, "Go ahead and kill me!"

Harry advanced closer while the man's back was turned, and he thought he saw the man suddenly raise the shotgun. Harry fired a shot, and the man fell forward through the French doors into the arms of the hysterical woman. Startled, she pushed him back and watched, her pretty face frozen in distorted horror, as he fell over the balcony railing to the ground.

Harry's mind shot back to the cheap motel room. The naked man in his memory was crying like a baby. It was his father, and another death.

The slam of a door behind him snapped Harry's memory. He looked across the street to see the dark house screened by three towering, cowering sycamores in the front lawn. There was no further sign of life. Funny, he thought, I didn't see anyone come out of that house.

Harry radioed for an ambulance, but he could tell from the hit that his marksmanship had been as precise as always and the ambulance would be superfluous. The pretty woman was leaning over the balcony, her jaw slack, her eyes bulging, looking at the dead man. "You killed him," she said, sobbing incredulously. "*You killed him!*"

Harry smiled to himself. "Yes, ma'am," he told himself, "about two-tenths of a second before he was going to kill you."

The light from the bedroom shone through her negligee, and Harry swallowed hard. She was showing more of her perfect body than he had seen of Lela's. He had seen a million of these bimbos, out for what they could get. Guys old enough to be their fathers. Bet she wasn't even married to him. Wasn't much different from Watts. Different color skin, bigger houses, but people are people no matter how you slice it. Scratch any of them and underneath you hear a heart ticking, "Me, me, me."

The ambulance pulled up and the paramedics got out and glanced at Harry with twisted lips and slitty eyes that told Harry he could not relax with them. The paramedics went over to the body, and with a cursory check, one shook his head and came back for a stretcher.

"We'll take him to the morgue," he said, sighing and shaking his head at Harry.

The other paramedic, short and perspiring, with muttonchop whiskers, came back and looked at Harry. He whistled through barely parted lips.

"You know who you bagged, trooper?" he asked.

"Never saw him before," Harry bristled, as though he were being accused of murder.

"Well, I wouldn't want to be in your shoes when they look into this one."

Harry looked at him, struck dumb by the accusation in his voice.

And, the paramedic told him who he had just killed.

4 THE mandatory three days off after being involved in a shooting and the requisite chat with the psychologist never sat too well on Harry. "Sure it's tough," he would respond about his 'feelings,' "but it would be a lot tougher if it had been the other way around."

After a couple more shootings the psychologist was saying, "Oh, it's you again."

And Harry would say, "Yes, and little as I like coming here, it beats getting my picture on the wall."

The fat folder sat on the desk in front of Frank Eberhart, Internal Affairs. He leafed absentmindedly through the stacks of papers, then straightened the edges neatly and stared down at the mug shot of Schlacter, Harry. The full lips twisted slightly in impatience, the round, recessed eyes drawn narrow by suspicion; the head of an athlete, Frank thought, and then, for some reason, perhaps a fleeting thought of his daughter, Frank was struck by the youth of the man, and he ran his hand quickly over his thin, gray hair, slicked back as he had always worn it, without concession to fads.

He shifted his narrow body in the institutional chair and looked across the aisle at the young secretary, who sat reading the paper. On the wall over her desk was a magazine advertisement showing the rear view of the bottom of a shapely girl with PEPE LOPEZ TEQUILA printed on her bikini panties. Frank had always admired the picture and the secretary, whose name was Lopez. It was a tossup as to which had the better behind, but admiring the picture was safer. He mused that some thought Internal Affairs was harder on sex offenders than on killers.

His colleagues were busy on the telephone, their desks shambles of papers strewn and intermingled with folders, pencils, paper clips. Mayhem. Frank's desk was clear except for the fat folder marked in grease pencil:

Schlacter, Harry

Frank rubbed his forehead with a slow, pensive motion. So many contradictions, he thought. How could one man be so good to some and so evil to others? Well, he thought, he would, as he had always done, make up his own mind.

He wanted to know as much as he could about Schlacter, Harry, so he was happy to get the case.

By the time Harry Schlacter walked into the Internal Affairs division, Frank Eberhart thought he knew him inside and out.

Frank smiled and rose to greet Harry. "I'm Frank Eberhart," he said, offering his hand, which Harry shook with a frown.

"Thank you for coming, Officer," Frank said. "Have a seat."

Harry regarded Frank with curious disdain. "I'll stand," he said curtly, looking down on the slight body with the gently sloping shoulders, the rimless glasses, the neat, inexpensive suit and plain tie. An accountant, Harry thought, then glanced quickly at the other two men in the room, both in shirtsleeves, one with the tie pulled open at the neck, the other with no tie.

Frank noticed the inspection, smiled to himself and then sat back in the chair as if the weight of the case put him there against his will.

Frank looked up at the strapping cop. More fit and muscular than he had discerned from the mug shot, but the smirk on the lips was the same.

"Sure you won't sit down?"

"I get nervous when I sit in one place too long."

"It's a little hard on my neck to look up at you. If you were only four feet tall it wouldn't be so bad."

Harry shrugged. "I'm not here by choice," he said.

Frank smiled as he looked up into Harry's eyes. "Neither am I," he said softly.

Harry looked away. Frank got to his feet. Harry looked back at him, his eyebrow arching.

Harry Schlacter wasn't sure whether or not he should regret procrastinating about meeting Lela's father, Frank Eberhart. He hadn't wanted to soil himself with any kind of intercourse with anyone from Internal Affairs; yet, surely, it might have made things easier for him today if he had.

"Well, I've been over everything," Frank said, dropping his hand to the folder. "Not just this incident, but all the others." He let the sentence hang, begging a response. None came. "When I finished it all the first time I said to myself, that's some cop. The magic word is more. Always more. When he was on traffic he wrote more tickets than anyone else, in the car he had more arrests, got more convictions because he never went to court unprepared, got more letters of commendation than I've ever seen for a cop so young. That's the plus side." He looked at Harry, trying to divine some reaction, but found nothing in that impassive face.

"But, he also had more partners, an average of three a week, and then there's the reason for the investigation: more killings..."

"Yeah, well, I don't need a recap of my career," Harry said. "They said you wanted to see me, so, what is it? I've got better things to do than amuse Internal Affairs." As soon as he said it, Harry regretted it. He wanted to make a good impression on Lela's father. Perhaps if Harry had made the effort to meet Frank before... But, he thought, at least I should be civil–but I'm more uptight here than I am facing a killer in the streets.

Frank looked at him, his eyes weary. "Every cop investigated is insulted. Why don't you try to make the best of it? I'm on your side. I'm a cop too, you know."

"Not my kind of cop," Harry muttered, tasting bitterness.

"Oh?" Frank said, eying him like he did everything else: gently.

Harry never knew when to keep his mouth shut. He was known for not only biting the hand that fed him but devouring the whole body as well. "You poques," he said, his cheeks contorting, "sit around passing judgment on the real cops like you're some high-and-mighty gods or something. And, how would you ever know what it's like on the street? Your books are written by the paper cops, who never experienced any more street than being the chief's chauffeur or moonlighting at funerals. You're wasting all this time hunting down cops when you ought to be out there fighting the real war."

Frank blanched. Harry hit a nerve. How could Frank explain? Harry was the last person who would understand.

Frank thought if he could only teach him a little restraint, Harry would truly be *numero uno*. Of course he realized that if you took the essence from the wine, you were left with vinegar.

"Now that you got that off your chest," Frank said, recovering and looking up at Harry, "can we talk?"

"I got nothing to say. I did my duty."

"It's not what you do always that gets you in trouble, Harry. It's how you do it."

Harry's eyes showed a flicker of surprise. "What's that supposed to mean?"

"Let's look at this incident," Frank said patiently. "You were out there alone–highly dangerous, number one; number two, against regulations; and number three, you didn't have a partner to back you up–to corroborate your story."

Frank looked thoughtfully out the window at the hazy city. He turned back to Harry. "You know, sometimes the word of two cops is taken over one citizen." He smiled ruefully, trying to win Harry's confidence.

"Yeah, sure," Harry said. "It's easy for you desk guys to talk department regulations, when you're not on the firing line."

Frank waved a weary hand at Harry. Didn't he know he had overworked that already? "Why did you answer the call?" he asked simply.

"We were three blocks away," Harry said, shocked at the stupidity of the question, and not hiding it from Frank.

"You were having dinner."

Harry shrugged. "Plenty of time for that."

"But your partner refused to go."

"That's his problem."

"You're entitled to dinner, Harry. You aren't the only cop on the force."

Harry snorted. "You ever see the West L.A. gang?"

Frank shook his head. "I don't care, Harry. You can't do it all. Everybody appreciates your zeal, but they want to play the game according to the rules."

Harry leaned toward Frank, poking a finger of a gun-conformed hand at his chest. "He was going to kill that woman if I didn't stop him."

"Too bad his shotgun was empty," Frank said, softly.

"Yeah," Harry mused, "isn't that a pistol? A real shame she didn't tell us that when she called in, so hysterical, he was going to kill her."

Frank nodded to encourage Harry to keep talking.

"Look," Harry said, the first plea in his voice, "I know what they're saying: the paper, the bleeding-heart liberals. I'm not trigger-happy. Why won't anyone believe that? I'm where the action is more of the time. I want to protect the victim. Sometimes an evil man gets hurt."

True, Frank realized, the harder and more effective you worked, the more results you got. He looked at the list of Harry's victims in his folder and read them aloud to Harry.

"One, a high-school kid in a high-speed chase. Dead on arrival. Car collided with telephone pole. Officer Schlacter shot out the right rear tire.

"Two, Watts sniper. Brought down by Officer Schlacter in the dark after his partner had been shot in the leg. Bullet entered the center of sniper's forehead. One shot.

"Three, armed robber who had shot and killed a liquor-store clerk, another high-speed chase. Officer Schlacter shot and killed suspect with a bullet through the back of the neck, severing spinal cord.

"Four, gang member firing on uniformed patrolman, unprovoked, as car passed. Followed by Officer Schlacter and pursued on foot after getaway car crashed into parked cars. One shot through the stomach."

Frank looked up, purring at Harry like some schoolmaster reserving his praise until the whole story was in. "Very commendable marksmanship," he said.

"Thanks."

Still reading, Frank said, "Officer Schlacter passed all the mandatory psychological testing after each incident and has returned to work in the three-day minimum."

Harry said nothing.

"And number five," Frank said, sighing, "number five, the big one. Rex Adams. Star of radio and television. Celebrity. Complicated by the fact that the victim was a visible and tireless cop-baiter. Unstable character perhaps, excessive drinking, fits of depression, but victim was shot from the rear: was naked and held an empty shotgun. Witnesses, wife and man across street from scene, swear Officer Schlacter's actions unprovoked. Widow suing city for four million dollars. District attorney investigating the possibility of a murder indictment against Officer Schlacter. Department very uncomfortable."

Harry would never understand administration and office politics, Frank thought–the necessity for public buffers between the public and police: Internal Affairs, Public Relations, Community Relations, lobbying at City Council, the police commission.

"And those are the only ones on the record. We aren't talking about Badeye Iler, for example..."

Harry just stared at Frank. Why couldn't he relax–ease up with the old man? He should be impressing Lela's father, not aggravating him.

"Harry," Frank pleaded, "don't you see the spot we're in? They want a citizen investigation into this. Every time there's a big one they say the cops can't prosecute their own. I want to clear you. You got to help me out a little. This guy was famous, Harry. He had that cop on his show dressed like a Ku Klux Klanner, telling how rotten we cops were..."

"I didn't *know* who he was," Harry shouted, slamming his palm on the desk in front of him. "You think I'm some kind of a hit man? I answered a call, he threatened...ah, what's the use. If you find any evidence I knew who he was, can me." For the first time Frank thought he noticed a sagging in Harry's spirit. "Why doesn't anybody believe me?"

"I believe you," Frank said, so softly Harry thought he heard incorrectly.

"What did you say?"

"I said I believe you. I know enough about you to believe you. I know you don't have a television, don't read the papers. You find all that stuff distracting from your purpose and depressing as well."

"How do you know that?" Harry was startled.

"My job," Frank said, "is investigation."

An unwanted touch of respect crept into Harry.

"But something bothers me."

"What's that?"

"I can't quite believe you never heard any of the department scuttlebutt about this hooded cop on the Rex Adams show."

"I don't listen to any of that stuff. That doesn't put anyone behind bars. Sure, my partner talked about that, but you desk boys don't even realize that when you get a call, they don't tell you his wife has one of these shyster Century City lawyers standing by to harass everybody into big settlements. They don't give you anything but the address and, if you're lucky, a name. If I knew who he was, should I stay away? But let me tell you something, Internal Affairs, I don't even listen to names. You got the President of the United States holding a gun on his wife, he isn't going to be too safe with me if I tell him to drop it and he points it at her instead."

Frank nodded wearily. He couldn't disagree with what Harry said.

"Look," Harry said, impatient with Frank's easygoing pace, "I got things to do, hoods to grab, contacts to make, informants to grease. I can't sit around amusing Internal Affairs all day. You don't like the results I bring the city, you get another boy."

Frank looked up at him, his mind drowning with all the answers he wouldn't make.

"Harry," he said.

"Yeah."

"Sit down, Harry. I want to talk to you about Lela, father to suitor—or is that too old-fashioned?"

At the sound of Lela's name Harry seemed disoriented. Amorphous symbols swam before his eyes. He sank into a chair, his tough-cop mask dissolving.

Frank sat on top of his desk, trying to be more informal—less official.

"I understand you've been seeing my daughter—quite regularly."

"Yes, sir, I have." Harry's attitude shifted on a dime. He was now the eager swain, calculating how to make the best impression.

Frank looked at Harry as though willing away reality. "You know how I feel about it?"

"Yes, sir, I do."

"You want your daughter to marry a cop?"

"I have great respect for the force," Harry said, then qualified it, "in general, that is."

"But specifically, let's say you were talking about a cop, oh, say, something like you. High-risk stuff."

"Hey, look," Harry said, shifting his dead weight in the chair, "I can understand how you feel. But, we're all adults. We got to make up our own minds, take our own chances. The thing is, can you understand how I feel?"

"How's that?"

"I love her. Lela's the most perfect human being I ever met. And, I understand how close you are. Lela worships you. But you don't want to clip her wings, do you?"

Frank studied Harry. A handsome man, he thought. No doubt about it. His grandchildren couldn't help but be adorable. If Harry lived long enough to produce them.

"And," Harry added, "she gives you all the credit for making her what she is—says you raised her single-handed."

Frank nodded slowly. "Let me tell you some things Lela might not have told you." Frank shifted his legs to emphasize how casual he was trying to be. "Her mother and I were in love like a couple of kids. Fights—so common to married couples—were almost nonexistent. Then, one night in the car we had an argument. It's hard for me to remember

46

what it was about. I should remember because we didn't often disagree. Lela was in the back seat, about four years old. I must have looked at my wife for a split second, when he came at us. I swerved to avoid him, but it was too late. He was drunk as a skunk, plowed into the front and knocked us right off the road. Ellen was killed instantly. Lela was thrown to one side of the car and back again. I had only a few bruises." Frank's eyes grew misty, as they always did when he so often relived this trauma.

"So you blame yourself," Harry said.

"Sometimes–but that's not the important thing. The important thing is Lela. Here I was a policeman with ambitions to climb up the ranks, visualizing medals for valor–kind of a Lord of the Streets kind of cop–when this happened and flattened me. I turned chicken. I was morbidly afraid something would happen to me." Frank pointed a finger at Harry, gesturing the firing of a gun, just as Harry had done to him. "You know, buy it for good and leave my little, helpless Lela alone. So, I put in for the soft stuff and, luckily, I always got it. There are more heroes around here than cowards. Oh, I wouldn't have chosen Internal Affairs, but they were running out of bulletproof duty to give me. I don't kid myself that anyone thinks it's honorable work, but I vowed I'd stay out of the line of fire until my girl was safely taken care of by a loving husband."

"I'd be flattered to be that man, you know."

"Yeah, you," Frank said, shaking his head. "Her first real love has to be a cop who is just the opposite of everything her dad wanted for her. A guy who has more bounty on his head than the rest of the troops combined."

"Oh, I don't know, Frank. That may be an exaggeration."

"Think so? Think the Whistler gang wouldn't plug you given the slightest go at you?"

"Why would they?"

"Oh, Harry, you aren't naive, are you? Badeye Iler. You think they have any doubt you blew him away?"

"Hey, I've heard that before. There isn't the slightest evidence of that."

"Yeah, sure. And, you haven't been arrested, have you? I'm talking about the gangs, and they don't need evidence. They are perfectly satisfied to go with their hunches." Frank shook his head, then found a fleck of lint on his sleeve, which he picked off and dropped to the floor. "Not a person in this building would give a nickel for your life, and my daughter has to fall in love with you."

"Well, I'm in West L.A. now," Harry said. "Nobody gets scratched in West L.A."

Frank sighed, found a little dandruff on his shoulder and brushed it off. "How long you suppose anyone's gonna want to keep you there after this one?"

"Damnit, Frank," Harry reddened and reverted to his defensive-cop stance, "what do the desk jockeys want us to do? I tell him to drop the shotgun he's pointing at the little lady's belly. He says, 'Up yours, fuzz,' and turns back to her. She is crying hysterically. Got the scene, Frank? What's in the new book? 'Sorry to give offense, sir. You are a rich and famous man, and I should have known better than to ask you not to shoot the little woman. What the heck, maybe the gun's empty and nothing'll happen.' You know, Frank, they didn't find many empty guns out in Watts."

"I know, Harry."

"So, I should say, 'You do what you think best, sir. I know a fella living in a big house like you got, and all, is a man of good judgment. And, even though the half-naked woman who's in there screaming called the cops her life was in danger, I expect this is a private argument, so I'll just leave my card in the mailbox if you should want me for anything, like bringing you a pizza or maybe mowing your lawn.'"

Frank groaned.

"That your idea of police work?"

"No, it isn't."

"Because sure as shootin' I do that, he plugs her and her relatives sue us for *twenty* million for me not doing my job–failure to protect."

"Yeah."

"And, hey, it would be super with me I had x-ray eyes and could tell if the gun was loaded. 'Course, the way that guy was carrying on, he could have just as easily killed her hitting her over the head with the gun. So, you call it, Frank. How many votes we get for walking away from the scene? Or, for waiting till he kills her to move?"

Frank shrugged his sagging shoulders. "Who knows...maybe today..."

"Yeah."

"So why don't you get out of it, Harry? It's not for you. It's too frustrating. Why not find another line? I'd give you my blessing in a minute."

"Yeah?"

"Yeah. Collect garbage. Anything where you aren't so liable to stop a bullet."

"It's in the blood, Frank," Harry said, as if resigned to a fate.

Frank sighed and stood up. He walked around the desk to where Harry sat. He stopped and stood facing the burly cop. "After the accident I devoted my life to Lela's happiness and safety. I know she's an adult now–gosh, she's been out of the house almost three months now–but I couldn't bear to have anything happen to her. I love her, Harry. I love her more than life itself. Can you understand that?"

Harry stared up from his seat at Frank. He nodded. "I can understand it, Frank, because I feel the same way."

"I should turn your case over to someone else. Conflict of interest."

"No need," Harry said. "I think I'd get as fair a shake from you as from anybody."

Frank shook his head. "I'm prejudiced, Harry. I want to see you off the force as long as you are dating Lela. How could I recommend anything else?"

Harry stared at Frank, then stood up to where he could stare down at him. "I'll take my chances," Harry said. "I peg you for a guy who strives to do the right thing. I don't want anyone else," he said, and walked out the door without looking back.

Frank watched the muscular back as it disappeared from his view. The gait was not as cocky as when he entered. But Frank realized that he too would walk out of there with less assurance than when he walked in.

5 WATTS never looked better to Harry. Going for love, not money.

The sun shone. The small houses, for the most part proudly kept, reminded him of any middle-class neighborhood. On the wider, busier streets the view was not so wonderful, but Harry knew how to take the back streets and avoid the war zones–like Whistler's Oak Terrace projects.

Harry could barely sleep at night for thinking about Lela. She was everything he always thought a woman should be. There was a soft innocence about her, a fine, sensitive intelligence, with no brashness, no coarseness. He couldn't wait to see her again.

It was a plywood and chain-link town. As though the whole thing had been dreamed up by Frank Gehry, the architect who liked to adorn his buildings with chain-link and plywood.

But, instead of decoration, the chain-link was used here in an effort to offer a semblance of protection to those within from those without. When it was not effective, the plywood was put up where the windows had been blown out. Put up sometimes behind the bars that protected everything but the glass.

Harry always thought a man could get rich having the chain-link and plywood concessions in Watts.

And after the plywood is put up, the spray-can army reconnoiters and spews its creative energy onto the boards in, as Harry put it, the language of the gutter.

Harry missed Watts. He missed the action. He missed the feeling that he was doing some good–making a difference.

Like Whistler's housing project, the 108th Street School was surrounded by chain-link fence. Of course, you could shoot through the chain-link, but Harry wasn't going to tell Lela that.

He parked his Bug at the curb by the schoolyard and made his way past the chain-link to the low, flat-roofed, one-story classroom where his beloved Lela had been ensconced as the full-time teacher.

50

"Why, Harry," she said, looking up from the stack of papers she was correcting, "how nice to see you. But you don't have to come out here."

"I want to," Harry confessed. "I can't wait to see you."

"Oh, you," she said, wrinkling her nose, rising to greet him, "I know you think I need protection, but I don't. Everybody here is quite wonderful, really."

"Not everybody," he muttered. "You'll promise me you'll never stay out here after dark?"

"Oh, Harry," she said, smiling her most loving smile. "You sound like my dad."

Harry winced. Had her father told her of their meeting? He was afraid to ask.

Lela poured forth her excitement about her classwork. How much she loved the children and how lucky she was to have the job.

"They're the lucky ones," Harry said, "to have you."

"Oh, Harry," she said, and they dissolved into each other's arms and kissed as though they were alone in the world.

The man had been on his way home from a lucrative transaction, when he happened to round the corner of the 108th Street School and looked in the window to see the white couple embrace. He would have known Harry Schlacter anywhere, from any angle.

"Whoo-whew," the whistling sound of Whistler was not heard by the happy couple.

Whistler backed around the corner and watched as Harry gallantly saw the pretty white woman to her car, then followed her in his Volkswagen Bug as she drove off into the sunset.

Whistler whistled again.

      ◌   ◌   ◌

Harry came back to Watts next on his day off. He was early for Lela, whose school was still in session. Harry was not a man who cultivated hobbies, and time hung heavy on his big hands on his day off. He decided to take the extra time to drop in on Maude Johnson.

Mrs. Johnson, as Harry always called her, managed a twenty-unit apartment building on 109th Street. It was the only building on her block not boarded up.

Her buildings were three two-story, stucco, flat-topped rectangles going back from the street. In every apartment you could look out the window and see another apartment. The grounds were one hundred percent covered with asphalt. The biggest days were when the mailman brought the welfare checks, and Mrs. Johnson was there for her rent.

The savings and loan association that repossessed the units had tried and failed with countless managers by the time the supervisor passed Mrs. Johnson's door. Mrs. Johnson met none of his requirements. She wasn't young, she had no man around the house to do handiwork. She hardly moved from her chair herself, but, he thought, out here you don't always get what you want.

The deal was struck, with Mrs. Johnson glad to save the sixty-five-dollars-a-month rent on her two-bedroom apartment for helping out.

As she told her new supervisor, waving her cane in the air, "I gots a cane—ain't gonna be nobody messes with me," and nobody ever did. Virtually all her rent was paid in cash, and she gave a tenant a few dollars to take her to the bank.

Harry called her "The Eyes and Ears of Watts," for she had given him help and encouragement as a young cop on the beat, when most people were afraid to talk to policemen. And he was grateful, treating her and her family like they were his own.

There was a ton of wisdom in the woman, Harry realized, and he just felt good spending a few minutes in her majestic presence.

He knocked at the screen door. She lit up when she saw his face. "Come on," the high-pitched voice sailed through the screen.

Harry came in and bent over to kiss her on her misshapen forehead. Maude Johnson was nothing to look at. Her head had come through the birth canal lopsided and just stayed that way. She had a dime-sized wart on her right cheek, and hairs poked out from it like hands on a compass.

Her height was average, her weight far above average. Her cane was always with her, not only to help her walk, but as a weapon of protection and an instrument of discipline for the passel of grandchildren she was rearing for her daughters–some from a working mother and more from a woman raising four of her own–a woman who couldn't say no to a man.

Welfare payments topped out at four kids per household, so it was not unusual for the grandmothers to take the surplus. As soon as one reached adulthood, another was found for "Gramma."

"How're you, Mrs. Johnson–you're looking mighty fine this

afternoon."

"No use complainin', Mr. Harry," she said.

It was a nice-sized room for the area–almost two hundred square feet, and against the far wall was the upright piano Maude Johnson had brought with her from Texas. Someone in her family had played it once upon a time, not she, but now it held the pictures of so many members of the family. In the center was an eight- by ten-inch picture of Jesus.

He was white.

The furniture was certainly serviceable, but no charitable organization would have been brokenhearted to part with it. Harry had never been in the room when the television was not on. There was some game show on now, and, since Harry had no television of his own, he was always ashamed that he was so intrigued by it.

"It's good to see you, Harry."

"Well, it's good to see you too, Mrs. Johnson."

"You know, what you done, Harry, we'll never forget. You made me one proud gramma."

"Now, now, you don't have to tell me every time I come to say howdy."

"Well, yes I do too. I don't want never to forget it. I just wants to keep reminding myself, and I does it by telling you every time I sees you. You give us all something to make us proud."

"Well, now remember, it was B.J. who did it."

"Nu-huh," she shook her misshapen head, "couldn'ta done it without you. B.J. knows that. Ever'body knows that."

"You're always giving me way too much credit."

"It's not only me, it's the whole black community owes you thanks."

Harry chuckled. "I think we could find a few don't agree with that."

"Who, the hoods? We don't care 'bout them none. You makin' this place fit to live for the decent folks. Can't 'spect the criminals be happy."

"Was," Harry said.

"Wuz? What you mean?"

"They transferred me to West L.A."

"Transfer? How come?"

Harry shrugged his shoulders.

"They can't do that. I'll call the chief an' tell him so myself." Mrs. Johnson shook her head. "Seems ever you get something good they take it away from you." She sighed so her body trembled. "The Lord giveth and the Lord taketh away," she said it to herself, and while Harry was tempted to point out there was no Lord in this transaction, he kept his peace.

"How's your Luke getting along?" Harry asked.

"Oh, dat one bad, Mr. Harry. He runnin' wid a *baaad* bunch."

"Don't let him. See that he amounts to something."

"Oh, I so wishes I could."

"Well, I guess they can't all be doctors."

"No, sir, ain't that the truth?" She chuckled to herself at the thought.

The door opened and a hulking, lumbering lad bursting to get out of his teens came in. He moved with a purposelessness born of studied insouciance.

"Oh, well, speak of the devil," Mrs. Johnson said, looking up from her chair at her grandson. "Say hello to Mr. Harry, boy."

"Hello, Mr. Harry," Luke said in perfectly flat tones, with care given not to have his greeting mistaken for anything friendly.

"Mr. Harry jest askin' 'bout you. Say you oughtta 'mount to sompin'."

The boy smiled in spite of himself. "Like I could be a doctor or sompin'."

"You could be what you put your mind to," Harry said. "Your sister did it."

"Yeah, my sister..." Luke trailed off as though paying a call on another world, and just as quickly decided his best move would be to vanish back out the door, which he did.

"Dat boy gonna be de death o' me," Mrs. Johnson said. "My girls give me some heartbreaks, but nothin' like dat boy."

"Don't give up on him, Mrs. Johnson. You can't ever give up."

Maude Johnson sighed and shook her head. "So what brings you out here if you're no longer working at the Southeast?"

Harry smiled his most sheepish smile. He had seated himself on the couch, opposite the stuffed chair Mrs. Johnson occupied as a throne. "A girl..."

"A girl?" and that old, misshapen face lit up with joy. "You finally got you'self a girlfrien'?"

Harry nodded.

"Well don't just sit there like the cat got yo' tongue. Start talkin'."

"She's a teacher at the One Hundred Eighth Street Elementary School."

"Oooo. Ooo. Ain't that nice though," she said. "You gonna bring her 'roun' to meet me?"

"Well, I sure will."

"Gotta put my stamp o' approval on her."

Harry smiled. He looked at his watch and stood up. "Gotta be going," he said. "School'll be out in a couple minutes."

"Well, you give her my best, ya hear?" Mrs. Johnson said. "Hm–mmm, 'bout time, you ask me."

"Yes, ma'am. Be seeing you. Take care."

"You too, Mr. Harry," and he was out the door.

Outside he passed Luke, who was keeping the front stucco wall warm. Almost as though he hoped to be the victim of a drive-by shooting.

"Don't take it too easy, Luke," Harry said.

Luke sneered and returned to the apartment to use the telephone.

Harry drove the five blocks to the schoolyard and arrived before the final bell had rung. He parked the Volkswagen at the curb and waited the few minutes for the bell.

⛨   ⛨   ⛨

Whistler was on duty at the projects' chain-link when his mother poked her head out of the open front second-story window.

"Whistler, you little shit!" she yelled. "Telephone!"

⛨   ⛨   ⛨

Frank Eberhart put the officers of Internal Affairs into several categories. First was the group who resented being there, who suffered the disdain of their fellows and who would gladly trade anything for it, even traffic. Frank thought Harry Schlacter would fit into this group, had he been in Internal Affairs.

The middle group were those who would have chosen something else but who realized the vagaries of assignments and tried to make the best of it. Frank, himself, fit here.

The smallest category was the handful of men who thrived on the assignment of investigating other cops. The power they felt was immense, and they even enjoyed being snubbed by their fellow officers because it gave them the sense of being in a position so powerful that it caused otherwise powerful policemen to fear and even hate them. The captain of Internal Affairs, Augie Templat, was such a man.

A tall man, he walked with long, lumbering strides, and he had a genius for getting on with his superiors by being, in his own words, "more of a butt-kisser than a boat-rocker."

Frank was neither. He did what he was told as best he could, never getting personally involved in his cases, never caring one way or another what happened to the people he investigated for drinking on duty, sexual misconduct, moral turpitude, excessive force, rank and repeated insubordination, burglary, narcotics infractions. He told his story at the hearing, he made his report; what they did with it was up to them. He had left no stone unturned, and they could take his word for it or they could disregard his work and base their decision on pure politics for all he cared.

Until this time.

Harry Schlacter was different. Frank had broken the cardinal rule of the department: don't get personally involved.

Frank had come to the office a half-hour early as usual. It gave him time to collect his thoughts for the day, and he always was at his desk when Augie Templat came striding in and always said good morning to him, and always first.

This morning he was marshaling his facts on the Harry Schlacter case because the captain had told him to get it all together and "run it past me so I can get a handle on it."

Augie Templat liked to talk in trendy jargon. Frank did not. To Frank, his boss had all the charm and grace of an Uzzi.

Templat came bounding into the room with his shock-absorber knees, carrying in his wake the strong smell of nicotine, smoke and coffee. "Come into my office, will ya, Frank," he said without the inflection of a question and without stopping as he passed Frank's desk.

Frank picked up the folder he had prepared on Harry Schlacter and followed Templat into the stark cubicle, turning over in his mind the pitch he had rehearsed.

"I just came from a meeting with the powers that be," Templat said, falling into his chair. "I know you've been burning the midnight oil on the H.S. case." He paused as if reflecting on some burdensome thought. "I can't think of his initials without thinking horseshit...!"

The color drained from Frank's face as he stood looking down at the slumped giant in the wooden swivel chair. The big man was stroking his neck rhythmically, looking off in the distance, as vacant as the cloudless sky outside, oblivious to Frank's reaction and almost, Frank thought, to his very presence.

"Anyway," Templat said, "they've decided he's through."

"What?" Frank staggered against the desk.

"Too much against it this time. I appreciate your interest. We all do... This time he just popped the wrong guy."

"But," Frank was shattered, "I can't believe it."

"Hey, Frank. What's got into you? Did I misread your report? I thought you wanted him out?"

Frank's face fell hangdog. "I thought I did," he said with a low helplessness.

"Every once in a while we have to throw the wolves a sacrificial lamb," the boss said. "I don't like it any better than you do..."

Frank looked at him and saw he didn't mean it. The check was always the same and would be, Harry or no Harry. "But why throw the wolves Harry? He's the best cop on the force."

"Yeah," he said, still stroking, "well, if he *was* the best, whoever was in second place just moved up."

"But they haven't even seen my final report," Frank said spiritlessly, waving the hapless folder at his superior, who wasn't looking at him.

"Wouldn't make any difference, Frank," he said, "this one's foreordained."

"You can't politic a man like that out of his livelihood."

"Ah, Frank, forget him. Everybody says he's a pain in the ass."

"I don't," Frank said, grasping for control of his emotions. "He's a maverick, sure, but he's what police work is all about. A man who gets the results we want...even if he doesn't always go about it the way we'd like. I'm convinced he did the right thing with that blowhard, Adams. Any of us would have done the same. You can't can a man for doing his job."

"Well, great. Maybe you want to start your own police force and hire him," Augie said. "In the meantime it's going to be your job to get enough on this big pain in the ass to discharge him for good. Until then, tell him he's suspended, pending blah, blah." Augie waved him away.

At the raucous blasting of the school bell Harry wanted to duck under the dashboard, for surely anything that obnoxiously loud must foretell the falling of a nuclear bomb.

Instead he watched the children tumble out on the playground and head for home, as though someone had spilled a cup of marbles.

Harry got out and locked the door. He hummed across the grounds–tattered grass and little else–toward Lela's room. He could have sworn he could tell the faces of her children from the others–they were so contented.

He found Lela at her desk correcting papers.

"Oh, hi, Harry," Lela said, her enthusiasm on the low burner.

"What's the matter?" Harry asked.

"Oh, nothing. Just a lot of work, I guess."

"Hm. Seems like you have something else on your mind." Harry sat at the small desk in front of Lela.

"Let's go outside," she said.

Harry thought she seemed afraid to be in a room with him. "Why?" he asked, his eyebrows arching.

"Sun's out," she said. "It's more pleasant. I've been in here all day."

The room was a veritable gallery of children's art and writing. Each desk had on top a self-portrait of the pupil and a short personal description. Around the walls were full-sized cutouts and paintings of each member of the class–all done in bright colors that gave the room the glow of good cheer.

Harry tried to plant a tiny kiss on Lela's cheek, but she turned with a quick motion that caused him to back off.

She led him to a wooden picnic table with attached wooden benches. He started to slide in the bench next to her, but she got up and sat across the table from him.

Harry's eyes narrowed, but he kept his place. "You aren't afraid to sit out here like this?" he asked.

She shook her head. "These are good people, Harry. Most of them care about their children, and they know I do. It gives me a sense of security, I guess."

"Yeah, but it only takes one crackpot..."

"But I'm doing a good job here, my best. If it isn't..."

"But reason doesn't rule these streets, Lela. You can't live your life being afraid. But you'll live longer if you're careful."

"Live longer? How long will you live, Harry?"

"Me?"

She nodded. "Dad says the gangs are out to get you."

"Oh, so that's what's eating you. Don't worry about me; I can take care of myself."

"He doesn't want me to be hurt."

"You?"

She nodded again. "By getting...too attached to someone I might lose."

"Lela, Lela. What is this? In life we don't know who will win and who will lose. Life is chance. Percentages."

"But it sounds like the odds are running against you. Oh, Harry," she said, reaching her hands across the table to hold his, "I think I love you. Dad means so much to me–I wouldn't want to hurt him for anything in the world."

"Not even me?"

"That's the problem."

"Did he forbid you to see me?"

She shook her head. "Dad doesn't forbid me anything. But I can't help feeling deep down what he feels. He says he's sure you killed that Badeye person."

"I've killed a few in my line of duty. You hear the mayor say he never pulled his gun? Times were different then. This is a different duty too. I haven't killed anyone who will be missed–even by their mothers."

She looked deep in his eyes and nodded once. "But can you take the law in your own hands–and survive?"

"Sometimes out here it's kill or be killed..."

"That's what he says. And he says they will surely get you if you don't get them first."

An involuntary laugh escaped Harry.

"And there are so many more of them."

"What are you saying, Lela? You are breaking it off? You don't want to see me again?"

Lela curled up her cute-as-a-button nose. "I don't know, Harry. Maybe I need time to think. Maybe we both do."

Lela had seen some moving shadows behind the corner of the

building she was facing, but her mind was on Harry and, ironically, his safety.

"I couldn't imagine living without you, Lela. So, even if I get killed tonight, can't we make the most of what time we have together? Do we have to waste it in disagreement?"

Lela started to speak, opening her mouth just a tad, not because she had an answer, but to keep the dialogue alive. She wanted to tell him she couldn't live without him either, but at that moment they came toward them and her mouth just dropped. There were three of them, but two of them were so large it looked like five. They had guns–one had a baseball bat or tire iron or something. It came down on Harry's shoulder with lightning speed.

Lela screamed. But screams out here were not that unusual. She couldn't help herself; the grisly terror she felt had to be vented. The sound built in her throat like a siren. Suddenly, a bison face reached out and clapped his broad, flat hand across her warm mouth, easily covering the lower half of her face. Another giant, with a severely disturbed face, the vacant eyes blank like a charging bull, bunched up a rag and stuffed it in her mouth and tied another rag around her eyes.

Harry felt molten lead shoot through his sinuses and tried to struggle to his feet. He got to his knees, when his face met an anonymous boot and he fell back.

"Okay," the tall one said. "Go to work, Bull."

Harry felt the crackling as though he were being run over by a bulldozer. As he slipped from consciousness, the last thing Harry heard was Whistler saying, "This is for Badeye–and it's only the beginning."

The last thing he saw was Bull and Moose working him over while Whistler held Lela in a choke hold. Her pretty face was tortured with panic.

The bull and the moose tied Lela's arms behind her back and then tied her feet with the end of the same rope. The blindfold and gag were tightened, muffling her screams as they forced her squirming body into the trunk of a car. Though the afternoon had turned cool, Lela Eberhart's body was soaked with perspiration.

Whistler slammed closed the trunk lid.

Harry's inert body lay on a bed of brown, indifferent grass. Whistler strode over and looked down at his victim–the dark-toothed grin lit up his black face.

"He still breathin'," he said.

"Finish him off," said Bull.

Whistler shook his head. "Too easy on him. We gonna hit Horseshid Harry where it gonna really hurt."

"Ah, get it over with," from the bull.

"Get in the car," Whistler commanded while Bull and Moose took one last longing look at Harry. "Come on, let's go," Whistler said, spitting on the unconscious policeman. They all climbed in the car and burned rubber.

Day 1

6   FRANK hadn't gotten much accomplished since he left Augie Templat's office. Frank was not a man to let his job get him down, ordinarily. Today, it got him down. With Harry off the force, his objections to Lela seeing him would vanish. But he wondered what kind of person Harry would be without his beloved uniform. Fish don't swim in the sand. Would that vital, hulking dynamo be able to keep his sanity selling insurance or working in the probation office?

Frank couldn't imagine it.

He looked at the clock on the wall. Almost four. Lela would be at home. He called. There was no answer. "This is your dad," he said sheepishly to her answer machine.

But why was he calling her first? Didn't he owe it to Harry to tell him before he told anyone else? Hadn't he gone back to his boss two hours after the decision was made and ask to be the one to break the news to Harry? Templat had no objection.

Frank devoted the balance of his day to contemplating the best approach to Harry.

He would begin by telling him of his change of heart. How he had finally decided that Harry was born to be a cop and there were certain risks and dangers that cops faced and in life you had to take your chances. He tried to imagine Harry doing something else and he just couldn't do it. Then he would give him Augie Templat's words verbatim.

With trepidation, Frank picked up the phone and dialed Harry's apartment.

No answer. And Harry had no machinery to record his calls.

He waited a half-hour and called Lela again. "Hi, sweetie," he said after the click and tone of her machine sounded. "If you see Harry, ask him to give me a call, will you? I'm at the office. I'll stay here until six."

When he hung up he had second thoughts about his message. Last night he had told Lela exactly how he felt about Harry. She had tears in her eyes and Frank felt terrible. He tried to tell her that her happiness was the most important thing to him. But it didn't come out right. Now he decided he sounded like an overprotective father.

Well, Frank thought, tonight I'll make it my business to apologize and to–as gracefully as I can–get out of her way.

When the trunk lid snapped shut on Lela she felt like Jonah in the belly of the whale. Blindfolded, hog-tied and packed like a sardine in with boxes and plastic bags, she barely had room to breathe.

"Dear God, help me," she cried to herself. Then she was ashamed of herself for not thinking of Harry first. She was at least conscious; he was unconscious and abandoned and maybe even dead.

Her thin body shuddered at the thought. "I must get to a telephone," she said, jerking on the ropes that bound her hands and feet. "Nine, eleven," she said to herself. "Nine, one, one," over and over, as though she might forget the number if she didn't keep repeating it.

The pounding of her heart reverberated in the trunk. She thought of Poe's *The Telltale Heart*. Now her adrenal glands responded to the alarm.

She realized to save Harry she was going to have to save herself first.

What did these people want with her? Were they going to kill her? Gang rape her? Anything was possible. Her father had warned her of the dire consequences of associating with Harry Schlacter, the scourge of the gangs. But what could she do? She loved him. Maybe it wasn't rational, but looking back she would do the same again.

But her kidnappers acted like such animals. Harry said the only way to deal with them was on their own terms–force was all they understood. Reason, sweet talk and salesmanship would fall on deaf ears.

She must save Harry. But when she thought about confronting and overpowering three giants, sheer terror rode roughshod in her bloodstream. One of them had arms like fire hydrants. Next to him she was a matchstick he could break in two with one hand. And there were *three* of them! "Nine, one, one," she said. "Oh, God, don't let Harry be dead...even if I will be..."

The trunk smelled like the rubber on the spare tire. She thought she would surely suffocate. She was always afraid of the dark as a child, and her father was careful to see she could always see light under her door. Now with her blindfold so tight, she was in pitch dark.

Thoughts, plans, plots, dreams spun feverishly in her mind.

"Oh, Harry, poor Harry. Nine, one, one..." She tried to slow her heart rate by inhaling deeply, but the smell of the rubber, and now gasoline, was too much for her.

Her poor children. What would they think? What would they do? She reluctantly realized a short time ago that most of them lived with violence as a daily staple. But what would happen to poor Ezra, who was so dependent on her–and little Felicity, who would barely speak to anyone else. She shed a tear for her children. She wanted so much to give them her best, and now she was snatched away from them. It wasn't fair–it wasn't right. She wanted to see that her third-graders wouldn't wind up like her kidnappers. And she hoped against hope that third grade wasn't too late.

The blackness was so frightening, she could taste her fear. She realized at once how unprepared she was to fight this battle. She had always been such a trusting soul. Except for the lack of a mother, her childhood had been idyllic–built only of love and trust. She was such an innocent and sweet child. Teachers adored her; her peers protected her. Her disposition was so sunny, people later said she couldn't be so happy and have any kind of an understanding of the realities of life. She was simply not prepared for the terror she now felt.

Where did these captors get a car like this? Money to put gasoline in it? Harry told her Whistler got his car as a gift. In gratitude for saving a man's life.

"How did he do that?" Lela had asked.

"He told the man, if he gave him the car, he would save his life–he wouldn't shoot him."

Lela permitted herself the hope that the car she was riding in was stolen and reported and some cop would stop them. But she realized how common stolen cars were, and how hard to trace. She knew she wouldn't be able to count on so simple a rescue. She would have to save herself to save Harry.

"Nine, eleven–nine, eleven."

How could she best three methodical criminals? The way they went about beating Harry was so calculated, it was almost as easy as painting by the numbers.

The first thing she did was analyze the journey: what kinds of roads were traveled, for how long. Of course, she thought, how foolishly academic if they just stop somewhere and unceremoniously shoot me.

She was cramped in the fetal position and tried to stretch a bit, but her movements were restricted by the small space, the bags and boxes, and the ropes. The blindfold was tight and the gag cut the corners of her mouth. But they couldn't tie her mind, and she was determined to fight to the death. Outlandish, she thought. A five-foot-three-inch, one-hundred-five-pound girl against three giants.

The car had slowed and now, she thought from the sounds of traffic, was pulling onto a freeway.

Lela's beating heart thumped against her perspiration-soaked ribs. She knew instinctively the only way to crowd out the terror was with an occupied mind. The first thing she had to do, she told herself, was to get the blindfold off, to get some sense of orientation.

She rubbed her head on the trunk floor, trying to pull the blindfold up over her eyes, but for her efforts she got only a chafed head.

She probed now in the blackness for some rough protrusion, moving as much as she could manage between the bags and boxes in the trunk. Every movement of her wet body caused her agony, so tight were the ropes.

After she managed a slight turn of her body, her head probed the lid of the trunk. At the back wall between the trunk and the car, her head touched a cold object with two rounded points. Slowly she positioned her head so she caught the blindfold on one of the points. She had a horrible fear that the car would stop suddenly and the metal would penetrate her skull as she tried to work her head into position between the trunk lid and what she now felt was the spare tire. It was as though she was standing on the precipice of death; as long as she struggled, there was always the hope of something better.

A great feeling of exultation swept over her as she felt the blindfold catch and pull up enough so she could see with one eye. She was surprised to see the trunk dimly lighted by the taillights, which had a clear plastic housing on the inside. Her eye focused on a small plastic wing nut, which held the plastic housing to the taillight.

Could she get into position to take the taillights out, in the hope some policeman saw it and stopped them?

Between the bags, she now saw held groceries, her eye fell on the car jack, fastened to the side of the trunk. She thought of all the uses to which she could put that, if only her hands were free.

With sharp pains coursing through her wrists, shoulders and

ankles, Lela forced herself around, reconfiguring bags and boxes, so her hands were touching the taillight, her body folded around the corner in an "L." She groped for the plastic nut that held the taillight unit and managed to get her thumb and forefinger around it and turn it a millimeter at a time until finally she freed the plastic housing, with its three light bulbs, from the taillight assembly.

Satisfaction cooled her body as she felt the sharp edge of the plastic. She turned and jammed the taillight unit between the back of the trunk and her back and began gently sawing her wrist ropes against the edge. Suddenly she gasped at a flash of pain burning into the flesh of her wrist as she realized she had broken one of the small light bulbs and cut her wrists.

The car was still speeding along the freeway, and she tried to get her fingers around her sweater so she could unscrew the two remaining light bulbs, but was unable to manage it. She had to pinch the bulbs suddenly with her fingers and try to turn them. After several unsuccessful, burning starts she managed to turn them off, let them cool, then remove them.

She took the bulbs from the sockets and rolled them away from her body so she could saw on the plastic housing without breaking them. She realized she would have to return the taillights before they stopped so they wouldn't be suspicious. Lela put the unit back between the car and her back and again rubbed the ropes against the sharp edge.

Since she could move only an inch at a time, the task took more than thirty minutes of concentrated effort, but Lela never wavered. While she was sawing she considered her alternatives for action and finally settled on what she thought Harry would want her to do.

She was lugubriously aware while she was forming her plans of the shadow of Harry and her father, Frank, looking over her shoulder, trying to help her.

Shadow. She almost said ghost.

She prayed to her God.

Dear God, please let Harry be alive–and all right.

She didn't know how anyone could sustain the awful blows she heard, each one resounding in her brain as though she were the victim, each one soliciting a desperate plea from her to stop. Stop!

STOP!

Even after the sounds no longer came strangled from Harry's throat, the blows continued.

Animals. There was no other name for them.

Atrocious animals.

Father would play it safe, take his chances, she thought. When you are outnumbered you don't do anything foolish. Harry would try to get control. If they want to kill you, he'd say, they'll kill you. They don't play by our rules, so when you play them you play their rules.

If they don't plan to kill you, they want you for something else–they want you alive, so chances are you aren't going to provoke them into changing their plans. And maybe, just maybe, these groceries meant they were planning to stay somewhere for a time–somewhere away from a store.

She could hear Harry saying those words, as if he were lying in the trunk with her (and, oh, how she wished he were), but they were her words–freely translated from Harry's ideas. She was thinking more like him than like her father, but then, she suspected, she always had, and her father always seemed to be trying to change her–even before she met Harry.

Well now, there was no doubt about it, the plans she had made were all Harry, and she'd have to take the consequences of any failure. But if you didn't live what you believed, you might as well not live. (Harry Schlacter, who else?)

When the last strand was cut and Lela freed her arms she said a prayer of thanks to God. The car had started to climb a long hill now and she sensed they were headed for the mountains. How long had it been since they left Los Angeles? An hour and a half? Two, perhaps three?

She was breathing easier now as she made her preparations. She took off the ropes, the blindfold and the gag and wiped the perspiration from her forehead on her sleeve and noticed the sticky blood on her blouse sleeves.

Her ears began to pop and she began shivering. Just a moment before, she remembered, she wanted to take her sweater off she was so hot, but couldn't move her arms. Now she felt almost giddy at the freedom of her body. She turned her mind to her plan. The execution, she realized, had to be perfect. She took the jack from its resting place on the wall of the trunk and settled herself back into her original position.

She exercised her muscles as best she could in the small confined space. She would need all her strength to bring this off, she thought, and it wouldn't do if she was so cramped she couldn't move.

Thirty minutes perhaps, not more than an hour, up the winding mountain road and they slowed and turned onto a bumpy road. Lela felt her heart stop. Oh, God, she said to herself, if I'm going to die before they open the trunk, I'll never know how I would have done. Can I really go through with this? Am I crazy?

Cold terror engulfed her as the car bumped to a halt and the engine was cut. Lie still, she commanded herself harshly, her heart pounding and her lungs heaving with fear. Surprise. It all depends on surprising them. It's a chance you must take, she told herself with Harry's voice echoing in her ear one of his favorite quotes: "There is nothing so necessary for the triumph of evil than that good men do nothing."

She tightened the grip on the jack behind her back. The blindfold and gag were in place, the taillight was back in its housing. The scene would flash before those tiny holes she poked in her blindfold for only an instant. How many would there be?

She heard the voices and crunchy footsteps. Then the metallic grating sound of the key being inserted in the lock. A quick supplication to God and Harry and the lid was thrown open.

One man loomed over her like a boulder blocking the mouth of a cave, and her escape from the trunk; the other one, off to the side. She saw deep, dark, thick woods, with towering pines and intimidating, ghostlike black cottonwoods, with only a rough road winding between them, covered with patches of snow.

"Moose is opening the house," she heard a voice. "We'll carry her in."

The man blocking her exit stood up a moment to listen to the voice. Lela brought the jack from behind her back and swung it at his midsection, slamming him with all her might. A startled rush of air shot from his slack, startled mouth. He doubled over like a collapsing folding chair and fell to the ground. Lela tore off the blindfold and gag with one motion and leaped from the trunk, gripping the jack tightly. The tall one was so surprised, he looked first at the pile on the snow, giving Lela just enough time to clear the trunk before he started after her.

She turned and swung the jack at him, but he sidestepped and took only a glance on the hip. Lela lost her grip and the jack went flying.

"Help!" she screamed. "Help, help, HELP!" at the top of her lungs as she ran down the road and veered off into the dark woods. The pine scent from the Jeffries and sugars burning in her nostrils with her quickening breath, she ran without destination, zigzagging to avoid any bullets that might be fired, but none were. The snow crunching beneath her feet, she ran and screamed without any feeling of how far behind her the tall one was. She didn't think she could afford the luxury of looking back, and soon realized, as she began to go hoarse from screaming, that there was only one flaw in her plan to run toward the closest light. There was no light in any direction, and she just ran, trying to follow the road, yet staying off it in the cover of the trees. The darkness was with her, but it took her too long to realize that while she was screaming for help, they knew where she was. Abruptly she stopped screaming and tried to change her course.

But it was too late. After twenty-five more yards she heard the sudden crackling of branches underfoot, and he swooped down on her like a famished carrion bird and with an adroit flying tackle brought her heaving body to the ground. Like the eternal pendulum, she couldn't stop, and brought her hands to his face and dug her long fingernails into his flesh and tore at the dark skin. He grabbed her hands and thrust his shoulder onto her neck, slamming the back of her head against the ground; the back of her neck lying exposed in the snow sent a chill down her spine. Instinctively, her hands left his face and went up to his shoulder to relieve the pressure on her neck, but her exhaustion was overcoming her adrenaline, and the weight of his body seemed immovable. She pushed against him in vain and struggled to catch a breath. A miscalculation, she thought. Oh, God, I should have taken my chances. This is surely it...when she heard Moose crashing through the forest. "You got her?" he said, breathless.

"Yeah," the tall one hissed with satisfaction. "Glad we brought along someone who could run."

"Hey, wait a minute," Moose protested. "I was on the porch."

"Yeah," Whistler smiled that gap-toothed smile. Lela saw through her bulging eyes his ears were like loving-cup handles and his nose–a broken porkchop. "You gonna be a good girl now?"

She tried to nod her head. Whistler Wagner eased up his thin body on her and Moose asked if he should work her over to calm her down.

"Naw," Whistler said. "We're gonna win this one with honey. I like a girl with spunk." He smiled again, showing her his rotten teeth and black space, and laughed as though he were gasping for breath.

Bull came with the rope and a black bandana, and tied and blindfolded her, the bandana crushing her ears against her head.

They picked her up, twisted her arms behind her back and marched her back to the cabin. "Nice of you to yell like that," Whistler said. "Had a hard time knowing where you were in this dark without your yelling. Yell all you want to here; ain't nobody gonna hear you.

We're miles from anybody. Miles. In the winter there ain't even nobody that close."

They marched in silence, Lela plotting another opportunity to escape. They hadn't killed her, and she had that good feeling you have when at great risk you make a decision and then discover you were right. If only she hadn't yelled for help. Still, maybe someone heard and went for the police. There was always hope.

"Now tell us, honey, how you got those ropes off."

She said nothing.

"Ain't talking? You got nothing to worry about, you learn to behave yourself. We ain't meaning no harm."

Lela felt her spirit pick up in spite of her fears. Maybe he meant it. But that was no cause to get off guard or let down any. All she had to do to keep alert was to think of the beating they gave Harry. Anyone who could do that and kidnap could certainly lie. Harry had taught her that.

It was a small, isolated white cabin that they went into, with a small porch. She felt herself pushed roughly into a chair.

Her blindfold cutting her eyes, her captors seemed far removed from any reality: voices without faces, sounds without bodies, coming to her ears from the depths of hell.

"Why do you want me? My father isn't rich. You've made a mistake."

She could hear the sucking sounds of Whistler laughing. "Ain't no mistake. Ain't money I'm after. You just had the misfortune to be in with the wrong crowd, you might say."

Lela asked the bodyless voice, "How can you be so evil?" Suddenly she felt a hand clamp her mouth shut.

Whistler sucked the air again in his nervous hilarity. "Evil? You might say it's the pigs. I was born and raised with the pigs...Miss Wills, like your lover boy. Bull!"

"Yes, sir."

"Put the gag back on her. We don't want to hear no more shit."

The gag tight on her mouth, she was unable to tell him she was not Miss Wills. Had he gotten the wrong person after all? And, who *was* Miss Wills?

She was dropped in a room the size of a closet and she heard the sound of a key turning in a lock.

Day 2

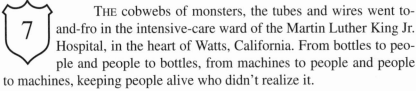

THE cobwebs of monsters, the tubes and wires went to-and-fro in the intensive-care ward of the Martin Luther King Jr. Hospital, in the heart of Watts, California. From bottles to people and people to bottles, from machines to people and people to machines, keeping people alive who didn't realize it.

It was the transportation business: transporting liquids, transporting electrodes. And always the monster webs, liberating to some, ensnaring to others.

Pieced together in Emergency as best they could, Harry Schlacter had not regained consciousness since the beating he absorbed at the 108th Street School.

Beside the shrouded Harry sat a figure in white, the brown identification tag above her left breast said:

B.J. Johnson, M.D.
Intern

and matched her smooth Hershey bar skin. Her cute, simple nose drew any lurking nonsense from her dark eyes, her silken hair the shimmering fleece of the black sheep. Pert and petite, she sat upright, almost stiff.

She looked like a black madonna sitting there at the bedside in Intensive Care. Her hospital whites couldn't obliterate her perfect figure, and the stethoscope that hung between her breasts glistened in the dim light.

The "child" on the bed was older than she was, and he wasn't a child but her benefactor.

Through her mind, as she looked at her wrapped companion, went the lines:

> *Oh, why should the spirit of mortal be proud*
> *In this little journey from swaddle to shroud?*

She couldn't remember who wrote the lines or where she first heard them. In college English, no doubt. Was it Thurber? Ogden Nash? Dorothy Parker? One of those funny exoterics, she knew; she just didn't know which one.

She said a quick prayer that shrouded Harry's journey wasn't over yet. She wouldn't dare to hope for anything until she saw how he survived the night, but she resolved to sit there to see that he got through, as though the force of her will would tip the scales so heavily weighted against him.

There he was, she thought, not taking her eyes off him, out of commission. She never dreamed she would see him like that. So vital he was–forceful. You always knew when Harry Schlacter was on the way–you felt the atmosphere make way for him, sucked into the vortex of his oversized personality. His style was unselfconscious, his character indomitable. Harry was always on the run; he wasn't meant to be in a coma.

She brushed her dark eyes with a knuckle, wiping surreptitiously at the tears in each.

Harry, Harry, she thought, I owe you so much. Did I ever tell you how much? Please wake up so I can tell you.

Then she shuddered. What would he think, if he were conscious, in his condition? So active in spirit and so helpless in body. The frustration would be unbearable. She had seen many less active people demoralized by incapacity.

The gaunt white man in white came through the door. "There you are," he almost shouted. He always talked too loudly, B.J. thought.

A.S. Baccus, M.D.
Resident

he was labeled, and he carried his sunken eyes and hollow cheeks like a burden.

"Okay, B.J.," he said, "you win the devotion prize. Now go and get some sleep so you won't be a zombie tomorrow."

"Zombie?" B.J. smiled wryly at him. "Look who's talking. At least I eat."

"I eat," Baccus said, sounding hurt.

"Yeah, bran flakes and skim water."

"Ah, I just avoid cholesterol like the plague. I've cut open too many cadavers with lima beans in their veins."

"I got news for you, A.B., you look like you already caught the plague."

"We're not talking diet," Baccus shouted. "We're talking your irrational vigil over this guy. He may have a five- or six-percent chance of pulling through, but your sitting next to him all night won't make a damn bit of difference."

Her smile was beatific, angelic. "Won't lower his chances either," she said.

The resident shook his head, not knowing if he should pity her or laugh at her. "You got something about this guy. What's so great about him?"

"I owe him something."

"Quite a lot, apparently."

"Everything."

"Okay, so hit the road to dreamland. There are plenty of watch-dogs here."   He was a student of old songs. He had a collection of old 33- and 45-rpm records that burdened the walls of his tiny apartment. And while he was thinking of old songs, he sang, "I'm just wild about Harry, and Harry's wild..." and stopped.

"Sh!" B.J. said. "Don't you ever keep your voice down?"

"Sometimes when I sleep. Listen, there's an old man out in the hall asking for you. Looks like death warmed over. Is it Harry's father?"

"His father's dead."

Resident Baccus looked at Harry. "That makes two of them," he said.

"Very funny."

"So why don't you mosey out there and see what this old geezer wants."

"I'll go if you stay," she said.

"Hey, I got a lot to do," he said, shocked at the suggestion. "I can't babysit."

"I'll wait till you have time."

"Oh, there are doctors and nurses all over this ward, around the clock."

"I'll wait," she said, folding her hands in her lap. "I just want to be sure."

She sat looking at her sleeping giant, remembering the incident she always thought of as the turning point in her life. Of course, no one would agree with her, she was sure. Who would ever believe this rough cop could have...?

She tried to remember how many checks Harry had given her, but all she could recall was how proud he looked at her graduation. He actually cried like a baby and had little success trying to cover it. Gramma was there, and Luke, and even Margie, giggling with another boyfriend, and more distant relatives, all bursting with pride, but none more proud than Harry. In the great sea of white faces, Harry told her he knew what it felt like to be black and accomplish something so big.

Her mind drifted back to the autumn evening in Watts outside Gramma's ground-floor apartment in the dingy stucco building where she had lived an unprecedented seventeen years. Harry was there to deliver his monthly check. Mailing would have been easier, more convenient, but he wanted to do it personally so he could get a progress report. It made him feel part of something good. He had stopped to make small talk about the weather and how they were boarding up the neighborhood, but this little twenty-unit building stood as an oasis in the desert, limping along abreast of the building and safety department.

He must have heard me sniffling a mile away, B.J. thought.

He turned to see B.J., her arms loaded with more books than she could control, coming around the corner. On seeing Harry she burst into great sobbing gulps. He came over to her and said, "What's wrong?"

B.J. was the one of the family who was blessed with not only the lion's share of the brains but the good looks as well. Her gramma could never understand the mysterious ways of God. Short and petite, B.J. had none of the broad racial features of her brother and sister.

She didn't answer Harry but kept blubbering. He took her arms in his big hands and said, "Hey, hey, what's this? Dr. Johnson doesn't blubber like an adolescent girl."

"Way I'm going, there ain't gonna be no *Doctor* Johnson."

And she spewed forth a rapid torrent of melancholia: She was inadequate to the task, she was not smart enough, as evidenced by her failing grade on her exam, and here she was only in the first year of medical school and already she was finding the going too tough for her; she even thought, in her darkest moments, that no black would ever be smart enough to be a doctor. Especially not a black woman.

"Hogwash," Harry shouted. "Get a hold on yourself. I never heard such drivel. If they didn't think you could make it, you wouldn't be in the class. And believe it or not, you won't be the first black doctor, and not the last, and that goes for women too." He took her by the arm and squeezed it for emphasis. "Listen, B.J., everybody around here believes in you, everybody is rooting for you. You've got responsibilities

74

to your people; you can do it. *I* know you can do it. And here..." he reached into his pocket and brought out the check and put it in one of the books in her arms. "I put my money where my mouth is."

She began to cry again. "Oh, Mr. Harry," she said, sobbing. "I can't keep taking your money. I just found out how much you make, and you're giving me more than half. How can you live on that much?"

"Shut up about that," he said, looking around, afraid someone would hear. "Do I look like I'm starving? I got an investment, is all. I don't need much now; when I get older I'm going to have this nice windfall when you pay it all back."

"Suppose I can't? Suppose I don't get through?"

"You'll get through," he said, remembering back to his days in the police academy with Charlie Rubenstein and a conversation not unlike this, but it was Harry whining to Charlie that he couldn't hack the academics and wouldn't get through. But Charlie said, "Nonsense," and tutored him through, and Harry, in exchange, taught Charlie to shoot passably.

"And I'll tell you another thing," Harry said, shaking B.J.'s arm, "I'm not taking a penny back from a shoe clerk or a cocktail waitress or a hooker. If you throw away your talent, I don't want anything to do with you–understand? Unless you're a doctor, I'm not touching a penny from you."

"Ah," she said, "you loan it to me; what do you care how I pay it back? And, I'll tell you this, Mr. Harry, I'm paying it back, no matter what."

"No," he shook his head violently. "This is not a loan; it's an investment in your future. If it goes sour, I'm out the dough just like I had put it in the stock market. But you know something? It isn't going to go sour. If you have a setback, you work a little harder; you don't give up. B.J., you're the hope of the world out here. You're going to be living proof the black doesn't have to limit herself to the dole and the streets. You're going all the way, and I don't care if it kills you. Now, cut the bad-mouthing and get in there and hit the books."

"Can't," she shook her head dolefully.

"What?" he shouted so loudly she jumped with fright and the second-floor tenants looked over the decrepit wooden railing with concern-covered faces.

"I mean," she said timidly, looking at her feet, "there's too much noise in there. I can only study in the library."

"Then get to the library," he yelled as though she were at the other end of the property. "What are you waiting for?"

Her face worked slowly until it turned up in an uncertain smile. "Okay, Mr. Harry, but I just want you to know something."

"What?"

"I'm way out of my class. I don't have the mental equipment for it. I can't continue for myself, that much I know. I don't have what it takes to do it for the black people or for Gramma. And I don't see any reason to do it for Luke and Margie, unless it's to take bullets out of his skull and babies out of her belly. I mean, I'm just not equipped."

"Baloney."

"Well, what I'm saying is, if I do do it, it won't be for anybody but you, Mr. Harry. I never had anybody believe in me so before like you, and, well, I guess I can't let you down..."

He turned his head abruptly from her so she wouldn't see his moistening eyes.

"Okay," he said, "cut the jabber and get to the library."

"Yes, suh," she said, slave-talking, and bowed low.

When he got himself under control and turned back, she was gone.

⛉   ⛉   ⛉

She came floating down the corridor like one of those ballerinas from the Ballet Russe, who moved as though they had pneumatic tires for feet. Dr. Baccus had reluctantly promised B.J. he would sit by Harry until she came back.

Frank sat with the look of a bemused accountant, with a pallor of face that bespoke his devotion to the great indoors. He looked as though he'd said something funny but thought it wasn't polite to call attention to it. He stood when he saw her coming; his stooped shoulders always made him look tired.

"You must be Dr. Johnson," he said, smiling that bemused smile and extending his hand.

"Why must I?" she said, returning his smile and taking his hand. "Because there aren't too many black women gotten up like doctors in here?"

"Goodness," Frank said, taken aback, "I'm sorry if I offended. I see you have a label that would bear me out. I...it is the middle of the night and you were coming in my direction."

"Quite all right. I meant nothing. I'm a little tired."

"I'm Frank Eberhart. I'm a policeman–friend of Harry's."

She eyed him critically. "You don't look like a policeman," she said. "You look more like an..." she paused.

"An accountant," he said, supplying the word.

"Yes."

"Did a young woman bring him in?"

"I didn't see who brought him. I heard someone in the neighborhood saw him and called the police."

"Nothing about a young woman? About twenty-two years old–petite...very...attractive?"

She shook her head. "You can check with Admissions."

"Already did." Frank looked down at his shoes. What had become of Lela? He had gone to her apartment. No sign of anything. At the school he found her door closed but not locked. Her purse was on her desk, untouched.

Martin Luther King was the first hospital he checked. He was being optimistic. He could have gone to the morgue first. He swallowed hard when he remembered his prophesy to Lela. And now some harm had come to her. It was his worst fear. Harry was his only link to the most important person in the world to Frank.

"Chances?" Frank barely whispered, terrified of the answer.

"Mister, I don't know who you are," B.J. said, "but if I could give my life for his, I would do it in an instant."

Frank peered at her over the top of his accountant's spectacles. "Oh," he said, "you're the one."

She stared back at him, her weariness subdued her emotions. She said without nuance, "I'm the one."

Frank stared at her. "If I've offended..."

She waved a hand to dismiss the thought. "I wish I could tell you what's going to happen. He's still alive, but it was an awful beating. He's in Intensive Care. If he wakes, we don't know if there will be any brain damage or even if he'll remember anything."

"I didn't come to talk about Harry," he said, his eyes glazing. "What can you tell me about the TRA LA gang?"

"I don't know the hoods, Mr. Eberhart."

"But your brother does. He's a member, I believe."

"My brother Luke and I are day and night. If you have a question about hoods, you came to the wrong sibling."

"I don't think so. Your brother isn't much of a singer. Never make the glee club."

She frowned. "So I've heard."

"All I'm asking is you use your influence with him. Get him to talk to me."

She laughed, a wide-ranged, musical laugh. "What influence? We don't even speak the same language. We stay out of each other's way. Maybe Harry can help you when he comes to," she said with a touch of hope in her voice. "If anybody can get through to Luke, Harry can."

"I don't need any help from Harry," Frank said. "We pretty well have it doped out. Harry would only interfere with the orderly investigation. It's like a well-oiled machine, Dr. Johnson," he said, wishful enthusiasm creeping from his pores. "A pleasure to see so many people doing their jobs smoothly within the rules and regulations of an ordered society."

Gee, B.J. thought, he's so defensive about Harry. What is all this rules and regulations stuff?

Frank regaled her at length, as enthusiastically as he ever spoke, which was to say his voice rose a pitch or two and his eyes opened a millimeter more. You still couldn't hear what he was saying if you weren't standing next to him.

He protests too much, she thought, and covered her intelligence with a sweet, naive smile, the same smile she had used so often to claw her way tactfully through the white man's world.

Frank left with a vague promise from her that she would mention the visit to Luke, if she ever saw him. When she got back to Intensive Care, Dr. Baccus was not sitting by Harry's bed.

Frank felt as deflated as an empty laundry bag as he slid into the driver's seat of his car. He sat staring out at the black of the Watts' night and thought none of this would have happened without Harry.

Frank thought of all the ifs. If he hadn't been assigned to Internal Affairs, if he hadn't been assigned to investigate Harry Schlacter, if Harry hadn't met his daughter. If she hadn't dated him, gotten involved. What was the use? he thought; you couldn't change anything now.

Frank realized he had been a little broad with the police talk to the young intern. But he was trying to justify his kind of police work as opposed to Harry's. But why should he need justification? He was still on his feet; Harry was not.

Almost reluctantly, he started the car, then turned it down the main street of Watts, toward his lonely home in South Pasadena. There was an unusual stillness on the usually sullen neighborhood, but Frank didn't feel it.

Anger. Frank chalked up his miserable performance with B.J. Johnson to anger. He had been right about what would happen to Harry, but he thought all that would happen to Lela was a broken heart.

Now he was sure the goons had taken her someplace to do to her God only knows what. He couldn't think about it without this lump constricting his throat.

Whistler, Bull and Moose were missing. No one had any idea where they could be. Frank's bragging to B.J. was hollow. The rules and procedures had produced little progress so far. Frank felt his entire life wrapped up in his daughter, Lela. If anything happened to her to ruin or end her life, he would not, he was sure, have the courage to go on.

He arrived home with a sense of hopelessness. Inside, he went to his bedroom closet and took down the carved mahogany box from the shelf.

He sat on the bed, with the box resting indifferently on his lap. The box had been a gift from his wife one of the early Christmases after Lela was born. Frank used to keep Lela's childhood artwork in it. He opened it now and saw the shining metal gleaming in the overhead light.

The gun had been a gift from his mother. It was the one his father used to shoot himself. His mother, in a fit of bitterness, had handed it to Frank, saying, "This is all he left us, Frank. You take it as a reminder of his weakness so you'll be stronger."

Frank was seventeen at the time. He had since come to believe his mother gave him the gun to remind him she was the superior parent. He had always felt a competition between them for his attention and affection.

He took the gun from the box. Under it was a pile of unmailed letters written to his wife–after she died. Nobody knew about the letters. They'd probably haul him off to the sanitarium if they did. But writing letters to his dead wife was what kept him *out* of the asylum. But why in the world did he save them all? He never reread them.

He held the gun in his left hand, caressing the gunmetal-gray barrel with his right. He passed the pistol to his right hand and raised it to slide the end of the barrel against his temple.

After a few seconds he removed the gun. He certainly wouldn't want to kill himself while there was still a hope of saving Lela.

Slowly, with exaggerated care, Frank placed the gun back in the box and closed the lid.

A moment later he had replaced it on the closet shelf and started going about the business of getting to sleep.

He undressed as he did everything: carefully. He hung his clothes neatly in the closet, brushed his teeth, turned out the light and prepared for another troubled, sleepless night.

8 MEN were fatally attracted to Whistler's mother. With downright cunning, Thelma Wagner was able to convince the two men of the double-egg incident that each had fathered the child. She, of course, told neither about the other. Both contributed to her well-being financially, and she contributed, as best she could, to theirs.

The one, the hardworking man, even lived with her and Jason until the "incident," and both men spent time in the house–the hardworking man after his six-day-a-week, ten-hour shift, and the fancy man in the day, when the hardworking man was at work. Both men thoughtfully disappeared when Thelma Wagner's public assistance caseworker came around to check under the bed for a sign of male shoes that might belong to someone capable of contributing to the financial welfare of the household.

The hardworking man went to work every day with his lunch in a brown-paper sack. The fancy man worked by night in a proprietary capacity in one of capitalism's oldest enterprises, where a woman paid piecework could earn a higher rate for her time than in any other calling. "The way of the world," Fancy Man said.

As they watched Whistler grow from a beginning burglar to an expert extortionist, both the working man and the fancy man said, at different times, "That boy born to crime." Whistler's mother didn't realize it, but the fancy man meant it as a compliment.

The hardworking man went to work on the bus. The fancy man drove a purple Cadillac. Whistler, a fast learner, spent all his charm on the fancy man. The hardworking man was bent on making Whistler respectable and not above stern measures to achieve his goals. Whistler was smart enough to realize that the right word in the right place might solve his problems. So one day, after a particularly heavy beating for some petty thievery, he told the hardworking man, "...You ain't shit next to Ma's daytime fancy man." After Whistler spit out the whole story, the startled hardworking man left, leaving Whistler's mother a bloody mess, and he never bothered Whistler again.

The fancy man reciprocated by teaching Whistler all he knew, and the boy, tall for fourteen, started his own service club. The bevy of beautiful black girls–some of them a little young, but timelessly virginal and in demand–adored him and called him "Daddy" and offered him anything in the whole world, but he couldn't get interested. He tried a few times and was so embarrassed by his inability that he decided to keep everything, to the girls' everlasting disappointment, on a business basis.

While he chastised himself for, what he considered, his emotional inability to make it with black girls, he congratulated himself on his realization that education was important. He wanted math because he recognized the power of quick calculation. He wanted reading so no one would put anything over on him with fancy words he would have to be ashamed to admit he didn't understand. He liked the lessons of power and politics he learned from history classes, and he wanted his history teacher, Miss Genevieve Wills.

One spring day Miss Wills asked him to stay after school, and Whistler considered it the opportunity of a lifetime. He sat slouched in his front seat, his heart pumping like it did after a quick escape from a burglary, looking at her frail body. Miss Wills was seated behind the table she used for a desk, dressed in her favorite gray suit, with the crossed thin blue stripes, almost lost in the fabric. Out of the jacket popped the frills of a white blouse. The way she dressed required speculation about her figure. She was in her mid-twenties, but already school-marmish, with her dull semi-blond hair pulled back in a bun, dull red lipstick and a smidgen too much color added to her high cheekbones. She had a carefree way of sitting, so careless about the position of her legs under the open table. Miss Wills' class was the only one in which Whistler sat in the front seat.

"Thank you for staying, Jason," she began in that soft and considerate voice that Jason was so unused to hearing anywhere else, a voice he tried to emulate. "We had a teachers' meeting this morning and the other teachers were complaining about how their terrible discipline problems seem to be getting worse. I was a little surprised to hear that, since my discipline problems have all but disappeared. Of course, I said something like that and someone said a little sarcastically that I had you to thank. Well, I asked him what he meant and he said, 'Just ask him!' So, I guess I'm asking you, Jason. Do I have you to thank?"

He shrugged.

"You don't know, Jason? Could it be a coincidence? In this school, where it seems to be one unending madhouse, am I just so scintillating everybody is interested in my subject?"

Whistler wanted to speak, but his heart was beating too wildly, like it was jumping off a track.

"Well, Jason," she said, eying him levelly, in a way that tantalized him, "I'm waiting." She had an enigmatic smile of self-satisfaction that drove him crazy, but he saw by her patient stare he was going to have to say something.

"You a' awful good teacher," he said, at last.

"That good, Jason? One of my fellow faculty members mentioned an incident about a boy who was mysteriously beaten–almost to death, I understand–and I recall the incident and that since then no one has so much as talked back to me. You know anything about that, Jason?"

"I sure like hearing about all them famous dudes," he blurted, "like big Julio Caesar 'n Napoleon Blown-apart. You make it real interesting."

Well, she thought to herself, pursing her lips, perhaps this is what it takes–order follows fear–it has in history, why not here? "I can't deny being grateful," she said aloud and sighed, "though you might accomplish it with less blood in the future, if I had my way. You have anything else to say? It seems I've done all the talking."

"No, ma'am."

"Well, if you ever decide to tell me to what I owe this favor, perhaps I could repay your kindness."

Jason felt his blood surge up his legs and almost burst through his head.

"But, Jason–"

"Yes, ma'am?"

"I could see how you could control your own class–but all my other classes? And you seem so soft-spoken; how do you do it?"

He shrugged modestly. "They just knows," he said.

"Know what?"

"What I want."

She cocked an eyebrow, soliciting a clarification on what he wanted.

Jason was on the verge of telling her, when the principal came in and he was excused.

"Causing you any trouble?" he heard the principal say from

where he listened outside the door.

"Quite the contrary," Miss Wills said, "Jason is one of my best pupils."

"Well, you must have a magic touch," he frowned. "That isn't what I hear from the other teachers."

In quickly receding days Whistler could think of nothing other than Miss Wills. He feared there was something wrong with him; maybe he was even queer or something because he had no reaction to black women. I mean, he thought, here I am almost fifteen years old and never been laid. If a couple girls hadn't lied for me, I'd be the laughingstock of the street. I'm beginning to wonder. But, hadn't Miss Wills asked what she could do to repay him? It should be simple to tell her and collect on her promise. But how? I can't just go up to her desk and say, "Hey, Miss Wills, wanna fuck?"

In two days that seemed like two eternities Jason worked up courage enough to consult his mother's fancy friend. He was lying on the couch that had movie magazines for legs. Jason stood beside him, looking down at his serene face.

"I got this friend, see," he began, "who needs advice. I tolt him you knew you' way roun' an' all, an' like I be glad to do him this favor, see."

"Sure, man. Shoot."

"Well, this guy..."

"'Bout yo' age?"

"Yeah. Well, he's got the hots for this here white lady."

"A bit older, I hope."

"Yeah...'bout ten year older."

"Um-hum."

"Well, I...I mean, my frien', he wants to know how to get her."

"Get her?"

"Yeah, you know," Whistler shuffled his feet uncomfortably, "ball."

"Oh, I see."

"I tolt him you knowed all 'bout dat stuff."

"You did, huh?"

"Yeah."

The pimp regarded the boy with amusement.

"Well," Whistler said, unable to wait any longer, "what shall I tell him to do?"

"Grab her," he said.

"Grab her?" his big eyes shot up like moons.

"That's it. No talkin' necessary, just grab her and put it to her–she'll love you for it."

Whistler swallowed hard. "That true?"

"Gospel."

"You mean you don't sweet-talk 'er nothin'?"

"Ken, if you want. Personally, I think it's faster just to grab–lot a women like to be grabbed–'specially them..." He looked slyly up at the boy, whose innocent eyes almost burst from his head. "Older women."

"Yeah?"

"Yeah."

"Well, I'll be damned."

The pimp smiled. "You go screwin' 'roun' with white women, you jest might be damned befo' yo' time, young stud."

"Me? Mmmmm, me?" Whistler sputtered. "I said my frien'."

"I hear you talking, stud."

In spite of the advice from a man whose opinion he valued and respected, Whistler just could not bring himself to grab Miss Wills. But, he wanted her more than ever. She had the world by the things. She could go anywhere, do anything. She was white.

Instead, Whistler watched Miss Wills leave her room and walk to the parking lot, where she got into her car, ever careless of her legs, night after night until, finally, driven almost insane by his fantasy, he got the courage to approach her.

"Well, hello, Jason," she spoke first on seeing him.

"Hello, Miss Wills," he swallowed the words.

She kept on walking toward her car.

"Miss Wills?"

She stopped and turned.

"Yes, Jason?"

"Could I talk to ya a minute?"

"Sure, Jason."

He suddenly lost his nerve and jammed his hands in his pockets, looking at the ground he kicked a stone.

"Did you want to talk to me, Jason?"

"Yeah, could I come home with you a minute?"

"Why?"

"To talk."

"Can't we talk here?"

"I'd rather come home with you."

"But I live a long way from here. How would you get back?"

"I take the bus."

Miss Wills smiled at him. She still couldn't understand how this tall, skinny, awkward boy could give her such a quiet classroom. "But what do you want at my home?"

"I got a problem to discuss."

"Well, let's discuss it right here."

"No, ma'am. I wants privacy."

"Let's go back to the room."

He shook his head shyly but stubbornly.

"Well then, I'll tell you what, I'll drive you home and we can discuss your problem in the car. That's private and you won't be stranded thirty miles from your home."

He looked down in her eyes to calculate his chances.

He got in the car and watched her legs as she slipped in the driver's seat.

"Which way do I go, Jason?"

"That way," he said, pointing.

She began driving, oblivious of her high-riding skirt. He said nothing.

"Well, what can I help you with?" she asked, smiling.

You can tell me how to be cool and white like you, he thought. But he said nothing.

"Am I going in the right direction?"

"Yes, ma'am." The world was here, he thought. The big, white, wonderful world, he called it. They drove on in silence.

"You live this far from school?" she asked.

"Yes, 'um."

"Aren't we getting out of the district now?" she asked a few minutes later. She wanted to give him all the time he needed.

"We just moved," he said.

"Oh," she answered skeptically.

"Cheaper 'n payin' rent," he said, and she laughed.

"Turn here," he said later, pointing to the left. She turned without paying any attention to the area, which was suddenly without habitation save for a poorly kept cemetery on the north and a lonely deserted house ahead on the south.

All Whistler's aspirations were deserting him. His models were falling in fear of the unknown and untried. He had no aptitude to sweet-talk her like television, no ability to dazzle her with his personality like the movies. But, maybe the pimp was right and he should just grab her like they did in those X-rated movies, where you had to be eighteen to get in. But hell, if he looked eighteen to them movie people, maybe he looked eighteen to Miss Wills. Lot of dummies in his class were a couple years older than him anyway.

As the landscape grew more deserted he knew he had to act fast. Jesus, he thought, we can't drive forever. Miss Wills won't believe I live in San Diego.

Just then his mind was made up when Miss Wills shifted in her position on the hot vinyl seat and her legs moved further apart momentarily and he took the opportunity to slam his hand up her dress. Life was a matter of seizing your opportunities.

She screamed.

Now Jason was in a milieu he understood: terror, panic, hysterical screaming women, and it emboldened him.

She fought his hand while trying to control the car with her other hand. He pressed on.

"Don't gimme no shit," he said. "You like it all right."

She screamed again and swung her arm, wildly glancing off his chest.

He grabbed the wheel and pulled the car off the road at the deserted house.

"What are you doing?"

"This is where I live," he said.

He grabbed the keys from the ignition and, while she reached for them, dropped them down the front of his pants.

"Give me those keys," she demanded.

"You know way dey is," he said, flailing his legs apart.

"Jason," she said, trying to put an authority in her voice she didn't feel. She looked him in the eye, trying to ignore his hand. "This is ridiculous. Take your hand off me."

"Off yo' what?"

"Jason."

"Say 'pussy.'"

"Jason."

"Pussy."

"JASON."

"PUSSY."

"Pussy," she murmured, deflated, but he grew stronger as she grew weaker.

"Say 'Feed my pussy.'"

"No, Jason."

"What's a matter, you don't like dark meat?"

"Jason, please."

"Please feed my pussy. Go on, say it."

"No, Jason, I–"

"Feed my pussy!" he demanded.

"No." She was shaking her head and sobbing hysterically.

He tore at her blouse now and ripped it open. She began screaming and kicking, and Jason's big hands clamped her shoulders and with all his weight he forced her over on her back in the seat. He got halfway on top of her, when she brought her knee up with all the force she could muster and rammed it between his legs. The thrust of her rock-like knee and the jagged steel of the keys on his sensitive groin sent him reeling and yelling in pain. With both his hands needed to assuage the pain and extract the keys, Miss Wills freed herself and ran frantically from the car, disheartened, disheveled and disillusioned, the half-mile down the road to the main street, where she tumbled into a gas station and called her roommate. Being of rather liberal persuasion, Miss Wills rejected the black attendant's suggestion she call the police.

When he recovered and dug the keys from his flesh, Whistler realized he still had possession of the car. He drove it straight to a wrecking yard, where a friend of his, who ran the machine that crushed autos into neat cubes, did him a special favor.

On hearing Miss Wills tell her hysterical tale, her boyfriend, who was opposed to her teaching in that school anyway, decided she had encouraged the boy and wanted nothing further to do with her.

Her roommate drove her to where she left the car and then to the police to report it stolen. It was never found.

Miss Wills didn't return to school the next day.

When Miss Wills did return, she found her classes to be unruly mobs which she was unable to control, and several days later she resigned her job at the suggestion of several giggling boys who brushed gleaming brass knuckles against her nose and other parts of her body.

It took her two and a half years to find another job–teaching nursery school–but she decided, philosophically, in the long run it was better than a nervous breakdown.

Day 7

LIKE the parts of God's assembly line, the moving parts of the intensive-care ward were interchangeable. The machines, the patients, the staff became indistinguishable to each other. New parts appeared daily, and the staff remained untouched by the personalities of the silent seriously to terminally ill. It was, after all, the same old game, only the players were different.

Amid all the shuffling of principals and equipment, B.J. sat steadfastly by her white knight as a friendly landmark in contrast to the suffocating impersonality all around. She was the statue where strangers met, the weather vane, the town-hall clock.

An intermittent but persistent low moan turned B.J. from her meditation. At first she thought it was the hum of a neighboring life-support system and paid no attention. Then the irregular sound took on a more human quality: Desperation intermixed with heavy air intakes turned her head toward Harry, on the bed beside her.

The groans formed around L's. "Llll. Leeee...Lllll." He began to move slightly, at first, then a weak thrashing.

"Leeeee."

"Laaaahh."

"Leeee....lah. LELA," he cried out, opening his eyes and trying to sit up.

Tears came to B.J.'s eyes. She stood and bent over him and put her arms around him, her cheek to his. "Oh, Harry," she cried. "You did it. You *did* it. I knew you would. Nobody else believed in you. *I* believed in you. You're going to *make* it."

She could see Harry was straining to sit up, and, though her medical sense told her to keep him in place, she wanted so much to help him do what he wanted, she tried to hold him up.

"Where is she?" he croaked. "Where's Lela?" He looked around, the pain from his head flashing in his eyes.

B.J. tried to soothe him. "Take it easy, Harry. You've had it pretty rough. One thing at a time."

"Lela!" he cried out.

"Frank was here to see you," she said. "He says the FBI and the police are doing everything humanly possible to find Lela. You shouldn't worry about anything now but getting yourself back together."

She felt his big body convulse in her arms and he darted away from her, trying to get out of bed. Instead, he fell on the floor.

Tears coursed down B.J.'s chocolate skin. Tears of joy running into tears of pity, then flowing to frustration and helplessness as she tried to pick Harry up but couldn't move him. Another intern came from across the room and helped her put the big, helpless man back on the bed.

He was still conscious, breathing hard.

"Take it easy, pal," said the other intern. He looked at B.J. "You gonna be okay?"

She nodded and he left, telling her to give a call if she needed him. "Maybe we'll have to restrain him," he said.

She shook her head. "Harry's going to be all right," she said. She patted the back of his hand. "You just get yourself on your feet, Harry. It's going to be a while, but you'll do it. You just have to take it a little at a time. They're doing everything anyone can do," she repeated.

"But they haven't found her?"

"Not yet."

"Any leads? Any word at all?" His head was pounding and it was an effort for him to speak. His eyes closed with the pain.

"Not that I know of," B.J. said.

Harry seemed to lose the fight and suddenly looked like all the life had drained out of him. "Ah..." he moaned. "Never. Never, never, never, never. This one," he said with difficulty, "I'm going to do myself."

B.J. looked down at his broken body and thought, I'd hate to think of what will happen to that poor girl if she has to wait for you to rescue her.

But she was not the first person to underestimate Harry Schlacter.

"Get me out of here!" he shouted.

○   ○   ○

Hospitals always smelled like ether to Frank Eberhart, even when they didn't. When they brought his wife, Ellen, to the hospital after the accident, it smelled of ether. That time it had been too late; she was, as the impersonals said, D.O.A., dead on arrival. He could smell the ether now as he strolled down the hall, vaguely aware of the din of shuffling nurses' feet, of carts rolling mercifully down the unimaginative corridors, of girls in starched white dresses doing good deeds, gray ladies, all helping people die gracefully, Frank thought, or forestalling the inevitable, signing a new lease on life–a second chance. But Frank knew it was for everyone only a matter of time. His wife's time had come too soon. But today he wondered if Ellen was the lucky one.

His mother and grandfather had both died in hospitals, a few years after Ellen and he settled in the little house in South Pasadena that was to be their dream house. Then there was the birth of Lela, when he rushed Ellen to the maternity ward, only to learn it would be a long, difficult birth, which resulted in many problems for the child. There were the many draining trips back and forth to the hospital to visit their baby, who the doctors doubted would live. It was all coming back to him: the torment, the terrorizing uncertainty, the exhausting pace.

But Lela made it. She was an awkward, not-very-lovely-looking girl until she entered her teens. Frank had wished Ellen could have lived to see the miraculous transformation. Sometimes he thought there was a lot of anguish in this life for a little pleasure, but doing his duty gave him pleasure, he mustn't forget that.

The sunny voice intruded gently on his reverie. At first he didn't realize he was being addressed.

"Here to see Harry, Frank?" He turned and recognized B.J.

"Hi, B.J.," he said with a laconic lilt in his gentle voice. "I'm going to see Harry," Frank admitted. "I'm thinking of forming a club–Cops Touched By Harry Schlacter. We'll have reunions every five years and swap Harry stories. Maybe even give a prize for the best one."

B.J. studied Frank quizzically. Why was he being so uncharacteristically effusive? Nervous about his impending encounter? He seemed to be walking very slowly when she stopped him, more slowly than usual. "My candidate," Frank went on, "is the one I heard from this old-timer from Fugitives. He comes up to me in the hall and says something like, 'Frank, old man, I hear your daughter is going out with Harry Schlacter?'

"I said, 'Word sure traveled fast,' and he said, 'Yeah, well, just don't let her drive him anywhere.'

"I asked why, and he told me.

"It seems some girl was driving Harry somewhere and she ran a red light and good old Harry gave her a ticket. She was so outraged, she never spoke to him again.

"But the kicker," he said, snorting as though he would never believe it, "was a couple weeks later, after the ribbing Harry took died down. He walks into the station and turns in his pile of tickets for the day–and it was always a pile, believe me–and on top is a ticket he wrote himself for running a stop sign. Well, the place just broke up with laughter, as you can imagine. Everyone, from the captain down; everyone but Harry. He wasn't laughing, and he insisted on paying it, and he did. 'Right is right,' he said."

On entering Harry's ward, Frank felt the fear creeping up his spine. Was he relying too much on this maverick cop?

How would Harry react when he told him he was suspended until further notice? And when he tried to explain the politics of the department, throwing him to the wolves? Would Harry believe that Frank resisted it? Would it matter? Did they really need Harry? How much could he know, taking the beating he did? How much would he tell? Would he cooperate at all? Probably not, and why should he?

Frank decided he wouldn't tell him the brass wanted to dump him for good. And he wouldn't tell him yet about his suspension. What choice did he have?

When he saw Harry asleep in the bed, Frank realized this time he was comfortable in the presence of Harry. He looked down on the immobile, swaddled cop in the hospital bed and got a lump in his throat.

He wasn't weakening, he reassured himself. It was just that with all the force and vitality gone from Harry, he looked just as unthreatening as anyone else.

Was he really sleeping, or only faking so he wouldn't have to face Frank in his helpless state? Well, Frank thought, I can use some time to get my thoughts together. What is it I want from this guy? Or better yet, what can I reasonably expect to get?

Seated beside the big, prostrate cop, Frank laughed a quiet, circumspect laugh, but it made Harry open one eye to see what was so funny. Immediately, the eye shut. He's playing with me, Frank thought. Well, buddy, he said to himself, in your condition maybe I'd want to cop out too. Frank felt superior. He was whole. Harry was broken. The right approach was grinding its well-lubricated, time-tested gears in its inexorable conquest of the wrong approach. The maverick adversary was down-and-out. Maybe for the count. Frank would triumph. It had pleased him, the thought of triumph over Harry, he couldn't deny it, and yet the lump was still in his throat.

There was a mutual suspicion between the two cops. Harry's bluster and Frank's coolness became masks for the doubts they had relative to the other's strengths. The diametrically opposite approach of the other produced in each a twinkling of self-doubt.

Frank didn't fear him now. It was the first day he was conscious and Frank had debated coming. On the one hand, he didn't want to appear weak. He didn't want Harry to think he was condoning murder or he was offering his daughter as a human sacrifice because Harry had the bad luck to wind up in this pitiful condition. But, on the other hand, Frank's sense of duty, of common decency, won out, and here he was looking down on the uncommunicative hulk on the bed.

Well, he thought, take the bull by the horns. Talk to him.

"How you doin'?" Frank asked with a boldness that surprised him.

Harry opened one eye again. Then closed it peacefully. "You got to get me out of here, Frank," he said, his voice weak, with a tremor that frightened Frank. "I'm getting poor medical advice. All they want to do is keep me in bed."

"What's the rush, Harry? You're covered by insurance. May as well make the most of it."

"The rush is Lela," he said. "Where is my Lela?"

"We're looking for her, Harry. Everything humanly possible is being done."

Harry opened his eye again for a brief moment, giving his skepticism a lugubrious platform. "Why aren't you out there investigating?"

"Because I'm in here investigating."

Harry waved a hand; pain shot through his shoulder and twisted his cheek. "I got nothing to tell you," he groaned. "You think if I'd seen what hit me I'd be in here? Must have been a whole army, anyway. But don't worry. I'll find them, and when I do there'll be no tomorrow for the lot. If any of them lays a finger on Lela..." his voice trailed off in agony.

Frank laid his hand reassuringly on the wrapped body. "You don't have to worry about a thing, Harry," he said soothingly. "I'm optimistic we'll break the case soon. The department has gone all out and the FBI has put fifty men on it. It's a great pleasure to watch them go at this so methodically, like a giant machine, with all those precision moving parts oiled with enthusiasm. Pictures and descriptions of Lela have been sent to all the police departments and FBI offices in all the Western states, Canada and Mexico. All known informants are being contacted. Lela's fellow teachers, students' families and acquaintances are all being interviewed. You can't imagine the effort being put into this one. I wouldn't flatter myself they are giving it that extra something because she's my daughter, but, just the same, it encourages me to think so. I'm optimistic we'll break it, Harry."

Harry opened both eyes and looked up into Frank's face, then turned away from him. "Ah," he grumbled, "I've heard that before."

Frank didn't answer for a long time. He saw that speaking was a great effort for Harry and didn't want to tire him. Finally, when he noticed Harry's eyes gently close, he asked, "So what would you do?"

Harry turned toward him, opening his eyes eagerly. "You got a pencil?"

"A pencil? Yeah, why?"

"You want to know what I'd do? Make a list. Get me this stuff." He was talking now like a runner full of adrenaline at the end of a race. "First, I want some of that fancy wiretap equipment that turns on when the phone is picked up and off when it's hung up."

"Illegal," Frank said, writing.

"Next, a telescopic rifle and ammo," Harry said. "I want the brass to give me the power to quash warrants and make plea deals."

"Hey, wait a minute, Harry. Are you out of your mind? They're after your neck, you know, for the Rex Adams thing. You can't expect them to break all the rules for you."

"You want Lela back, Frank?" Harry asked with annoying defiance.

"Don't embarrass me with a question like that," Frank said, wondering where Harry was getting the strength for this enthusiasm.

"So, how are the troops doing? What have you got under your belts so far? A week? What have you got to show for your procedures?"

"Takes time, Harry."

"Yeah, well, Lela may not have all that much time. Whoever did this to me isn't fooling around. Then," he added almost casually, "I'll need a couple ballons of heroin."

"Heroin?" Frank yelled. "Now you've gone over the edge, Harry. You've really flipped. If I didn't think you were crazy before, I have no doubt now. You think I'm a drug dealer? Where would I get ballons of heroin?"

"It's all over town," Harry said blithely. "Not that hard to get. You know that, Frank."

"You're trying to fight fire with fire again, Harry, and you won't succeed."

Harry rested his eyes again. Then, as if he had expended too much of his strength already, he opened the lids to half-mast and spoke wearily.

"Well, you've got a choice, Frank. If you're satisfied with your results without me, don't get me the stuff." Harry's lids closed heavily, probably, Frank thought, the result of heavy medication.

Frank looked bleakly at the list in his hand. Harry was so outrageous, he thought. Is he serious, or is he just putting me to some bizarre test? But, do I have any justification for turning down any offer of help?

He looked out the window. The sun had slipped behind the clouds again. How did he get himself into all this just when he'd sworn off Harry for good? He was so sure the department and the FBI would have gotten some solid leads by this time, but there wasn't any use kidding himself. There was nothing. Harry had worked miracles before. Frank had to admit the Badeye collar, with all its illegality, was a magnificent work of art. Maybe—maybe not. Harry was in no shape for anything now. Maybe the rule-book boys would still triumph. He knew Harry would not give up simply because Frank had let him down. So, Frank thought, he might as well at least keep the lines of communication open.

"I'll see what I can do," he said.

But Harry wasn't listening.

Day 8

10 LELA'S initial terror on being thrown into the suffocating closet had turned to feverish calculations on how to save herself and reunite with Harry.

Everything ached. She feared she would be permanently deformed being tied by the ropes in these painful positions. Whistler let Moose take her to the bathroom. Moose told her not to worry, "Girls isn't my thing," he said.

On the second night, when the radio was turned off and all was quiet in the outer rooms, her door was stealthily opened and she felt a hand between her legs. She twisted herself suddenly around and whimpered through the gag.

"Lie still, bitch," she heard a gruff voice say. "Teach you to come on strong wid Bull," he said in a cretin's innocence. He hit her about the face and she felt her clothes being torn off her. Is this part of it? she wondered. Will they take turns? She wiggled her body so her bound feet banged on the wall, an automatic gesture for she had little hope of rescue. Icy terror shot up her spine as the huge man fumbled with his pants. Just as she felt him crash on top of her, she heard the voice of Whistler.

"What you doin', boy?" he asked angrily. The next thing she knew, the weight was lifted from her and she heard the sounds of flesh being slapped and whimpering.

"Don't you ever touch her again," Whistler said.

He bent over and took off the gag and asked her if she was all right. She just stared at him, without realizing she couldn't see through the blindfold and he couldn't see her eyes. "I'm going to leave this off from now on," he said, "so you can call out if you have any more trouble."

Whistler had checked to see that the microphone was hidden in the shade of the lamp on the end table next to the couch. The lamp base was a hollow, gray, ceramic item in the shape of Dumbo the elephant. Moose had taken out the eyes to enhance the sound, so Dumbo looked especially stupid. The shade was made out of some silky-looking material everyone hoped was fireproof. The mike had been adroitly wired there by Moose, with the wire running through the lamp and under the carpet to the tape recorder in the phonograph console on the wall bookshelf.

They were in the caretaker's cabin, but he only took care of the big house, out of sight up the road, in the summer. He wintered in Palm Springs, taking care there. Outside, a light snow was falling. Inside, the smell of mothballs was fading. The cabin had two small bedrooms, a living room, bath and kitchen. Lela was kept in the closet in the small bedroom, where Bull slept. Everyone agreed because of Moose's "orientation" he should sleep alone in the living room. He was an early riser and could start breakfast without disturbing them.

The walls were of a material known in the building trade as drywall. They had a coat of mushroom-colored paint, and the workmanship in installing them had not been expert, so the taped seams were visible everywhere.

The bookshelves were made of unpainted pine boards, and held tools of the caretaker's trade, foodstuffs, towels, soap and even a few books–*Reader's Digest* editions mostly, as well as a respectable collection of *Hustler* magazines. Bull, alone among the residents, devoured them voraciously. The drooping couch, with its dirt-brown plaid upholstery, faced the fireplace, framed in more drywall, with a pine-plank mantel. On each side of the couch, at ninety-degree angles, were chairs, one a slat-backed wooden chair, the other stuffed, in a brown floral pattern, well-worn in the vital spots. Seated on the soft one was Moose. He was crocheting.

It was Theodore Roosevelt's Bull Moose party that was the inspiration for the names. On other occasions he referred to the pair as his "Brawn Trust." Miss Wills had been his favorite teacher and she taught his favorite subject: history. He loved best of all Teddy Roosevelt, and for years he would say: "I feel like a Bull Moose," whether it was relevant or not. Moose did the cooking and housekeeping, and, though his physique was such you'd keep your distance, he had a high, squeaky voice and was painfully effeminate.

Bull, the errand boy and muscle for the outfit, had the mind of a not-too-bright eight-year-old child, but the qualities that endeared him to

Whistler were his super strength and his childlike obedience. He was lying now before the fireplace, on the honest-to-goodness bear rug, reading a comic book, occasionally asking Whistler or Moose the meaning of a particularly hard word that he would spell slowly.

"Everything ready to go?" Whistler asked Moose.

Moose looked up from his crocheting as if scorning the question. "It ain't fo' nothin' I'se the greatest wire-'n-tape man." Then he went back to work and snickered. "Fo' all da good it do. Dat filly a quiet one. Jest sorta give you the feeling you was da scum of de earth."

"Closemouthed bitch," Bull said, twisting slightly on the floor. "What does f-a-n-t-a-s-t-i-c spell?"

"Fantastic," Moose answered.

"She'll talk," Whistler said. "She'll say something we can work with, sooner or later."

"Ask me," Bull said, "you overdo dat guest shit. I say hit her hard, she'll fold in two minutes. Be eatin' outta yo' hand, no sweat."

"Yeah, you tried that, remember?" Whistler's smooth, impassive face curved in a smirk. "And you're not trying it again, if you value your life at all."

Bull grunted and looked back at his comic book.

"How much longer you figger she'll hold?" Moose asked.

"She'll be comin' 'round anytime now," Whistler said. "You got somethin' better to do?"

"No, boss, I'se just wantin' to plan da meals right. 'Bout time we lay in some more provisions."

When Moose was assigned to do the cooking, he made it clear what his tastes were. "I don't cook no black food: no chitlins, no grits, no blackeyed peas. I cooks white food exclusive; I just want to be straight 'bout dat up front. I does me a rack o' lamb an' a beef Wellington–I does high-class foods exclusive. Stuffed mushrooms an' veal chops, cherries jubilee–I don't do no cheap food."

Bull grumbled. He missed the food he was used to. But Whistler wasn't about to cook himself *or* turn the task over to the cretin...fancy food wasn't important to him though. Peanut butter, popcorn, potato chips, vanilla ice cream would keep Whistler happy indefinitely.

And Moose was as good as his word, and the food was good.

"Okay, make your list, Moose," Whistler said, waving a hand, "Bull can go to the store."

"Aw, gee, boss," Moose whined. "He ain't got no eye fo' quality like I does."

"You're needed here," he cut him off, "to work the tapes."

"What tapes? She ain't said nothin'."

"She's thinkin' though. It don't take long for captives to start depending on their captors. It's scientifically proven fact. Ain't we feeding her? Ain't we give her a place to sleep, lots of care? Won't be long, she'll be falling in love with me."

"I wouldn't be holding my breath for dat one," Moose said through the hair on his face: two eyes, a nose and hair.

"Wait and see," Whistler said, unruffled.

"How long you figger on waitin'? Been over a week already."

"Whatever it takes. I get that Horseshid Harry off my back, once and for all."

"You really got it bad for dat Harry," Moose said. "My momma allus said it a waste o' time to hold a grudge. She ain't seen nothin' next to you."

"Yeah, well, maybe she ain't seen Horseshid Harry." Whistler shook his head, then sank out of sight in reverie.

"You know, he was a nice kid, Harry was. Happy-go-lucky kinda guy. No Worries Harry–I called him. Happy Harry. He weren't the kinda guy who'd ever get a hard-on 'bout nothin'. Then when his brother bought it from some silly-assed wannabe gangbangers, I saw that change. Man, it was like lightning struck. Alla sudden he's got this bug up his ass 'bout the brothers."

"Mean prejudice?" Moose asked.

"Nah, can't say Harry ever prejudiced. More like the criminal element. The bad-blood brothers. I knew right then–Harry was gonna wind up a cop. I mean, I felt it in my bones. Before all that business, Harry'd be lucky to get outta bed in the mornin'."

"Sounds almost like you was sweet on him," Moose suggested.

"Oh, shut up that fag mouth of yours. What the hell would you know about men's friendships, cocksucker. We were friends, I ain't ashamed of that. Sure, he was a honky, but that didn't mean shit to us schoolkids. That racial shit is from the grownups, you know that, Moose."

Moose nodded. "So you so buddy-buddy, how come you is up here wid his girl–vowing to finish Harry off, once and fo' all?"

"That's 'cause he shit on me back in high school, an' he ain't let up since." Whistler's face showed Moose the difficulty he was having talking about the memory. "I had this deal, see," Whistler said. "Make us both rich. Harry didn't have to throw the game or nothin', just keep the points in the spread, see. I mean, I'da made him more for that ten min-utes work than his old man made in a year! Sombitch coulda gone to col-lege on it. Everything goin' nice, ya dig? I mean, the game is almost over and we is three points to the good in the spread. I mean, we coulda kicked a goal and still we'd be in the gravy. Know what the sombitch does?"

Moose shook his head in sympathy. "I can just imagine."

"The sombitch runs the goddamn ball seventy-some goddamn yards for a fukkin' touchdown!"

"Oh, boss," Moose commiserated.

"An' that ain't all. He calls the cops on top. They picks me up and don't my ass wind up in the slammer, thanks to my friend. An' you know what the fukkin' last straw is?"

"No, boss."

"The sombitch comes to visit me in the stir. Don't that beat all shit? 'Nothin' personal,' the fukker says. Shee-it!"

"Dat a long time ago," Moose shook his head.

"Yeah, well, you been eating good since then; I put a lot of white food in that fat gut of yours, you ain't got no complaints."

"I ain't complainin'," Moose said, his voice squeaking.

"They put him on this here gang special force, an' he comes after me like lightning. I mean, you'd think I was the only gang leader in town, you get me? Come after me in a little transaction, heists the stuff off me and the money off my frien', and the judge throws the case out but decides not to return my goods, see. So ole Harry, I make him a casual proposition: Twenty grand if he returns to me what is rightfully mine. I mean, the case was *thrown out*, you understand. And, that's as much bread as he sees in a year. So, what's he do? Throws me a hay-maker in the hall of the courtroom. Knocks me flat on my ass. That's the kind of gratitude I get for tryin' to make him rich..."

"Ain't no justice, boss," Moose said without looking up from his crocheting.

"But, boss, didn't I just hear you tell a kid to join the Boy Scouts–make something of hisself. I mean, he was beggin' you to join."

"'S different!" Whistler snapped. "The brothers do it on their own–'s fine. We just don't want no more subjugation from no honky cops. I mean, theys gotta be *some* advantages to emancipation."

"Yeah."

"I tell you, Moose, in this life you can't show no weakness. Soon's you do, you are dead in the water. Power to the people, Moose, ain't no other way." Whistler sighed as though a burden had lifted. He often felt his boys were his burden. "Black man's burden," he called it.

Whistler looked into the fire. "We gotta take care of Harry. May take some time, but we're going to turn this here Lela, Harry's special girl, and we gonna use her to get him where he belongs."

"Where's dat, boss?"

"In the slammer. He ain't nothin' but a common criminal with a badge," Whistler snorted. "Gonna be a sex toy for one of them big, black muthafukkers."

"Yeah," Moose said, "maybe so, but the cops ain't too swift 'bout indictin' dere own."

"True enough, my man," Whistler agreed. "So I just gotta dramatize the issue a bit. Get the public on my side. Keep his girl until they all cave in. She might even fancy me 'fore it's all over. Scientifically proven that girls become dependent on their captors. Even to falling in love..."

"Yeah, well, as I said," Moose said, his voice an eerie female twitter, "on dat dere one, I wouldn't hold mah breath."

"Okay, you want to put some money on it?"

"Oh, no, my momma tell me never to gamble. Never win, she say. Only thing she say it was safe to bet was if someone bet dey could turn you white. Said if dey did turn you white and you lost, it would be worth da money."

Whistler laughed, showing decaying teeth. "She's ready. I feel it in my bones. Today we're gonna get something from her we can use."

Moose grunted.

"Everybody ready? I'm going to get her out."

〇   〇   〇

The closet was bare except for the horizontal bar at the top for hanging clothes and the clothes hook screwed into the wall. On the floor Lela was bound and blindfolded. The gag had been removed after the second night's incident so she could call out in an emergency. After five days of good behavior Lela was rewarded by tying her hands in front of her rather than behind her back, and she considered it a great luxury, for which she was very grateful, though she still held back from expressing her gratitude.

It was her major dilemma: How to get what she wanted from them without giving them what they wanted. She had been keeping time by scratching the door molding with her fingernail, at first every time she got sleepy, then when she heard the radio turned off. It wasn't too accurate, but it was better than nothing.

She vowed to keep her sanity and her independence, and she kept her mind active by thinking about Harry and her father and how best to escape. She remembered the discussion she had with Harry, walking on the beach in the bright sun one Sunday, when he asked her what she would do to save her life. Lie, certainly–steal, assault, would she murder? Harry, of course, took the position that to save a worthwhile life you would do anything. Would that include sleeping with Whistler Wagner? Would that be worse than murder? She feared that to Harry it would.

Well, she *was* grateful that Whistler was treating her so gently. On the second day, he asked her to think over a few things while she was in the closet. First, she could, if she wanted, make a tape to send to her father and boyfriend, saying anything she wanted to let them know she was alive. Though she considered their feelings and peace of mind, she suspected some trick and was not sure she should so rapidly agree to anything Whistler proposed.

Second, he wanted her to explore her feelings about black people. Did she feel they were equal to whites? Did she think she could ever have a black friend? A black boyfriend? Could she ever come to feel kindly toward him? Could she ever love a black man?

Next, he asked her if she thought policemen should be subject to the same laws as other people. It was easy to see the answer Whistler wanted, but she wanted to be sure that she got something in return.

Lela tried to figure who Miss Wills was, what she was to Whistler and what it meant to her. A former girlfriend, perhaps? But, why call her "Miss"? Some authority figure, maybe, who dominated his early childhood. If she only had a clue. Lela thought the key to her freedom might lie in that enigma.

Her muscles and joints ached and her skin chafed under the ropes. She thought if she couldn't get some freedom of movement, the numbness would cause everything to atrophy. If only she could get out in the house, with her blindfold off, she could get a better sense of time and place and, hopefully, see tracks in the snow outside to give some hint of which way it was to the nearest living person.

One thing at a time, she told herself. She couldn't be too in a hurry or she would seem too transparent. But now, as she felt fingernail-carved ridges in the doorframe, she realized the time had come for step one of her plan. So when Whistler came to the door, she told him that she was ready to make the tape.

Day 14

THE smell in the hospital therapy room offended Frank. Clean should not smell, he thought, yet antiseptic filled the air. Frank felt like he had a nose full of mothballs.

He saw Harry across the room, his wrapped, unsteady legs relentlessly pounding the pedals of a stationary bicycle, his face reflecting the torture of muscle and nerve, the black-and-blue spots had begun to yellow, while his legs refused to give up the cadence. It was two weeks, to the day, since Harry's beating, and he was pushing the healing process without mercy.

The resident-in-charge, his doctor and B.J. had all warned Harry he was overdoing the rebuilding process and could easily reverse his condition if he persisted, but Harry had only responded that those who were satisfied with half-measures were doomed to live half-lives.

Pity welled again in Frank's breast as he saw Harry across the room. Even before he reached him, Harry yelled, "Hey, Frank, you got the stuff?"

What a question, Frank thought. Have I got the stuff for what? The stuff he asked for, or the right stuff, the stuff it takes to make it?

"I gotta see you privately," Frank said, clutching a briefcase under his arm.

"Privately?" Harry asked, suspicious of the briefcase. He had never seen Frank carry one before. "We're among friends here," he said.

"Privately," Frank insisted with a gentle firmness. "When you hear, I'm sure you'll agree."

Frank noticed Harry's body twist with pain as he got off the bicycle. "Give me a hand, old man," Harry said, and leaned on Frank.

The only sound from either of them as they struggled toward Harry's now semiprivate room was that of Harry's labored breathing.

When Frank helped Harry onto his bed, he noticed an old party in the bed by the window, looking not unlike Somerset Maugham just before his final statement.

"Who's your friend?" Frank asked.

Harry sat on the edge of the bed, moving his outstretched arms in small circles. "That's Willy. Don't worry; he can't hear a thing."

Frank opened the case and took out a tape machine and set it on the bedside table, noticing for the first time the photograph of his Lela in the black drugstore frame. B.J. had brought the picture from Harry's apartment, where it had resided on his bedside table. Frank had to move it to set up the tape machine, and he did so gingerly, as though the world might crumble under his touch.

"What's up?" Harry asked, looking at the machine, still rotating his arms.

Frank switched it on and thought what an eerie quality the voice had.

"Greetings from liberation land." It was Whistler's voice; Harry knew it immediately.

"Our honored guest is Lela Eberhart, daughter of a cop, girl-friend of another cop–just how close a friend of Harry Schlacter will remain to be seen.

"We have brought her here as our guest to liberate her from the sinister influence of the police, who murder anonymously and with impunity. It is these wrongs we seek to right. Ours is a holy mission. We want no ransom money; we want only what is right–justice for all people, black-skinned as well as white.

"The price of Lela's release will be disclosed in a few minutes. You will all agree, it is a reasonable price–all, except the murderer himself."

Harry dropped his arms to his sides and listened with a pain-caused ironic smile. He remembered how Whistler used to talk street-talk, and grudgingly gave him credit for learning the language.

"Money is not involved," the voice continued in measured, reasonable tones, almost scholarly, without emotion, "only justice. Since we are asking something of the police, we are, naturally, offering something in return. We are offering the freedom of our guest, and, to convince you she is alive and well-cared-for, she has asked to speak to you. Here is Miss Lela Eberhart." Whistler sounded like the master of ceremonies at a stag banquet.

"Hi, Harry and Dad," her voice sounded tired, but not defeated. "I'm alive. They feed me all right. I hope they'll let me go soon."

Frank watched Harry fall back against his pillow, relief flooding his face. That quickly gave way to a frown of contempt for the captors.

"Well, Lela," Whistler's kindly voice was heard again, "that's going to be up to your friend Harry Schlacter and his employers. We want to let you go as soon as they want to have you back. It's as simple as that. We have only two requests. The first is to expel Harry Schlacter from the police force for his many offenses against humanity, like his wanton premeditated murder of our colleague Badeye Iler. After that is accomplished and we get word on the radio–the same station that you hear this tape on–we will give you our second request. Of course, there is no hurry. We're all happy here, aren't we, Lela?"

"Yes."

"You being treated well?"

"Sure."

"Food good?"

"The food's excellent."

Frank watched Harry to see if he was picking up on the jarring sounds. Harry was clenching his fists.

"Lela, what's your feeling toward blacks?"

"They're people like anyone else. Some good–some bad."

"Think you could be friends with a black person?" The voice came through obsequious, and yet with childlike anticipation.

"Sure."

"A black man?"

"Maybe."

"Fall in love...with a black...man?"

Her tone was seductive when she said, "Why not?"

He giggled. She laughed.

"Have I been nice to you?"

"Real good."

"You got any complaints at all?"

"No."

"That's good, Lela, and I'm never gonna give you any cause to complain. Let me just get your feelings on one more thing, Lela, before we sign off. Do you think policemen should be subject to the same laws and punishments as the rest of us?"

"Yes."

"And would that include your boyfriend, Harry Schlacter?"

"Yes."

"So you see, Harry," Whistler purred, "the rest is up to you."

Harry lunged at the tape machine and fell on the floor. Intern B.J. came in and helped Frank put him back in his bed.

"You're going to set yourself way back, Harry Schlacter, if you don't calm down," B.J. said.

"I got to get out of here."

"Easy, Harry."

"It's got to be a fake," Harry cried. "That can't be Lela."

"It's Lela," Frank said, quietly.

"No."

"But it's a fake too. It's a patch job. They used the same 'yes' a couple times, then spliced answers to questions. I ran it through the lab. It's an amateur job."

Harry leaned back, deflated, and groaned. "Who is going to know that?"

"We know it."

"There be a press release on it?"

"No. We don't want them to know what we know. Don't want to inhibit them in any way."

"Any postmark on the tape?"

Frank shook his head. "Dropped in mail slot at the station–in the middle of the night."

"Could be local."

"Or mailed it to someone to drop."

"Check the gang?"

Frank nodded. "Nobody's cracking."

"Informants?"

"Nothing."

Harry bit his lower lip. "You get the stuff?"

"Not much."

"What'd you get?"

"I got the telescopic rifle and the ammo."

"That's all?" Harry didn't hide his disappointment.

Frank nodded. "And that's the good news."

"And the bad?"

"The brass. Not only aren't they interested in your requirements for solving the case, they want your neck..."

"In answer to that garbage?" Harry said, pointing contemptuously at the tape machine.

"That's only part of it. Actually, it's an embarrassment to them. They wanted you out before they got the tape. Now the *Times* is screaming to get you; their cute cartoonist has drawn another dilly, showing you on all fours, salivating like a rabid dog–real subtle, that guy–and the department doesn't like bad publicity. But on the other hand, they don't want to knuckle under to some hood's pressure."

Frank looked at the floor, exhaling his exasperation. "They've put me in charge of your Badeye investigation now that they don't feel they have grounds on the Rex Adams thing."

"How can you talk like that?" Harry yelled, slamming his fist on the mattress, then recoiling with pain. "Your daughter could be murdered–or worse," he said, pausing pitifully. Frank noticed Harry's suffering when the line "fall in love with a black man" came across the tape. He knew Harry's fetish for chastity; he knew all about Harry. The guy he didn't know about was himself.

"He may sound reasonable on the tape," Harry was saying, "but Whistler is a madman. Nobody knows him like I do. Instead of helping me find her, you are going to investigate me for some hood's murder?"

Frank looked away, out of the window, and saw those ridiculous palm trees that always made him think he should be in the South Pacific somewhere instead of among noisy automobiles and stucco houses, asphalt streets and concrete sidewalks. Cement city with *Washingtonia robusta* palms.

"The reason," Frank said, without turning back, "is if we get enough to discharge you, he'll release her."

"Sure, take a hood at his word. They murder, but, for some reason, no one suspects them of lying. And, what about his second demand? Probably wants the chief to commit suicide at the Music Center. Will he go along with that?"

"Harry," Frank said in his gentle tone, weighted down by the ironies of his world, "they want you to resign."

"Resign?" Harry fell back on the bed, stunned.

"So much simpler," Frank went on wearily. "It won't look like they are caving in to criminal ransom demands. More like *you* were doing it selflessly. You know, heroics to save the girl."

A desperate gurgling sound escaped Harry's throat.

"Look, Harry, you went too far. Everybody knows you hit Badeye, and some don't blame you. But the department is on the defensive so much that it can't look the other way any more."

"Anybody shedding any tears for Charlie Rubenstein?" Harry asked, his chest heaving, his fists clenched beside him.

"He's gone, Harry."

"And he gets less sympathy than his killer. Maybe we ought to put Badeye's picture next to Charlie's, with the dead cops at the Southeast."

Frank shook his head. "And we don't want to find your picture there either, and, if we don't get you off the force soon, no one doubts you'll wind up there. You just missed it this time by a fraction of an inch," he said, looking at the big cop sprawled helplessly on the hospital bed.

"The Hall of Shame?" Harry asked.

"Fame, Harry; we call it the Hall of *Fame.*"

"Shame," Harry repeated stubbornly. "Any cop who gets shot it's shame. You can shoot in the line of duty, but you don't get shot unless you're asleep. It's no honor to be up there. It's a disgrace."

Frank stared at his fellow policeman. "That's a little strong, Harry."

"Maybe, but if you think I'm resigning because you scared me about being shot, think again. I can take care of myself."

Frank stared at Harry, then, as if blinded by some tragic reality on Harry's face, turned suddenly and kicked the toe of his shoe lightly on the wall, a huge emotion for Frank. "I couldn't tell you, Harry. I begged to be the one to tell you. They said okay–then this happened," he said, pointing at Harry. "I couldn't tell you."

"Tell me what?" Harry squinted up at Frank.

"After the Rex Adams thing–you know, the case they gave me–our first meeting?"

"Yeah."

"Well, I told you I wanted you off the force, remember? And I said you should ask for another, unbiased, investigator?"

"So what?"

"They decided to suspend you–*against* my recommendation. I went to bat for you, but they said, essentially, that's politics–the way the cookie crumbles, ball bounces–lot of meaningless clichés." Frank took a deep breath, his face twisting in the pain of the memory. "Now, I should have told you before this happened–but I couldn't. Now everybody is embarrassed. On the one hand, it would be simple to have you turn in your badge because of Rex Adams, but it would look like the department was caving in to Whistler and the hoods. But even if they did, it wouldn't satisfy Whistler. The blood he wants is for his buddy Badeye. Nothing else will do."

"Oh, man..."

"Yeah. We have nothing. But now they want me to investigate that–to show Whistler we're working on it."

"Oh, Frank..."

"Well, it could prolong Lela's life...until we can get her out."

"Okay, if you want to play charades," he shook his head. "What an awful pity you have to waste this valuable time like that."

"Will you cooperate? Tell us what you know?"

Harry picked up his pillow and threw it at Frank, who stopped it with his abdomen. "I won't resign, Frank. And I won't tell you anything either. I'm tired of being reprimanded like a child all the time, then begged to solve the tough cases."

"Harry, Harry, we both want the same thing–Lela. We ought to be able to work together."

"Together, ha!" Harry snorted. "What is your part? A rifle, and I do the rest? Real swell, Frank," his thick voice trailed off. "Real swell..."

"Please, Harry," Frank said, ashamed of himself for begging. "Don't make it harder for me than it already is. Everybody is working real hard on this, but there might be something missing. You might give us that big break. She's my daughter, Harry. I raised her alone. I love her more than anything in this world. What do you want from me?"

Harry looked out the window at the palms swaying in the breeze. He thinks *he* loves her, he thought. He turned his steely gaze on Frank's watering eyes.

"Let me tell you a story, Frank. One of my favorites."

Frank nodded. He couldn't believe Harry could tell a story, but he was grateful for the break.

"There was this chief of police in a small town, looking to retire, and he wanted to pick a successor from his troops. There were only about ten or twelve cops in the burg, and the chief narrowed his choice to three, but he couldn't decide among them. So he called them into his office, one by one, and told them a story about a farmer, explaining that they would each be asked to ask the farmer only one question.

"The story went like this: There was a farmer who went to his barn to shoot a pigeon, and, after firing, a spark caught the hay and the barn burned down.

"What question would you ask the farmer, Frank?"

Frank looked at Harry, shook his head and smiled. "I don't know. I guess–did he get the livestock out alive?"

"A good question, Frank, and one of the cops answered it that way. Another one asked if he was insured. But the third, the guy who got the job, asked: 'Did he get the pigeon?'"

Frank laughed, "Good, Harry, very good. We don't have the pigeon, yet; I don't have to tell you."

Harry nodded. "I'm not in the greatest shape, Frank, maybe you guessed. But I don't want to sit around here much longer. I could use a driver..."

Frank's eyes filled with liquid gratitude.

○   ○   ○

The distinguished-looking man in the black morning coat and broad, silk, gray-striped tie came in the door, carrying a thick attaché case.

He nodded briefly at Harry, who was sitting up exercising his neck by rolling his head back and forth and from side to side.

"Mr. Schlacter, I presume," he said.

"Yeah," Harry didn't stop rolling his head.

"I'm Mr. Anfuso from Dimwidee and Seafurth."

"Yeah, have a seat."

"Our pleasure," the portly, balding man said, looking around at his newfound surroundings, leaving no doubt he didn't mean it. "I must admit this is my first hospital assignment. Oh, I've gone to homes and offices, generally Beverly Hills and Century City, but," he cleared his mouth of some bothersome flavor, "never to a hospital."

"Yeah, well, thanks for coming."

"I suppose, when people are in the hospital," the man said, making his best effort at being friendly, as if trying to erase what he realized was a snobbish-sounding beginning, "they want to get out before making any definite plans." He looked at Harry, trying to appraise his condition.

"Yeah, well, when I'm out of here, I won't have any time..."

"And, then, as I told you on the phone, we can make a selection, but we can't fit it without the young lady present."

"She can't be present right now," Harry said shortly, "so I'll estimate, and *we* won't make any selections, *I* will."

Mr. Anfuso looked abashed but recovered nicely. "Of course, forgive me, just my manner of speaking."

Harry waved his hand in a gesture of summoning the opening of the attaché case.

Mr. Anfuso did so, showing a sparkling array of diamond rings. Harry's eyes popped and his head stopped rolling. He passed his eyes critically over the merchandise for a few seconds, then pointed at one of the rings.

"You want us to make this and hold it for a fitting?"

"No," Harry said, "she's about five-foot-three, a hundred pounds." Harry had never asked her, but learned to estimate physical statistics of suspects within five percent, another of his many job assets, self-taught.

"Most unusual," Mr. Anfuso muttered politely.

"Yeah, well, I'm going to see the lady and I want to surprise her with the ring."

"I see," he said blindly, raising an eyebrow. "I hope you find her." This last was in the form of a naughty confidence.

Harry jumped. "I'll find her. Don't you worry about that!" He shouted as though Anfuso were stone-deaf.

Mr. Anfuso had heard the tape, as had most Los Angeles residents, so much play was given to it, and so, contrary to all good rules of gem salesmanship he had lived by in the name of Dimwidee and Seafurth for eighteen years, Mr. Anfuso made exceptions to the deposit requirements, the restrictions against credit, the qualifying procedures for a purchase, because Harry had told him his story, and he had never been so moved. It was told with less grace and more emotion than any story he had ever heard, and he promised to deliver the ring in half the ordinary time, at the smallest markup.

He didn't really expect to collect on the note, but Harry knew he would pay the price, far in excess of his means, if it took him the rest of his life. Now the only thing he had to do was make sure he lived long enough to pay the debt, and make sure Lela lived for him to give her his gift.

Day 17

12 AMID the suffocating smell of her own unwashed body, Lela fought to ward off the creeping sickness she felt in the pit of her being. She fretted her mind into hopeful activity. She must not, she told herself, give up. As a reward for making the tape Lela's blindfold had come off. For all the good it did her. She was in the closet most of the time, and when she was out in the house, the shades were drawn. Not that there was anything to see outside. The night they arrived and she ran from her captors she sensed the isolation.

Whistler promised her she could have a bath any time she wanted it–under one condition: He wasn't leaving her alone in the bathroom. There was a window she could get out, and who knows what else she could cook up after all she had accomplished in the trunk of his car. So, yes, he would be right in there with her–watching.

The mere idea revolted her.

She wondered why Moose couldn't guard her in the bath, but was afraid to risk offending Whistler by asking. But as one desperate day fed anxiously into the next, Lela's calculating turned into conniving. Then she moved on to deception, and, with a pose she could only hope was convincing, she told Whistler she would like to take a bath–with him.

His rotten teeth flashed in a sudden smile, then it disappeared just as suddenly, and Lela feared she'd made a mistake.

"We'll see about it," Whistler said, and left her to finish her lunch in the company of Bull and Moose.

        ⛉   ⛉   ⛉

Lela sat in the old-fashioned large tub in the small, wainscoted bathroom, luxuriating in the steaming water and bath oil Whistler had brought her. On the hook on the bathroom door were the clothes

Whistler had brought to replace the ones Bull had torn. Personally selected to his taste, there was a peach-colored Quiana stretch, slinky dress with ruffles on the bosom, underwear of cliché pink with generous frills. On the floor was a pair of high-heeled pumps, liberally laced with sequins. The entire ensemble a whisper from whoredom.

Whistler sat on the closed toilet lid, watching Lela. He had often pictured Miss Wills in frilly clothes like these, and was anxious to see how Lela would look in them.

Lela didn't know how to take him. She looked for some weakness that she could exploit, some crack in his courtly facade, but she found none. So she realized his only moment of weakness might come on the "Big Night," and she would have to point her efforts in that direction.

When she got herself out of her bath she stood before him and dried herself leisurely, throwing her head back as if to abandon all fear. She watched his eyes play on her body. His muscles seemed to twitch, and Lela experienced a sudden fear and drew back, covering herself with the towel. She stepped into the frilly underwear and pulled the peach Quiana slinky, shiny dress over her head and fluffed out the appliquéd ruffles about her young bosom.

"Nice dress," Whistler said.

"I'm glad you like it."

"We getting any closer to the Big Night?"

"Looks that way," she said, demurely cocking her head to the floor.

"You gonna tell me when you're ready, Miss Wills? I don't want to push you none."

Lela looked startled. There it was again, she thought. "Who is Miss Wills?" she said carefully.

"Who?"

"Miss Wills," she said. "You called me Miss Wills again."

"No, I didn't," he said, cutting her short.

She began again to wonder about Miss Wills. At first when he called her that, Lela thought she might not have heard what she thought she did. Now she was sure he had called her Miss Wills. If only she knew why. It made her think he was crazier than he otherwise seemed.

"I'll be ready," Lela said, "when I can feel like a person." If she could buy more time, she might solve the mystery of Miss Wills. It might help her escape.

Whistler stood up and motioned for her to go to the living room, where he seated her on the couch. He sat on the floor, the concealed microphone in the Dumbo lamp between them. The old wooden radio on the bookshelf was playing loud rock music.

Whistler smiled, showing his bad teeth. Lela always blanched when she saw those teeth. She could take his looks until he opened his mouth. If she could counsel him, it would be to never open his mouth...or to take some of that ill-gotten gain from God knows what illegal enterprises and have his teeth straightened and capped. "Have you thought about love since you been here?"

She took a deep breath and smelled the cooking odors coming from the kitchen. "I told you, Mr. Wagner..."

"Hey, wait a minute, I told you, you gotta call me Whistler. Mr. Wagner, that's talking down to me."

"I'm sorry." She looked down at her thin fingers, caressing the arm of the couch, "I meant it to be respectful."

He waved his hand as though he didn't believe her. "I don't need that. I got all the respect I want. What I'm looking for is something else."

"Love?" she asked.

"Yeah."

Bull came in from outdoors, carrying an armload of logs he had just chopped for the fire. He set them in front of the fireplace.

Moose came from the kitchen and asked, "How you like yo' steak cooked, Missy Lela?"

"I like it medium-rare, thank you. May I help you with something?" she said, rising.

"I don't need no help," he shouted, reacting violently to her innocent suggestion. "You don't like my cooking?"

"Oh, Moose, I love your cooking."

"Then why you want to meddle?"

"I wouldn't presume to interfere with your creative cooking; I just thought I might save you some work with something menial, like cutting carrots or something."

Bull looked up and said, "You can cut the cheese," and sniggered and giggled, sucking air in infantile abandon.

"Sit down, Lela," Whistler said gently. "I don't think we are ready to put a knife in your hands yet. Maybe in time."

Moose returned to the kitchen and Bull went back outside. Lela asked Whistler, "How did you happen to bring these particular men along on this errand?"

He stared at her a long time before answering, as if trying to determine some hidden meaning to her question.

"They good boys," he said at last. "Moose got a lot of skills."

"But he's so effeminate. I must say, I don't picture his kind in a gang."

"I don't think of my boys as a gang like the cops do. More a business enterprise, where each contributes according to his lights. Moose's sex habits don't affect us at all. What he does, he does well."

"But that creature, Bull. He has the mind of a child. Surely he has no skill."

"Strength. That's his asset. Almost superhuman strength. And obedience." He smiled. "The Mafia live or die by their enforcers. Let me tell you a little story: We all come from the same neighborhood–the Compton-Watts area. Some of us made a success of ourselves, and those who couldn't, joined the police."

Lela blinked back an incredulous gasp when she realized he was not joking.

"We all about the same age–Harry and Charlie Rubenstein were classmates. I was a classmate of Bull's until we got business in our blood. Badeye Iler, the guy Harry murdered, was, you might say, my teacher. I met him in stir and he taught me a thing or two. Said the Snorkles were getting a little heavy in their turf and they wanted to hit the leader. I was so wet behind the ears, I didn't even realize they had territory in the stir. Anyway, Badeye says to me they been watching me and want to put me to the test. When I heard what the test was–they wanted me to stick an ice pick in this here guy's heart–I sez no thanks, it's very flattering and all, but I just didn't want to go around killing people with all these witnesses and all those gang guys knowing it. Badeye says, 'Okay, stud, you think about it. You do the job, nobody knows nothing. You don't want to do it, we have it done an' got four witnesses swears you did it. Maybe don't even use the witnesses, just pass the word to the Snorkles. Like a leak to the press.' Yessir, that half-white dude taught me everything. When we got out, he took me under his wing, and things went so well for me I got promoted to the top, sort of chairman of the board, you might say, and, not being one to forget his friends, I made Badeye my vice president."

"The man who taught you everything?" Lela asked.

"The very same dude who blackmailed me into murdering a guy I didn't want to hit. He must have known I'd never forget that favor, and when I got suspicious he was playing footsies with another business who was muscling in on our turf, I asked my very good friend Bull to see to the problem. Somehow, Badeye was expecting it, got the draw on Bull and did this to him," he waved his hand toward the outside door with contemptuous resignation. "'Course, he was no genius before that bullet hit him there, but now he's got the mind of an eight-year-old, and not too smart an eight-year-old at that. But he hasn't lost any of his strength, no sir; if anything, he's stronger. 'Course, he's sorry for what he done to you on one of them first nights, but he'll never do it again." Whistler frowned. "Well, I can't turn my back on him. But, I owe him. Even though he didn't get the Badeye job done, I got a loyalty to my boys. And he's still useful."

"But," Lela let the word hang there, perplexed like a disoriented sparrow in a cloud.

"How did I get Harry to do the job for me? Simple. Harry's best friend was Charlie Rubenstein. He grew up on the street with us, but he was an oddball. Liked the books, studious type. Athletic too. An all-round Jew, I called him. Charlie got a little close to some of my associates. Well, I had to show him that we didn't cotton to no proselytizin' from the fuzz. I tried to get him to lay off, peaceful like, but he was stubborn, that one. Now the Badeye thing had been giving me ulcers anyway, and it was like a perfect marriage. So, I gave Badeye the job to hit Charlie."

"And he did it?"

"Oh, I gave him a choice. He said, of course, he wasn't hittin' no cops. Only morons did that, and I should send Bull on that errand, but I didn't like that smart-mouth stuff, and I told him he could make up his own mind. Either he hit Charlie and nobody knows he did it, or we have it done for him and leak word to the fuzz he done it." Whistler giggled, proud of himself.

"So he did it?"

"Amazing how fast he caught on. So, now I got my problem solved. Solved itself, you might say. Badeye skedaddles to Frisco, so he's outta my hair. I get word to Harry, Badeye done the deed, and Harry does the rest."

Whistler looked at Lela and saw raw outrage on her face. But, she held her tongue. A girl with style, he thought–real class–like Miss Wills.

"So the moral is, the boys who stay loyal, like Bull, get my undying loyalty in return. Those who cross me, like Badeye, Charlie Rubenstein and Harry, got to take their just deserts sooner or later.

Badeye goes back fourteen years, but I got him. Now, there is something Harry loves more than life itself, and that's being a cop."

Lela whimpered.

"Oh, you didn't think I knew that? I didn't get where I am by being stupid. The way to hit Harry isn't to kill him, it's to take his job away from him, and that's what we're doing. That's our first request. Notice I don't say 'nonnegotiable demands' like those hotheads. My operation always had a little more class."

Lela watched him as he bragged, all full of himself. Pride goeth before a fall, she said to herself, then added, I only hope.

It was only a few minutes later that the all-pervasive radio startled Lela with the special bulletin:

"A spokesman for the Los Angeles Police Department said today that Officer Harry Schlacter has been suspended from the department, after he refused to resign. Schlacter was the officer the kidnappers of Lela Eberhart demanded removed from the force. The ransom tape, played exclusively on this station, spoke of a second demand after the expulsion of Officer Schlacter, and we will report to you as soon as we get any word on just what that second demand will be."

Lela was nauseated at the carnival-huckster tone of the announcer, how he seemed to be enjoying delivering the message, the messenger for evil intended and evil transported and evil achieved. All in a day's work. He had a sickening pride in his exclusive, with no concession to the principles or anything but his own gratifications.

Up to that moment Lela had hope that Harry would save her. She felt that he was truly the super-cop. Her father gave her that idea. Now with him off the police force she suddenly had all her hopes shattered, and that left the solution up to her. There was still the FBI and the police. But how long did it take them to find Patty Hearst? Years. It was a very depressing thought.

That evening, after dinner, sitting on the couch by the concealed microphone, Lela broached the subject of the Big Night. Whistler was delighted because of Harry's suspension. It was time to make another tape, and they were running low on usable material.

"I've been considering what you asked me to consider," she started badly, she thought. He'll know I'm not sincere, I'm just trying to use him, to trap him really. I've got to put him off yet keep him interested. My timing is wretched. So obvious right on the heels of Harry's suspension. But Whistler didn't seem to notice; his elated eyebrows arched in interest. He got up and turned off the radio.

"What did you consider?"

"You know. The Big Night."

"Oh," he nodded, sitting back down, "the Big Night."

There was a roaring fire in the fireplace, outside the snow was blowing and drifting. The flickering shadows from the fire danced on the wall, having an almost hypnotic effect on Lela.

"If I was to agree, do you think I could stay out of the closet after that?"

Whistler pondered the question. "Well, I wouldn't rule out the possibility," he said finally.

"And have you thought about sending the boys away?"

"Hm," he considered. Whistler was not one for quick answers, and waiting for his response made Lela uncomfortable. Moose had taught him it was easier to edit the tapes if there were breaks between speakers.

"I mean, I don't want an audience. You realize, I hope, that this would be my first time."

"Is that so?" Whistler's face bounced expectantly. Why, she wondered, should that seem to make him so happy? She had heard of a premium being put on innocence, but she thought experienced men preferred experience. Whistler seemed enchanted.

"Then couldn't they go for a ride? Do some shopping or something?"

Whistler nodded, not in approval, merely in consideration.

"Because if you don't trust me," she said, "I'm not ready to do it." She giggled uncomfortably. "I don't know if I'm ready anyway, you understand, I'm just discussing it."

"I understand," Whistler said with, Lela thought, a peculiar tone of relief.

"And another thing I would have to have your absolute word on."

"What's that?"

"You'd have to promise never to tell Harry or my father. I mean, I would just die if they knew. Harry would kill us both, I think. He's an absolute nut on purity." She giggled again, nervously. "We both know that's old-fashioned, of course, but Harry's Harry."

"You don't have to worry none on that score. Whistler don't tell nobody nothing." His lips twisted in a smirk. "Least of all the fuzz."

"Well," she said to break the long silence that followed, "what do you think?"

"I think," Whistler laughed, "you starting to sound awful anxious. I'm a little suspicious."

"What are you suspicious about?" she cut in too quickly. Then, trying to cover up, "Girls have normal desires too, you know, and you said yourself that the captive becomes dependent on the captor for the creature comforts in life and, when they are satisfied, feels gratitude. It's a textbook case, Whistler. You have been awful good to me. I mean, I know how much worse I could have had it and all..."

"But that doesn't mean," he said, careful to enunciate clearly for the microphone in the lamp, "that you have to hop into bed with me, does it?"

She frowned. "Isn't that what you want?"

"I only want it if you do, Lela. I want you to work out all your feelings. I don't want you to come to me because you think you owe it to me or because it will help you get out quicker. And I don't want you to come with Harry Schlacter on your mind. When you come, it must be with Harry no longer the object of even a small part of your love. When you come, it must be because you love me."

Lela's mouth hung speechless. Whistler was not going to be the pliable fool she hoped, and she'd spent a long, sleepless night troubling over her next move when the next morning she gave him the line for the tape he was waiting for.

"Harry's finished, done for. I'm not interested in him any more. Now I'm only interested in you."

Whistler just looked at her and smiled.

Oh, Lela thought, those horrible teeth. She smiled sweetly back at him.

Day 22

13 THE two cops in the shadows looked like a pair of crippled, shivering squirrels, crouched behind the midnight-blue garbage bins, their pistols at the ready.

They were enveloped in the malodorous bouquet of putrefying garbage, left in the bins because of some snafu in the pickup schedule or perhaps an overdue bill or a less than conscientious truck driver, each contributing in its own small way to the quality of the local environment.

Harry had checked himself out of the hospital this morning over the strong objections of his medical advisors, who insisted six weeks was the absolute minimum required for healing.

Harry halved it. Three weeks and he was gone, not feeling like a million bucks, nor looking like it either.

The officers were in mufti, Frank because he preferred plain clothes, Harry because he had been suspended.

Frank was holding his thin body with uncomfortable stiffness, the result of wrenching his back while painting his house for the third time in as many years. Harry was still walking with an awkward limp from the beating he'd sustained when Lela was kidnapped, but he kept to himself the luxury of a grimace from the lingering pain when he was sure Frank wasn't looking.

They waited expectantly in the cold, silent night.

The full moon illuminated a splash of colors rising behind them on the two-story, brick warehouse wall. The mural tribute to barrio life–a mother seated at a wooden table with her children sprawled on the floor, playing in quiet contentment–painted by a talented Chicano lad, was defaced with the standard black spray-painted graffiti, the work of some anonymous, untalented vandal.

MARIE SUCKS
RUIZ
DARK HART

The black scrawl letters stood as mute testimony to the counter point of thoughtful artistic expression and mindless destruction.

"This may be the dumbest thing I've ever been snookered into," Frank said, blowing on his hands while rubbing them together nervously in front of his face, his mind on the cold and the extra pain it caused his back.

With his thin, gray hair and matching skin, Frank never looked more the accountant next to the young football hero with the thick neck and bulging, but aching, muscles straining at the cheap detective's suit he'd had to swap for his beloved uniform.

Gently and swiftly the sky went dark, the storm clouds covering the moon and turning off the spotlight on the barrio brood. After suffering the complaints of drought, God was working up to one of His rainiest seasons for Los Angeles.

It was almost one o'clock in the morning in the East-Central industrial district, and quiet. No cars moved in the streets, no trees grew from the ground–nothing but buildings–brick, mortar, glass, *cemento* and the two steel boxes of blue with "Downtown Trash" stenciled in white across them.

Behind the bins, Frank had never felt so cold, and made the mistake of mentioning it. Harry said, "You're a cop." As though a cop couldn't be cold, Frank thought. Harry had taken to pointedly reminding him that Frank was a policeman; the unspoken reference to Harry's suspension cut like an accusation through the muddy water between them.

Frank groaned. Without looking at Harry, he said, "You know something, Harry?"

"Hm?"

"My back's not too good. I hope this is an easy collar. I don't think I'd be much good to you if we had any rough stuff."

"Yeah," Harry said, not bothering to hide his antipathy. "You were the one who wanted to come along."

"Come along nothing," Frank protested. "I wanted to find Lela. I didn't want to play cops and robbers at a drug bust."

"*This* is how we get Lela," Harry said as though he were instructing a child with a learning disability. He looked down the street. "I know you're only interested in your pension."

Frank felt that one right through to his back. A little cruel under the circumstances, he thought. "Yeah, and before tonight, I thought I'd live to see it."

Behind them the askew eyes of the big Mexican momma were

cast down at her brood and seemed to be looking at Harry and Frank in disapproval.

"So how about letting me in on it, Harry," Frank said. "How do we use this bust to help Lela?"

"Sh!" Harry snapped. "I hear something."

A maroon Mustang pulled into the parking lot, with a short, squat white man at the wheel. His eyes darted around as he backed between two trucks and cut the engine. He sat, watching and waiting, a wary cat in the jungle.

Harry smiled and threw Frank an exaggerated wink. Frank looked away in disgust.

Without taking his eyes off Shorty in the Mustang, Harry said, "All right, when the buyer comes we wait for the transaction, then we go after him."

"What about the seller?" Frank asked.

"We don't need money."

"What?" Frank asked, thinking he didn't hear right. "What did you say?"

"Sh! Here he comes." Harry tensed every raw, stinging muscle as the tall, thick-shouldered black with alert, darting eyes sauntered into the lot. After a pounding beat of Harry's heart, the tall one got into the car with Shorty.

Harry, the predator, crouched, tightly wound, ready to spring. "It's him," he hissed darkly.

Harry and Frank watched as Shorty took something in a bag and handed it to Thick Shoulders, who looked inside it. The black took an envelope from the inside pocket of his yellow jacket and handed it to Shorty. He glanced inside the envelope, then pocketed it, and turned on the engine.

"They're driving away," Harry said, astounded.

"What did I tell you?" Frank said.

"Let's go; pull your shield." Harry got up and pointed his gun at the car, which had come in their direction now.

"Stop!" he shouted. "Police officers!" Frank waved his shield, feeling the pain shoot through his back, and then fell back just in time to avoid being struck by the car and the bullet that cracked from it.

The shot hit the barrio momma in her mural eye, and the clouds parted briefly to throw a sliver of moonlight on the chipped brick to make the poor woman appear cross-eyed.

"Let's go," Harry shouted, and started running to where their car was hidden in the next lot. Frank couldn't run. Harry angrily started the car and came to pick him up. "Get in," he yelled impatiently. The Mustang had a good lead on them, but Harry drove fearlessly, aided by his siren and the empty streets, and he soon closed the gap to a block or so.

Shorty wasn't worrying about stoplights or other traffic and had a few brief encounters with parked vehicles as he made turns. He led the police car down secondary streets through the industrial section to Little Tokyo, and turned south.

God turned on the valve marked "heavy rain" and poured water hard and fast on the streets under them.

"Lord, look at this rain," Frank groaned.

Harry ignored him.

"He's taking us to Watts, Harry. You think we'll have another riot?"

Harry stepped on the gas.

"I'm too old for a riot," Frank said, reacting to every swerve of the car with heavy, labored breathing and near paralysis.

"Nobody riots in the rain," Harry said impatiently.

A misjudgment on the slick, wet street sent Harry and Frank to the sidewalk in front of a row of dingy dry-goods stores and dusty pawn-shops, causing an inconvenient meeting with sheets of plate glass and parking meters, setting the pursuers back a few blocks and wrenching Frank's back, causing him to shriek with pain.

"Let him go, Harry," Frank pleaded through a painfully contort-ed mouth, his eyes wide with terror. "It's crazy driving like this in this rain. You'll get us both killed."

Harry was no quitter, however, and chase was once again given.

That settles it, Frank thought. He didn't want his daughter to have anything to do with this madman. She could marry the head of the Mafia for all he cared; he just prayed he would live to see it.

"There he is," Harry shouted to Frank, who was bent over, his eyes closed. "He's getting out!"

Frank opened his eyes, but couldn't straighten up. "Who?" he groaned.

"The buyer. He's running into that apartment."

Harry pulled the car to the curb, ran out, and shouted at Frank "Let's take him!"...and Harry disappeared across the asphalt lawn of the two-story apartment on 103rd Street near Central.

Harry hadn't really seen the buyer enter the apartment, but he saw a door close, and he took his chances on the third dirty door on the left. He pounded on the door and said, "Open up, police officer."

He got no response. He put his ear to the door and heard sounds of female moaning. "Okay, open up," he shouted. "I'm counting to ten before I kick it in. One. Two..."

In the car, Frank's pain was so excruciating that he couldn't move, let alone drive the car. He lay down across the front seat, his back causing him to sob intermittently and say prayers.

Suspended Officer Harry Schlacter kicked in the door and found himself with his gun pointed into a dark room filled with the smell of chitlins. The instant he crashed through the door, the moaning-female sound stopped. All Harry heard now were the occasional sounds of the internal-combustion engines in the street and his own heavy breathing.

Keep your back to the wall, old boy, Harry told himself while his eyes adjusted to the darkness. The man he chased into this black, malodorous apartment reminded him of Whistler, and the urge to kill that adversary that he had experienced so often welled within him once again. He must be careful, he told himself. First, the man was not Whistler; he was away somewhere with Lela. The thought of it, combined with the smell of the chitlins, made him want to vomit. He had come no closer to imagining a killing easier to justify than Whistler Wagner's. Someday, he thought, there would be the ultimate confrontation, after which only one would walk away alive, and Harry felt, in all modesty, that God was on his side and, for now, he would be satisfied if he accomplished his mission in this broken-down apartment. It would give him a big boost in his quest for Lela.

Harry heard the muffled sounds of the neighbors looking out to see what the commotion was. He heard only selected words, whispered in the night. Words like "cops," "fuzz" and "pig." "He in Miss Sarah's digs." He could feel the cold eyes on the broken door, and he hoped there wouldn't be a riot. If only Frank were able to help. He realized he shouldn't be in here alone. Too risky.

His eyes were beginning to focus on the sparsely furnished room and the myriad of strings strung across the ceiling like man-made cobwebs. He was sick to his stomach. Was it the chitlins or was it his fear?

Still no sounds from within. Harry made his way along the wall to the small, square hall, where he found two doors: one open to the bathroom, the floor studded with missing tile; and the other closed. Bracing himself with his back on the wall, Harry threw open the door and flipped on the light switch next to it, illuminating a black couple, naked on the bed, the girl on top, frolicking through the motions without, Harry noticed, apparent connection. Piles of clothing were strewn around the fringes of the playground, and, without a break in the routine, the girl looked over at Harry and said, "What you want, man, can't you see we busy?"

The face of the man was still obscured by the woman, and Harry hoped he had not gone into the wrong apartment.

Ignoring the shapely buttocks waving in his direction, Harry bluffed. "Okay, pal, it's cute, but it won't float."

"Heee, hee, hee." Harry heard the throaty, derisive laughter. "He just jealous o' yo' size, honey," she said. "All those white boys is." She flashed her abundant white teeth at Harry. "You got a warrant, man?" she hissed. "'Cause iff'n yo' don't, yo' just haul yo' lil'-white ass right outta my digs."

"Where's the stuff?" Harry found his tough-guy voice.

The man appeared for the first time from under the girl to stare straight at Harry's gun. All pretense behind him, he rasped in his husky voice, "You got a warrant, muthahfukkah?"

Harry cocked his gun in front of the man's nose. "The balloon or the morgue?" he said. "You decide."

The man looked at the muzzle of the gun and then at Harry, as if to decide what his chances were. "Man, you made one big mistake dis time. I don't know what you talkin' 'bout. I here wid my girl–you seen me."

"Just gimme the stuff," Harry said, holding his hand out.

The man and the woman continued to deny any knowledge of any balloon of heroin, so Harry tore the place apart while keeping the gun on the couple.

"What you doin', man? I didn't take nothin' from no car tonight. I been here screwin' my gal. You seen it wid yo' own eyes. You don't believe me, ask her."

The girl nodded heavily.

Harry pulled drawers, looked under the carpet, took them through the apartment so he could tear apart the kitchen. Nothing. Back in the bedroom, with the bedclothes strewn over the floor, the mattress torn apart, all the bureau drawers emptied, Harry began to worry. He looked at the man. There was a smug smile on his face. Then, he looked at the woman, and she wasn't smiling. Her expression, so different from the man's, set off a spark of suspicion in Harry.

"Okay," he said to her. "Bend over."

"I *beg* yo' pardon?" she said, trying to sound outraged.

"You heard me. Bend over."

The man spoke up, the smug smile sailing from his sweaty face. "You don't talk to my girl like that," he yelled. "Just because she ain't dressed. She ain't no whore like you bang. You take me in, okay. You big hero. Then maybe you want to come back with a search warrant, okay. You let my girl alone."

There was just enough fear in the man's voice to make Harry smile with suspicious satisfaction. He grabbed the girl and said, "Okay, lay down and spread your legs."

She did not oblige, so Harry threw her on the bed and pried her legs apart, using the pistol as a wedge.

The edge of the balloon was just barely visible in the generous tuft of black hair. Harry forced her legs further apart and took the balloon.

"Douche?" he said.

"Sachet," she replied.

"Touché."

"Nazi pig," the girl hissed, and spat in his face.

Harry was too preoccupied with his cache to wipe his face, which broke into a broad grin, the spittle dripping from his chin. He swung the little balloon between his fingers and thought of all he could do with the white powder contents–all the doors it would open in his search for truth and justice.

"I could get you twenty years for this," he said.

Floating fear swam in the man's eyes. Harry waved the balloon as if daring the couple to make a move toward it. But they were as marble statues, their dark bodies glistening with perspiration in the dull light of the naked ceiling bulb. It was as though they had all simultaneously come to understand that their fates hung delicately in the balance of that little balloon dangling between Harry's fingers, and yet they all realized he had said the word "could." Not "I *will* get you twenty years for this," as was more Harry's style, but "could." The air in the dusky room seemed to thin with relief, then, just as quickly, cloud with suspicion.

Harry pocketed the balloon and announced, "I'll have it tested. Maybe it *will* turn out to be douche powder." He started backing out the door, still holding the gun on the couple.

The girl said, "Hey, aren't you going to..." but was cut off by a kick from her man.

Harry looked at them and laughed. "Stay local," he said, "in case

I need you."

In the car, Frank was in pain when he saw Harry limp toward him and get in the driver's seat.

"Wrong apartment?" he asked.

Harry shook his head. "I got it," he said.

"It?" Frank asked, perplexed.

Harry produced the balloon.

"What happened to the suspect?" Frank worried aloud. "You didn't kill him, did you, Harry? God, Harry, tell me you didn't have to shoot him."

"I didn't shoot him. He's back in the apartment."

"So why didn't you make the collar?"

"Me?" he said in mock horror. "I'm not police any more, remember?" He chuckled to himself. "If they only knew. Asked me for a warrant. Geez."

"But, I...I thought you were going to take him in. I mean, I could have written it up..."

"What for?"

"Well..." Frank sputtered. "I mean, a crime has been committed." Then, as if understanding for the first time, his body tensed like a coiled snake. "Wait a minute, Harry–you can't–hey, wait–you're not–hey, hey, I can't let you *do* that."

"It's done," Harry said flatly, and started the car and pulled away from the curb.

"Yeah, but wait a minute. This is against the law. You want to become a heroin dealer?"

"Aw, Frank," Harry said, fed up, "shut up. You want her back, don't you?"

"I want her back, sure, but I'm not dealing in drugs to do it, and I've come here with you. You said you were making a bust. I..."

"I made it."

"Yeah, but I... Oh, God! Where is the collar?"

"Wait a minute, Frank. You're a smart man. What did you think I was doing in there? Think about it, Frank. A suspended cop? Use your head."

Frank shifted as though he had sat on something aggravating. "I...I thought maybe a little blackmail for information. You didn't tell me too much," he added half apologetically.

"Blackmail?" Harry said, throwing his palm to his forehead in mock horror. "That's illegal."

Frank squirmed. "Well," he said uncomfortably, "it's not drug dealing."

"Oh, degree again," Harry said. "I asked you for heroin; you didn't produce it. *I* produced it for our holy cause. You think I want to shoot it myself?"

"Harry," Frank apologized openly now. "I'm an old guy. I'm near my pension." His voice had a pathetic pleading quality. "I don't want to blow it. I couldn't live with myself anyway."

"You don't want me to free Lela?"

"Yeah, I want it more than anything, Harry. You know that. And if it came down to a choice of me blowing my career or saving her, I wouldn't hesitate to save her. But you're way down the chain here. It's only a start, and it may be a false start, and it may get you in more trouble so you can't do anything. A blind alley. And, God, here I am an accessory if I don't turn you in."

Harry slammed his fist against the steering wheel. "Frank," he yelled, "I don't want you bugging me. You were the one who wanted to help me. Now you got cold feet already."

"Yeah, but I didn't know you were going criminal on me."

"Damnit, if you want everything nice and orderly and strictly procedural, stick with the cops and the FBI. What is it now?–over three weeks, and nothing. Not a sniff of a clue. The only evidence you got was that embarrassing edited tape that took *my* job away from me. You got some nerve sniveling about *your* job in front of me."

"Harry..." Frank pleaded, a beaten man.

"So go ahead. Go your own way. I'll go mine. We'll see who gets to her first."

Frank said nothing, but stared blankly through the windshield at the street and wondered if it was raining where Lela was, and if he would ever see her again.

14   THE huge block letters that spelled "HOLLYWOOD," braced against the mountains, had been restored by a well-meaning chamber of commerce, sparing no expense. Brass stars had been embedded in the concrete sidewalk, with the names of the great and near-great and, because there was so much sidewalk, even some lesser lights who had the bucks to promote themselves; but, Harry thought, as he threaded his way purposefully over the brass stars, between the hopheads, homosexuals and hookers, precious little has happened to restore the tinsel town to its once glory days.

Oh, periodically there was a big press about a Hollywood cleanup and cops were everywhere, but there were thousands of law-breakers ducking in and out of hovels, like mice in season. Increase the force all you want, Harry thought, the criminals would spawn faster.

He passed a theater whose marquee displayed five bold X's. The poster advertisements for the film showed a black man wrapped around a white girl. He looked quickly away. He didn't dare think of Whistler and Lela. If he found out Whistler laid a hand on Lela, he would not be able to vouch for his sangfroid when he found him.

He turned up a side street and walked past boarded-up store-fronts to shops that sold tee-shirts specializing in risqué slogans and vulgar gestures. Harry paused, dumbfounded at the path of society. He read:

SKIERS GO DOWN FASTER

PILOTS STAY UP LONGER

PILOTS' DAUGHTERS HAVE BETTER COCKPITS

GAS STATION ATTENDANTS PUMP HARDER

ALL FISHERMEN ARE MASTER BAITERS

SEX IS LIKE SNOW. YOU NEVER KNOW HOW MANY INCHES YOU'LL GET OR HOW LONG IT WILL LAST

IN CASE OF RAPE, THIS SIDE UP

Harry shook his head in disgust at the cement-colored face of the proprietor, a day's growth of beard and a cigarette that was largely ash hanging from his cracked lips.

"How can you sell stuff like that?" Harry shouted. "Don't you have any sense of decency? You like kids looking at this stuff?"

"Up yours," the man growled, the ash falling on his chest, gray snow on a dirty slope. "It's a free country."

Harry ran up the steps behind the shop and knocked on the second-floor door.

"Who's there?" called a male voice.

"An old friend," Harry called back.

The door opened a crack and Harry saw a slip of his prey: a pockmarked, undernourished sad sack, under five-and-a-half-feet tall. Harry looked down through the crack. "Hi, Killer," he said, "good to see you again."

Before Killer McAuley's shock of recognition could be transferred from his dim brain to his raw nervous system, Harry had slammed his foot in the door. A second later, the door broke clean when Killer slammed it toward Harry in a futile effort to close him out.

Harry seemed to fill the doorway, and it didn't take Killer much longer to recognize the hopelessness of the situation. He turned his back fatalistically on Harry and dragged himself across the small, dark, sparsely furnished room to his torn and filthy mattress. Harry noticed the slogan on Killer's dirty tee-shirt:

Don't fuck with me

The killer dropped his emaciated body down and said, "Jesus, Harry, what do you want from me now?"

"Want?" Harry said in mock indignation. "It's just a social call, Killer."

Killer rolled over, turning his back to Harry. "My ass," he muttered.

"You're looking a little thin, Killer," Harry said. "Probably not eating right."

"Eating?" his voice croaking as though strained through crushed granite. "What's that?"

Harry took a twenty-dollar bill from his pocket and threw it, crumpled, on the distressed dresser. "Here's beans for a week or steak for a night."

Killer rolled back to look at the twenty spot. There wasn't any doubt in Harry's mind that the twenty looked good to him, but he did a manly job of hiding it.

"I'm tired of you, Harry," he said in a voice affirming the statement. "You and your constant bugging. I get the word now you're ex-fuzz." His vacant smile startled Harry, his teeth seemed somehow worse than before: stained, crooked, rotten, a few mercifully missing. "Now buzz off..."

"Aw, Killer. I'm a friend."

"My ass. So show me a warrant or something." He coughed a dry laugh. "Or even a badge?"

"Killer..."

"Don't bullshit me, Harry. You want to pump me for something to get yourself back on the force, then come back with a warrant."

"Okay, Killer, if that's the way you want it." Harry started out the door, then turned to pick up his twenty. "Guess the Red Cross can use this more than you, huh, Killer?"

"Jesus, you got balls comin' in here tryin' to buy me for twenty bucks."

Harry didn't look back. "I'm not buying, Killer. What would I do with a guy in your shape? You don't eat something soon, you're going to be a bad buy at any price." Harry turned abruptly to face him, startling Killer. "Where's Whistler?"

"How would I know?"

"You know," Harry said.

"What's it worth?" Killer asked, grinning and showing his remaining teeth.

"Worth? I come as a friend..."

"You expect a lot for twenty bucks. You never heard of inflation? I get five hundred easy for less important stuff."

"Well, this is a private job, Killer. I'm not counting on reimbursement, and you know how ex-cops aren't exactly rich."

"Shit, with all you took? Don't shit me, Harry," Killer said, not even realizing there was no truth in it. "'Sides, I finger this one and I won't need nothin' but a undertaker."

Harry took out his gun and pointed it at Killer's eyes. "You'll need one sooner or later," Harry said. "Let me lock him up. He won't know where I got my stuff."

"He'll know."

Harry shrugged. "Up to you, Killer," he said, cocking his gun. "Maybe there's more dignity dying of a police bullet." His lips twisted ruefully. "Ex," he added.

"You wouldn't kill me, Harry," Killer said, beginning to have some doubts.

"No?" Harry asked. "Would anybody miss you here?"

Killer McAuley eyed Harry in an effort to calculate his chances. He fidgeted. He'd heard rumors Harry hit Badeye. He wasn't sure.

"So take a chance, Killer. Maybe Whistler will get out someday and come looking for you. If you don't die from undernourishment and you keep your nose clean, you'll buy a couple more years with the info. That beats five hundred bucks any day." Harry shrugged his muscular shoulders again, like a cement truck vibrating its fluid contents. "Maybe he'll be cut down before then...in the line of duty or something. One shot and you're gone today."

Killer wet his lips with his tongue, which, for him, was not as easy as it sounds. "Okay," he said. "I guess you are crazy enough. What the hell do I owe Whistler anyway? I did some time for him because he had a better lawyer." He waved a yellow hand at the giant looming above him like a marble mountain. "Put the gun away," he said. "I don't know much, but what I know twenty bucks isn't going to buy. You got some nerve offering twenty, the fix I'm in."

"What's the price?"

"You got some real shit, I hear."

Harry watched Killer, his breathing labored, perspiration forming on his lips and forehead. Not from the gun, Harry was sure. He had put the word out to the junkies that he was willing to compensate the appetite of anyone who kept his ear to the ground and provided him with a lead. In spite of Harry's reputation for a hard-liner, hope springs eternal and, when the need is great enough, any chance will be run to obtain the necessary relief. So there were a rash of informants, but after the first one proved false, Harry dispatched him with a rather impressive beating, and word quickly spread that this time Harry was crazier than ever and it would be better to commit suicide than play with him if you couldn't deliver the goods.

"If I put my hands on some, what could I get for it?"

"Your twenty, for starters."

"Thanks. And?"

"And–a name."

"A *name*? What do I want with names? I want to know where he is."

"I don't know that, Harry," he said wearily. "This is the closest secret in town. I just happen to know something 'cause I did a little business with a guy and I overheard somethin'."

"What is it?"

"Maybe nothing," he shrugged.

"What?"

"Where's the shit?"

"Aw, who's on first, the chicken or the egg? Suppose you tell me what you know; it checks, I give it to you."

"Screw you, Harry," he said, turning his back. "My need is now, not two weeks down the road. I'm all fixed, I don't talk to the likes of you." Killer McAuley spat with just enough venom to make sure Harry understood his distaste, but short of shutting all the doors.

Harry looked down at the miserable worm, squirming now without any control. My timing is good, Harry thought. Real good. He calculated. He knew Killer McAuley was reliable. When he had something, he didn't exaggerate its importance, he didn't build you up for a letdown. A name he had. It was better than nothing. Harry wasn't going to use the heroin himself. So why not?

"Okay," Harry said. "I arrange a little for you. I give it to you. I get the name *before* you shoot."

Killer trembled in the affirmative. "How long will it take?" he asked eagerly.

Harry reached in his pocket and pulled out the balloon. Killer's eyes burst from his head. "Jesus, Harry." He salivated and whispered hoarsely, "You had it all the time."

"What do I get for it?" he said, dangling it before Killer's nose. Killer reached out for it and Harry withdrew. "Deal's a deal." Harry watched him. "Just tell me what I am getting. Not the name. What the name means."

"He's the contact with the man who's got the place," Killer said, his breathing harder and harder now, in short gasps. "I don't know who got the place. I don't know nothin'. I tell you who knows who got the place."

"What place?" Harry pressed his advantage.

"The place Whistler got the girl." He couldn't wait much longer. He reached out. Harry withdrew again.

"Let me get it straight, Killer, then it's yours. You're going to tell me who knows the man who knows where Whistler is?"

Killer nodded up and down, up and down, like a broken cuckoo clock. Harry handed over the balloon. Killer shot for the bathroom. Harry grabbed him. "Not so fast, Killer. The name."

He looked up at Harry, his voice parched with thirst, his throat raw with fury. His eyes bulged from his head like overripe olives.

"Luke Johnson," he croaked. Harry let go. Killer disappeared into the back room, and Harry heard a deep breath and a long sigh.

Luke Johnson. It couldn't be. B.J. Johnson's brother. The most closemouthed of all the gang. No junkie, no drunk, no nothing. No weak spots that he knew. Only reticent. Never a decent stool. Harry knew no one he'd less rather tackle.

Harry left the hovel with Killer McAuley sighing in the bathroom. Downstairs, when he turned onto the street, he bumped into a boy with an acne-infested face who was checking out the merchandise in the tee-shirt-store window.

Day 26

WHO WILL SHEPHERD YOUR SALVATION?

SMIRNOFF VODKA
IT LEAVES YOU BREATHLESS

The two billboards' juxtaposition on the freeway made Harry laugh out loud. He was driving with his radio on toward the 109th Street, Watts apartment of Maude Johnson, trying to formulate a plan to get through to her grandson Luke.

"Fifty-three," he said to himself, then looked at the speedometer. Fifty-five. "Not bad," he told himself. When he was on traffic, Harry could estimate the speed a car was traveling within three miles an hour. He had trained himself, he said, because if you are purported to be an expert on speed, you should *be* an expert.

Ideas were coming to him. He would not have been disappointed if the contact had been someone easier than Luke Johnson, but at least he was that much closer to Lela than he was a day ago. There wasn't anybody who couldn't be reached, but he couldn't think of anyone offhand harder to reach than Luke.

A car passed him with a bumper sticker that read, "Honk if you love Jesus." An elderly man was at the wheel, with a woman his age next to him. A young, plain-looking girl honked her horn. Just then Harry noticed a boy with a pockmarked face in another car looking at the girl and waving wildly to her. Harry noticed he had a bumper sticker too. It said, "Honk if you're horny." The girl turned red in the face, and Harry noticed the boy was trying to signal her to get off the freeway. Harry passed the boy and cut him off from the girl and boxed him in until the girl was out of sight. He wanted to give the boy a lecture about reckless driving, about morality and all sorts of things, but he didn't have time.

Harry hated himself for having the radio on. It came in the used car he'd bought and he never listened to it before now. But now he was

136

as hooked as the general public on hearing the next utterance of the famous Whistler Wagner.

Harry was still on the freeway when the station began playing Whistler's second tape. He felt like something with huge claws was tearing at his heart as he heard Lela say Whistler must promise never to tell Harry, "He's an absolute nut on purity. We both know that's old-fashioned, but Harry's Harry."

Harry was driving so slowly now, people were honking their horns, and he got off the freeway without realizing where.

Then she said, "Girls have normal desires too, you know," and, "You have been awful good to me." Harry felt like throwing up.

But when she said, "Harry's finished, done for. I'm not interested in him any more. Now I'm only interested in you," he stopped the car in the middle of the street and narrowly escaped being rear-ended.

He pulled over to the curb and sat in a daze. He barely heard Whistler speak his second request: "I say, if justice be done, Harry Schlacter be arrested for murder and held without bail, just like my people is." Harry didn't know how long he sat there contemplating giving the whole search up. If Lela really felt that way about Whistler, he'd be crazy to interfere.

But maybe she was brainwashed or acting to save her life. He had to get to her, he thought, before that madman destroyed her.

He had been reluctant to lean on Maude Johnson to get through to Luke, but now he was so angry, he thought he'd do anything to get Lela out of the clutches of Whistler Wagner.

Harry pulled in front of the Southeast Division station house, where he had spent most of his years as a cop. Good years, he thought, doing my duty. Now they were settling for mediocrities. Guys who didn't make waves.

The plan he decided on needed cooperation, and he wasn't sure he still had friends at the Southeast. It was no secret nobody wanted to work with Harry. Too gung ho. A real pain. But surely he could find someone to go along with him. It wouldn't be more than a day or two, he was sure. Maybe only one night.

Lieutenant Flagg was a hairy monster who knew how to get promoted. His rapport with his superiors was far greater than it was with his men. When Flagg was Harry's sergeant, Harry liked to berate him for, what he considered, this grievous shortcoming. Flagg had always answered simply, "You see who's the sergeant, don't you?"

He had no sympathy for Harry's zero aptitude for political

savvy. He was always shocked by his total lack of understanding of the niceties required for advancement. What he didn't understand was that Harry liked his station and would have been happy with an occasional pat on the back. But Harry's was a very hard back to pat.

Harry later wondered why he even asked Flagg. He was a hundred percent certain he would refuse to go along with his ruse, and he had indeed unceremoniously cut him short.

"I don't want to hear any more of it, Schlacter, the answer is no. You're not impersonating a police officer with my stamp of approval, and that's that. The matter is closed."

Always repeats himself, Harry thought, but he realized that Lt. Flagg was not among the select minority of the force that was sorry to see Harry suspended. He must look elsewhere and work around Flagg's duty shift.

Sully Wilson was his answer. A dedicated black cop who grew up with Harry, who shared Harry's zeal for jailing cons. Sully, who took a lot of flak from his soul mates for turning traitor. "No brother of mine," he heard again and again. Now he was fortuitously on desk duty at the Southeast while riding out an injury he'd sustained in making a spectacular armed-robbery arrest.

Harry found him where he looked first–at the schoolground, shooting baskets with the neighborhood kids.

When he heard Harry's scheme, Sully broke into a broad grin. "I gotta hand it to you, Harry," he said. "You're all right. 'Course, I could get busted myself for this..."

Harry watched the smooth brown face working in speculative thought, and when he saw the crinkles around the eyes, he knew he had him. It would all have to be precise; when Flagg was gone and Sully was on. It would have to be completed on one shift, or a major move would have to be made. It was a tremendous gamble for both of them, but it was the best Harry could come up with.

Sully went on duty in a couple more hours. Harry said, "Look for me when you see the back of that goldbricker Flagg riding into the sunset."

The apartment building on 109th near Central hadn't changed in the seventeen years Harry had been going there. A building that needed paint seventeen years ago needed paint still. The battered industrial buildings in the neighborhood looked the same, and the other apartments on the street were still boarded up. Instead of grass, there was asphalt; instead of trees, six-inch steel poles filled with concrete to keep the cars off the asphalt yard.

Maude Johnson had named her grandson Luke. His sisters, Margie and Barbara, had come to her already named, but Luke was just a newborn infant when Maude's daughter decided child-rearing was not in her best interests.

It was this little Luke–not three years old when Harry first laid eyes on him when he went for his first interview with Gramma Johnson in quest of his newspaper route–who was the target of Harry's hopes today.

He thought back on the polite little boy who would say, "Mornin', Mr. Harry," and, "'Scuse me, Mr. Harry," every time he walked in front of him, and he wondered how he had slipped from his grandma's control. Harry knocked on the battered door. "Come on," came the familiar high-pitched voice, almost a whine.

"Well, Mr. Harry," Maude said happily, "we been 'spectin' you."

She was seated in her usual partially stuffed chair, clutching her cane to her abundantly fleshed body and smiling broadly; the black-gray hair knotted loosely against her misshapen head. Some new additions to her heterogeneous collection of used furniture crammed the room, making it difficult to maneuver without some close encounter with a coffee table, odd chair, television set or the focal upright piano, which was just as Harry remembered it from his first visit: full of photographs of black "relations" and the large central picture of the white Jesus.

The blue carpet, as well as the machine-brocade blue couch and chair, was covered with clear plastic, and there were small children everywhere–great-grandchildren now–and they were forever saying, "'Scuse me, Mr. Harry," as they walked past him. If they should forget this litany, Gramma would give them a gentle but purposeful reminder with her cane.

"How you doin'?" Harry asked, sitting on the couch, across from her chair.

"I ain't gonna complain," she said. "My legs ain't too good, an' sometimes my arthritis bother me some, but it don't do no good to complain. B.J. tell me you been feelin' poorly."

When Harry told her his plan, she shook her head sadly, causing his heart to sink.

Then she spoke.

"All you done fo' dis family, ain't nobody gonna say no to nothin' you ask, Mr. Harry. 'Cept Luke, o' course...an' I fix him."

As if responding to a stage cue line, the front door flung open and in walked Luke Johnson, dressed in baggy pants and white tee-shirt, balanced on a pair of high-topped sneakers. He stopped short when he saw Harry.

"I don't know nothin'," he said, a twinge of nervousness betraying itself on his wide lips. "I'm tellin' you now so dey don't be no mis-unnerstannin'."

Harry nodded. "I don't blame you," he said. "I just came by to take your gramma in."

"In? In where? Take her where? What fo'?"

Harry studied the boy, nineteen now. He had a well-proportioned body, a broad, flat nose, tiny ears, but his best feature was his mouth. He knew how to keep it shut. He wasn't very bright, but he was smart enough not to say anything when he didn't know what to say, which was most of the time, and Whistler was not alone in mistaking it for sophistry.

"Nothing we need to bother you with, Luke," he said easily. "I'll get her the best public defender. I wouldn't expect it'll cost more than a couple years."

"Years? Hey, what is this, some kinda scam?" He looked to his grandma for some sign, but she only stared straight ahead.

"They was some business a time ago," she said with convincing monotone. "I didn't want to bother you none 'bout it, Luke. I needed some money to buy you some things you wanted. It weren't nothin' much at the time, but Harry here, he don't miss nothin'."

"Hey, hold on," Luke said, starting a smile of relief. "You full of it, man. You suspended. Think I'm stupid or somethin'? What you doin', makin' a citizen's arrest?"

Harry said, "Why not? I got thirty days before my suspension takes effect. I'm just rounding up the loose ends, my boy. 'Course, if you should happen to stumble on something about Whistler's whereabouts, Gramma will be free as a bird."

"I don't know nothin'," Luke insisted.

Harry nodded, projecting his lips in a that's-your-story attitude. "'Sokay, Luke. If you change your mind before we arraign her, we'll be over at the Southeast."

"You ain't been with the Southeast for months, Harry. What kinda shit you tryin'?"

"Not with them now either, it's just the closest slammer. I want to make it easy for you. 'Course, we don't see you tonight, she'll probably be transferred out to the downtown facility in the morning."

The tiny dotted balloons in Luke's eye sockets were clouding with doubt. He couldn't imagine his grandma in trouble, but here she was not denying anything. "Hey," he said, "you ain't takin' her nowhere."

"Why not?"

"She sick. She ain't walkin' hardly 'tall."

"We'll get her a wheelchair, don't worry."

"She needed here. She got grandchirruns."

"Yeah, well, we'll see they're taken care of."

"How that?"

"Juvenile hall. They give them birthday cakes on their birthday. Donated by rich folks. Sometimes they even thaw them out first. Not like at home, but it isn't that bad either."

"Uh-uh," Luke said, shaking his head. "No juvie hall fo' dem kids, they gonna 'mount to sompin', and dey not gonna 'mount to shit in juvie hall."

"You know we'll go as easy on her as we can."

"Yeah, well, she ain't up to it, no way, Mr. Harry." Luke was persuading now, perspiration stood out on his upper lip. "She ain't seein' so well nowadays neither."

"Well, that's all right, Luke, where she's going there isn't all that much to see," Harry said, then turned to Maude Johnson, sitting proudly regal on her upholstered, puffy chair. "Well, come on, Mrs. Johnson. You want to take anything?"

"No," Maude said, "I'll be along. You just let me have a few words with Luke fo' a minute."

Harry stepped outside and walked across the asphalt, turned, and leaned his back to the wall. He wasn't afraid, just careful.

It seemed an eternity until the high voice called him back in. Inside the little, crowded room, Maude said, "He want to know what gonna happen to him, in case he find anything out 'bout dis business."

"Nothing," Harry said. "No one will know. You got that promise."

"Huh," Luke kicked a foot over the plastic floor. "You come here like a big shit broad daylight. They *gones* 'spect sompin'."

"I could have sent a platoon of uniforms," Harry said. "Nobody will suspect anything. We're taking your gramma in, that's all."

"An' if'n she get out, dey know I da stool."

"You can eliminate that danger by giving me what you know now."

Luke thought a minute. "An' you leave Gramma alone?"

"Forever. You give me this one, Luke, you never have to do another thing–long as you stay clean."

"Shee-it," Luke groaned, kicking the plastic again. "I don't know nothin'," he said, and walked out the front door.

"He thinks we're bluffing," Harry said to Maude with a wink. "Let's go."

Harry helped Maude to her feet amid the sudden appearance of endless little children, who somehow realized what was happening. As Maude made her way to the door with the help of her cane and Harry, they began pulling on her shapeless gray dress, crying and pleading, "Doan go, Gramma, doan go. Please doan go."

Outside they caught a glimpse of Luke, crouched behind a car across the street. Maude called out to him: "Luke, look after the babies, hear?"

Luke turned his face, hoping she hadn't really seen him.

"This don't look like no po-leece car," Maude said when Harry helped her into his car.

"Isn't. It's mine," Harry said, sensing her disappointment.

Harry led Maude to Sully Wilson at the desk. Five minutes was all he allowed for Lt. Flagg to leave his post, but Harry knew his man.

"When Luke comes in," he told Sully, "and asks for his grandma, tell him she's been booked. Then call me before you bring him down."

Sully nodded. "You mean *if* he comes."

"I mean *when*," Harry said.

Downstairs, Harry was solicitous of Maude's comfort. He bought her favorite candy from the candy machine and even found a beat-up portable TV set in somebody's bottom drawer and plugged it in and turned it to her favorite channel where *The Wheel of Fortune* would be on later. Harry sat down with her.

"He tell you anything?"

She shook her head. "I don't know what he knows. He says if he knows anything he's afraid it ain't enough for you. I say, 'Just tell Mr. Harry what you know. He's been good to yo' sister, he ain't gonna go back on his word.'"

Harry nodded.

The sun disappeared and the moonless sky dampened Harry's spirits. "You think Luke's going to make it soon?" he asked, trying to hide his anxiety.

"He'll make it," she said, munching a Hershey bar.

"Sure?"

"'Course I'se sure. Ever since he born I take care of dat boy. He may not be grateful, but he doan wan' to get a wuppin', an' he know I'd give it to him."

Harry fidgeted and looked at the clock. A little short of four hours left before the shift changed. Luke seemed a little big to take a wuppin' from this sickly old woman, but he didn't doubt she would give it to him.

Harry's fingers danced on the desk. Maude sat watching the portable television.

"You go on, Mr. Harry," she said. "No use stayin' roun' here. Someone else take care of Luke when he come."

Harry shook his head. "Nobody else can take care of Luke," he said.

Day 26

16 THE stale air in the closet smelled like the inside of a sleeping bag. In the darkness, Lela felt her body with her hands. Was she going soft? The confinement and deprivation of exercise had taken its toll. Her time was a series of eternities, suffocating her in blackness. Her body ached in every muscle, her spirits sank to floor level. Still she had in her a spark of survival. Stay alert, she told herself. Opportunity may knock and you must be ready to answer. But it was getting harder all the time.

Without being able to actually hear the words spoken or the music played on the radio in the cabin, Lela could feel the rhythms of the station–the portions of time devoted to talk; the rock music, with its incessant, monotonous bass. She even felt the station breaks, and was able to use them as a crude measurement of time. Conversations between her captors, which she struggled to hear, were mere muffled and indistinguishable sounds over the thumping bass of the cheap radio.

Then one day she heard the starting roar of the car engine. She listened acutely to the diminishing sounds of engine and tires kicking up loose gravel. Before, the car had always returned in a few hours. This time, the hours passed with no sound of the car coming back.

What did this mean? she wondered. Who went where, and why?

She kicked the closet door three times with her shoe–her signal that she needed to go to the bathroom.

Moose opened the door, untied her and helped her get to her feet.

She always thought Moose became especially prissy when he had to take her to the bathroom. Whistler insisted Moose stay in the tiny room with her, and Moose didn't like it. He filled the room, but turned his back to her.

Now, with Whistler gone, he stood outside the half-open door.

"Moose," she called to him.

"Hm?" he answered, without looking in the door.

"What's your real name?"

"Johnny, why?"

"Wouldn't you rather I called you Johnny?"

Moose shrugged his massive shoulders. "Don't matter none."

But she thought that it did. "So you wouldn't mind if I called you Johnny...like you were a person, instead of an animal?"

"If you want, don't matter to me."

"What about Bull?" she asked Moose. "What's his name?"

Moose laughed. "I don't know if he remembers his name."

The toilet flushed and Lela appeared at the door and looked up into those black eyes she always thought were so soulful.

"I don't see why you aren't the boss, Johnny. You are bigger and stronger than Whistler, and, far as I can see, smarter too."

"Oh, Missy, I ain't smarter," he said, shifting his feet at the compliment.

"And Bull's so much stronger. Why aren't you two in charge?"

"We need a leader," Moose said. "Whistler's a leader. You know, to be the leader, you gotta want to. I'd rather just follow along. Lot simpler."

Lela looked across the living room, through the kitchen door at Bull, slurping sugar-coated Froot-Loops. She hoped to see a flicker of interest on his part, but decided there was just nothing there.

At lunch, Lela asked Moose if Whistler had gone somewhere, but Moose was not talking. "Got my orders," he said.

Wheedle as she did, Lela was unable to break the confidence. She tried another tack. "Johnny," she said, "since you're the new boss, how about letting me out of the closet?"

"No way."

"You know you can trust me."

"Can't trust your own mother, this world."

"Please."

Moose pursed his lips and shook his head. "Whistler say to keep you tied up in that closet, an' that's all there's to it. Now, you can nag me if you want, but I ain't budging."

"Can't you at least let me untied?"

"Oh, Missy, I know how you feel, but I got my orders."

"Orders? Aren't you in charge?"

"I ain't the boss."

"You are while you're in charge. Come on, Johnny, what can it hurt to untie me in the closet? You can still lock the door. Really, Johnny, where am I going to go? After all this time I can't be trusted that much?"

Moose furrowed his brow. "Oh, all right. But you breathe a word of this to Whistler and I'm in the soup."

"Don't worry, Johnny. I'm on your side."

"My side? Who's on the other side? I'm on Whistler's side. If you on my side, you on Whistler's side, and that doan seem right to me."

Lela smiled. "You know, Johnny, you are a handsome devil."

Moose eyed her with sloe, seductive eyes, and she wondered if she didn't see a spark of interest there.

"Yes, 'um. I knows what you mean. I expect things be different, could sure go for a girl like you."

So much for that angle, she thought. If I had oodles of time, I might be able to work it. But Whistler will surely be back before I have time to reverse Moose's ingrained preferences for his own kind.

Back in the closet, hands and feet unfettered, Lela was a woman with a new lease on life. She pondered what chance she might have to turn Moose on Whistler–or to help her escape.

Lela used her new freedom to explore the closet with her hands. At eye level she felt a metal clothes hook. She unscrewed it from the wall and ran her thumb over the sharp point of the screw. She thought how becoming it would be protruding from Whistler's heart.

But how to get it there?

In the long hours of confinement, Lela thought of her school-children and their faces, silently saying each of their names to keep her mind from atrophying.

Should she teach them survival? Probably out of her thirty-two kids, none of them would ever need it. Why should *she* need it? Oh, she thought, but I do. I am simply about to go stark-raving mad. It is all right to decide to go along–cooperate–with your captors if you are dealing with rational people–but these people haven't shown any signs of ratio-nality. Harry called them "psychotics"–born and bred without con-science. Lela thought she was doing well not to break under the strain, but the last few days had nurtured intensified self-doubt.

Now Whistler was gone, but where, and why?

After praying to retain her sanity, Lela would write letters in her mind to her father and to Harry.

> *Dear Daddy,*
> *Why has this happened to me? Whistler is such a strange man. He's certainly not stupid, but, I suspect, there is a strange emotional void in him, and I don't have the key to it. I still haven't found out who Miss Wills is. When I ask Moose, he just*

ignores me. I asked Bull once, but he just tittered like the village idiot.

Whistler is so strange. He says he wants me to love him, but if I get too close and accidentally touch him, he jumps away. He's so tall, he's awkward. Before he stopped seeing me, he was aloof in a way and tried to force a friendliness that makes me uncomfortable because it seems so unreal. He seems all in some strange turmoil. I lied to him and told him Harry meant nothing to me, and I haven't seen him since. It's like a big competition thing and all he wanted was me to forget Harry.

He seems easily in command of his cohorts, but uneasy with me.

Dear Harry,

My memories of you are getting me through my nightmare. I am slowly beginning to understand all you have been telling me. When I visualize a court scene, with Whistler looking dapper and contrite in front of a sympathetic judge who gives him perhaps nine months, I want to kill him. I hope you'll understand, if I have to make love to him to kill him, I'll do it. I'll love the three of them at once; anything to save my life so I can be with you again.

I know how you feel about that, and I dread to think what will happen to us if it comes to that, but if I don't survive, it will be academic anyway. The question is, I guess, do I want to survive if I have to live without you?

Life was so sweet with you, I can't bear to think that this madman might keep me from ever seeing you again. If there is one thought that keeps me going, it is that you will come and save me, Harry. I will do my part, I promise. I'll keep from going to pieces. I'll try to escape, but can I do it? All I know is you can save me, and that keeps me going.

I miss you so, Harry. I hope you think of me once in a while. I need you so.

All my love.

That night, at the kitchen table, as Moose was clearing the dishes and Bull was methodically licking his fingers, Lela screwed up her courage to ask, "You think I could get a book from the shelf?"

Moose frowned. "What for?"

"It gets a little boring for me. Bull can read his comics; I have to stay in the dark."

"Just a precaution, Missy. Ain't nothing personal."

"Can it hurt?"

"I'll get you one."

"Oh, couldn't I pick?"

"I got my orders," he said, but she could see he was questioning them.

"Please?" She tried to make slinky eyes at him, then smiled at the irony of trying to flirt with a homosexual.

"Oh, all right," Moose said, pursing his lips like a reluctant schoolmarm.

"Oh, thank you," Lela said, clapping her hands. She turned to the bookshelf and made a pretense of perusing the few titles. She could feel Moose's eyes on her back.

She took the tissue-wrapped clothes hook out of her pocket and pretended to wipe her nose with it. She took a book off the shelf and turned to see if Moose was watching. He was.

"This looks like a good one, Johnny," she said. But she couldn't read his expression. Was that suspicion she saw there?

She put the book in the hand with the tissue-wrapped hook and slipped it back in the shelf, blocking it from the view of Moose with her body.

Lela took another book from a higher shelf, fanned the pages and said, "I like this one better." She turned and found Moose scowling. "Oh, thanks so much, Johnny. I feel so much better already. You've no idea how important these little pleasures have become."

Deep down, Lela felt he knew what she had done. Would he tell Whistler? Would he just leave it there? Or would he extract the hook from behind the book and not tell anyone? He didn't say anything, but he sure looked at her funny.

The book she'd chosen was small consolation. It was a *Reader's Digest* condensation of some popular novels of a decade back. She only stared at the pages when Moose came by, to prove to him she needed the door open to read.

She was congratulating herself on the freedoms she had accomplished in less than two days when Moose came to tell her she would have to be tied again and the door closed. Her protests and wheedling didn't move the man-mountain this time. The thudding of the door and the click of the lock plunged her into her deepest depression, having this almost-human existence briefly and then having it taken away.

She was fighting, but it was getting harder with each succeeding hour of solitude, building like stones on a wall, sealing her in forever. She felt herself weakening. Would a real God let this happen to her? What sign was this? What in her life called for this punishment?

And so it was, with her spirits scraping the bottom of the dark, musty well, that she heard the dim sound of a car engine approaching the house. Then the sound stopped and she felt tingly all over, as though she were anticipating the arrival of a long-lost loved one. It seemed like hours before the door to her cell opened and there stood above her the tall, stately god–gracious, courtly, solicitous gentleman. He crouched down with the ease of a gentle furry animal and untied her hands and feet, then extended his smooth hand to hers and lifted her up.

He was, at that moment, the consummate artist. There was the evil of the closet and the good embodied in him, silently extricating her from her solitary hell.

"Where have you been?" she asked eagerly, a flood of gratitude washing her eager words.

"Did you miss me?" he asked casually.

"Oh, yes," she cried, and dropped her head to his chest. He put his hand gently on her blond hair and stroked it slowly. It sent ice water down her spine. Oh, dear God, she said to herself, don't let him sense my revulsion.

He stepped back to study her silently. Finally he nodded, then led her into the bathroom for a bath, then handed her a robe, which she put on. He took her to the living room, where she first noticed Moose fussing over a table of cosmetics.

The room looked bright and cheery to her, like waking up from a nightmare and finding everything you cherished in place. The sun on the snow outside shot a blazing light through the windows and made Lela's head reel. She pinched her eyes shut to get used to the light more slowly.

Whistler sat her on the couch. The radio was, thoughtfully, silent.

Whistler started as though he were acting some role in a small theater where the actors were larger than the stage. "I been away on a business trip," he said.

"Oh? Successful, I hope."

He nodded that high, sloping forehead of his. It wasn't the seed of the hardworking man that struck the responsive chord in Whistler's mother's womb on that night of nights; it was the planting of Fancy Man, with the high, sloping forehead and the arched, insouciant eyebrows.

"What did you do on your business trip?" Lela asked brightly. So happy was she to be out in daylight, her eager attention was almost unctuous.

He studied her again, as if trying to recall a memory. "Tied up some loose ends," he said vaguely. Suddenly, he became more expansive, as if brought to life by a thought. He broke into a self-satisfied grin, baring all his dirty teeth. Lela felt uneasy in the pit of her stomach. "Took care of my competition," he said.

"Oh?"

Whistler nodded a curt, smug nod. "Harry's dead," he said. "So they won't be nobody standin' in the way o' our marriage."

Lela felt the sickness rise from within her like some abortive rocket launch, lurching drunkenly upward, the sourness splaying over the landscape in utter defeat.

Whistler stared blankly at the mess, then, the reality gripping him, he shouted to Moose to clean it up. Moose suggested Bull, and Whistler said, "I said *you* do it, Moose, now do it."

"My, my, boss, you is gettin' edgy," Moose mumbled.

While Moose was doing the job, with his nose pinched, he looked like a dowager changing a diaper. Whistler asked Lela, "What's amatter, you don't want to marry me?" It was more of a challenge than a plea.

"Oh, it's not that," she said, feeling her life gone out of her with Whistler's news. No, now none of her inhibitions would get in her way. Her plans intensified in those few seconds–solidified. I must do it myself, she thought. I must kill him. I must cooperate. Kill him, cooperate, do as he asks. Cooperate, then kill. Kill, kill, *kill* !

"I hope you're not disappointed," Whistler said. "I wouldn'ta had it done if you didn't tell me Harry meant nothing to you and you were through with him." He sucked in the air through his decaying teeth to fuel his lugubrious cackle.

She summoned all the intuition she ever had about acting. "I'm glad he's dead," she said, and Whistler smiled. "I'm just surprised...and flattered you want to marry me. I had no idea..."

She thought Whistler's baring of those ugly teeth connoted some pleasure, but she couldn't be sure. Because, strangely, she thought he might be masking pain with that ghoulish grin instead.

They sat her down on the same couch after Moose cleaned it. It was still damp and she could still smell her vomit. She wanted to ask if it would be all right if she sat in a chair, but she thought she'd better not do any boat-rocking. Not just yet.

"Look here," Whistler said to Lela, "I want you to try and scrunch the side of your mouth like this," and he demonstrated, contracting the left side of his mouth, the way Miss Wills had done.

Lela frowned. "Is this something that other person did?"

"Just do it," he snapped, frightening her. She tried the contraction and she made a passable pass at it, but it wasn't the same for Whistler.

The kitchen table had been brought in and was placed on her right. On it were a basin, a bottle of Clairol hair coloring and assorted makeup kits. Moose hovered over the table with maternal care.

Whistler sat in his usual chair and faced her. He must have smelled the sour smell of her spilled soul, but said nothing. "Moose gonna doll you up a bit here. Make a new woman outta ya. Ya tired of the closet, ain't ya?"

"Oh, yes."

"Well, I'm gonna start from scratch. Moose, do the honors."

"Yes, boss," Moose said, putting a towel around Lela's neck.

When Moose started applying the dye to her hair, Lela wondered why they didn't carry this operation out in the bathroom. There just weren't any logical answers to anything.

She looked out the window at the lightly falling snow and the huge mounds of white, like clouds kissing the trees, and she felt so good she could imagine no higher aspiration than to sit here, out of the closet, and look out on this Currier and Ives print.

"When are we getting married?" she asked Whistler wistfully.

"Soon's you ready," he said.

"Who's going to do the ceremony?"

"It's all arranged," he said.

She wondered if a justice of the peace would come to the house or they would go out. She prayed for the latter, but would have been satisfied with bringing someone in. But surely, Whistler wouldn't be so stupid as to bring in someone he couldn't trust.

Her new-color hair was dried, and Whistler studied the color, then said to Moose, "I think it's a little too red. A little more brown."

Moose nodded and mixed another potion, then brushed it on her hair until, with several more suggestions of Whistler, they arrived at the satisfactory tint.

God, Lela thought, what are they doing to me? He doesn't like me as I am. What's next? I wonder if I'm going to have to have plastic surgery?

As Moose began applying the makeup, under the strict supervision of Whistler, Whistler asked, "You do any more thinking about my questions?"

"Oh, yes," she said, starting eagerly, wanting to talk. She wanted to say all that she had rehearsed to win his confidence. But she was unable to speak the words with the sincerity she practiced and they came out, at first, by dull rote, then, later, more trance-like.

"I used to be ashamed in school because my father always came in his uniform. That's before he got promoted, when I was just in first and second grade. And, I mean, he came to everything. Sometimes I'd have one line in a classroom play–not for the whole school, you understand, just some reading exercise–and he'd be there. Sometimes he was the only parent, and he smiled and beamed, he was so proud. I was so embarrassed. I'll never forget, one day one of my classmates said, 'Hey, Lela, is that cop your dad?' and I turned away from her suddenly and didn't say anything, because I was too honest for an outright denial. Everybody had a mom; I had a cop.

"Then later I got engaged to a public defender. He didn't think too much of cops, and a lot of that rubbed off on me, I guess. I sat for hours and listened to his patronizing my father and other cops and, finally, I thought, gee, this doesn't seem to make my father too happy, and, since he was all I had and he had been good to me, I fell for another cop, but I did it mainly to please my father," she added hastily. "I never really liked Harry."

"Why not?" Whistler prodded.

"Oh," she said, as though searching for the answer she had rehearsed so many times, "he was so old-fashioned. He had a moral sense that seemed so out of date." She caught herself speaking of Harry in the past tense and, for a moment, couldn't go on. When she got hold of herself, she said, "Puritan is what he was. I mean, we'd go to a movie and he'd apologize for the language to me as though I had never heard those words before. We also saw a movie where a couple was making love, and he took me by the hand and dragged me out of there. He said it was disgusting, they weren't even married, and he let me know that he would never even consider marrying a girl who wasn't pure."

Whistler chuckled softly. Moose was applying makeup to her cheekbones and Whistler was directing him to put it higher and make it heavier.

"So what do you think about cops being above the law?" Whistler asked, like feeding Pablum to a baby.

"No, no, no," she shook her head, causing Moose to pull his hands away from her face and step back.

"Mustn't shake yo' head like dat," Moose squealed in his high-pitched voice.

"Sorry," she said.

Whistler smiled and Lela was pleased with the effect she was having. But every time she thought that Harry might be dead, her voice turned to a trancelike drone.

"I'm glad he's dead," she repeated dully. "An eye for an eye, a tooth for a tooth. If a man kills, he deserves to be killed, whether policeman or ordinary citizen. No one is above the law." And now, she said to herself, the person who killed Harry must be killed. It is a never-ending chain. A Möbius band.

"Harry's dumb," Whistler said flatly. Lela looked at him for an explanation. Moose applied dull red lipstick to her lips, and Whistler decided it was too dark, so he wiped it off with a tissue.

Bull sniggered and clapped his hands. Lela thought he was reacting to Whistler's statement about Harry being dumb, but it was just some funny in the comic book he had propped on his belly on the floor.

"He'da never found you," Whistler went on without taking his eyes from Moose's hands working on Lela's face. "I used Luke Johnson as the contact–right under his nose. So obvious and yet so remote. You know about the thing Harry had for Luke's sister B.J. Black and white don't mix in Harry's world, but you bet he was gettin' his."

Lela wondered why he was telling her this. If Harry was dead, was it necessary to downgrade him more? Was he trying to brainwash her?

As if reading her mind, he said, "I only had him hit 'cause I didn't want you having second thoughts 'bout our marriage."

"Oh, no," she assured him. "I was through with Harry," she swallowed reflexively, unconsciously, "before I fell in love with you." There, she had gotten the words out. She studied his face for his reaction. She didn't think she'd done too badly. He was showing her his miserable teeth again.

She felt Moose's fingers on her cheeks now. The lips seemed to win Whistler's approval, but the cheeks needed some renovation. Oh, God, she thought, on my way to my final degradation I can't even have the satisfaction of being desired for myself. He wants someone else, and he's making me over to look like her.

"Luke wouldn't talk to his own mother," Whistler said, as though there had been no break in his conversation. No cop has ever got nothing outta Luke. He'd take a bullet before he'd talk." He chuckled softly again, proud of his stroke of genius.

Moose tied her hair in a bun on the back of her head and pinned it in place. "Bring the clothes," Whistler barked at Bull, who jumped from the floor and went into the bedroom and returned with a gray gabardine suit with a tiny blue horizontal-and-vertical stripe and a white blouse with broad ruffles in the front.

Lela undressed and put on the blouse and suit and noticed the hemline was fifteen years behind the times. That awful peach floozy dress had no effect, she thought. Now he's making me look like a schoolmarm.

Whistler smiled at her. He asked her to turn around so he could see all the sides, and she did so, twirling her arms out like a model.

Lela was fed dinner alone. Whistler watched her with a morbid fascination that made her uncomfortable. When she tried to ask him questions about the wedding date, he held up his palm to silence her. His silent stare made her squirm.

After dinner she was escorted back to the closet by Whistler and Bull. She started to cry in protest, but Whistler said nothing until her hands and feet were tied and Bull had pushed her roughly back into the dark cell. There was no blindfold to mess the artistic makeup.

"Good night, Miss Wills," Whistler said sweetly as he shut the door on her.

In the closet, with the lock thrown heartlessly into place, Lela sobbed, "Oh, God, he's made me into someone he wants to bury and he's burying me. He can't have liked this Miss Wills. He still didn't touch me, even after I was made over. If he liked this woman, why would he dump her in this stinking hellhole? Oh, God, oh, God..." she gasped through her sobs, her hopes squelched by the man she was now convinced was totally mad. I must kill him, she thought, I must.

In the living room, Whistler made his final "request," into the microphone, for appending to the third tape, to be aired on Lela and his wedding night.

He was so proud of his work.

Day 26

 LUKE felt trapped. Inside the Watts apartment, the walls seemed to be closing in, crushing the life out of him. The babies were yelping and tugging at his pant leg, crying, "I wan' Gramma," and he responded gracelessly, "Ain't nobody wan' Gramma mor'n me."

The television was on at full volume, but nobody was watching it. They were instead bugging the bejesus out of Luke, pounding the venerable piano, making the central picture of Jesus dance lightly in the dead air. Luke couldn't understand how Gramma could control them so successfully. She could hardly walk, and he was a big, strong man and completely helpless.

As the grandchildren passed beyond the welfare range, younger kids were added to Mrs. Johnson's care. She just kept getting older, but her charges always seemed to regenerate. Margie's ma was still spilling babies, and Margie herself had developed into a chip off the old block, and the mélange at Luke's feet were of a mysterious origin. Luke had no idea whose they were. Even Mrs. Johnson had trouble keeping track.

There were four from their own family in there somewhere, but, with the extra neighbors' kids, they seemed like a regiment to Luke.

It was the worst possible time for B.J. to drop in. Luke started on her before the door closed behind her.

"'Bout time you showin' up. Dese here babies need lookin' after by a woman's touch. Jest be movin'," he said hopefully, starting out the door.

B.J. threw out her arm and stopped him. "Wait a minute. I can't stay here. I've got a job to go to." Luke understood her implication: that while she had a job, Luke did not. "I just came to see Gramma. Where is she?" she asked, looking around the disheveled room.

"Ha," Luke snorted, throwing his head back in scorn. "'Sif you didn't know."

"Know what?"

"Harry took her to da slammer."

"Slammer? Gramma?" She was wary of her brother Luke. "What for?"

Luke eyed her with contemptuous suspicion. Then he paced the floor, agitated, kicking the plastic coating on the blue carpet. "Look, doan gimme no shit now, sis, I can't take it. Dese here babies drivin' me up the muthahfukkin' wall, an' you come roun', big as you please, playin' stoopid."

"But..."

"Another thing I meanin' to talk at you 'bout...doan go 'Hiya Luke'in' me front o' my men." He hung his head. "It's embarrassin'."

"A doctor?" she asked, her eyebrows shooting up. "It's embarrassing to have a doctor in the family?"

Luke looked grim. As though he couldn't understand why she would find that strange. "Nothin' wrong wid bein' a doctor, I guess. But, you stay outta my way."

"So what's wrong with me saying 'Hiya, Luke'?"

"How you got to be a doctor's what's wrong."

"How? Like anyone else. I went to medical school, I worked my tail off, it almost killed me."

Luke shook his head. "*Un-uh*, doan feed me no stuff, sis. I know all 'bout Harry givin' you da bread."

"Loaned it."

"How you repay him? Wid you' body, that's how...an' sellin' out you' gramma."

"I sold out Gramma? What you talkin' 'bout, boy?" B.J. lapsed into her native tongue, a luxury she did not often allow herself. "Nobody prouder'n this family o' me bein' a doctor than Gramma. How you say I sell her out?"

"I tolt you. She in da slammer. Harry put her dere."

"What for?"

Luke shrugged. "Some business. You be da first to know."

"Listen, Luke," she said, flaring in anger, "I don't know what you think about Harry, but he's the most decent person I've ever known. I realize to someone with your mind it must look like I'm sleeping with him, okay. It isn't true, but I can see why you'd think that. But to think I'd sell out Gramma, that's just plain stupid."

"Doan you go callin' me stoopid. What's stoopid is to think Whitey just hand out da bread, no strings 'tached."

"Well, that's what he did. All he ever asked was that I didn't give up."

"Dat's bullshit, B.J. No whitey give no money to no niggers 'less he gets sompin' better in return. I knows you humpin' him."

"No, Luke," she said, in quiet control now. "I know it must be hard for you to understand. I admit it was a little hard for me in the beginning, and I was more than a little suspicious, but he never asked me for anything. Nothing."

"Well, no*body* gonna believe Whitey just drops all that bread on ya for nothin'! Nobody ever gonna believe dat, so just be careful who ya 'Hiya, Lukein' me in front of in da future. Unnerstan'?"

She looked at him dumbly.

"Jest doan go advertisin' you my sister."

She shook her head slowly, side to side, in amazement. "I wonder, Luke, do you think there is any possibility we had the same father?"

The 1600 shift at the Southeast was almost over when Harry got the call from the desk. "Hold him, Sully," Harry said, "I'll call you when you can bring him down..."

Harry was working under a disadvantage. He didn't know Whistler told Lela he was dead. The hit was really only a contingency plan. If Whistler's demands weren't met, he would achieve his goal, and save face, by having Harry hit. Never before had Whistler experienced such power within the enemy camp. He adored it.

In the downstairs detectives' room, with the scarred furniture and the off-green walls, Harry unplugged the television set and replaced it in the bottom drawer of the desk, he picked up the candy wrappers and stuffed them in his pocket. He grabbed the keys to the lockup and ushered Maude hurriedly to the cage, where he sat her down on the chair and said, "Now look like you're crying your heart out to get out of here."

"I doan know, Mr. Harry, if I kin play this trick on my grannson."

He waved a hand at her. "'Sokay, I'll let you think about it. I could always just leave you, then you wouldn't have to do any acting."

"I unnerstan', Mr. Harry," she said, nodding her head in doleful resignation. She was from the old school. If a policeman said it, it must be true.

Harry picked up the phone and dialed. "Sully, it's all clear. Bring him down."

Luke came sauntering through the room a half-minute later, looking like a troubled man, trying to throw it off like an extra hair shirt. He glanced over at his grandmother in her cell, then looked back at Harry.

"Kin I talk to her?"

"Sure, Luke. Visiting hours anytime, here with our friends. Downtown, they're a little fussier, but we hope it won't come to that."

Luke went over to the cage. "Gramma, what I do wid dem kids when Margie goes out?"

"You stay wid 'em, boy," she said.

"Me?" Luke protested. "I ain't no babysitter."

Gramma shook her head. "Sho wish I could be wid dem chirruns," she sighed a distant sigh.

Luke kicked the bars and circled the room, jamming his hands petulantly in his pockets, his shoulders hunched, his face downcast.

Harry watched him, and when Luke kicked the legs of the desk and started out the room, Harry, seeing his plans go out with Luke, jumped up and followed him.

"Okay, Luke," he said, grabbing hold of his arm, "we're going to have to book you too. Sorry."

"Fo' what?"

"On suspicion of conspiracy to commit kidnapping," Harry said. "Material witness. Anything strikes my fancy."

"You can't hold me," he protested.

Harry looked at the street-wise kid. He knew too much to fool. "We can keep you twenty-four hours," he said. "That's enough."

"Fo' what?"

"To get word to the street you came in to sing."

"That's a lie."

"Kidnapping's worse. I'll go you one better. Knowledge of a crime, unreported, is worse than a lie."

"You stink, Harry."

"Yeah, real bad."

Luke considered. He looked down at Harry's tight hand on his upper arm. "An' if I know sompin'?"

"Luke, like I said–nothing. I'll do my own investigation and it's all unofficial."

"I don't know nothin'."

Harry squeezed the arm tighter and shook the lad. "You don't seem to understand, Luke. This isn't some penny-ante crime we'd like to tidy up to make the records look better; this one I'm tasting. This girl is important to me. You guys were stupid to blow away Charlie Rubenstein. He was a good cop, good for you. He was a lot better for you than what he replaced, and miles better than what's coming after. Whistler's stupid if he thinks he can bring this off. It was stupid to kill Charlie. If only for your own sakes."

Luke spat on the floor. "Dat Charlie a case. Worked me over–worked the kids over. Didn't unnerstan' we doan want no white boy tryin' to make us white boys."

"Yeah, well, Charlie didn't get his so nice, Luke." Harry shook his head slowly, "Not nice at all. We got a thing about that, Luke–thinking it might happen to us, you know."

"I didn't do nothin'. I know nothin'."

"Come on, Luke," Harry said, backing him against the wall. "You know something. A guy with your weight has to know something."

"Shee-it. You haul my gramma's ass in here like you wuz Mod Squad or sompin', an' you ain't even a cop. That gotta take da cake." He shook his bewildered head.

Harry increased the pressure on his arm and moved his menacing head within an inch of Luke's. "Let's have it, Luke. I know you know the contact for the place. You know I know. So who is it?"

"I give you dat, I mi's well give you mah life."

"Okay," Harry said, releasing him and backing away. "Have it your way. I'll just get word out you told me. I'll throw you in the slammer for twenty-four and send the word you squealed to get released."

"Hey," Luke said, his eyes lighting with an idea, "wait a minute. If'n you don't know where Whistler is, how can you say I told you?" A sardonic smirk of satisfaction crossed Luke's lips.

"I'm going to crack it, Luke, don't you worry. And when I do–wham!" Harry slapped his fist against his palm, too close to Luke's nose for comfort. "I don't forget those who cross me. I'll just say we are waiting for a little supporting evidence–we have to have that, you know–and that'll give them time to think–how long would it take them?"

"Huh? To put my lights out? Ten minutes," Luke said, snapping his fingers.

"Shall I get him first? Before he has the ten minutes?"

"What you mean, 'get him'? Kill him?"

"Naw," Harry said with a smirk that baffled Luke. "Policemen don't do that."

"Shee-it. You ex..."

Harry grabbed him again and slammed him against the wall with a reverberating shock that brought a detective from the next room. When he saw Harry was in control, he popped back where he came from. Harry stared hard at the sullen brown eyes. His elbow worked its way to Luke's throat. The pressure was applied, gently at first, to communicate the idea. Luke squirmed, but was no match for Harry's overwhelming strength.

"Let's have it," he said.

"I...I got nothin'."

Harry applied more pressure; Luke gasped. "Nothin'll hold in court," he said, covering himself.

"I'm not going to court," Harry said, releasing the pressure.

"I weren't dere. I can only tell you da jive."

"Don't gimme that, Luke. I know what you know. The name. Let's have it."

"An' my gramma gonna be let go?"

"Yeah."

"An' let alone–fo' ever?"

"You got it."

Luke looked around the corridor, to make sure they were alone. "You sure you ain't jivin' me? You gonna keep dis unner you' hat?" His dark face was drawn under the strain.

"Yeah, yeah, come on, Gramma's getting cold."

"Well," Luke said, whispering hoarsely, "de jive is Ching got him stashed."

Harry nodded in mechanical disgust. The machine was getting rusty. Why didn't I think of that? he mused. Ching.

"Where?" Harry pressed.

"Don't know. Only Ching know dat."

"Who's with him?"

"Hey, you want a lot fo' you' money."

"Who's with him? Don't crap me any more, Luke, or I'll choke you right here. You gave me the biggie. These are crumbs. Who's there?"

Luke felt the tightening of his throat again and croaked, "Bull an' Moose."

"That's all?"

"Far's I know. Far's I know," he repeated in relief as the hold on his neck was released.

Harry unlocked Maude's cell and gave her a hug.

He called Sully to arrange transportation for them home in an unmarked car. He looked at the clock on the wall. It was after eleven. Less than an hour and the shift would change. He'd just made it.

Although it was eleven at night and Mrs. Johnson had great difficulty walking, they asked the young officer to let them out of the unmarked car two blocks from home. They would gladly walk the rest of the way.

Day 29

FRANK Eberhart wrote excellent reports.

The table he sat at in his new detectives' squad room would not stop any heartbeats in Goodwill's used-furniture department. He missed his plebeian steel desk and the feeling of anchored permanence it gave him. He missed the serenity and cama- raderie of an office. He even missed the picture of the bikini rear with PEPE LOPEZ printed across it. He even missed Pepe Lopez, or whatev- er her name was. And he was amused at his new assignment–on loan to the downtown detectives, charged with the responsibility of nailing Whistler and his gang–before Harry did.

He looked down at the report he had just finished.

HOWARD CHING
CONFIDENTIAL

Officer Harry Schlacter, LAPD, was assigned to Special Gang Detail after Officer Jack Bach was slain behind the Watts pharmacy of Howard Ching. Officer Bach was working undercover and was making a buy when an unknown assailant shot him in the back of the head. Howard Ching was interrogated, then released.

Harry spent a lot of time auditing Ching's business records and the records of the drug companies who sold to him. Harry bugged the department to go after Ching and trap him, make a buy, just haul him in and intimidate him, but they gave him a million excuses for doing noth- ing. Harry thought it was because they were afraid to lose another under- cover man.

The squad room was empty. Outside, it was dark and rainy. Frank picked up the phone and dialed the number from memory. A case- hardened voice answered:

"Ching Pharmacy."

"This is Frank Eberhart again. Is Mr. Ching available yet?"

"He's filling a prescription. Can he call you back?"

"Well, I called before and he hasn't called me back. I'll wait for him this time."

"Can't tie up the phone. I'll tell him you called again," and the line went dead in Frank's hand.

He replaced the receiver and nodded his head. His hand crossed the folder gently.

Filling a prescription, he said to himself, nodding again. How respectable. A public servant, ministering to the ills of mankind. Where you draw the line between legitimate ills and illegal ills may blur with time. The report on the desk told of Ching's beginnings: when he opened the pharmacy in Watts and lived in Inglewood. A conscientious professional, Ching made a good living on welfare and Medicare and Medi-Cal, and sundry social-assistance plans, with the great volume of lucrative prescriptions he filled on the public weal for those whose lives centered about their illnesses, real and imagined.

He picked up the photocopy. Was it naive to hope that Ching would call him back? He was beginning to think so. Yet nothing creates suspicion like a citizen, presumed innocent, of course, refusing to return a perfectly harmless call from the police. He would wait another ten minutes. Harry would have stormed the pharmacy with guns blazing just to ask him a harmless question if he hadn't returned his call. Frank realized that was not his style, never could be. He dismissed the idea of a trip as making too much of it, causing suspicion and clamming him up.

In the hope that another reading would provide some clue, Frank looked again at the report.

Ching, Howard, age forty-eight; married to Viola, age forty-two. Two children: Mark, fifteen, and Philip, thirteen. Owns and operates pharmacy at One Hundred Third and Broadway, Los Angeles. In 1982 sold house in Inglewood for thirty-five thousand dollars and bought home in Palos Verdes for six hundred fifty thousand dollars. Owns Rolls-Royce Silver Arrow, license HWC; Mercedes-Benz 500 SLC, license CHING; Porsche 911, license HOWARD. House is walled in with six-foot cement-block walls, except front, which has six picture windows facing street. The drapes on these windows are never opened. All callers at the home are screened through an intercom. The house has a swim-

ming pool, tennis court, Jacuzzi, sauna, and is lavishly furnished with expensive antiques.

When Ching was questioned about how he achieved this in a few years in a pharmacy in Watts, he answered, "I work hard."

Intelligence sources suggest the following story, gathered by rumor, fact, conjecture, much of it unverified:

Ching experienced in the early years of his practice of pharmacy in Watts a series of drug burglaries. His insurance premiums and deductibles skyrocketed, so that Ching was paying from his own pocket for most of the losses. No matter what he tried–security guards, burglar-alarm systems, even guard dogs–he still sustained staggering losses.

Subsequent to these losses, Ching was visited by a local gang leader, Jason Wagner, a.k.a. Whistler, a.k.a. Richard Wagner, a.k.a. Honus Wagner. It was suggested that Whistler knew a way to stem the tide of robberies and make Ching rich in the process. Ching listened suspiciously to the young, brash black man's simple plan. All Ching had to do was supply Whistler with the drugs that were being stolen, at a handsome profit to Ching, and the robberies would cease. Ching balked, saying he was a respectable, hardworking man with a family and he wasn't interested in drug dealing.

"Hey, wait a minute, man," Whistler protested. "Nobody asking you to deal. You got a license to sell the stuff, I got the cash to buy it. All legitimate like."

Ching answered that it sounded good to him, all Whistler had to do was bring him the prescriptions. Whistler said Ching would have to do something for his money. He would have to take care of those minor accounting details.

Ching got the message. Why should he cooperate with the police? he asked. What did the police do for him when he had all those unsolved robberies?

Frank closed the folder, pushed up his glasses, rubbed his eyes and dialed Howard Ching one more time.

Charts, graphs, notebooks and folders were spread everywhere: on the worn carpet, on the cheap pressboard coffee table, on the rental couch in Harry's apartment.

Frank thought his only chance to get Harry to open up was to lay out what he had and hope it would precipitate a comment here, a revealing question there that would lead to some exchange of information.

Frank had come unannounced and had to wait almost three hours for Harry to return to his hillside apartment in the Mount Washington area, the same apartment he lived in when he went to the nearby police academy. Harry had been anything but cordial, and only let Frank in when he told him he wanted to give him all he had–all the results of the department and FBI efforts in the search for Lela Eberhart and her captors. Harry looked over Frank Eberhart's thoroughly documented investigation reports and the splendid visual aids he'd produced.

Unspoken between the two policemen were pervasive thoughts of Whistler's hideous second tape that they heard, separately, on the radio.

"We have interviewed all known contacts of Whistler Wagner," Frank was saying. Harry flopped back in a poorly stuffed chair and Frank was pacing the dead carpet, stopping to emphasize points he thought would get through to Harry.

"We've run title searches on everything that might be connected to Whistler and any of his known business acquaintances. We've even gone to the partnership papers to see if they have any hidden interests in anything.

"Motor Vehicles has been furnishing us daily reports on any cars registered to anyone in the gang, any of their friends, acquaintances, business associates. Stolen-car descriptions are put out regularly in case they are moving and switching cars." He looked at Harry, whose face showed only blasé impassivity.

"We've flooded the country with pictures of Lela and Whistler and a couple of his gang who haven't been seen around. Bulletins and descriptions have gone to all Western states, Mexico and Canada and major Eastern and Midwestern cities. Our information is voluminous."

Harry grunted. "So why have you come here, Frank? You want to take the credit for it when I find her? Make it look like, with these piles of trivia, you helped me crack the case?"

"No," Frank said simply, trying to assure him. "No credit. If the brass knew I was doing this, I'd lose my job."

"So why are you? I thought we had a contest going. See who got to her first. Now it looks like you are throwing in the towel. What do you want in return?" Harry asked.

Frank smiled thinly. He had done a lot of thinking about Harry's reaction. Harry wasn't stupid. He saw right through the ploy.

"I want my daughter," he said with a catch in his thin voice. "I'm having a devil of a time getting cooperation from our fellow cops. I get the cold shoulder. It's as though I'm responsible for you getting the ax. A lot of your old enemies feel you are getting the shaft. Called you a real pain in the rear a couple weeks ago, said you deserved anything that came to you. Until the suspension was announced so graciously on the radio; a real cave-in to the hoods, they thought. I guess they can see their wives and girlfriends getting snatched and as a result getting booted out of their livelihoods." He paused, looking at Harry for some reaction, but seeing none, he plowed on. "Maybe you could at least get the word out you aren't working against us. You know, so I could get some of those hard-nosed cops to loosen up a little." He stopped pacing and stood in front of Harry, looking down at the big man, curved into the chair. There was a plea of desperation in his voice.

"You think we'll ever find her?" he said.

"*I'll* find her," Harry said, a man exuding more self-confidence than he could justify.

Frank bent over, putting his face closer to Harry's. "Can't we at least swap information, Harry? We wouldn't have to work together necessarily, but it ought to be a big help for both of us if we traded what we have."

Harry nodded his head like a ball bouncing gently to a standstill. Frank took encouragement. Mistakenly. "Nice try, Frank. You boys put a lot of effort into that stuff." He waved his hand at the written material, graphs, charts and papers all over the room. "Make a nice impression at some used-car-dealer's sales conference. But you're a little short on results, and what we care about here in the good old LAPD is results. Effort doesn't mean a thing."

Harry stood up now and paced over to the window, looking out as though he were expecting to see something sinister. He turned to face Frank. "Every time I try to work an informant or even ask a little favor of the police, they gleefully ram my suspension down my throat. It's hard enough in the best of circumstances, and now both sides are against me. No, Frank, it was a clever idea, I'll give you that. If you ever had enough data to interest me, you wouldn't show it to me. You wouldn't have to. Tell them I compliment you all on your effort and it won't be long now you'll be praising me for my results. But this one, Frank," he said, poking a finger at the spare, lean chest, "I want myself."

Frank Eberhart barely nodded, more in understanding than in approval.

Now he pleaded softly with the big, rough "suspended" cop towering above him, seeming to engulf him in his vitality. "Promise me one thing–for old times' sake."

Harry just glared with a look that let Frank know he was not a promiser.

"If you do get to them first, be careful, please. I don't think I could make it if anything happened to Lela."

Nothing more was spoken. Frank gathered his papers and walked out the door, his shoulders stooping, an aging man carrying the burden of failure.

Day 30

How nice it was to know that in spite of all the people he had rubbed the wrong way, a guy as rough-and-tumble as Harry could still count on a few kindred spirits. Harry inspired a confidence in fellow mavericks few of his blander colleagues could command. At the same time, he irked the high command of the force, so they wanted his scalp and all that went with it.

It was a guy in the property room that got the recording device to Harry, along with the hookup and instructions for its use. A guy named Steve Pennington, who had been dumped in the windowless basement of the Parker Center, downtown, for sassing a commander who came down on him for an irregular street arrest. Pennington was a soulmate of Harry's, and he smoldered so long before he said, "Look, Commander, I appreciate your viewpoint, but you've never been on the street. Never been out of your air-conditioned office. You know what they say: 'If you don't play the game, you shouldn't make the rules.'"

"All in good fun," Steve Pennington told the review board, who thought they were doing him a favor banishing him to what he called "The Black Hole of Calcutta."

It took Harry two days to connect with Steve, and it took Steve another day to get the little box to Harry. Steve had a friend at the phone company. The friend had access to the cable books which showed you all the tricks on reading phone wires. Sure, a bug in the phone instrument would be better, but breaking into Ching's fortress pharmacy was too risky. Of course, what he was doing was risky enough.

Steve laid it out for Harry. "This little caper could cost us both ten years in the slammer and ten grand. Your patsy has any trouble with his phone, they go to the box, you're history. That's why I never met you, and I never even heard of you."

Harry took a level measure of the guy. "So why are you sticking your neck out for a stranger?"

Steve rolled his eyes upward. "I want to see you pull it off, Harry. I want to see you beat the bastards upstairs. Most of the coppers do. The brass are big on taking credit. But just let a poor patrolman need a little help in a jam, they never heard of you," he said. "I'm rooting for you, Harry. Go get 'em. Just be damn careful."

While he was downtown, Harry drifted into the locker room, where he was confronted with the sign that always irked him:

LOCK YOUR LOCKER

Harry remembered the sign he had painted on his own locker door in big, uneven letters:

THIS LOCKER REMAINS UNLOCKED AT ALL TIMES AS AN EXPRESSION OF TRUST IN MY FELLOW POLICE OFFICERS.

Harry had hand-lettered the sign on cardboard three times, and each time it was torn off, before he decided to paint it directly on the door.

Harry stood in the center of the locker room, and tried to remember what it felt like to be just a cop, unhurried and unharassed. He couldn't remember.

Suddenly he felt a clap on his back and turned to see the hefty, sweating figure of Billy Bartholomew, his former West L.A. partner. "Harry, old pal, good to see you." Harry always thought one of Billy's assets was his ability to glad-hand. A perfect attribute for West L.A., he thought.

"Billy," he said in simple acknowledgment.

"Christ, I've been working my ass off down here. They got me on the freeway therapy. You know, lose a few goddamn pounds, and it's fukkin' killing me. Too much pizza and beer," he smiled an engaging, open smile.

"And too little action in West L.A."

"Yeah, well, I just wanted you to know I heard the news, and I think you've been royally fucked. The assholes gave you a real shitty deal."

"Watch your language, Billy. You're a police officer. Talk so you won't be ashamed to hold your head up."

Stunned, Billy's jaw dropped. "Jeeesus Chreeist," he said. "You don't have one goddamn fukkin' social-grace bone in your fukkin' body. A little cussin's not murder," he said with a sour vengeance that failed to turn sweet for him. "You sure got a way of turning away every friendly hand. Well, you can stick it up your ass," Billy said, giving Harry the finger and walking away.

"So long, fatty," Harry called after Billy. "Pay for your own meals and you won't eat so much."

〇   〇   〇

The machine beside Harry on the front seat of his car was smaller than a cigarette pack. Harry didn't look on it as a machine as much as the supreme informant, never intimidated, never compromised. Technology, Harry thought, could never be put to better use than the solving of crime.

"Thirty-five," Harry said to himself, then looked at the speedometer. Thirty-five it was. It gave him satisfaction. Expertise always did. To think of the sophistication of the device on the seat next to him that recorded phone conversations automatically, gave him pleasure.

He was heading south now on the Harbor Freeway. A gentle rain was falling. "Fifty-five," he said. Fifty-seven. Not bad. He glanced in the rearview mirror and had a strange feeling that the two men in the car behind him had been there since before he got on the freeway. He pulled over to the right lane. They followed. Then he stopped at a call box. They stopped.

He picked up the phone to avoid suspicion, and when the woman came on the other end, he said he was sorry, he thought he needed help, but the trouble seemed to have corrected itself, and he got back in the car. Driving fifty-five steadily in the right lane, all the cars seemed to pass him except the one with the two men behind him.

What now? Harry wondered. These two young bucks looked more like cops than cons. Why would cops want to follow me? Sure not too subtle about it, but maybe that was their instruction. Maybe they have the wrong guy. It wouldn't be the first time, with the guys they are hiring nowadays, and these look still wet behind the ears. They both have the obligatory mustache–all the young cops wear them nowadays to look older. And the old cops wear them to look like the young cops, who are trying to look older.

He turned off on Manchester; they turned off too. Maybe they're trying to get something solid on me to can me. He looked down at the

170

wire-recording device. What could be better than to catch me breaking the law? Unobtrusively, his hand circled the machine and he slipped it to the floor, where he pushed it under the seat with his foot.

He brought the car to an abrupt stop before a manufacturing plant with no windows on the street. He got out slowly, locked the car and sauntered into the factory, noting, with satisfaction, the troops had stopped a half-block away and had made no move to get out of the car.

Harry walked through the factory as a man who knew what he was about and, other than a few routine "hellos," he met no resistance. He walked out the back shipping entrance, jumped down the loading dock and circled around the block until he came to the place their car was parked on the main street. He felt for his gun automatically, then walked between two dingy commercial buildings and spotted the car a few cars to the right. He drew his gun and walked up in the blind spot, where the rookies were intent on watching the entrance of the factory.

Tap, tap, tap went the barrel of the gun lightly on the window of the passenger side of the car. When the men looked startled at the noise, Harry was pointing the gun between the passenger's eyes. Harry opened the door and said, "All right, one at a time. Out."

The passenger got out and Harry pushed him against the car. "Hands up. Atta boy." Harry kept the gun at his head, frisked him, drew a gun and handcuffs and asked the other gentleman to step out for the same.

"Hey," the driver said, "you're making a mistake. We're police officers."

Harry chuckled. "Police officers don't go following police officers. I'm a police officer."

"Hey, wait a minute," the passenger said, ruffled. "No one told us that. We can prove it." He started to reach for his pocket, but Harry hit his arm with the gun.

"Hold on there. Don't move."

He told them to get in the car and, while he held the gun on the passenger's head, he instructed the driver where to go. It was just getting dark and the rain had stopped, but the streets were still slick. Harry said, "Drive nice and easy and nobody gets a bullet in their head."

The passenger was perspiring freely now, his black hair matted like a helmet on his head. "We're fukkin' cops, man."

"So what are you doing following me?"

"Christ, you aren't gonna shoot us, are you?"

"If you clean up your language, you might have a better chance.

I've always favored cops you could look up to, not guttersnipes who talked like cons."

"Okay, okay, I'm sorry. Jes...geez, where are you taking us?"

"You'll see. What were you after?"

"We don't know anything. Just keep an eye on you and report your movements."

"How long you been at it?"

"Just this shift. This was our first action."

"Some story."

"You don't believe we're cops?" the perspiring passenger asked incredulously.

Harry didn't answer, but in a few minutes told the driver to pull the car over in front of a deserted warehouse. He took them inside, the driver doing his best to remain cool, the passenger making no pretenses.

"Who you working for?" Harry asked.

"I told you, we're cops," said the perspiring man.

"Who you taking your orders from?"

"Don't know him. Just assigned to him on a one-timer. Name's Frank."

Harry clamped his jaw. Frank. *My* Frank? "Eberhart?" he said aloud.

"Yeah, you know him?"

"In a way."

Inside, Harry found exposed pipes to handcuff the young knights to, separating them on different floors. "To cut down the profanity," he said. "If one of you has to filthy mouth, at least the other won't have to hear it."

He drove the car back, parked it on a side street, locked it and pocketed the keys. He got back in his car and looked at his watch. Not bad. Only a little after six. Pharmacy closed now. He had time to kill anyway, though he was going to spend it casing the place.

He drove to Broadway and 103rd and looked over the neighborhood. The rain was steady now, and the one-story, stucco pharmacy, with the flat roof, looked insignificant in the darkness. He sat across the street on 103rd and watched the building for an hour. On the left side was a boarded-up two-story apartment. On the right, an abandoned gas station. No sign of any activity. The building was locked with steel grates over the doors and windows. Harry wondered how Whistler's gang had managed to penetrate all that armor without setting off the alarms. Never underestimate Whistler, he thought ruefully.

Harry spotted the telephone box on the left side, near the back. After the hour was up, Harry stealthily left his car. In his pocket were the tiny recorder, a screwdriver and pliers. As he approached the telephone box, he noticed it was padlocked. With his screwdriver, Harry took off the hinges and managed to gain access without disturbing the lock. He set the recording device in place, connected the wire as Steve instructed him, said a prayer that it would still be there when he got back, replaced the hinges and, when he satisfied himself he was not being watched, got back in his car and drove home.

He parked his car in his carport and walked up the steps to his apartment, when his eye caught two unsavory-looking men, eying him.

He inserted the key in the lock and carefully opened the door and turned on the light. On the floor was a plain manila envelope. He locked the door behind him, picked up the envelope and tore it open with his finger.

A glossy eight-by-ten photograph of his friend Charlie Rubenstein's body with the ants crawling all over him, just like they found him, with the flame-and-crossed-sword symbol of Whistler's TRA LA (The Revolutionary Army of Los Angeles) gang carved in his chest. But Harry's police mug shot had been cut out and pasted over Charlie's head. The caption, in block letters cut from newspaper, was:

YOUR NEXT PIG

♢   ♢   ♢

Day 31

DRAMATIS PERSONAE: The Deputy Chief. A rugged-looking man, a softening around the edges. He had been one of Harry's paper cops, beginning as a chauffeur and rising through the administrative ranks, where the highest physical hazard was a bruised ego. Widely touted for the top job; the highest ranking cop Frank ever met with. Frank realized the necessity for such men, the foolishness of putting a man with administrative capabilities and designs on the street on some dangerous assignment. Frank knew from his own experience that the stresses of administrative work were no picnic, and he smiled at the hale and hearty greeting he got now, as though the deputy chief were saying, "I'm just one of the boys." The deputy's sphere of influence in the department was Public Relations.

The Police Commissioner. One of those men who, because of erratic diet, vacillated between a cherub and a dried prune. His face was beginning to crumple again, the once-tight flesh sagging, making him look like the patron of a rather inept plastic surgeon. Frank thought it was a good thing he didn't have to pass the academy physical.

Captain of Internal Affairs, Augie Templat, a.k.a. Uriah Heep, smiled ingratiatingly, his hefty body ill-at-ease in the institutional chair.

Frank sat looking at the three VIPs across the table. The seating in the airless room struck him as peculiar. Frank seemed to be the focal point. Instead of them all sitting in a circle or around the table democratically, befitting the jolly-good-fellow handshakes and the you're-one-of-us slaps on the back, the three bigwigs peered across the caste barrier at the poor cop who had nothing more to show for his twenty-plus years in service than a clean record. Did they mean for him to feel like he was on trial? Frank wondered.

The deputy chief (PR) opened the meeting. "This is an informal meeting, Frank. Off the record. You understand?" he said in the halest of friendly voices.

Frank nodded. You got nowhere saying you didn't understand, and, in spite of the uneasy feeling he had, the presence of so much brass made him feel curiously important.

After the introductory banalities, Augie Templat said, "Well, Frank, I've been tapped to carry the ball here. We've all heard the second tape. Everyday the pressure builds—from the press, from the community. Now, we've been through it with this guy Schlacter before, and we're all strung out. You asked to help him before; you can help him again."

"How?" Frank asked innocently.

"By bringing him in."

"How will that help him?"

"Save your daughter. He wants that too. And wouldn't that be better than surrounding his place with SWAT?" Augie was as ingratiating as a Dutch uncle.

"Look better for the department, I guess," Frank allowed.

"That too," the deputy chief spoke. He had a kindly, paternal voice, like everybody's idea of God the Father. "This guy just doesn't have any conception of the kinds of pressure we're under. Seven thousand men or so in the department. It's like a small city, Frank, and in any city there is a good and bad, but the good doesn't excite the press. Drama, corruption, killings, that's exciting. The percentages are minuscule, but to read the papers you'd think Harry Schlacter was the whole force. Oh, once in a while they start out saying, 'We realize the majority of police are honest,' et cetera, but nobody pays any attention to that. Now look, Frank," he spoke warm and friendly, "we know he killed Badeye, don't we?" If he hadn't asked the direct question, Frank would not have contested the statement. All the eyes were on Frank, begging his response.

He began slowly, uncertainly, "Well, I think he did. He's never admitted it to me though, and I have been wrong before when I've been just as certain." He paused deliberately, without completing his thought. Then added almost inaudibly, "Then there is the presumption of innocence."

The group shifted in their seats, almost as a body.

"Well, Jesus, Frank," Augie spoke with the cocked head of a cynical disbeliever, "he's a loose cannon. What he did to those two cops who followed him yesterday. How much more of that shit you want us to put up with?"

As soon as the shift was up, the boys' watch commander had contacted Frank. He didn't seem surprised. He knew Harry, and found his cops in under four hours. But it was one of the operation's worst fiascos. Tailing Harry was simply a bust. The problems (many) versus the results (few) were not worth the effort.

Frank shrugged his shoulders. "When Harry goes after a pigeon, I don't want to be in his way."

"Now, Frank." It was the aging, crumpled face having at him now, but reasonably, oh, so reasonably. "Let's look at it the other way then. It's a ransom condition we can meet. Oh, I know all the arguments against it, but this Whistler Wagner has been playing with us too long. We've got to show some results. It isn't going to hurt anyone to lock up Schlacter a little while to see if Whistler means business."

Frank blinked at the primitive logic. "It'll hurt Harry," he said softly.

"Jesus, Frank!" There was a jarring sound in the room as Augie Templat pounded his fist on the table, giving Frank the sensation of a mild earthquake. "This mealy-mouth crap is driving me right up the wall. You'd think you didn't want your daughter back–as if we didn't all know she had you wrapped around her little finger."

Frank looked to the other two men to see how they stomached

Augie's outburst, but their stares were loyally firm. In spite of himself, Frank was blushing. He never had been too fond of Augie Templat, and he couldn't see anything here to change his mind. Unfortunately for all concerned, the jowly captain of Internal Affairs got Frank angry. The room was silent. They were all looking at him and seemed to expect him to speak. He got the uncomfortable feeling he was no longer the guest of honor but the object of an uncanny sort of third degree.

"Certainly I want my daughter back," he said much louder than before. "I miss her terribly. Everything about her–even that little finger she wraps me around." He looked squarely at Augie, who diverted his eyes to his interlaced fingers on the table.

"Nobody has more faith in the department than I do," Frank went on. "But it's been over a month and we don't have anything but a couple of embarrassing tapes."

There were coughs all around and the sound of chairs shifting. No one interrupted Frank, so he went on.

"We all know Harry is in love with my daughter, Lela." He pronounced the name with a wistful nostalgia in his voice, pausing for only a moment, as if for his own private memorial service. "And we all know Harry...we know that Harry won't rest until he cracks this thing. And, of course, he's doing it without any help from anyone, without even the security and comfort of the basest membership in the police department." Frank paused, but the steely eyes across the table remained constant. "I'm just wondering," he said with his disarming slow, soft voice, "if the reason you want to bring him in isn't to prevent the embarrassment it would cause the department if a canned cop solved the case, saved the girl on his own, when all the resources of the FBI and the LAPD failed to produce a single lead."

There was sputtering from the judges, denials from the gods. There was more talk, but not much more said. Frank was at last assured that if he brought Harry in and Whistler did not keep his word and release Lela, they would release Harry. In exchange, Frank agreed to follow orders and arrest the best cop on the force, Harry Schlacter.

◊   ◊   ◊

That night, Harry checked the tape from his tap on Ching's phone. The good news was the little recorder was working. The bad news was there was nothing on the tape remotely incriminating. Harry put the recorder back in place and went on his way.

"Thirty-three mph," he said in his Beetle.

Thirty-three it was.

THERE was a knock on his door, but Harry wasn't sure he wanted to answer it. The knock was gentle, not threatening or insistent, but Harry didn't feel like moving from the chair he had slumped into.

He wasn't really much closer to Whistler than he was when he heard that debilitating tape. So much now depended on Ching, but Ching was not a man to cooperate, unless there was no other way out. Harry's nightly audit of Ching's phone conversations had yielded frustration and heartbreak, but no leads.

The gentle knock was repeated. For some reason the sound of the knock took him back seventeen years, to a fateful knock of his own: He was eleven years old and riding his bicycle down Figueroa, weaving in and out among the broken bits of glass, trying to avoid a flat tire. He had some important news his mother wanted him to deliver since the bartender had said his father wasn't there when his mother called, in that tone he used when he *was* there.

The Fig Bar, on Figueroa near Rosecrans, was a hardly lit, low, stucco building, sparsely peopled with hod carriers, truck drivers and an assortment of unemployed. No one made a fuss about Harry being under twenty-one when he strode in and asked Jake, the bartender, if he had seen his dad.

Jake shook his head with a solemn warning, unspoken.

Harry couldn't see his father so he started to go outside. A slight and stooped hod carrier, whether taking pity on the boy or out of some streak of meanness, followed him out and looked down at the tousled blond hair and said, "Looking for your dad?"

"Yes, sir," the boy answered politely, taking the man aback with his manners. "I have an important message for him."

"Important?" He scratched his head, weighing the conflicting merits of the case. "How important?"

"Very important, sir."

It was the second "sir" that got him. "You might find him out back," he said, waving a hand at the row of dirty motel buildings behind the bar. "Try number B."

"Thank you, sir." Harry ran off.

"But, ah, I'd knock first," the man added as an afterthought.

Harry got to B. The door was scarred and streaked and the purple paint was peeling. Harry knocked. There was no answer. The lights were not on. He knocked again. Harder. He heard his father's familiar gruff voice. "Go away. I'm busy."

Harry was about to go away, but he remembered his mother's urgent admonition that he was to bring his father back with him. If he didn't succeed, his father would never forgive him when he sobered up.

So Harry knocked once more before he tried the door and found it open. The light from outside flooded the double bed, its covers strewn on the floor like spent spectators at a wrestling match. On the soiled sheets that covered the lumpy mattress was Harry's father, naked, wrestling with a young black girl, also naked, except for a black garter belt and nylon stockings.

His father's eyes focused on the boy. "Get out of here," he screamed.

Harry didn't move.

His father seemed frozen in space.

Harry said, "Mom wants you," without feeling, without knowing where the words came from. That wasn't his message at all. Why did he say, "Mom wants you?"

"Tell her to go screw," Harry's father said. The black girl tittered and said, "You tend to yo' own knittin'!..."

"She wanted me to give you a message."

"Well, give it to me, goddamnit, and get the hell out of here."

"I...I think I should give it to you...alone," Harry said, his speech halting.

"Give it to me now," his father roared, "and give it to me fast, or I'll beat your ass to hell and gone."

Harry gasped for breath, looked again at the black girl and tried to absorb the meaning of the scene. He wasn't sure what it meant, but he didn't think it was very good. He was sure his mother wouldn't like it. He heard his father scream. "Out with it, you little shitass!"

And Harry blurted it. "Your mother's dead," he said a bit more harshly than he had rehearsed, and he was sorry for it as soon as he said it.

His father sat up on an elbow, apparently not hearing correctly.

"Is that *your* mother," he asked with a fateful pause, "or mine?"

"Yours," Harry said, relieved that he could report that alternative.

His father fell back and the sobs welled from his beer belly like hateful hiccups until his whole body shook.

Another knock, much louder this time, at Harry's apartment door pulled him back to reality. Harry dragged himself to his feet and went over to the door. "Who is it?"

"Open up in the name of the law." It was Frank's voice. "We've got the place surrounded. I'm going to count to ten," he said.

"Without making a mistake?" Harry asked. He opened the door and Frank walked in, his steps heavy with age, still dressed in his suit and tie, carrying a newspaper and an official envelope.

"The news isn't good, pal," he said, sitting down and spreading the newspaper on the couch. "Take a look at this."

There was an editorial calling for his dismissal and a cartoon showing an ape with a police uniform, holding a gun in both hands and pointing it at a naked, bound, scrawny man. The caption:

HOTSHOT

"And here's the official word," he said, handing Harry the envelope. "They've decided they have enough evidence to discharge you from the police force."

Harry opened it and saw his cold dismissal in frozen official jargon. He let the letter drop to the floor, as if that would somehow nullify it; if he didn't touch it too long, it wouldn't become part of him, wouldn't take effect.

Frank tactfully folded the newspaper, closing in the unfavorable comment. "How've you been, Harry?"

"Peachy."

"What you up to?"

"Getting by."

"Any breaks?"

Harry shook his head. "Do your own legwork, don't try to ride in on my coattails."

"It's not that simple, Harry."

"No?"

"There's a part of Whistler's tape the station agreed to leave off. Said he wanted his friends to make a citizen's arrest if the cops didn't do anything. You know, bring you in–dead or alive."

"Nice."

"Not only are you off the force, the brass wants me to arrest you." He shrugged, as if unable to make up his mind. "I want to find her, Harry. I want it more than anything."

"Listen, what can you arrest me for? Newspaper editorials and cartoons? The word of a hood like Whistler? You can't just lock people up on flimsy rumors."

"I have more than that, Harry."

Harry looked shocked. "More? What have you got?"

"Do I really need to tell you, Harry?"

"Yes, you really need to tell me," he said, mocking Frank's sadness.

Frank looked at Harry silently for a moment, as if trying to understand how he could be asking for this. Then, satisfied he had to do it, he began, being careful not to look at Harry, except for an occasional glance to see that he hadn't shut him out.

"Well, there's a cop named Folk who will testify he told you when he was releasing Badeye. In the middle of the night, as it turned out, to minimize publicity. Then we have a tenant in your building here who saw you go out at twelve-thirty on that very same night dressed in your uniform. Now that wasn't your shift, Harry."

Harry didn't flinch. Frank could tell his mind was working.

"I'll bet," Frank went on, his quiet voice quavering lightly, "you even knew his real name was Earnest and made some comment about it. Maybe even called him Earnest instead of Badeye. His mother was probably the last to call him that."

Harry couldn't help admire Frank's uncanny ability to get into other people's minds. When Frank seemed to wind down, Harry jumped up and went over to him and bent down, wagging his finger at him. "Frank, ole buddy, your daughter means more to me than anything in this world. Life itself. A couple years ago if anyone said any girl could do that to me, I'da laughed him outta town. I'm going to get her out of there safely if I have to *kill* everybody who tries to stop me. And I mean *any*body. Cops and robbers alike. You heard Lela. There's no difference. My God, how he must have brainwashed her. I hate to think of what goes on there. I don't dare think of it, I'd be stymied crazy, I couldn't function. Just don't let anybody stand in my way, Frank."

"Me too, Harry? You gonna kill me too?" Frank had a small, inquisitive smile on his lips.

Harry stared down at him. "Just don't tempt me," he said.

"Harry, Harry," Frank said, "calm yourself. I don't blame you for being upset."

"He doesn't *blame* me for being *upset,*" Harry cried out. "Look what they're doing to my girl. Did you hear that tape?" Harry hadn't wanted to talk to Frank about the tape. It just slipped out.

"Some of it was edited," Frank said.

"*Some* of it?"

Frank nodded sadly. "A lot of it was intact, Harry. I ran it through the lab. A lot of it was just consecutive." He shook his head. "I'm sorry."

"Sorry, sorry? *You*'re sorry? Let me get him. I'm getting there. Leave me alone," he begged. "Let me get her out of there and you can do anything you want. Just don't get in my way now."

"But the trouble is, Harry, you're doing anything you want to get her out. End justifies the means."

"Some ends justify *some* means," Harry said. "And this end justifies *any* means."

"I wish I could argue with you, Harry. I've got my job to think of too. He hasn't killed her yet. It looks like he isn't going to. She may suffer some miserable degradation, but Lela is strong. She'll bounce back."

"If there's anything left to bounce after you get through trying to inhibit me."

"Harry, we've got to rise above the scum. We can't go after them with their own gutter methods."

"It's all they understand."

"You can't fight a fire with fire. It only spreads the evil, it doesn't eradicate it."

"Well, you watch me, Frank," Harry said, striding away from him and pacing the floor like a caged panther. "You go back to the mealy-mouthed brass, who take their marching orders from the Whistler Wagners of the world, and you guys read all the laws and all the procedures written by guys who never saw the streets, and you get Lela out of that miserable hell she's in. You've had all the facilities of the department and the FBI, and what have you got? Whistler is thumbing his nose at you. He says, 'Fire a cop,' you fire him. He says, 'Jail a cop.' No evidence, all conjecture in a detective's head, wouldn't stay in court five minutes and you know it, Frank, and what do you do? Jail the cop. Well, don't you think Whistler knows whose face he's going to see first, mine or yours? Is he afraid of the rule book, or is he afraid of me? What was his demand? Burn the rule books, pick up Frank Eberhart, or jail Harry Schlacter?"

"The only way to prevent chaos, Harry, is with rules and order. That's what the police are all about. Jailing people is secondary. Law and order, an orderly society where decent citizens play by the rules. If we act like the cons, you soon can't tell us apart. We must be better."

"Very nice," Harry said, "when this is all over you can start your own religion. Count on me for a small donation, but don't look for me to join up."

Harry stopped his pacing, made a hopeless gesture with his hands and sank into a chair, in deep despair. "What has he done to our Lela?" he said, his voice breaking in a sob. "How did he get her to talk all that suggestive talk?" he said with harsh distaste. The tormented thoughts he had held in so long burst forth as water from a broken dam. "He must be holding a gun on her."

"Maybe he is. Maybe he had her read a script or something."

"Ah," Harry said, jumping up, "I'm not taking any chances." He began the march of the caged black jungle cat again.

"Harry," Frank pleaded. "Give me a break. Won't you cooperate with me?"

"Cooperate? Let you arrest me? Is that what you call cooperation?

"Well, he said he'd release her. If they don't have anything on you, they won't be able to hold you. In the meantime she'll be home, safe and sound."

Harry slammed his fist on the wall he was passing. "Frank, how can you believe that? You believe that...that animal? Well, if I believed it, I'd turn myself in. He's a murderer, a kidnapper, a drug dealer and God knows what else; you don't think he might tell a little lie now and again? I got a better one, Frank. Why don't you *tell* him I'm in jail? Whistler, I mean. Get word to him I'm in jail; see if you get her back."

"We couldn't do that if you weren't in jail."

"Why not?"

"Isn't honest."

"Agh," Harry shook his head and stopped to look out the window. There he saw two hoods sitting in a car across the street. "Come here a minute, Frank."

Frank came to the window and looked out where Harry was pointing to the car.

"Those yours?" Harry asked.

Frank shook his head. "No mustaches." He put his hand on Harry's shoulder. "Don't make it hard for me."

Harry took the hand gingerly and dropped it from his body. "One of the big troubles today, Frank, is we want to believe everybody is equal. We swallow that baloney we're fed in court that a criminal's word must weigh as heavily as a policeman's. But don't tell me you're believing it. That would be too much for me to take."

"We've got to *prove* we're better than them, Harry. We've got to beat them with superior methods, morals and mentality. Not in the gutter."

"Well, if you want to fight them on the church lawn, you'll be alone, because they're in the gutter."

"Harry..."

"Don't 'Harry' me, Frank. I went along with the system as long as I could stand it. More than any man, until they got my buddy Charlie and all the rules turned on me. Everything I did against the murderer seemed to be wrong. Nobody cared he was the one. All they care about was what I did to bag him."

Frank put his hand up to Harry. "I'm about to come apart. Nothing means more to me, either, than getting my daughter back, and since we've shot over four weeks, as you generously point out, my resistance to your method is crumbling. Just don't shove it down my throat, Harry, I've got a lifetime of beliefs at stake. I'm not built to use illegal procedures; just the psychological implications of the reversal of all I've stood for, believed in, in my lifetime would ruin me."

"Well, Frank," Harry said, "it looks like it's you or me. The lines are pretty clear. We both want the same thing, we just go about it a little different, is all. I'll fight you fair and square; we'll see who wins. You take me in, I don't give Lela much hope. Give me a chance, Frank," Harry pleaded. "Give me a couple more days. It won't kill you."

Frank looked into the deep eyes of the man possessed. Then he vacillated. There were too many inconsistencies clouding the issue, just like their first meeting, when he'd seen Harry's dossier: more arrests, more tickets, more calls answered, more letters of praise, more complaints, more partners. Could anyone be as good and bad in one body?

"Hurry up, Harry," he said at last, turning to go. "I don't know how much longer I can stall them."

Day 35

THE Mercedes 500 SLC with the CHING license plate was parked behind the pharmacy. The lights were still on inside, but Ching was not in evidence. Maybe he's in his office, on the phone, giving me something I can use, Harry hoped.

It was raining again, lightly, but enough to slick the streets and dampen the spirits. Harry wondered if Lela was having rain where she was, if she got to see it, to walk in it. Then his mind turned to Ching again. He mused at the expensive car sitting untouched in the high-crime neighborhood. Never a hand laid on it. If you were driving a Rolls-Royce or a Mercedes SLC in Watts and a cop saw you, you'd better have convincing identification and registration papers. On the other hand, if you stole a Ford or Chevy, you wouldn't get a second look.

Harry decided to cruise the neighborhood to give Ching all the time he needed to do something incriminating on the phone. He drove over to the football field where he starred on the Centinela High team, where Whistler tried to bribe him to shave a few points, and he relived the game where he beat the point spread with a spectacular touchdown in the last minute.

He drove on to the white clapboard corner church where he took his first communion. Inside, a wedding rehearsal was in progress. They were all black now. The neighborhood had mutated from a mixture when he was growing up to almost all black. He remembered his mother singing with the choir in her purple robe, and he sat in the front row, alone. Nobody wanted to be up front in church, only in the theater and at sports events, as though the further you were from God, the less likely He was to see your defects.

Harry remembered the first and last time his father went to the church. It was in his coffin. Harry, now that he was older, suspected his mother did it out of some dark, instinctive spite. She always said he thought he was God, "So let's give him a proper send-off."

He had died so simply. Harry was graduating from high school, and Easter had fallen late in the year. To celebrate both occasions,

Harry's mother, Sally Ann, had bought a spectacular Easter bonnet. When Elmer, her ornery husband, saw the bill for the hat on Good Friday, he exploded–had a stroke and died on the spot.

Sally Ann always said that, in spite of Elmer's exalted opinion of himself, Easter came and went without his being resurrected, and she wore the bonnet triumphantly at his funeral, though its bright spring flowers and pastel straw were hardly in keeping with the traditional widow's weeds.

"Twenty-five," Harry said aloud as he cruised back to the Ching drug shop. He looked at the speedometer. Twenty-five it was. He passed the neighborhood where he grew up, the small one-story, stucco boxes that housed their families: his, Charlie Rubenstein's and Badeye Iler's. Whistler Wagner had lived in a number of apartments. He looked up at the ridiculously tall palm trees and mused that there were a lot of people in the neighborhood whose eyesight wasn't good enough to see the little green sprouts on the top.

By the time Harry got back, the pharmacy was dark. After parking his car, he stalked carefully to the little phone box in the back, took off the hinges again with the screwdriver he brought and replaced the little tape with a fresh one.

In the car, on the way back to his apartment, Harry inserted the tape in the portable machine he had beside him on the front seat. There was a series of monotonous calls from doctors' offices for prescriptions, drug companies with questions on orders, salesmen, even Mrs. Ching with a complaint about the children and her inability to cope with the oldest boy. Then Harry was shocked to hear the familiar voice, so painfully abject in its desperation:

"Mr. Ching, this is Frank Eberhart, LAPD."

"Yes, I know you. I'm sorry I didn't get to return your calls, I've been so swamped." The voice had a smooth, ingratiating quality.

"Quite all right, I appreciate you talking to me now."

"What can I do for you?"

"A great favor, Mr. Ching. You may have heard my daughter's been kidnapped by Whistler Wagner."

"Yes, a terrible thing."

"I was hoping you could help us locate her. Some tidbit of information perhaps, some clue as to where to look, some person to contact."

"I wish I could help you," was the edgy, educated reply, "but I don't know anything about it. I'm a pharmacist who happens to practice in a high-crime area. I wish I knew half the things the police think I

186

know; I could make my living as an informer." He laughed lightly, almost falsetto.

Harry could hear Frank heave a heavy sigh on the tape. "Mr. Ching, I know you're crooked and you know I know it."

"Careful what you say. I may have to bring an action for slander."

"No you won't, Mr. Ching, because the infallible defense against slander is truth. Nobody sells the volume you do legitimately."

"Look, Frankie," Ching said with a deprecating inflection, "I'd like to talk to you all day, but I don't have the time. I've cooperated with your investigation all I could. Now if you think you have something that'll hold water in court, come and get me. Otherwise, I've got to go."

"Ching," Frank said with painful urgency, "I'm asking you a small one...my daughter's life is in grave danger. Whistler is an erratic, explosive person, you know that, you've experienced it first-hand. You have children. I know it was your fears for your family that put you in the spot you're in. I sympathize with that. That will mitigate anything we do. I'm asking you a little favor as one parent to another. Give me a break. A hint. Anything."

"Do I understand you're offering me some kind of deal? Immunity?"

"I'll give you anything I can. Tell me what you know."

"What can you give me?"

"I'm not the boss." Frank's voice trailed and hit bottom.

"Well, it's academic anyway. I don't know anything."

"Wait a minute," Frank begged, "don't hang up. I'll see what I can do for you. I'll talk to the D.A. He makes these decisions. I just can't promise you anything right now."

"Why not?"

"It's not legal."

There was a stunned pause. Then Ching said, "Well, thanks for calling. I wish I could help you, but I can't," and hung up.

Harry was furious for poor Frank. He didn't know how to handle a bum like Ching. You didn't get anywhere with that parent-to-parent-plea stuff. Whistler Wagner knew how to get to Ching. Harry knew how to get to Ching. With maximum fear. No friendly, sympathetic, fellow-man baloney. Ching was casehardened. Frank was too soft. No deals, unless you held all the cards.

There were other insignificant calls, and nothing among them that Harry found elucidating until he heard this strange exchange:

"Uncle Sam?"

"Yeah."

"Swimming hole."

"Yeah."

"Fruity."

"Jake."

"Old Rowley's place. Down from my shop."

"Give my regards to Broadway?"

"Mine too. A dozen times holy."

"Roger."

Harry listened to the portion three times and had it memorized. What it meant was another matter. He was pondering the possible meanings and their implications when he pulled into the carport at his apartment. As he stepped out of the car they lurched at him. One black, one white. One with a tire iron, the other a chain.

Off guard, Harry was lucky to sidestep the first thrust with the tire iron from the black, who could have been a stuntman stand-in for King Kong. The white was less menacing, looking like the Hunchback of Notre Dame, except he had never seen the inside of a church. He was, however, able to swing a mean chain, and he caught Harry across the shoulder. But Harry, too dense to know when the odds are impossible, Harry, who was obsessed with the triumph of good over evil, let fly a fist that caught King Kong in the neck and sent him gasping backward, an advantage Harry pressed, and climaxed by breaking the ape's jaw. The chain was coming at him again, and Harry ducked, missing it by inches. The chain crashed into Harry's windshield and threw the deformity off balance long enough for Harry to pounce on him and break one of the hunchback's favorite arms.

Harry didn't expect any trouble from his attackers in the disconnected shape they found their bones, but, to be safe, he took the chain and wrapped it around the victims and from the trunk of his car took a padlock, which he inserted in the chain, which he attached to the pole that held up the carport.

Harry brushed himself off and thought how similar this all was to the cop tail. Handcuff to pipes, chain to posts. They can keep coming as long as we don't run out of pipes and posts, he thought.

He walked wearily and warily up the steps to his door, unlocked it, gun drawn, and threw on the light switch and didn't go in until he was satisfied he wasn't being set up for another ambush.

Inside, he locked the door, sat down and thought, I gotta get out of here. But where? It's easy to disappear in this town if you're loaded with dough. I'll find another way.

He went over in his mind the dialogue on the Ching tape again. Certain things were falling into place. Of course, it was just speculation. He could be wrong. And yet...

Day 36

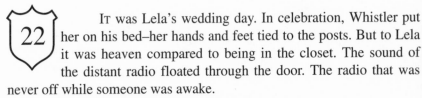

IT was Lela's wedding day. In celebration, Whistler put her on his bed–her hands and feet tied to the posts. But to Lela it was heaven compared to being in the closet. The sound of the distant radio floated through the door. The radio that was never off while someone was awake.

Looking out the window made Lela feel reborn. She was very grateful to Whistler for her relative freedom. Even a small thing like allowing Lela to look out the window brought joy to her heart. And now she was going to marry him–the man she hated more than anyone in the world.

She looked outside at the surreal black-and-white landscape–so symbolic of the marriage. There was nothing out there but snow, white snow, and tall, bare, black trees penetrating the white snow. There would be no white wedding gown for her marriage, but the snow would symbolize her purity.

The snow was everywhere. There were no streets, no paths, no footprints out her window–only snow, and it looked to be about three feet deep. How could she run anywhere in that? She'd sink in up to her unloved breasts. Even if she could get her hands on the car keys, she couldn't drive the car an inch in that much snow. Besides, she couldn't find the road. Everything was going against her.

She could continue to insist Bull and Moose go away so she and Whistler could have the house to themselves for their "celebration," but where could they go? They couldn't move in all that snow.

Lela lifted her head the few inches she was able to and stared outside and felt her fate sealing her in suffocating silence. No wonder Whistler had finally settled on this day for the wedding. He had outsmarted her.

How could she kill him with Bull and Moose in the next room? She could possibly seduce Bull, but Moose was immune; she might wound Moose, but Bull could break her in two with two fingers if someone told him to do it. But if Whistler was dead, would Moose tell Bull to hurt her? Could she seduce Bull and turn him on Moose? But what if she made him so angry he would just kill her in an irrational rage–before she had time to seduce him?

All the carefully laid plans she had agonized over for weeks, nullified by the weather. She was now without the luxury of time to lay a contingent plan.

The smoky smell of the fire in the living-room fireplace seeped under the door and filled Lela's nostrils. Her plea to be treated like a human being before she could love fell on the deafest ears.

As long as she had breath she would never give up, but looking out at the hopeless depth of the snow plunged her into despair. Bull still came in to check her every fifteen or twenty minutes, though God knows where he thought she would go.

When Lela asked Whistler how they would get to a minister to perform the ceremony, she was told Moose was a minister of some strange, unheard-of sect: Assembly of Evangelicals, or something. So she could eliminate the hope of any help from strangers.

Suddenly her ears caught the sound of a muffled harmonica covering the sound of the radio. She couldn't make out the tune, but it took her a moment to realize–it must be coming from inside the house.

The marks on her closet doorframe added up to thirty-six, and the lack of communication from any loved one, familiar face or trustworthy source had taken its toll. Of all the lies she had been sure she had been told, the one she refused to believe was that Harry was dead. But he might as well be, she thought, when he hears what is going to happen to me.

Smells from the kitchen were wending their way to her now. Moose was baking chocolate chip cookies for dessert, her favorite. He had whispered to her that he was going to do it.

Desserts–"stressed" spelled backwards. It was as though they were preparing a last meal for her before her execution.

The harmonica was sounding morose now, like a funeral march. Lela was convinced she was going to die.

She felt as though someone had taken sandpaper to her nerve ends. She thought of the wedding day she had dreamed of, a girl in white gliding down the aisle of her church on her father's arm, pride in her heart, her friends in the pews, her tall, strong and handsome bridegroom waiting at the chancel rail. Her childhood minister asks Harry if he takes

Lela and Lela if she takes Harry and there is a long, tender kiss and music and flowers. Afterwards, a joyous reception and a wedding trip to Santa Barbara, La Jolla or even Carmel.

Perspiration soaked her suit as she rehearsed the scene she planned for after the wedding. So much depended on unknowns. Would the hook still be behind the book? Would there be an opportunity to get it? And then get it into Whistler's heart? What would the Bobbsey Twins, Bull and Moose, do?

I've got to put on a good show, she thought, I've got to convince them he fell on the hook. She was involved in her plans when the door opened and Moose stood there, all hair and eyes, with a blond wig in his hand. He looked her over and said, "We ready fo' you, Miss Lela, just as soon's I get this wig on you."

He untied her and she sat on the edge of the bed while he pinned her hair back and put the wig on her head. Then he tied the wig hair in a loose bun in back. Moose stepped back for a critical look. In answer to Lela's questioning stare, he said "Whistler not satisfied with the hair color, he got you this wig instead."

Moose made some adjustments to the wig, pushing the generous bangs back underneath the sides. "Now I just gots to do a little more makeup," he said. He pulled the makeup kit from the battered bureau drawer and went to work.

"Am I getting a wedding dress?" Lela asked.

"This is yo' weddin' dress," Moose said, looking at the gray gabardine suit. Whoever it was I'm supposed to look like, Lela thought, had an awful old-fashioned taste.

Moose left her alone in the room. Untied. Her mind raced. She looked at the window. Easy to open. She went over to it. It was nailed shut. Break the glass? Could you break glass silently? These little panes, you'd have to break out the wood frames too. Too risky. Better stick to the original plan. "I must not fail," she said to herself over and over. "I must not fail."

She was becoming mesmerized by the thick, drifting, unfamiliar snow when the door opened and Bull stood there grinning that evil, frighteningly memorable grin of his. Oh, no, her first thought was a further trick of depravity: I'm marrying Bull.

But Bull held out his hand to her and waved a harmonica with his other hand. "Come on, Missy Lela," he said, and she smiled, thinking to herself, some choice. To be relieved to be marrying Whistler when it could have been Bull the cretin or Moose the homosexual.

The living room looked warm and friendly to her. The fire was roaring in the fireplace, paper dolls had been cut out of brown-paper shopping bags and strung across the room. It was homey to Lela after what seemed a lifetime in the closet. She might almost mistake it for her schoolroom.

"Looky what I found," Bull said, showing Lela the harmonica proudly. "I gonna play 'Here Come de Bride.'" And it was a good thing he told her what he was playing, because she wouldn't have recognized it otherwise. He got the rhythm close, but the intonation was hopeless.

When Bull started to play, Whistler came from the kitchen dressed in clean Levi's and his best leather jacket over his Pendalton shirt. On his head was tied a bandana. His wide belt had a silver buckle with a big "W" inlaid with turquoise. "W" for "wow," Lela thought. She smiled at him, but he didn't smile back. He must be taking it very seriously, she thought. A strange primitive of a man–an emotional pygmy. The range he had shown her so far: one note. The depth of his character: about a quarter of an inch.

The sound of the radio, playing inappropriate music, followed Whistler into the room.

Lela's heart pounded as Moose went to the bookshelf and took out a book. She was flooded with relief when it turned out to be a distance from where her hook was, she hoped, still reposing. He opened the book as though it were the Bible and nodded at Bull, who took Lela on one arm and with the other moved the harmonica in his mouth for a repeat of his facsimile rendition of "Here Comes the Bride." Richard Wagner, she thought, was a lucky man he wasn't here to hear it.

When Bull deposited Lela beside Whistler and stepped aside, Whistler took her arm grimly in his. He didn't look at her or acknowledge her person in any way. Lela was smiling brightly if painfully. Moose began:

"Brother an' sister, we're gathering here in the sight of God..."

How could God be watching this and letting it happen? Lela thought.

Bull was standing with his back to the kitchen door. The sounds of the radio were coming through faintly.

"Bull, you got that radio so's you can hear it?" Whistler asked, his eyes squinted in that stern-father squint he reserved for the important stuff.

"Sure do," Bull acknowledged.

"Don't miss nothin', hear?"

"Won't."

"Just tell me right away, you hear something."

"Told me a hunderd times," Bull pouted.

Moose continued: "To join together you two dudes in holy matrimonial. So to get right to da point, do you, Whistler Jason Wagner, take dis here woman, Miss Wills, to be ya lawful wedded wife, to have an' to hold, for riches or for poors, in sickness and healthy, till death do you part?"

If it works, Lela thought, death will do us part tonight.

Whistler answered with an "I do" that sounded almost grisly to Lela.

"Do you likewise, Miss Wills?"

Lela said nothing. She looked at Whistler for some reaction, some flicker of interest in her–or the fabled Miss Wills, for that matter–but caught only a whiff of whiskey. Fortification, no doubt. She didn't know where the words came from or why, but she said, finally, after Moose asked her again if she did likewise:

"My name is Lela Eberhart. Not Miss Wills. Do you want to marry me or some phantom lover? I mean, if this is all a joke, I can go along with it, but I have to know what's going on."

Moose frowned at her. Whistler squeezed her arm until it felt numb, but he didn't look at her. These people are crazy as coots, she thought.

"Well," Moose prodded. "Do you? Just say 'I do.'"

"I do," she said with a mechanical rapidity that stunned Moose.

"Okay, produce da ring."

Whistler dug in his coat pocket and brought out a small velvet-covered box and opened it. Lela looked down on an enormous diamond, the size of which startled her speechless. Whistler slipped it on her finger slowly, then closed her hand over it. It was the first tenderness she'd felt from him.

"With this ring, I thee wed," Moose said.

"I do," Whistler said.

"In the name of da Father, da Son and da Holy Ghost. You wanna kiss da bride?"

Whistler looked at Lela for the first time in the ceremony. "Later," he said.

The reception was a joyous affair for the guests. Whistler still seemed preoccupied. Whenever the radio music stopped and the talking began, Whistler would "sh" the wedding guests and listen. Then when the music began again, his face melted in disappointment.

The dinner for two, intimate by the fireplace, was delicious and bountiful: rack of lamb with little paper panties, squiggly mashed potatoes squirming around the edge of the plate, mint jelly, string beans almondine, cherries jubilee. All the supplies laid in for the big event before the white shroud of snow wrapped the tiny cabin as tightly as any mummy. Moose had put a record on the ancient record player–but under Whistler's instructions, it was turned so low he could still hear the radio playing in the kitchen.

Whistler's face contorted. He remembered when the three men had been sitting around the living room, looking out on the devastating snow, while Lela was in the closet.

"Some snow job," Bull had said, and sniggered.

Moose asked, "What you want to do 'bout da meal, boss? We gettin' real low. You wanna hold back on da stuff I plannin' for da weddin' banquet?"

"No. Miss Wills and I feast."

"Yes, boss. Bull an' I'll eat in da kitchen. Short rations."

Whistler didn't argue. "How much we got left?"

"If you eat big tonight, we might stretch for half a day."

Whistler nodded. "Not a word to her," he said. "If we have the wedding feast with a slice of bread, she's gonna be suspicious. I expect we'll have our answer on the radio tonight. You *did* send that tape all right, Moose?"

"Yes, sir, but we sent it to Texas, remember? Make it look like we was moving."

"Your brother *is* reliable, you told me."

"More'n anybody I know. He sent it. I called him from San Berdo. He mailed it all right."

"Maybe the station didn't get it yet."

"Been nine days," Moose said. "We use overnight mail."

Whistler nodded and licked his lips apprehensively.

Bull looked out the window. "I can get out," he said. "I'll walk to the village for food."

Whistler shook his head. "It's a small store. It'll alert them to blacks–strangers here. Can't say we're passing through. No one's passing in this shit."

"Well, we gotta eat," Moose said.

"We wait. Maybe it melts soon."

"If it don't?" Moose asked.

"There's some snowshoes here," Whistler said. "I just don't take no chances till the last minute."

They were sitting alone now, Whistler in strange silence and Lela trying to animate the conversation, eliciting only grunts and nods from Whistler. Lela stood and pretended to peruse the bookshelf. She pulled out the special book and took the brass hook out of its tissue wrapper. Lela was flooded with relief when she felt the hook, cold in her palm. She quickly shoved it under the cushion of the tattered stuffed chair and returned to her chair at the table. She visualized luring Whistler to the easy chair. She would sit on his lap, kiss him, get the hook and stab him unaware.

Whistler turned and yelled through the closed kitchen door, "You got the radio on, Moose?"

"Yes, boss."

"Anything yet?"

"No, boss."

"You tell me soon's you hear."

"Yes, boss."

"What's on the radio?" Lela asked.

"Nothin'," Whistler said with a snarl that begged the finality of the question. He sat, silent, morose and pensive. What did he want? The question screamed inside her.

"Whistler," she said gently.

"Hm?"

"Who is Miss Wills?"

He looked startled at first that she should have such effrontery, then he relaxed and studied her. "You are," he said simply.

"I mean, who was the real one, the other one, the one you made me look like?"

He looked at her a long moment, then looked away, as if trying to divine if her question would conjure up the distant Miss Wills or make her disappear.

The cherries jubilee, flaming in all its glory, had been eaten. "Down in flames," Lela had said. The dishes had been cleared; Whistler stood as he took off his jacket. Lela gulped as she watched him lay it over the back of the stuffed chair before he sat back down at the table. The hurricane lamp still burned between them, filling the air with the odor of kerosene. Music came from the phonograph on the bookshelf. Bull and Moose were still imprisoned in the kitchen. Not much protection, Lela thought, an unlocked door.

Lela reached out to take Whistler's hand, settling for resting hers on his clenched fist.

"Was she a great love of yours?" Lela asked gently, trying to gain his confidence.

Whistler nodded, bleary-eyed.

"Do you think I can take her place?" she said, rubbing his fist with a gentle, slow, circular motion.

"Hope so," he croaked.

"Was she...white?"

He nodded again.

"Do I look like her?" she asked, pursing the corner of her mouth like Whistler taught her.

He considered, looking her up and down. "Some," he said, disappointed.

"Where did you meet her?"

"School."

"She in your class?"

Whistler shook his head. "Teacher," he whispered, as though he had explored some primitive depth for the first time.

"Oh," she said with gentle encouragement. "What did she teach?"

"History."

"You must have loved her very much," she said.

She heard the palm slam the table and felt the lamp rattle before she realized he had jerked his fist from under her tender hand. "I don't wanna talk 'bout it no more," he said.

"I'm sorry," she said. "I didn't mean to pry. You're just so moody tonight, I thought I might help you."

He looked at her again. He mumbled something she couldn't understand.

"You know, sometimes I hear you talking jive talk–other times you talk more...normally."

"White, you mean?"

"Well...like I do anyway. Like they do on television."

Whistler grunted.

"Why is that?" she pressed gently.

"Dunno."

"Come on, Whistler," she said, "I think you are a lot smarter than that."

He shrugged his shoulders.

"No, come on, I'm interested. I see in my third-graders some of the same thing. They talk normally to me, then slip into this street talk with their peers. It's almost as though they are afraid to stand out. Like they'll have less hassle if they play the dumb kid." She looked levelly into his eyes. "You ever feel that way?"

He looked out the window to the darkness lying on the virgin snow. "Maybe," he said.

"Did you ever play the dumb kid with adults? To maybe get what you wanted?"

"Maybe," he said. "So why you askin' all these questions? You writin' a book about me?"

She tittered, "No." Then she took a moment for a second thought. "Might not be a bad idea though. Help pass the time here. Would you give me a pencil and paper?"

"No."

"No?" she said, her eyes shutting, as if stuck by a sudden blow. "You mean, I'm going to be your wife and I can't even have a pencil?"

"Don't want nothin' written 'bout me."

"Well, okay. Can I at least write a letter to my father to tell him I'm married?"

Whistler shook his head.

There was something missing here, Lela thought. Not just the warmth and affection one might expect from a wedding dinner, but even a reluctance to exhibit any kind of concern or even acknowledgment that anything had happened.

Lela looked across the table and there for the merest instant she saw Harry–tall, handsome and smiling, his lips parting over straight, white teeth. She reached out her hand and touched his. At that moment he was gone, and her hand rested on Whistler's hand. She fought the impulse to jerk her hand back, and hoped Whistler didn't feel the twitch of revulsion she felt.

Suddenly Whistler withdrew his hand, and she slid her hand back into her lap without taking her eyes from his averted eyes. "Now,

Whistler, what's wrong?"

"Nothing!"

"But *some*thing *is* wrong. This isn't a normal wedding night. You're barely speaking to me."

"Dunno normal. Never been married."

"Well, I haven't either," she said, "but it doesn't take much imagination to realize it's got to be a little friendlier than this."

Whistler twitched his cheek, then looked down at the bare scarred table.

"I want to please you, Whistler," she pleaded. "Just tell me how."

"Why you want to please me?"

"I'm your wife. Isn't that what wives do?"

Whistler shrugged, and his cheek twitched again.

Lela stared at Whistler, forcing a slight, seductive smile to her lips.

Whistler frowned, his cheek twitched and his eye closed in a forceful wink, the wink of fear, not seduction.

Lela drew in a breath in the hope of fortifying her flagging spirits. The flame on the wick of the hurricane lamp on the table between them flickered.

"Whistler?" she started, then faltered. "Can we...talk?"

"'Bout what?"

"What we're going to do. I mean, now we're married I...well, I wondered what you had in mind for us." Maybe, she thought, I won't have to use the clothes hook.

"I mean, are we going to just stay here the rest of our lives?" She suddenly got another idea, "Or are you just going to kill me?"

Whistler's cheek twitched.

"Where will we live when we go back–*if* we go back?"

"We'll see," he grunted.

"Where," she said, brightening, with a slow smile, her foot moving under the table to rub against his leg, "will we spend tonight?"

The cheek twitched again, as though the groom were in excruciating pain.

"What's wrong, Whistler?" she asked. "Are you sorry we're married?"

Whistler frowned, then he fidgeted. He had had good success with his tapes–two tapes played on the air out of two sent. It wasn't right

DAVID CHAMPION

that this tape should be ignored. Maybe asking for Harry's execution was going a little too far. But no one could tell Whistler Harry didn't deserve it.

Something was going on. Here he was, snowed in in the wilderness, out of food, and the fuzz ignoring his negotiations. All of a sudden it had all turned sour. Now here he was, married for strategic reasons to someone who suddenly didn't appeal to him.

What was it? Lela was nice enough, and damn good-looking by any standards, any color. Maybe the problem was she was so goddamn white. She was educated, well-spoken, had been sheltered and coddled like she was some goddamn rare flower or something–never needing to get dirt under her fingernails, never having to start hatching babies at fourteen. Never having to do anything–just getting by on the goddamn whiteness of her prissy-assed looks.

Now, that Miss Wills was some kinda broad. Mysterious-looking...it wasn't all right up front for everyone to see. Well, he tried, but he just couldn't turn this baby-faced prissy-ass into the sophisticated Miss Wills. He could dress her, get her a blond wig, pull it back in a bun, ladle on the makeup, but it just wasn't in her. She didn't talk like Miss Wills, she didn't walk like her, think like her or do *any*thing like her. The whole venture was a flop.

"Why don't you talk to me?" Lela noted. "Here we are, married, and I don't even know anything about you."

"What you wanna know?"

"Well, *every*thing," she said. "Do you like movies?"

"Don't go to no movies."

She noticed how his grammar slipped again.

"Television?"

"Some–watch some."

"What?"

"Whatever's on–*Miami Vice* was good. *L.A. Law. Hill Street Blues* used to be okay. Sometimes a soap if I'm real bored."

"How about your business. What do you do for a living?"

He turned quiet again. "I get by," he said.

"Oh, I think you're being too modest. Why, just look at what it must take for us to be here. I mean, the logistics of the operation." She paused. "Drugs?" she ventured with less bravery than she hoped.

"No worry of yours," he said, "I does all right."

"I'm sure you do," she said, hoping she had massaged the ego sufficiently. "Whistler, is this marriage just for some kind of show?"

"Why you say that?"

"Because it's so strange. I mean, here we are, married, and you don't seem at all interested."

"Got lot on my mind."

"Tell me what," she said. "Maybe I can help you with it."

He shook his head.

"Moose!" Whistler yelled at the kitchen door when he heard voices after the radio music stopped. "What they talkin' about?"

"Nothin', boss," came the retort through the closed door, "just the traffic."

Whistler slumped back in his chair under the weight of his depression.

Lela studied the sad black face, ravaged with discouragement. She wanted to cheer him up. She tried to look sultry when she asked, "So where are we going to sleep tonight?"

The smallest twitch jerked Whistler's cheek.

"You don't mean I'm going back in the closet?"

Silence, then the twitch.

"Please, no, oh, please...no!"

The only sound from Whistler was the audible intake of air he afforded himself, as though that would get his exacerbated twitch under control.

"Oh, no," she wailed, then broke into tears, followed by loud sobs.

His cheek convulsed. "Sh! You want the boys to think I'm hurting you?"

She shook her head. "But you *are* hurting me."

"I'm not laying a hand on you."

"Don't you know you can hurt a girl without hitting her? Don't you know about feelings?"

Whistler abruptly turned his head away.

Lela glanced quickly at the chair. It was at the same place, the cushion was undisturbed. But how could she be sure the hook was still there? she wondered.

Why wouldn't it be, silly? she chided herself. No one has gone near the chair since I put the hook under the cushion.

"Whistler," she said after a moment of awkward silence, trying to make her voice purr, "what can I do to make you happy?"

"Dunno if you can."

Lela almost giggled aloud at her thoughts. Here she was, trying desperately to promote a courtship *after* the marriage.

"Well," she said brightly, rising, "shall we try? Let's go over to the soft chair."

He looked at her as if he didn't know what she was talking about.

He didn't move.

She looked down at him, now beside her, and put her hands on his shoulders, then ran them slowly down his chest. He seemed to freeze in place. Like a snowman who had never experienced warmth.

She started unbuttoning his shirt. He stopped her hand.

My God, she thought, if he sits there all night, I'll never get my chance. She slid off the gabardine jacket, then started unbuttoning her blouse. She took off the blouse. Then the brassiere. She bent over to touch her delicate breasts to his cheek. He stared hard at her, as though that would help him overcome his inhibition. It didn't. She was trying to be seductive. One instant she was a woman more bent on survival than pleasure; the next she was suspicious of the strange stirrings she was beginning to feel inside her. Whistler's insouciance to her tingling feelings told her her slinky seduction was working more on her than it was on him. Whistler seemed oddly distracted. Like the radio was his elusive, hard-to-get lover. Lela was available. The radio was the challenge.

Lela's skirt and panties slipped off her with a fluid grace that surprised her. Her feelings were all mixed up as she slid gently onto his lap.

"Don't you like me?" she purred, as she imagined he must have fantasized his teacher doing. "Don't you think I'm attractive," she said, "for a teacher?"

Whistler turned to ice. Lela gritted her teeth. Now what? She looked quickly at the chair with the hook buried under its cushion.

Whistler frowned. "What you looking at?"

Lela's eyes darted to Whistler's face. "What? Oh, nothing." Oh, God, she thought. If he suspects... If he looks...

Then, the record came to an end and suddenly Whistler said, "'Scuse me," and leaped up, dumping Lela on the floor, and headed for the kitchen.

Lela panicked. Was he going for a butcher knife? What good would a clothes hook do against that? She picked herself up.

There was the sound of a muffled argument in the kitchen before Whistler returned with the wooden radio and set it on the shelf next to the phonograph. He hastily plugged in the radio, and the rock music suddenly invaded the room, as if to bless the union with a more realistic turmoil.

Whistler shuffled back to his kitchen chair at the table, a man weighted down with sad realities. He slumped into the chair and kept his dull stare fixed on the old radio, as though by sheer force of will he could coax from that antique wooden box the sounds he wanted to hear.

Now, she said to herself, now! She bent over the soft, cushioned chair and took the hook in her hand. It felt rough and awkward to hold. Could she get the grip she needed to sink the point into him? Would she have sufficient leverage to make the plunge pay off?

Well, she decided, there doesn't seem another option. He was loonier than a jaybird to start with, and it's been steadily downhill ever since.

Lela stood trying to focus her bleary eyes on the spot on his back to plunge the hook into. Now was her chance. He was slouched, bringing the target of his heart closer to her striking range.

Could she do it? Did she have the strength? The will? How could she kill her husband on their wedding night? But he wasn't really her husband, was he? What if she tried and failed? What would be the consequences? Stop this! she commanded herself. Do it! Don't just sit here shivering. Do it!

The fire had gone out in the fireplace. The room was starting to swim in Lela's head, or she was starting to swim in the room, she didn't know which. The light from the hurricane lamp was ghostly, and put her in mind of all the stories she had heard about devil worship.

Her husband was acting crazier all the time. What was this fetish with the radio? Was he possessed by the devil? Lela was so mixed up, she couldn't make sense of anything. All she could remember was she had to kill him...but she couldn't remember how she was supposed to do it.

Human sacrifice? Was she losing her mind? Nothing going on here seemed in the slightest contact with reality.

She was in a cocoon–this tape and nail-popping drywall room. She felt like the moth whose attraction to the light was so strong it would kill her.

Hunched in deep concentration, Whistler seemed to her the

crazed inmate of an asylum expecting to hear broadcast news of his release.

Censorship is what it was, Whistler thought. That's un-American. I got my rights of free speech like anybody else. God, something better happen soon, this cabin 'bout to make me stir-crazy. Who'da ever thought we'd have a goddamn fukkin' snowstorm to break every muthafukkin' record on the books?

"Goddamn fukkin' snowstorm." Whistler pounded his fist on the table, sending that hurricane lamp on a jolly dance. "I wasn't snowed in here, I'd show 'em..." he trailed off, as though returning to sanity.

"Husband!" Lela yelled in a throaty, domineering black voice she'd heard the mothers of her schoolchildren use. "What you so mad about?"

"Nona yo' business," he grunted without looking at her. Standing beside him, she placed her hand gently on his shoulder, trying to gain his attention. The full moon cast shadows of the window frame on her naked body.

On the radio the announcer was saying, "And with the stroke of twelve we pass into another day bringing you the finest in rock and news."

Now, Lela commanded to herself, do it!

Whistler jumped up and picked up the radio and smashed it against the wall. It fell, splintered and silent, to the floor.

Lela's hand tightened on the hook. It was as though she saw herself as that radio. It was only the first target of his rage. She would be the next. Do it!

She moved slowly, with an unconscious deliberation, to where Whistler was leaning, still hunched over the shelf. She raised the hook in her hand, but laid her other hand gently on his back. It was a loving gesture.

He turned suddenly, to see the hook fall from her hand to the floor.

His eyes were miles wide with confusion at first, then closed in understanding, then suddenly pinched but open in rage.

"Bitch," he hissed, striking her hard on the mouth. She gasped, and blood came immediately. "I don't want to kill you," she cried, "I want to love you." He proceeded to beat her about her face and defenseless body. The blows rained on her like the judgment of an angry mob. "Don't do this, please," she gasped. "Don't hurt me..." Her screams of agony were ignored in the kitchen, where Bull and Moose minded their own business.

When the final blow toppled Lela to the floor, Whistler fell on top of her, opening his pants with great urgency and wanting more than anything in the world to follow the savage beating with a savage raping.

"Oh, please don't," Lela sobbed. "Not like this. Be gentle. I want to...please...I want to make love to you. Don't kill me. Save me. I want to live. Please...Whistler."

Suddenly Lela realized Whistler's ambition was not being realized. What she realized instead was he was seized by a sudden sobbing fit, his chest heaving like intermittent tidal waves on a calm sandy beach. Then he was hissing and snarling like some chained beast, and his erratic behavior terrified Lela more than the beating had. He took her neck now in both his hands and started to apply pressure until she could no longer breathe. Her mouth fell slack. Her eyes exploded.

"Now hear me, and hear me good, bitch," he said, releasing the pressure for a moment while she sucked in the air, holding to the thin thread of life he left her. "You breathe one word of this to anyone and I'll kill you so fast...I mean, if I even *think* you gave the slightest hint, I'll kill you. You understand?"

She nodded her head in eager comatose agreement.

"*I'll kill you*," he shouted, foam trickling down the sides of his mouth.

"Bull! Moose!" he shrieked, and the door opened instantly. They both looked at the beaten girl on the floor and felt their faces drop.

"Tie up this frigid bitch and throw her back in her cell."

When she had been once again bound and gagged and blindfolded, she dissolved into body-quaking hysterical sobs.

Day 37

THE walls were lavender when Harry moved into his furnished one-room apartment. He had asked the manager if they couldn't paint the small room white, and the manager, an aspiring Hollywood star, said, "It's a funny thing about apartments. They have vibrations. And when I have someone in an apartment, with bad vibes, I paint over those vibes to contain them as soon as they move out. But if I have a tenant with good vibes, I want to keep them bouncing around in there, so I don't paint over them."

So Harry said, "I'll paint it myself," which did not seem to disturb the manager's vibration aesthetic.

The walls were white now. Cool and white like snow. Outside he could see two cars with two men in each of them. One car with mustaches; one without. It wasn't only the mustaches that gave the policemen away, it was the less expensive car. The goons were in a purple modified Lincoln. It wasn't the two who'd jumped him. The rain had started a few hours before, and was now coming down like water from the hoses at a five alarm fire. It cast a gloomy pall on Harry.

Harry was weary of trying to plot what seemed a hopeless escape. They were throwing more and more stumbling blocks in his way. Only his idealized visions of Lela kept him going. The apartment seemed constructed so all the rent-jumpers would have to sneak past the manager's office. There were no adjoining roofs to hop over, little shrubbery to hide in and, if that weren't bad enough, the one driveway exit for his car was watched.

He had decided against a big B-movie gun battle, when he heard a knock on his door. His first thought was the boys were getting impatient and had come to get him. The frustration made him snap up his pistol and throw open the door without even asking who was there. Catch them by surprise. One threatening move out of them and he'd shoot.

Instead, there stood a shadow of Frank Eberhart, soaking wet: pale, wan and drawn, like an undercooked, soggy pretzel.

Frank looked at the pistol. "Way I feel, you might be doing me a favor." He pushed past Harry and came into the room. "How about this rain?"

Harry looked outside, up and down, for signs of more adversaries, then closed the door and locked it. He walked back, with the gun hanging limp, to the open flight bag he had on his kitchenette counter.

"I see you're packing your bags," Frank said. "You must have known I was coming."

"Yeah. Thought I'd take a little vacation."

"Oh? Where you going? Sing Sing?"

"Very funny, Frank."

"Not so funny," Frank said. "There's the little matter of you overlooking turning in your shield. They didn't go for that too big downtown."

Harry tried to stare him down. Frank shrugged it off.

"And when you are on a tail and your subject ambushes you and humiliates you, afterwards you don't take too kindly. And a lot of cops don't like to see it. Makes 'em squeamish. Especially brass. So finish your packing."

"Wait a minute, Frank, you aren't serious?"

Frank nodded his weary, chalky head. "'Fraid so. Worst job I ever had to do. Figured you'd rather me than some pair of uniformed rookies, wet behind the ears, a little heavy-handed maybe..."

"Frank, I'm on to her. I've got to have time..."

"Now, Harry. Those are my orders."

"And abandon Lela?"

Frank winced from the pain. "Tell me what you got, Harry. We'll take it from here."

"Ha! So the cavalry can race in, in the last reel? No, thanks. I'm seeing this one through myself. The cops would bungle. Sacrifice results for methods. I'm too close for that. All I need is a couple days, Frank. I swear to you."

Frank shook his head. "Don't you see, Harry? The brass think you're thumbing your nose at them. Think you are bigger, more important than the whole force. And if it turns out you are–if you go find Lela–that will be the last straw that they don't want to chance."

"How about you, Frank?"

Frank dropped his head. "Harry, don't make it hard. Please," he pleaded with him. "You think I don't want my daughter? I'm going to tell you something I'll deny if you repeat. I've come a long way around. I think you've got a better chance of getting her out with all your lousy rule-breaking than we have going at it the right way."

"Right way? You still call it the right way, you haven't come too far."

"Go easy on me, pal. My whole life has been out of the book. Don't push me too far. If this were anyone but my daughter, I wouldn't have come this far."

"Yeah, don't forget every victim is someone's son or daughter."

Frank looked sharply away.

Harry said, "Two more days, Frank. All I'm asking. You'll have her back, I swear to you."

Frank smiled the smile of a man caught in the answerless dilemma. "They want me to bring you in, Harry. I don't do it today, they'll send the troops. I just gave you a couple days, remember? And I don't do my job today, I may be out of it tomorrow."

Harry slapped the wall with his open hand. "Frank, you're being shortsighted. I'm there, I'm telling you. You want her back. I want her back. I'll bet even the department wouldn't mind having her back."

"So tell us what you got. We *are* on the same side, aren't we?"

Harry shook his head. "You'd bungle it. I know you would. I'm doing some things–okay–you wouldn't do. We both know I'm going to do it. Can't you turn your back one more time?"

"You know where she is?"

"I will, Frank. I'm on the threshold."

"Ah, Harry, it's more promises. We've had the same highs in the department. Nothing came of them. Nothing." His despair touched Harry. He went over to where Frank was sitting, with his hands dropped between his knees, and put his hand on Frank's shoulder.

"Frank, pal. You don't believe if you lock me up, Whistler'll let her walk out of there, do you?"

Frank took a deep breath, then shook his head. He decided not to tell him about the third tape, which called for Harry's execution; a tape unplayed on the radio.

Harry squeezed the bony shoulder gently.

In the confining silence that followed, Frank looked into Harry's pleading eyes, then down to the floor. "It's no good," he said finally, miserably. "All my life I've followed orders."

"And where has it got you, Frank?"

Frank let his breath escape, as though all the sadness would be purged with it. "Where I am," he said flatly.

Harry changed the gentle grip on Frank's shoulder to a tight, shaking thrust. He shouted, "Frank, don't be stupid. I'm going to give you your daughter in two days. You know me, Frank. I don't make extravagant promises. Weigh that risk with what you've got. You want Lela as much as I do. Let me get her. Two days, Frank. I'm not asking for the moon."

Frank slumped back, trying to escape Harry's gripping hands. Finally, the fear drained out of his bloodless face, he looked up and said, "You want to beat me up and escape?"

Harry looked at his friend and felt a sickness circle his throat and body. "And have those dogs eat me alive?" he said, waving in the direction of the cars lying in wait. "That some kind of trap, buddy? Beat you up and run out of here like a sitting duck at a shooting gallery?" He looked down at his friend and said softly, "I couldn't do it anyway, Frank. I couldn't lay a hand on you to save my life."

"But Lela. To save Lela's life," Frank said hopefully. "You could do it for Lela. You said," he was almost begging now, "you'd do anything to save Lela. Nothing would stand in your way..."

Harry stared a long time, but couldn't answer. Instead he got an idea, which he communicated to the weakened Frank, who mumbled about risk, but Harry was in command. He stood over Frank, who could barely hold his head up, and repeated the details like a top sergeant shouting orders to raw recruits.

"Can you handle that, Frank?" he roared in his ear.

Frank looked at Harry, bleary-eyed, and nodded. Then croaked hoarsely, "But I gotta know, Harry. I gotta know what's going on, where you are. I can't lose my job for insubordination."

"I did," Harry answered grimly.

Frank was about to protest weakly that he didn't lose his job for insubordination but for murder, but then considered and decided he might be right. The insubordinate things he had done might have stuck sharper in the craw of the brass than the murder.

The shot rang out as if from nowhere, a harsh, fatal snap, as a woodsman's ax striking a time-honored tree.

Frank jumped and clutched his chest. Harry slumped to the floor, the gun thudding at his side.

Back in the closet, her "privileges" taken from her–the privilege of being treated somewhat like a human being–Lela was demoralized. Her spirit was broken–she was at the lowest ebb in her young life. She had fought her best fight, she thought, and it failed. Her hysterical sobs gave way to the resignation of her abject failure.

The next morning, it seemed it took longer than usual to get her out of the closet for the bathroom and breakfast. She was filled with anxiety and didn't mind putting off facing Whistler.

But it was Moose who finally opened the door. Gone was his gentle prodding, "Come along, Missy." Now he grunted and pushed her into the bathroom before her eyes could get accustomed to the light.

But the biggest shock was the breakfast. It was a glass of water and a slice of bread. Lela ate and drank without comment. Not only didn't she want to give them any satisfaction, she no longer cared, and she ate mechanically, just as she would have had they served her eggs Benedict.

It gave her an idea: a hunger strike. The next thing she knew, she was pushed into the closet with a thump.

At lunch, Lela was again alone with Moose. Lunch was another piece of bread. Moose leaned over Lela to whisper in her ear:

"Done a foolish thing, Missy. Don't nobody go messin' wid Whistler an' live to tell 'bout it."

"You call this living, Moose?" she whispered hoarsely. "How long you think I'll last on these rations?"

"Sh! We all eatin' light. We's outta food. I gotta snowshoe outta here an' gets some food 'fore long, the snow don't clear."

Back in the closet, Lela was no stronger, but Moose's whispered confidences made her feel almost human.

Though her spirit was crushed by her failure to kill her captor, this small human contact gave her a straw of hope.

If only Moose liked girls.

〇　　　〇　　　〇

Frank tumbled down the stairs as a man born to tragedy. He ran to the two mustaches and yelled, "Come quick. Harry shot himself rather than be taken, I gotta get him to the hospital. I need you to put him in my car."

210

The two men followed Frank back up the stairs and into the apartment, where they picked up the blood-soaked, groaning Harry.

"He's delirious," said the handlebar mustache.

"Yeah," said the walrus. They picked Harry up gently and carried him back down the stairs.

"My car," Frank said.

"You want us to go along?"

"No," Frank said. "You stay on the house till the end of the shift. Report anybody that comes or goes. Anybody that does anything to his car." The men nodded together.

Frank looked over at the purple modified Lincoln. The misshapen faces in it were smiling.

He drove into the hospital emergency entrance and two orderlies came out with a stretcher, on which they loaded the bleeding Harry.

Frank followed them inside, where he put in a call for B.J. In a minute she was down, her brown face broken in a friendly but suitably somber smile. "What have we here?" she said, looking down at Harry.

"Shot himself," Frank said. Then added, without conviction, "Accidentally."

"Looks serious," she said. "I'll take him to Operating." She motioned the orderlies to follow her, and they went a short way down the corridor and turned into a room. Frank tried to follow, but B.J. blocked his way.

"No, Frank," she whispered. "I'll take it from here."

"Wait a minute," he said, "the deal was I could stay with him."

"It wouldn't look right," B.J. whispered. "Cause suspicion. I'll keep you informed and deliver him to you after the suitable time." She went through the door and closed it in Frank's face.

In the operating holding room, B.J. wiped the blood from Harry's face. "Clumsy," she said. She looked at ease–in charge. Harry thought he'd made a good investment–and a good decision to count on her for help.

"Listen," he said, sitting up, "I need you now like I never needed you before, B.J. Can you get me an ambulance and an orderly uniform in it? Take me out on the stretcher and have the uniform in the thing? Two men I'll need. And can I stay at your grandma's place for a while? Can you call her and arrange it?" Harry was talking so fast he was sputtering.

"I think we can arrange..."

"And can you get my car?" He dug in his pocket for the keys. "But wait till I tell you. It's probably being watched. If you're followed, try to lose them. If you can't lose them, take the car and park it in some parking lot where we can get it later. I doubt if they'll keep a twenty-four-hour on my car, but if they do, I'll just have to get another."

She smiled. "You finished, soldier?"

Harry was on his feet. "How long do I have to wait for the ambulance?"

"That's easy, it's the uniform that'll take a little time. What's your size?"

"Forty-four long," he said. "Where can I hide until you get it?"

"Hide? You're hidden in here."

Harry shook his head. "Frank'll come busting in here any minute. I'm surprised he hasn't yet. He isn't going to let me out of his sight if he can help it."

"How about the morgue?"

Harry shuddered. "Wasn't exactly what I had in mind."

B.J. nodded, resolved. She reached out and took his arm and led him back to the table and made him lie down. She took a sheet and covered him with it. "Now lie still," she said. She went out for the orderlies. "Take him to the morgue," she said, "but don't put him in a locker. May he rest in peace."

She leaned down. "I'll be in touch," she said.

The orderlies wheeled the sheet-covered body out the back door and toward the service elevator.

A moment later, Frank came bursting into the operating holding room, to find it empty. He ran out the back door and almost tripped over two orderlies wheeling a sheet-covered body down the hall. B.J. saw him and called out, "Hey, Frank."

He turned and ran back to her. "What's going on? Where is he?"

"He?"

"Harry. He. Come on, you know who."

"I thought he was with you. Didn't you see him?"

"What are you trying to pull?"

"He went out to find you. Were you in the waiting room?"

"I...what...? Of course I was in the waiting room."

"Well, you aren't now. Maybe he passed you. Why don't you go back and look for him?"

Frank knew when he was being flimflammed, but she was so convincing he went back through the operating holding room to the waiting room, just as the orderlies entered the elevator with their stiff.

The elevator stopped in the basement and the orderlies wheeled

212

their charge into the morgue, where they left it, and returned upstairs.

Harry remained under the sheet.

Minutes later, two attendants came to the morgue, and the one said to the other, "Hey, someone left a stiff. Let's get him in a locker." One of them opened the locker and they both reached for Harry. As soon as he felt their hands on him, he jumped up and yelled, "Don't touch me," and the two attendants shrieked and ran from the room, their hair standing out like quills on frightened porcupines.

Five minutes later, the orderlies were back, and the blond one winked at the black and said, as they started to wheel Harry out, "This is the one for the crematorium."

"You got the wrong boy," Harry said, muffled through the sheet, hoping to scare them as he had the last time, but they burst out laughing. "All set," the orderly said, and they wheeled him to the emergency entrance, where they loaded him into the ambulance, closed the door and got in the front seat.

Harry changed clothes and put his street clothes in a paper bag they brought.

When they pulled up in front of Gramma Johnson's apartment, Harry went in first, the door open by prearrangement, then the other two followed, one at a time, one with the bag of clothes.

After a suitable interval, the two left together, taking time to tell the gathering crowd that they had the wrong address.

No one seemed to notice that three went in but only two came out.

"BURN, baby, burn" had been the cry in Watts in 1965. And, oh, baby, did they ever burn. They burned not only their neighborhood buildings but the livelihood of their brothers and sisters.

One of the most successful assaults was on Rowley's supermarket. It had been gutted and leveled, reminiscent of Dresden after the war.

With tax incentives, low-interest loans and other forms of coercion, Uncle Sam convinced White Honky to rebuild. After all, there were the jobs of twenty-seven blacks lost with the firebombing, each of which profited more from the operation than their white exploiters.

Actually, though it was not generally known, the insurance check, along with the tax writeoffs, made it the biggest year for Rowley's Watts store.

Harry sat in his car in the parking lot of the rebuilt store, watching the entrance to the lot. Rain was coming down and the water was jumping over the clogged drains. B.J. had gotten his car for him in the middle of the night and had no trouble with tails.

Harry had gone to Ching's pharmacy at eight and waited for him, but saw no sign of any of his cars. With his disguise–heavy sunglasses, chewing gum and a hat covering his hair–Harry went in and asked for the owner and was told he was not expected that day.

Instead of being able to follow him to his rendezvous, if any, Harry would have to take the chance on his decoding of the message, and so he sat now at Rowley's, in the hope that he had understood it.

"A dozen times holy" he hoped meant twelve o'clock Sunday. Since Rowley's closed every night before midnight, he was banking on the "dozen" being noon. He looked at his watch. Eleven-fifty. "Swimming hole" was code for pool, an eight ball, a measure of cocaine, he hoped. "Fruity" he couldn't figure, but thought maybe the meeting place was at the fruit counter. "Old Rowley's place. Down from my shop. Give my regards to Broadway"...the Rowley's on Broadway, close to Ching's drugstore.

Maybe. He had told Frank he was so sure two days would do it, but now that he sat here, the closer it got to the time, the more doubtful he became.

The rebuilt store was twenty-five years old and looked shell-shocked. The war was over, but the battles continued: heavy shoplifting, vandalism, robbery. It was a continual fight to keep above ground. The market got a lot of use, the prices were high, but there still wasn't much profit.

At two minutes to noon, with the precision of a Swiss cuckoo clock, Ching pulled into the parking lot in his Porsche 911. Some guts, Harry thought, coming to this kind of assignation in so distinctive a car. Guts.

Harry felt for his gun and his shield. He smiled with heartwarming satisfaction; he had, after all, gotten this far. Now be careful of over-confidence, he told himself.

He got out of his car and walked into the store and stood just inside the glass door, leafing through a magazine he had picked up with a cover story on police brutality. Why are we always portrayed as brutes? he wondered. Why not guardians of liberty or something glamorous? Why? He knew why. It was anything *but* glamorous being a cop. He checked the parking lot. A few minutes later Ching walked into the market, without an umbrella. He strolled past Harry and took a cart and pushed it deep into the bowels of the humming grocery section.

Harry followed. He took a cart and put a few items in it on his way to the tables laden with oranges, grapefruit, tangerines, apples and assorted vegetables. He parked himself behind a pyramid displaying cat food cans, and waited. Ching was fingering apples, as though looking for ripe ones, when a stocky, too-fat black man with a frightening scar on his left cheek came into view, pushing a shopping cart. The black put some oranges in a bag, then moved to where Ching stood beside his cart, fingering the apples. Both men put a few apples in a bag and put them in the cart. For a moment Harry was confounded as they started to part, until he realized the beauty of the transaction. Each man had carts with identical items in them, they pulled up next to one another, took the same items–the apples–and put them in the other cart. Now they would check out, with the cache in a box of Aunt Jemima pancake mix, and be on their way. Can you be arrested for shopping? What requisite probable cause could a policeman have to make an arrest?

Harry flew after the scar-faced black man and poked his pistol in his ribs. "Freeze," he said. "I'll take the cart, you step over here."

"Hey, wait a minute, pal, what's comin' down here? I ain't done nothin'. You makin' a big mistake."

"For your sake I hope so."

Scarface started to make a run for it. Harry dashed after him and tackled him, throwing the black man against a shelf of canned goods, rattling cans of Campbell's beef stew.

Harry took out his handcuffs and cuffed the man, whose pores were oozing, to a refrigerator door. He then took off after Ching, who was already in the check-out line. He showed him his shield. "Would you mind stepping out of line a minute, sir?"

Ching's face twisted into the frozen, painful smile he wore when panicked. "Shopping illegal now?" he asked with that saccharine condescension Harry remembered from when he audited his operation.

"Depends what you got in the cart," Harry said, trying to ape the smile.

"I don't have to stand here and be insulted like this. If you have a warrant, let me see it. Otherwise, I'm walking out of here and you can pay for the groceries yourself."

"With what's in the pancake mix?" Harry bluffed.

It worked. Ching's eyes cantered.

"If you're looking for your partner, he's looking over the milk supply." Harry pulled the gun. "Just for convenience sake, let me have the pleasure of your company while I go over your haul here."

"Haul? What *is* this?" Ching demanded. "I've never been so insulted."

"Is that so?" Harry said skeptically, with an arched eyebrow. "You're lucky."

He tore open the boxes. Dear God, he prayed silently, don't let there be a mistake.

It was the box of Froot Loops cereal that solved all Harry's problems. "Well, looky here," Harry said, pulling out stacks of packed bills, "this is better than Crackerjacks any day. Hundreds too. Hey, I'm gonna start buying Froot Loops."

Ching looked at the bills. "I must have gotten the wrong cart," he said.

"Yeah, this one must have been mine. Well, here's the other one," he said, pointing to the cart Scarface had taken in exchange. "Let's see what you had to give for all this dough."

Harry tore into the Froot Loops box in the other cart and hit pay dirt. "Fruity." Cute, Harry thought. The packets of white powder told

Harry he was home.

Instinctively, the shoppers parted and gave Harry a wide berth. The checker's eyes never left the duo.

"Nice work, Ching. You've graduated from uppers and downers, I see. It's a good twenty years, pal. That's easy."

"I don't know what you're talking about."

"I'm sure." Harry pointed his gun in Ching's face and said, "Let's go outside and talk it over." Gathering up the cash and the packets, stuffing them in his jacket pocket, they walked through the check stand and Harry said, "Police," waving at the carts. "Bill us."

Outside, Ching dropped all pretense. "Listen, you cheap little son of a bitch, I know a setup when I see one." They stood under an overhang. The rain in the background was chilling and cleansing.

"Ho, ho, very nice, Ching. Prove that and you'll be home free." He grabbed the little man by the shirt front and shook him against the outside wall of the market. "Where is she?"

"She? Who?"

Harry shook him so his head hit the wall. "Don't 'who' me, Ching. Lela! Where has Whistler got her? You're the man who knows; you're not getting anywhere alive without telling me, and telling me the truth. You trick me, and I swear you won't have a family to go home to. That's if you survive to go anywhere."

"Are you threatening me?"

"Any fool could tell that," Harry said, tightening his grip. "But threats aside, Ching baby, drug dealing is frowned on, even today. I said twenty years, and that's minimum for this stuff. You're through, pal.

"'Course, with your supplies cut because you lost your license, you'll have to go into the hard stuff heavier, and that's so risky. Well, you can always open a classic-car museum."

"Listen, wiseass, don't shit me. I know you're impersonating a police officer, and I'll see your ass in jail for that. You've been canned, Harry, everybody knows that."

"Ah, so? Did you see the shield? You want to see it again? Closer?" Harry pulled the shield, while still holding Ching's shirt with his other hand, and thrust the cold metal in his nose. "Get a good look, pusher, twenty years is a long time."

"So you stole the shield or kept it. You're no longer fuzz."

"So you want to take that chance?"

Ching didn't answer. He was thinking.

"Ever hear of undercover?" Harry asked him. "A nice little ruse, don't you think? Broadcast on the radio, 'Harry's canned, you don't have to be afraid of him any more.' Nice, huh? Just ask yourself, did I get you or did I get you? Your first boo-boo, Ching. Of course, if this stuff turns out to be baby powder, we let you go."

Harry tightened the hold on Ching's shirt and pushed him against the wall again. "Be nice for the kids, just growing up and all, to sit in court and hear the testimony. So if you don't believe I'm a cop, you got to admit it's one whale of a citizen's arrest. Where is she, Ching? You gave Whistler the place. Where is it?"

"I don't know anything."

"You want to chance it? Your buddy in there cuffed to the refrigerator already sang. All your fault, he said. He didn't want any part of it. You told him it was foolproof. Kinda mad at you now. It'll be twenty for him too. He looks mad enough to kill you. Or maybe slice up the missus again."

Ching shot a hateful glare at Harry. "How did you know about that?"

Harry laughed. "That's easy. That's Whistler's style: winning by intimidation. Any cop with half-decent sources knows a lot more than is on the police reports. It was a lot harder knowing about this. But, now I got the goods on you good, Ching. I said twenty years, but I'm being modest. That's a liberal judge–the *most* liberal. More like life, with any luck at all."

Ching licked his lips. His cheeks were twitching.

Harry pressed. "I'm taking this stuff with me and I'm letting you go."

"What?" Ching was sure he misunderstood.

"That's right. I'm leaving you here. I'll even throw in the key to the cuffs. You can unlock your buddy."

"What?"

"All I want from you is the location. Think on it good, Ching. Cheap. But think fast, because there isn't any more time to waste. Where is she?"

"No arrest?"

"Nothing. I'm keeping the stuff, of course. I don't want to see it in some little kid's blood; keep you honest too. Crime shouldn't pay, though God knows you've done well enough."

Ching licked his lips again. He looked back toward the door, as though someone might run from there and save him, but in this high-crime area, a policeman making a bust was hardly worth a second look.

Harry bared his teeth at him in his imitation Ching smile. "You can always tell them I threatened to kill your wife and children," he said, "which is, of course, what I will do if I get the wrong information."

Ching panicked. Perspiration bathed him, though a chilling wind was blowing through the parking lot. He told Harry what he knew. The place belonged to a friend of his. He had never been there, but he thought he could draw a map.

"Of course," he said, "I can't promise they're still there."

Harry waved the packets and the money at him. "This is all the guarantee I need."

25   HARRY drove from Rowley's market to his Watts hideout. He was feeling pretty good for the first time since Lela had been taken. "Pride goeth before a fall, Harry boy," he said aloud.

The cash and cache were on the seat beside him. The afternoon was cool and the rain was still coming down like there was a terrible leak in the sky, and the neighborhood had that faint garbagey smell, like the steaming of rotting compost.

He turned from Avalon to 109th, when a black child shot into the street in front of the car. Harry jammed on the brakes and swerved, narrowly missing the child.

"Hey," he shouted out the window, "watch where you're going, you could have been killed."

The boy grinned at him, then Harry recognized him. It was little Matthew, one of Gramma Johnson's charges, of indefinite relationship. He was soaked to the bone, but unwavering in his duty.

"Gramma tell me to stop you an' tell ya dey's two men watchin' da front. Say you kin get in da back bedroom winnow. We make a fuss out front an' distrac' 'em."

Harry opened the door for the boy, who climbed in the seat beside him. When he saw the money, in bundles on the seat, his eyes wanted to get out of his head.

Harry tousled the boy's hair and smiled. He took one of the hundred-dollar bills and folded it in the boy's hand. "There," he said, "that's for risking your life to save mine."

The boy's jaw dropped to his chest, his eyes clouded over. "Man, is dis real?"

"It's real, all right. You give that to Gramma to keep for you. She can break it on her next trip to the bank. I don't expect you'd have too much luck trying to break a hundred yourself."

The boy smiled so hard his face was nothing but teeth.

Harry calculated as he made a U-turn and went back on Avalon.

Should he try to go somewhere else? But where?

"Is B.J. there?" he asked.

The boy nodded, still studying with fascination the hundred-dollar bill in his hand.

She would help with the preparations, Harry thought. He knew already the local heavy rains meant heavy snow in the area of the map he had in his pocket. He would need cross-country skis and snow clothes. Money, he had. Time and efficiency were important now. He knew it would be hard to get into the cabin with the snow, but thought it would also be hard for them to get out. As long as he could get there and watch it.

He drove down the next street and into the alley behind the apartment. He looked down the side yard and saw a dog tied outside the Johnsons' bedroom window. Should keep the snoops from the bedroom window. But Harry couldn't leave the car. That would tip them off for sure.

"You know anyone around here you can trust who has a garage?"

The boy nodded. "Ole Mr. Lindsey, he got a garage. Got a car in it too."

"You think you could ask him if I could rent it for a while? Nobody gotta know."

The boy nodded eagerly. "I kin arrange it, Mr. Harry. I kin."

They drove down the alley and around the corner, and Mr. Lindsey came out to check the car. A stooped black man with a friendly face, he refused the hundred-dollar bill Harry offered him. "Heard too much 'bout what you done for B.J.," he said, waving his hand. "Glad to do this fo' ya, and dey be no charge."

Harry tried to insist, but Mr. Lindsey said, "Please don't argue none. I be insulted."

Harry and the boy walked back to the alley behind the three stucco buildings. The boy told Harry to wait while he went into the apartment, and came out with three friends and a dog leash. He went around the front to the side and took the dog, on the leash, across the street to where the two officers sat in the car, stroking their mustaches.

Harry crept around the back of the building, out of sight of the car, and while the dog jumped up on the passenger side of the car and the two officers regarded it uncomfortably, Harry crawled in the bedroom window.

The apartment had no windows on the street. All the units were built alike, and in the postwar building boom that spawned these units there was no time for custom niceties. Besides, windows on the street in this neighborhood connoted a security flaw. The apartments would have been hard to rent.

Inside, Harry and B.J. were plotting the job. He gave her numerous instructions, which she cheerfully wrote down.

Gramma presided over the apartment like a Buddha. Harry felt at home in the cramped quarters. The piano still dominated the room, and Jesus still dominated the piano.

Harry peeked out the window at the cop car. Both cops were white. He couldn't say much for the hiding job, but, then, it was awfully hard to hide two young white cops with mustaches in this neighborhood. He wondered if it was Frank's doing. Nothing like making it obvious when you want the suspect to relax—or maybe get away? He knew Frank had mixed feelings, but who else would have thought to put the troops looking for Harry Schlacter out in Watts? Who else would have even realized he had these connections?

Matthew came bursting in the door, whispering hoarsely, "Man commin'!...man commin'!"

Harry got up and went into the bedroom where Margie was fooling around on the bed with a black who looked, to Harry, in the last stages of a high. The room was littered with clothes, bottles, jars, a bicycle, and there was barely room for him. He closed the door all but an inch.

B.J. came back and joined him. "It's Frank," she whispered.

Gramma answered the door with great difficulty; her legs were giving her more trouble.

He heard Frank's voice. "Hello, I'm Frank Eberhart," he said kindly. "I've been looking for my friend Harry Schlacter, and I thought he might be here visiting you."

Oh, God, Harry thought. How clever. She'll just say, "Com'on in," and bring me out. Oh, God...

But he heard her say, "Ain't seen Harry in some time now. You see him, you tell him I miss him. 'Specs him to come by more often just to say howdy. Why, I know'd dat boy since he been eleven year old. Used to deliver da paper for me. Best little boy I had too. You tell him Gramma say hello."

Harry looked at B.J., a strained admiration crossing his face. It was going to be a battle of wits, and Gramma was proving no piker.

"Well, you wouldn't mind if I took a look around then, would you? I mean, in case he left some message for me or something?"

"Glad to have you come in an' make you'self at home, but the fact is, the place is a awful mess right now...ooo, oooo, dese kids nowadays don't have no respec' fo' cleanliness, and I'd be shamed to have a gentleman like you to see it. You wanna give me some time to clean up, you surely welcome."

"How much time you figure?"

She sighed, wrinkling her broad, flat nose. "Way dey got dis place lookin', I 'specs it be da better part of a day 'fore I could make it presentable. But I'se glad to do it."

"Hm," Frank said, gleaning suspicion from her tone and adding distrust to his. "I guess I'll have to wait then. You wouldn't mind if I just waited right here, would you? I mean, I don't have to disturb you, I'll stay in the car."

"Dat's fine, you just make you'self at home. I'd sure invite you in, but you might slow up da cleanin', ever'body havin' to be polite and say 'scuse me ever'time dey pass. I guess it'd be best on da street, if you don't mind." Then, as if an afterthought so unimportant to her, she said, "I suppose you got a warrant."

"You want a warrant, ma'am?" he said.

"Be best," she allowed.

Frank smiled, a mixture of the admiration and frustration he felt.

Just then he saw B.J. come into the living room. "Hi, Officer," she said. "Good to see you." She stepped outside on the asphalt, drawing Frank away from the door.

Inside, Harry had already seen the back window was being watched by one of the mustaches in the car.

Outside, Frank had bawled B.J. out for double-crossing him, and she apologized. "Harry left," she said, "but before he did, he wanted me to give you a message."

"What's that?" Frank couldn't help letting his interest slip.

"He says he's home. Just sit by your phone in case he needs help, and he'll bring her home."

"How soon?"

"A couple more days."

"A couple more days?" Frank exploded. "He said that yesterday–when you both deceived me. Let me take him in. Let me talk to him at least."

"Gee, I would, but I don't know where he is."

"Can I have a look around?"

"Gee, Gramma is so sensitive about the mess."

Frank's eyes were sagging. "I don't blame you," he said at last. "I guess you have a small debt with him."

She smiled, her sparkling eyes a glimmer of light in the rain. Frank had no choice. He had to follow the rules, live by the regulations. He went to the car and told his two stakeouts that he was returning to get a search warrant and that they should make sure that no one with white skin left that apartment until he got back.

B.J. went back inside. Gramma was sitting, bent over her cane. Harry was raving about the superb job she did with Frank. He turned to B.J.

"We gotta move fast, B.J. Are you still available?"

She smiled. "Sure, Harry. You name it."

Harry told her where to leave the car. He gave her a pile of the hundred-dollar bills, left five of them for Gramma for the "rent" and gave Matthew another one to take to the man down the street with the truck. Then he put five hundred-dollar bills in an envelope and gave Matthew his instructions.

"Now move it," Harry said, "I've got to get out of here in less than an hour. Frank'll be back with the warrant and I'm afraid I riled him once too often. You got any tools, Mrs. Johnson?"

She nodded and told Harry to ask Margie. In the bedroom Margie untangled herself from her friend and she showed him a box in the closet where the tools were kept. Harry selected wrenches and a screwdriver and went back to the living room.

"Mrs. Johnson," he said, "I'd like to borrow your piano." And he told her what he had in mind. She laughed and thought it was the best idea.

"You think it'll work?" was all she asked.

"Better," he said, and he took the pictures of the family and friends and Jesus off the top and went to work.

When he was finished the piano was gutted. The soundboard and the keyboard and action were spread out on the floor.

"Better get a blanket to cover them up," he said, "just in case someone comes snooping."

"Margie," Gramma Johnson yelled. "Get dat blanket out here, hear?"

Margie came dragging out with a blanket and threw it in Harry's direction. He covered the innards and climbed inside the piano case to test it for size.

224

"Not too bad," he said. "It's a nice place to visit, but I wouldn't want to live there."

Outside the rain had subsided to a light drizzle. When the truck pulled up, Gramma leaned on her cane and rose up to go to the door. With great effort, she went outside and talked to the man. In full view of the stakeout team, the truck driver took an envelope from his pocket and counted out five one-hundred-dollar bills. She motioned him inside and he motioned to the truck for his two friends to come in.

In a moment the piano appeared at the doorway and was negotiated over the stoop, down the asphalt and onto the sidewalk, where they managed to push it up the wooden ramp to the back of the truck.

Across the street, the stakeout team watched with interest. The driver said, "Man, keep your eyes open, this could be some sort of diversionary tactic."

"Yeah," said the passenger, stroking his mustache. "I know what you mean."

"Why don't you get out and watch the back? You'll have a better view. I'll stay and watch the front."

The passenger, feeling more comfortable in the car, couldn't argue, being the junior man on the team. He got out and walked over to where he could see the back window better. The rain suddenly increased and pounded his yellow slicker.

The three blacks on the truck tied the piano in and got in the cab to drive off. The police-stakeout-car passenger was still rubbing his mustache; he couldn't figure what it was, but something bothered him. He crossed the street as the truck drove off, and heard Gramma Johnson telling one of the tenants, an undernourished man with three days' stubble of beard, "I got five hunert dollar fo' dat ole piano."

"No," he said, and shook his head in amazement.

"An' it hardly play 'tall."

Day 38

 FRANK whistled softly to himself as he drove from the judge's house to Gramma Johnson's apartment. He had sworn out a search warrant on a Sunday in under two hours, portal to portal. He had, as always, gone by the book.

He realized, of course, that had the situation been reversed and had Harry been in pursuit of Frank and Harry thought he was in the apartment, never in a million years would Harry have gone for a warrant. He would have kicked in the door and worried about the formalities later. When the D.A. would rag him for his sloppy police methods, Harry would say something like, "I brought him in, didn't I? You find a way to make it stick."

Perhaps that was the hardest thing for Frank to take about Harry–he didn't give any quarter. He was so sure of himself all the time.

Frank felt good. He always felt good when he thought he had done his duty as the law wanted him to do it. He hoped he wasn't feeling good just because it was finally Harry, just because he had turned the tables. But it was a textbook example of how to follow procedures and still bag the suspect.

He pulled his car right behind where the stake car was parked. He was happy to see that one of the men had the nerve to stand outside the car on the sidewalk to get a better view of the back window.

Frank went to the car, and the sidewalk man came over to him, keeping an eye on the back.

"Everything quiet?" Frank asked.

"Quiet," the man standing next to him nodded, feeling his mustache to see if it was still there.

"Nobody went in or out?"

"Nobody." The driver looked up in his eyes. Frank noticed the frown and looked back with a questioning glance.

"Well, there were three guys who went in, but they were the only ones who came out again."

"Three guys? Did you get a good look at the three who came out?"

"Yeah," the standing man answered. "All black."

"You got the mug of Schlacter. Couldn't have been in blackface?"

"Naw."

Frank turned to investigate for himself. "What were they doing?"

"Just hauling out an old piano. Heard her say she got five bills for it."

Frank closed his eyes slowly, as if to shut out a blinding light. "Piano?" he whispered hoarsely.

"Yeah, piano, but they were all black. There was no Happy-trigger Harry there, that I'll swear to."

But Frank was across the street, knocking on the door. Maude Johnson opened the door. Frank showed her the warrant grimly. She barely looked at it, waved her hand and said, "Shucks, Mr. Frank, you don't need to get no warrant to see me once the place is clean. Come on in."

Frank's shoulders sagged at her ebullient hospitality. It was a great effort for him to step over the threshold and onto the plastic-coated carpet.

"What happened to your piano?" he asked.

"Oh, I sol' it, Mr. Frank. I got five hunert dollars fo' it."

Frank walked to the corner and picked up the blanket. He nodded his head, all his worst fears crashing down on him.

"You sold it without the works," he said, not asking a question, not really making a statement, just experiencing a nightmare out loud.

She nodded with pride. "Didn't work too good nohow, Mr. Frank," she said, "but it sho' was a beautiful case."

"Yeah," Frank said, and walked out of the apartment without putting his search warrant to use.

⛉   ⛉   ⛉

The light was fading and the rain was lighter as Harry cruised across Cement City. The long, thin skis, white with a little red and blue rooster on each tip, were attached, with the ski poles, to the ski rack on the roof of the car. The new license plates had been put on–switched with a friend of B.J.'s for a few days, with a couple of crisp hundreds for his trouble. The broken windshield had finally been replaced in a junkyard by a friend of B.J.'s.The chains were in the trunk, with three five-gallon cans of extra gas. The telescopic rifle was at his side, along with detailed maps of the area and some emergency rations. In the back seat, a pair of snowshoes and miscellaneous supplies.

Harry patted his pocket for the wad of hundreds he would use in doing his job. Then he would turn the money in. Harry never considered using it for himself. Money and its uses meant little to him. Of course, he could pay off the engagement ring–the box of which he now felt in his other pocket–but he wouldn't consider that. The white powder was in the glove compartment. Harry was taking, he realized, a terrible chance of getting caught with it, but he couldn't think of any place else to put it. He didn't want B.J. to have to risk having it, and he couldn't trust the sanctity of his apartment from the bad guys or the good.

The snaky mountain road loomed before him now like a bolt of indecisive lightning. Harry began his ascent and downshifted the little car.

He asked himself what it was all about. Why am I running? This is the first time I can remember I had a personal stake in my job. Sometimes I think I'm a madman. Am I trying to prove to myself I'm alive? Take Frank, he thought. Frank is a man at peace with himself. He does his job, takes what's given. Doesn't rock any boats. Smooth and cool.

Up ahead the snow was deep in the road. Harry stopped to put on the chains. Having little experience in snow, Harry had some difficulty, but managed to get the chains around the tires and connected. As he drove on he wondered if Lela could really fall in love with Whistler. The thought of it made him taste bile. He was afraid she had been brainwashed and might even be armed and try to shoot him. He would have to be awfully careful not to hurt her. He had almost come to terms with losing his job on the force, but losing Lela, he knew, he could never survive.

It was easy for him to understand why policemen have such a high suicide rate.

Harry wanted Lela so badly he began to think of ways he could change to accommodate her. Anything.

He drove as far as he could and found a small snowed-in motor court and saw a suggestion of life.

The proprietor had a bad case of shingles, a face that was beginning to curdle, and was hard-pressed to think of a reason why he couldn't rent to Harry. When Harry told him what he needed–the highest cabin that had a view of the road up the hill–and flashed five crisp hundred-dollar bills, laying them on the counter, the man shook his head, almost frightened at the sight of so much power.

The clerk wet his lips and stared at the money. Harry pushed it across to him. "I would appreciate it if you forgot you ever saw me and pay no attention to anything that goes on."

"Well, wait just a minute," the clerk spoke slowly, slurring his words a trifle. "I don't want no trouble 'round here." Harry smelled the whiskey fumes and wondered if he had made a mistake. But, as he calculated it, this must be the last outpost before the kidnap cabin, certainly he could drive no further on the snowed-in road, and he wasn't going to be too fussy about the personal habits of the innkeeper.

"You won't get any trouble. Any trouble or damage will be compensated." Harry peeled off another five hundred. "Here's another deposit. Good-faith. Non-refundable security. Whatever you call it."

The man gulped, envisioning the stream of booze it would buy. But he shook his head. There were, after all, a few bottles still on the shelf. Enough to get him through to the next thaw.

Harry produced his shield and flopped open the leather case. He watched the proprietor's eyes and he knew he had scored.

Harry left the money on the counter and went to his room. It was a dingy little thing the size of Rex Adams' walk-in closet (may he rest in peace). But Harry barely noticed it.

It was too dark to do any exploring so Harry tried to sleep, but couldn't keep his mind from buzzing about his goal.

◌   ◌   ◌

Day 39

He was on his skis at first light. He skied cautiously about two miles before he came to the small, white, snowbound cabin on his map. He skied as close as he could through the bare trees without being noticed and took his binoculars and looked at the cabin. He saw nothing but a wisp of smoke coming out of the chimney. There was no path to the door, no clearing for car movement and the car itself was so deeply buried in the snow that Harry couldn't identify it. He debated going closer, but didn't want to risk his tracks being noticed too close to the house. He tried the binoculars again, but the light was reflecting off the glass and he couldn't see inside.

Harry skied back, the cold, brisk air caressing his face, sensitizing his nerve endings and making him feel acutely alive.

He observed the small general store and speculated on how much food they had at the house. The man at the store said he hadn't done any business with strangers for three or four days and he hadn't had any black customers since the family with three children a few weeks ago. Harry wondered how they could be getting food. Where did they go for it? Was it a Ching trick? Would Ching take that risk? Surely he knew he'd wind up a victim if he led Harry on a goose chase.

The storekeeper said the roads had been closed ahead for four days and it didn't look like there would be any more clearing for a couple more days.

Harry went back to his cabin and looked out the window and waited. He couldn't go to sleep. Whistler was liable to send someone out on snowshoes to knock off the store.

〇 　 〇 　 〇

Frank was feeling none too good in the wake of Harry's escape. He was in the squad room, brooding about the latest tape from Whistler. Would they really have gotten married? His darling girl and that criminal?

Whistler had sounded like a man at the end of the line, who, realizing he was going down, wanted to be sure to take everyone down with him.

To Frank, Whistler was a man sorting out the keys to his future from the debris of his past. But on that third tape he sounded simply desperate and deranged.

The first tape recording had been dropped through the mail slot of the radio station. This last one was postmarked in Texas, over a week before the police got it.

The station had agreed to hold off playing the tape for forty-eight more hours, until a psychiatrist could render an opinion of what playing it or not playing it might mean to the safety of the hostage. But the time was up. The station didn't broadcast, and Frank feared Whistler had, in an insane rage, killed his precious daughter.

Without a word to anybody, Frank Eberhart dragged himself home, took the mahogany box from his bedroom closet shelf, unlocked it, took out his father's suicide gun, then laid it on the nightstand. Fatalistically, he collapsed on his bed and looked over at the gun, then closed his eyes and released his body from all its inhibiting muscular tension and let it quake with nerve-rending sobs.

〇 　 〇 　 〇

Inside the cabin in the mountains, hunger was unraveling the troops. The surreal calm that had prevailed was coming apart at the seams.

Now in the second day without food, the snow was showing no sign of melting, and the goddamn sky was looking like it was just getting ready to crap on them again.

The boys were starting to get on each other's nerves. Moose was agitating to move out. They had, he said, devoted way too much of their lives to the enterprise. He was sorely missing his "gentlemen frien's," and unless somebody wanted to make it up to him, he was "'bout ready to bail outta this situation."

"Come, come, Moose," Whistler said. "You are a loyal soldier. Don't talk nonsense."

"Not nonsense. We don't get us some food, we all gonna starve to death. I can't guarantee nothin' with our guest," he waved his hand toward the closet, "she awful weak."

"Don't care 'bout her."

"Yes, sir, I knows that–but you care 'bout us? is the question."

"'Course I do."

"Den we gots to get us some food."

"Too dangerous," Whistler said. He was morose since the "wedding." "We can't move the car in this shit and would be lucky to make it to the local store an' back on foot. Even if you got there, we'd be blown."

"Not necessarily," Moose argued.

Whistler nodded his head. "The curse of being born black," he said. "Ain't no hiding. Cops be here in minutes."

"How they know where we are?" Moose asked.

"How you gonna explain you walking into a store like that in the wilderness?"

"Maybe I drivin' and got stuck."

"And don't want anybody to pull you out? And here you are, buying enough food for an army."

"Well, that may be all logical an' all, but we's *starvin'*, and you can't stay alive on logic," Moose said. "Look here, times is changin'. They's black people all over."

"Yeah, but there ain't even any white folks 'round here now. Look outside, it's a thousand feet deep and snowing again."

"Okay, boss," Moose said, deflated by Whistler's logic. "I'm takin' my chances. You da boss. You decides. You wants me to try an' buy some food an' come back, or you wants me to leave permanent? Either way, I is goin'. 'S up to you."

Bull's eyes bulged at Moose's audacity. Bull was in his favorite position: on his belly, on the floor, a comic book in front of him. "I'm awful hungry," he said apologetically.

"Sissies!" Whistler hissed. "My luck to be up here with sissies!"

"Aw, boss," Bull said, "I ain't no sissy."

"Look," Whistler said. "Things get too bad, we cook the girl."

"Boss!"

"Aw, lots of folks done it. The Donner party comin' to California. The folks' plane crashed in South America. It's not that unusual."

Moose was shaking his head vigorously. "Not me. Not me."

"Come on—you're the world-class cook," Whistler snickered. "White food. This is *real* white food. You could cook up a sauce make us think we eating chicken."

"Sauce, outta what?" Moose asked. "Her blood?" He shook his head again. "Any cookin' dat girl, you'se gonna do it. I goin'. You decide if you wants me back."

○   ○   ○

Sequestered in the darkness, weak from hunger, despairing of ever being saved and having given up hope for her life, Lela was awakened from a restless sleep by a sound in the room behind the closet: Whistler's bedroom.

Never before had she heard anything other than Whistler's footsteps from that room. All the conversations took place in the living room or kitchen, as far from her hearing as possible. But now she heard this low, moaning sound and then what she thought were the whispers of men's voices. She couldn't make out what was being said, but the moaning continued, low melodies of strange timbre. At first, Lela thought she must be dreaming. But then she satisfied herself she was awake. But what did it mean? Some sickness, some conflict—some weakness in their front? Was someone inflicting pain? Was Whistler sick? She hadn't laid eyes on him since the "wedding night." Were they simply weak, as she was, from hunger? Did she have any rational reason to hope? But if she failed to accomplish her mission at full strength, what could she reasonably hope in her weakness?

The next morning, in the bathroom, Lela was alone with Moose. He was muttering to himself a lot of babble Lela couldn't make out. Then suddenly he was bent over her, whispering in her ear.

"I tells him da truth. He's not made impotent you tryin' to off him. No–he's impotent 'cause girls is jest not his thing. After all that talk 'mong his whores he can't do nothin'–turns out he can do sompin', jest not wid no bitch, ya hear? Pardon my French, 'course." Moose was breathing the reckless breath of excitement.

"So I give it to Whistler. I shows him what paradise's all 'bout. All along he thinks he wants a bitch, he really want me. I showed him, I did. There ain't nothin' lak it in dis whole messed-up world.

"Funniest damn thing–he's callin' me 'Miss Wills' alla time he's doin' it," Moose chuckled.

Lela was relieved and disappointed. Relieved she wouldn't have to touch him–disappointed she had lost the last leverage she thought she had.

Day 40

27 THE glistening snow had crusted from the cold night. Harry sat in the cottage looking out and wondering how long he'd slept. Getting soft? he wondered. In the old days he wouldn't have dozed. He hoped he hadn't missed any movement from the cabin up the hill. There was nothing to do but set out on the skis again and see if there were any tracks from the cabin.

The crisp morning air made him feel sanitized and eager. He was getting accustomed to the skis and managed to stay on his feet, though he hoped he would never have to chase anybody over the snow on them. The ice crust underfoot was slick, and he moved faster but less steadily. When he got to his lookout, he noticed the smoke from the chimney had diminished significantly, the car was still covered with snow, in the same place, and there were no tracks in the snow at the house. He tried to guess who and how many were inside, what they were planning and how much food they had, but he couldn't. After watching through the binoculars without seeing anything, Harry considered moving closer. But the fear of being seen and forfeiting the element of surprise kept him back. Since he didn't know if Lela would come out shooting to save her own life, he thought he'd better play the waiting game.

After an hour he skied back to his cottage. In the afternoon he went to the store and bought some food. He returned and pondered the possibilities. He was beginning to like the feeling of quiet and seclusion, and couldn't understand how a city boy, used to hustle and bustle, could find this anything but boring. I'm burning out, he thought, before I'm thirty.

I wonder, he said to himself, if I could be wrong? That car could belong to some native, some caretaker, some other visitor. Ching could have sent me up here on a wild-goose chase, giving him time to cover himself. Harry's only hope now was in Ching's fear of reprisal. He knew he wasn't afraid of being arrested; he could afford lawyers much better than any assistant D.A. fresh out of law school. No, Ching was in the spot he was in because he didn't fear the law as much as he feared

Whistler Wagner. The only fear that registered with Mr. Ching was a physical fear. Harry wondered if he had sufficiently imparted that to him. If he hadn't, he could sit here a long time before he saw the faces he was looking for.

Harry made two more ski trips with his binoculars that day to make sure there wasn't some other way out and to see if there were any tracks, but there were none.

He had ascertained that the storekeeper stayed open until five. He looked at his seventeen-dollar watch and saw the hands creeping to four. Harry had about decided if he were to have any encounter with any or all of them while the roads were closed, it would have to be in day-light. They couldn't risk breaking into the store, the community was too small, they would be hunted down. Their tracks would give them away. No one was coming from anywhere in this weather, so they would easily find them. Maybe. Anyway, Harry hoped he was right. He was getting tired already. He couldn't stay awake much of the night again. He thought it was because of the quiet. You can't stay awake when there is nothing to keep you occupied. His longest stakeouts hadn't been more than twelve hours: eight hours of his duty shift and another four volun-teered.

He looked back out the window, about to give up hope for another day, when he saw a peculiar apparition stumbling its way down the hill in the clearing that was the road before the storm.

Harry's heart leapt to his throat; adrenaline shot through his body. He grabbed his binoculars and focused them on the figure. It was a black man on snowshoes that he couldn't handle very well. A bearded face. As he came into better focus, Harry thought he recognized one of Whistler's gang–the effeminate one they called Moose.

Unhappily, in his present predicament there was nothing of a moose about him, and he could not keep his footing in the snow. He fell and sank in, twisting his snowshoes, and Harry felt his body relax as he assessed the athletic prowess of his prey.

Moose was making slow progress toward the clump of buildings that included the small general store-gas station, but was still slipping and falling when Harry went outside and clamped on his skis. He started down from his cottage, at right angles to Moose. He wanted to reach him before he got to the place where the road was cleared and he could man-age to stay afoot better.

The sun had softened the crust and Harry occasionally sank him-self on soft spots. The euphoric feeling he had outdoors, surrounded by the complete white purity, returned to him. The cold, clear air made him feel like a cleansed god on his way to some heavenly glory. Harry felt momentarily sorry for mortals who never experienced the exhilaration of the complete bright whiteness. Up ahead, Harry saw Moose struggling to keep his balance, then one foot sank into the snow and the moose man fell over as though shot through the heart.

The handgun was inside Harry's parka, as were the handcuffs. Harry also brought his shield: the shield that was no longer his. When Moose looked up from his prone position in the sunken snow, relief flooded his bearded face. He thought the nice-looking white man on skis was a heaven-sent ski patrol, come to save him.

Moose said, "Oh, man, is I glad to see you. I'se so hungry, ya got any food?...I can pay." Then he got a closer look at the man bent over him and recognized Harry. He started to fumble in his jacket for his gun, but Harry smiled and said, "Better let that alone, Moose. You don't want to try and outdraw old Fast-draw Harry, do you?" and Moose was, before the sentence was over, staring at the barrel of Harry's gun. The perspiration forming on his body made him feel clammy in the freezing air.

Taking Moose's gun was child's play for Harry compared to getting the lumbering, awkward, clumsy man on snowshoes up to Harry's cabin. Moose just couldn't seem to stay on his feet.

Finally, inside, Harry handcuffed Moose to an exposed water pipe, stood over where he was huddled up on the floor trying to hoard some warmth and shot questions at him.

"How's Lela?"

Silence.

A kick from Harry. Ribs.

Grunt. "Doan know nobody that name."

"Ever hear of a Whistler?"

No answer.

Another kick.

Groan. "Ya got any food, man?"

"Give me some answers, you'll get food. Lela? She alive?"

Moose looked up at Harry as though he were good enough to eat, his tongue running timidly over his lips, the perspiration dripping from his beard.

He considered his answer. Moose was not a stupid man, and he calculated every answer and what it would get him, from both Harry and Whistler.

Harry was in no mood for subtlety however, and, his patience running out, he reached over and grabbed Moose by the neck and began applying pressure.

"All right, blubber, let's have it, and let's have it now. Is Lela alive?"

Moose looked, terrorized, into Harry's hard eyes. Was he really going to kill him? He had heard about Harry in the street, but had had little personal contact. Harry's target always seemed to be Whistler. The word was "dat fuzz don' take no shit from no one." Moose opened his mouth to speak, but couldn't get the words out of his constricted throat. Instead he tried to nod his head. Harry thought he saw a barely perceptible move in that direction. He released the pressure. Moose gasped for life.

"Alive?"

"She alive..." he said between gulps.

"How many you got watching her up there?"

"Hey, how many questions you gonna ask 'fo' I gets some food?"

Harry looked at the pathetic animal-like creature at his feet and went over to the bag he had on the table and took out a box of crackers. With deliberate slowness he opened the box and the inner wrapping and gently lifted the top cracker off and watched Moose salivate as he handed it to him.

"Jeesus, one cracker," he croaked as he gulped it.

"One answer, one cracker. Like to try for two?"

"Listen, man, I a gourmet chef. I makes beef Wellington, I makes veal Cordon Bleu, I makes cherries jubilee, oysters Rockefeller," Moose was going on quickly, as if the repetition of dishes would fill his empty belly. "I makes white food exclusive. I don't make no black food. I be a good cook for you, Mr. Harry. You sees."

Harry was the killer-whale trainer, giving the leviathan a reward for each trick performed. "How many?"

"Dey's de duck ala orange, one of my specialties, beef matambre, and my pastas are out of this world." It wasn't working. Moose was eying the crackers as though they were caviar.

"How many?"

"Two mo'," he croaked. Harry fed him a cracker.

In that painful manner, Harry extracted from the reluctant captive information about the house, the arsenal and how, after the wedding ceremony, Lela was back in the closet. The wedding ceremony angered him. But if she was back in the closet... He thought that meant she had resisted Whistler. His second greatest fear.

Moose was clever enough not to tell him Lela's condition, thinking it would force Harry into some precipitate action.

"Far's I know she fine," he said in answer to Harry's question on her condition.

"Food supply?"

"Ain't none. Dat's why I out walkin'."

"Where'd you get it before...the food?"

"San Berdo. Don't do no shoppin' here, don't want to tip nobody off wid no black mens. But dis here snow ain't give us no choice."

Harry brought out a jar of peanut butter and a knife, and at that moment Moose would have been willing to trade ten beef Wellingtons, medium-rare, for that jar of peanut butter.

As Harry watched Moose wolf down the peanut butter crackers, he calculated how weak and hungry Whistler and Bull were. Eerily, as though he were reading his mind, Moose said, "Don't you go gettin' no fancy ideas 'bout stormin' da house. Whistler is gettin' ravin' mad over de snow an' all an' de way things turn out wid Lela, them not hittin' it off like he 'spects dey would, I mean, and dey's armed to de teeth, an' Whistler, he jest hates you mo' dan any man in dis world."

Harry looked out the window at the blanket of white, glistening, powder-like gems, relief flooding his muscular body.

"Mutual," he said, wondering how long it would be before the next one came down the road and thinking how much better off he was with the information Moose supplied him, believable or not, than he would have been if he had just shot him, as he might have a few months earlier.

Moose was beginning to feel better, gaining his strength and other appetites.

"Harry?" he said boldly.

"Mm?"

"Anybody ever tell you, you a good-lookin' man?"

The high, effeminate voice and the implication flared Harry's fury, then he laughed aloud, more in anger than amusement.

"Why you laugh? I know how to makes men happy. I been cooped up in dat cabin wid two crazy mans, an' I got my appetites too. I could get her outta dere fo' ya," he said eagerly. "I get yo' Lela fo' ya."

Harry stared at him and held himself from punching Moose in

the mouth. Lord, Lord, he said to himself, I've done everything else to save her; I said I'd do anything. But every man must have some limits. I wonder, Harry thought, revulsed, if I believed that was the only way, would I do it?

He said nothing, only stood impassively, looking out at the snow.

Day 41

BULL, Harry knew, would be another problem. A cretin-like fellow of enormous strength, he would not be as easy a mark as Moose. He would react with animal-like instincts of self-preservation, would certainly be more wary since Moose did not return, and he would be armed.

Not long after sunup the next day, Harry, sitting at the cabin window, saw the tiny distant figure through his binoculars. He also saw a rifle braced across his chest. Harry could, of course, take his telescopic rifle and shoot him, but he knew he couldn't chance storming the cabin if there were the slightest risk to Lela.

How easy it would be for Whistler to shoot Lela at the slightest provocation. Might even have to serve a few months in jail, Harry thought ruefully.

Bull was making unsteady progress. He was staying on his feet and close enough now so Harry, weakened from loss of sleep, could see the cold steam coming in puffs from his brown mouth. Bull was moving with more strength and determination than Harry thought he should if he were weakened with hunger.

Bull would not be taken easily. In this white terrain, the cretin with the rifle on his chest would be able to see Harry approaching and get off a good shot before Harry, whose expertise on skis was still short of perfection, could collar him. And if Harry shot him with the telescopic rifle, some oily defense attorney would say Whistler feared for his life. After all, his comrade had been shot down in cold blood...

Shooting in cold blood. They had always accused him of that, Harry remembered in his woozy state. He had never looked at it that way, was sure it wasn't true. And yet...was there a thin line there? Did cops really aspire to kill people? Put away the bad for good? Did he? Lela had asked Harry. Harry denied it. But he secretly wondered...about other cops. But he feared Lela secretly wondered not about other cops, but about him. He wanted no cloud on his claim. He would not shoot Bull.

Soon the bundled-up black man with the rifle across his chest would be to the part of the road that had been plowed and would be able to walk without snowshoes.

In the summertime, Harry thought, he could have hidden in the shade and underbrush of the giant aspens and cottonwoods. Now it was a vast defoliated jungle, and today's bright sun highlighted any moving creature. If he could only sneak up behind Bull and get him to drop his rifle. But legend had it that Bull was too stupid not to whirl around and shoot. The plain, most disturbing fact was that there was no place for Harry to hide to surprise Bull.

The landscape was a Frasconi woodcut: the white floor, unsullied by man; the dark pillars supporting the sky. And the one intruding black man, destroying the serenity of the picture, hobbling along, inept but inevitable, bounding across the white, now stopping and looking at the tracks going to Harry's cottage.

Oh, no, Harry thought. Why didn't I realize? You can't get anywhere in this snow without making tracks. Bull had followed Moose's tracks and come upon the spot where they had their scuffle, and now, instead of going to town, the tracks are leading to the cottage. Harry watched through the binoculars as Bull's body seemed to go rigid. What would he do? Go on to the food, come and investigate, or go back and report his finding to Whistler and await further instructions? Harry could imagine the difficult calculations going through Bull's feeble mind. But when an animal is hungry, he doesn't risk unknown dangers to save a fellow, he goes to satisfy his hunger first. And so Bull headed toward the road. He could investigate the tracks much better on a full belly.

It was a break for Harry. But now surely Bull would be even more wary. Once again Harry felt a flush of anger rise to his cheeks. You can stand here and speculate all day. It won't solve your problems. He turned to Moose, snuggling the floor like a furry animal. "Take good care of yourself, Moose, I shall return." He took the jacket off the big wooden clothes hook on the wall, put his arms through the sleeves, strapped on his backpack, then took his skis and poles and went out the door, locking it with the key. Well, if Moose has the strength, on that little bit of peanut butter, to pull the pipes out, a locked door may slow him down another five or six seconds. But it's all psychology anyway.

Harry skied down the gentle slope, under cover of the cabins, until he was hidden behind the cabin closest to the plowed road. It stood about forty feet behind the line where the plow had stopped and the snow was piled to the side, but, he could see now, not high enough to hide him. He looked around the cabin and saw Bull approaching, his steps more labored now, as though each leg were filled with lead.

Speed and surprise were Harry's big hopes. He counted on Bull bending over to take off the snowshoes when he came to the clearing. He hoped Bull would loosen his grip on the rifle. Perhaps set it down, but he thought there was little chance of that, especially after discovering the tracks. Bull was looking furtively toward the direction of Harry's cottage and the tracks. Harry thought, if Bull thinks the bogeyman is up there, it will help the surprise.

Surreptitiously, Harry peeked around the corner of the cottage to see the weary but wary traveler make his way to the plowed section of road. Harry glanced over at the manager's cabin, hoping he wouldn't give the game away, hoping the booze had sufficiently enervated him. Hoping.

Bull stood now on the plowed road and paused for a triumphant breath of cold, fresh air. He looked around him three hundred sixty degrees, then concentrated on the cottage at the top of the hill. The one the tracks led to. Harry glided his way to the other side of the cottage, where he would be behind Bull if he bent over to take off the snowshoes and faced his destination.

Harry pulled his gun, took off the safety, pointed his skis toward Bull and at the moment the huge man bent over, Harry pushed off. He would have to push and glide for forty crucial feet. The gun was pointed at Bull's back, but Harry wanted to make no sound until he was closer, with a chance to get the skis off, especially if Bull had taken off the snowshoes. Perfect timing would be when Bull had taken off one, but not the other. Maximize his awkwardness. He couldn't go anywhere. In the snow he could sink in; in the plowed snow he could barely navigate.

Harry was within ten feet before Bull had straightened and whirled around, and Harry shouted, "Freeze." But Bull didn't freeze. Instead he gripped his rifle and whipped it up to meet Harry, who skied into him, knocking him over while the gun went off, the bullet almost making acquaintance with Harry's scalp.

Harry whipped his pistol at Bull's head, and the loud crack that resulted didn't seem to faze the huge animal panting for air. They grappled in bittersweet burlesque, one man in a pair of long, awkward cross-country skis, the other with one round, stubby snowshoe.

Neither was laughing.

Harry jabbed the pointed end of the ski pole in Bull's midsection and a whoosh of air came tumbling out. Harry thought if he could get his skis off, he would have the advantage, but Bull was not giving him the moment's peace required, and before Harry realized it, the rifle was coming around the side of his head and, ducking, he lost his balance and fell.

Bull, also off balance, recovered and brought the rifle back around, and Harry deflected it momentarily with the ski pole. Unhappily he realized the bull was not having the same compunctions about shooting him.

Harry got a quick jab with his pole in Bull's groin and caught him off balance enough to grab hold of the rifle barrel, twist and pull it to throw Bull completely off his balance and bring him down on top of Harry.

Bull was grunting and snorting, and Harry cracked the pistol across his throat, causing a desperate gurgling sound to escape, followed by a trickle of blood, but not relieving him of any of the weight of the black man.

Using his rifle barrel as a rod, Bull turned it across Harry's throat and began applying pressure. Harry gasped but no air came. The pistol had wedged under his back and it took all his strength to raise himself enough to free it. All he could think of was the trouble he had gotten himself into by not shooting Bull in the first place. In the back, if necessary. Was this chivalrous to be on the ground under a man choking you to death? He brought the pistol up until the end of the barrel was against Bull's temple.

Bull did not relent; the pressure continued; Harry panicked. He would black out and die. What would become of Lela...? With his last bit of strength he slid the pistol away from Bull's temple and down to his thigh, where he pulled the trigger.

The shot ripped through the big man's leg and knocked him back off Harry, groping at the pain. Harry was sucking in air as fast as he could to restock his oxygen-deprived body with life.

But not fast enough for his animal adversary, who, not sharing Harry's civilized reserve about killing, took his rifle and pointed it at Harry and pulled the trigger.

Harry squirmed just in time. The bullet passed over his head and Harry plowed his shoulder into Bull's gut, in his famous off-tackle play, knocking the big man back into the snow. Harry took his gun and slammed it into Bull's temple. Bull gave a little start, but three more blows to the head were necessary to render him finally unconscious.

Harry caught his breath again and mustered the strength to handcuff Bull's hands behind his back. Then he took off the snowshoe remaining and buckled it and the other one to Bull's belt loops under him and with great effort made the slow and arduous journey back up to his cottage.

After he pulled him up the two front steps and in through the door, he heard Moose groan in ultimate resignation.

Harry dragged Bull into the bathroom and handcuffed him to the exposed water pipe, realizing if Bull were conscious and up to strength, he would easily pull it from the wall. He used a towel and tightened it around the upper thigh to stop the flow of blood. He cleaned the wound with a small washcloth and decided it wasn't too serious: no artery had been severed. When the blood stopped, Harry left Bull in the bathroom and went back to Moose.

"Okay, pal, the game is up. You want to change anything you told me?"

Moose looked hurt. "I tol' you da truth, man."

Harry took some cloth from his bag and tied it around Moose's mouth. Then he blindfolded him. Moose grunted. Harry said, "Moose, I don't want to hear a peep out of you. Bull comes to, I don't want him to know you're here. If he finds out you're here, you're a goner, you understand?"

Terrorized mouth quavering, eyes twitching spastically, Moose nodded. From the backpack Harry took some rope into the bathroom, where he proceeded to tie the unconscious Bull for good measure.

Then Harry sat on the toilet lid and waited, thinking. After he thought he knew his next few moves, Harry hastened Bull's reawakening by dousing his face with cold water.

Blinking open, the eyes seemed so childlike. Not the eyes that an hour before had the glazed look of a jaguar bent on a kill.

"Got a message fo' ya," Bull said groggily.

"Better be good," Harry said. "I saved your life just to hear your sweet voice."

"Whistler gonna kill you, you don't get him outta dere alive."

Harry laughed out loud. "Not doing too good so far," he said. "How's Lela?"

"She ain't good."

Harry's body tightened. This was not the news he got from Moose, but Bull seemed more eager to talk.

"What's the matter with her?"

"Got a pretty bad beatin' from Whistler."

"Why?"

"Dunno," he shook his head as if to say, the less I know, the better I like it. "She sick too."

"What?"

"Dunno what. Kinda bad cold. Pneumonia maybe. We been havin' it rough. No food. Say, you wouldn't happen to have a little sompin' I could eat, would ya?"

"Sure do, Bull, and I'm going to feed you, just as soon as I get some more answers."

Bull's childlike eyes lighted up. His tongue ran across his lips in abandoned anticipation.

"Who's left up there? At the cabin?"

"Jest Whistler an' Miss Wills."

"What's this 'Miss Wills' stuff?" Harry pressed.

"Nothin'. Only Whistler's name fo' her. Called her dat. Liked it better. That's 'fo' he beat her pretty bad. Doan call her nothin' now but 'dat slut.'"

Harry stiffened and felt his fist bunching. Then he relaxed. Mustn't blame the messenger for the message, he thought.

"Who was Miss Wills?" Harry asked. "Where did he get the name?"

"Some history teacher or sompin'."

Harry remembered the story vaguely. Attempted rape. No charges brought. God, if the savage did that to Lela... Harry jumped up.

"Hey, man, da food. Where you goin'? You gonna get me da food?"

"When I get back."

"Back?"

"Yeah. I'm going to get Miss Wills out of there."

"Hey, no, man. Doan do dat you wanna see her livin' 'gain. Whistler he a mad dog when Moose didn't come back. He knows it's yo' work, Harry. He knows it's you. Da cops woulda circled the house wid da bullhorn an' all dat shit. He know."

"Moose could have gotten lost, frozen to death, lot of things could have happened."

Bull nodded. "Could. But now I don't come back, he know it's you. He know you, Harry. He gonna kill dat girl. You jest ain't got no chance. He glad to die, he see dat girl dead first. Dat's my message. He up dere right now wid a gun at dat girl head. And she ain't none too strong nohow seein's we been out of food last few days, and Whistler he ain't give her none. Water's all she get. An' da pipes is froze and dat snow melt slow, so they ain't too much dat."

"What about those tapes you sent? Lela sounded happy. She's on the floor with a gun at her head?"

"Moose done dat. Real good wid tapes. 'Course, she was a lot friendlier befo' Whistler beat her like dat."

"I'll be back to feed you, pal."

"Not if you go near that cabin, you ain't. Man, gimme little just in case you don't make it back. I could starve to death before anybody find me here. Where you got Moose? You kill him?"

Harry stared down at the cringing figure. "Just pray I make it back," he said, and left, taking the key from the inside of the bathroom door and locking it from the outside. He picked up his supplies—the telescopic rifle and binoculars—and, after checking Moose, went out and locked the door from the outside and put on his skis and began the trek to the lookout point near the cabin.

When he got there he realized he could go closer this time because Whistler wouldn't be coming after him. He skied through the trees and got to where, with the help of his binoculars, he could make out the dark figure of Whistler through the windows. Suddenly the figure made a jerking movement and Harry instinctively sought cover behind a tree.

The front door of the cabin opened and Whistler came out on the porch, dragging a heap of rags at his feet. It took Harry a moment to realize the heap of dirty rags was his Lela. Whistler was pointing a pistol at her brain and holding her as a shield for his own safety.

"I know you're out there, Harry," he screamed. All of the calm grace that snowed the police brass on the tapes was gone. Not a trace of the contrite, humble Whistler who appeared in court vowing to turn a new leaf and who, more often than not, got through to the judges. Now he was a rabid dog: hungrily salivating, eyes sunken in fear and hunger, hanging on by the one thread of barter still left to him: the girl he was holding up like a limp rag doll in front of him.

The morning sun glistened on the sparkling snow surrounding the house like melting cotton candy. There was no sun under the big, bare trees where Harry stood, and he felt himself tremble with the biting cold. He could still feel his wounds from the beating Whistler's boys had given him.

"I know you're out there, Harry, I can smell you from here. What you done with my boys? You waste 'em, Harry? I got your girl here, Harry. You be careful." Whistler squinted into the sunlight.

"Now hear me, Harry, and hear me good! You get me some food and you get me safe passage outta here an' you get the girl back– what's left of her."

Harry could see the pistol trembling at Lela's temple. He prayed it would not go off, though it looked like Whistler had little control. Harry looked through the telescopic sight of the rifle and fixed the cross hairs on the middle of Whistler's forehead. He could get a clean shot, he thought, but Whistler might pull the trigger, either voluntarily or involuntarily, and that would be the end of Lela. Besides, Whistler was jerking around too much and Harry was liable to miss. Harry could not put any hope in Whistler's will to live. He thought he still had a shred of it, but Bull said he didn't care. Perhaps he was right.

"You get me some food now," Whistler screamed. "You hear me, Harry?" Harry didn't answer. "You get me some food now or I gonna have to eat me some pussy." He shook Lela in front of him, like a quavering leaf in the wind. Whistler peered out into the desolate snow-covered woods.

"Okay, listen up here, Harry Horseshid," his voice cackled hysterically, "I know you're out there, I can see that shit-ugly face, don't try to jive me. And get this straight, muthafukker, I'm wasting this no-good bitch, then I'm layin' on the sword like them samurais Miss Wills told me about done, before I'm giving up to you. Now you send my boys back here with some food, or you ain't never seeing this here filly alive."

Whistler shook the rag doll at his side. Harry thought he heard her whimper.

"And I don't want to see your ugly mug anywhere near here, you hear? You come back here and I'm wasting the bitch. Then'll just be you against me to the end. 'S all right with me. I always dreamed of a showdown with you, Harry."

Harry considered his options: the benefit of remaining silent versus confronting the hysteric. It was a close call for him, but he finally came down on the side of speaking, reasoning that a man losing his grasp, as Whistler seemed to be doing, might respond better to the voice of authority, no matter how hated, than to uncertainty.

Harry's voice boomed through the woods as though it had been acoustically designed to maximize its impact. "Okay, Whistler, you misunderstand one thing–you are trapped in the woods and you are starving. You aren't in the driver's seat any more. I found you. Your boys are all right. Eating a lot better than you are. Just surrender now and you'll be eating too in ten minutes."

A low, guttural response built in Whistler until the pitch raised to a hyena laugh, eerily piercing the still woods.

Lela cried out a weak, "Harry, Har..." before Whistler clapped his flat hand over her mouth.

Whistler's body shook on the porch, his feeble fist shaking the pistol, his other hand covering the trembling mouth of Harry's beloved Lela. The gaunt figure of death, ranting, raving, empty, and yet presiding with a strange, undeniable power over the very life he seemed to reject.

"I'm going, Whistler. You take good care of that girl, you hear? I'll get some food back to you, but if Lela is harmed *in any way*, you'll be the sorriest man on this earth."

"Horseshid!"

"Next to you, Charlie Rubenstein will have had a peaceful death."

With a flourish of more strength than should have been left in him, Whistler Wagner backed through the door, dragging the lifeless girl behind him.

Harry heard the crack of the door slamming. He turned on his skis and returned to the cottage.

Day 41

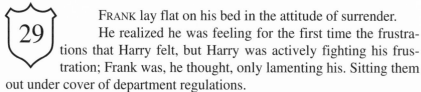

FRANK lay flat on his bed in the attitude of surrender.

He realized he was feeling for the first time the frustrations that Harry felt, but Harry was actively fighting his frustration; Frank was, he thought, only lamenting his. Sitting them out under cover of department regulations.

He had gone through the motions the last three days: gone to work, sat, stared into space, and gone home again to lie down next to his father's gun. Today he lasted only a couple hours, told them he was sick, and left. No one questioned him.

Slowly, with less resolve than he had hoped, his hand groped the night table for the gun. He curled his fingers around the butt and brought it over to his head.

Los Angeles was overcast that day and the gray gloom penetrated Frank's spirit. "Wrong, wrong," he muttered. "I've been wrong." His finger felt the cold curved trigger.

The sound shot stridently through the quiet bedroom, piercing the silence of death. The telephone was ringing.

The only telephone in the mountain cottages was in the manager's cottage, and Harry didn't want any eavesdropping, so he went to the general store.

The old-fashioned enclosed booth stood outside the entrance to the store, which looked to Harry like a photographic blow-up of a miniature general store: everything neatly in place, unmoved, without any internal animation.

He stood in the booth, shifting from one foot to the other to warm himself, and listened to the rings. When he was impatient for an answer to his calls, he would pick up counting the rings after five or six had gone by, estimating generously how many there had been. He began doing so now. Twelve, thirteen, fourteen, he counted in unvarying, monotonous rhythm. "Frank," he screamed into the phone. "Frank, it's Harry, answer the phone, Frank." Seventeen, eighteen, he banged his palm on the black instrument, hung on the corner of the booth. He counted thirty-five rings before he hung up and put in a call to the police headquarters building, special gang detail.

In a falsetto voice, Harry said, "I've been raped by a gang–would that be the gang detail or the rape squad?"

"I'll connect you," said a timidly officious voice. You never knew when the outrageous calls were serious.

"Special gang detail, Conahan speaking."

"Yeah, Conahan, Frank Eberhart there?"

"I'm sorry, sir, he isn't here, may I leave a message for him?"

"You seen him?"

"No, sir."

"Anybody there seen him?"

"Just a minute, please." There were muffled voices and Lt. Abrams got on the phone. "Frank went home, may I help you?"

"Home? I called him at home. He's not at home." Harry was dancing faster now, the excitement of talking to someone who had seen Frank agitated his movements.

"Listen, I saw him leave. I was right here when he left, and he said he was going home."

"How long ago?"

"Maybe an hour. Maybe he stopped off for a few beers." Abrams laughed. They both knew that Frank would never do that. "Hey, Harry, is that you? Harry? Where are you?"

Harry got nervous. He didn't want the call traced, he didn't want SWAT and the helicopters, but he needed help. "Harry, let me have your number, I'll have him call you. Harry?"

"Tell him Harry Clymer called, will you?" Harry was disguising his voice. "His pinochle buddy, we got a game tonight." Harry hung up.

Immediately, he picked up the phone again and dialed Frank's home number, which he had memorized.

He started counting at eight rings, saying to himself, eleven, twelve. Harry slapped the black box again, as though some genie inside, if awakened, could summon up Frank.

Eighteen, nineteen, twenty. "Frank," he yelled. "Frank, answer it. Please, God, let Frank be at home. Frank. I need you, Frank. I can't do it without you." Such were the depths of his despair that Harry asked, for the first time in his life, for help.

He stopped counting in the mid-twenties, while he tried to think of his alternatives if Frank could not be reached. Every suggestion he made himself he rejected as being too dangerous for Lela. And yet he couldn't wait forever, she was up there starving to death with a madman who very easily could kill her for food.

"Thirty-three, thirty-four," he said, guessing. He decided he would let it ring until Frank answered or the phone company came to disconnect the phone. He might be in the shower, out in his yard, painting his house for the twenty-seventh time. Harry would just wait.

He was testing and rejecting alternative courses of action when the ringing stopped. The groggy, dispirited voice on the other end said, "'Lo," and Harry didn't recognize it.

"Frank? Is that you, Frank?" Harry said, trying to understand. Had he really counted over seventy-five rings? Does persistence pay, or was this a wrong number after all that?

"Yeah."

"Frank, you sound half-dead. Are you all right?"

Tiny ripples curled Frank's lips. The insistent ringing of the phone had sucked him back from the whirlpool of indifference that had made him caress the pistol. He released the grip now. He thought after so many rings it must be about Lela.

"I found her, Frank."

Frank leapt out of bed, instantly a new man. "Where? Harry, where are you?"

"Hold on, Frank. I've got conditions."

"Anything, Harry. Anything you say."

"I need you, Frank. I need you, you understand? I can't do it alone. I found her but I can't get her out. But if you bring anyone else, it'll blow it. You must come alone, get me, Frank?"

"Anything, Harry. *Anything*. Tell me where."

Harry gave him directions. "Frank, I'll be watching. If there's any sign of anyone else, helicopters, any other car, all bets are off."

"Trust me, Harry. Your way, sure. How is she?"

"She's alive, Frank. I can't talk any more. Put on the siren. Get here as fast as you can. Turn it off when you get to Arrowhead. I don't want anybody out here alerted."

"Harry..."

"Yeah."

"I love you, Harry..."

He broke the connection and returned to the cabin to feed his prisoners and wait.

Frank drove the first ten miles in seven minutes flat. The siren screaming above him gave him a euphoric feeling of rebirth. Funny, he thought, regulations would suggest only a red light in this circumstance perhaps, but Harry said turn on your siren and I turned it *on*.

On the seat beside him, Lela's warmest wool overcoat. Dear Lord, thank you for that call. Harry was right. Harry got the pigeon. The FBI and the cops, we fell all over our procedures, but Harry triumphed. Harry, oh, Harry. You got the pigeon! And Harry was big enough to call me in. Could he have known how close I was to not answering the phone? Suppose Harry had only the patience of the average person and hung up the phone after five to ten rings. Frank didn't want to think of that now. Harry had helped him overcome it. Unorthodox Harry. Insubordinate Harry. Troublesome Harry. Freewheeling, wild, undisciplined Harry. And Frank. What of Frank? he asked himself. The man so secure in his procedures. A man so cocky his latest failure almost killed him. It was the last straw. Revenge. He never cared for it. But now his thoughts segued to the backyard behind his tiny house in South Pasadena. Lela was eight years old. She was seated at a small table with two of her dolls, having a tea party. She was dressed in one of her mother's dresses, with high-heeled shoes that kept falling off her feet, and she asked her father a question that stunned him with the strange maturity he read into it.

He was painting the house for the umpteenth time. He had painted it less than a year earlier, but it was his most effective therapy. His neighbors thought he was crazy. He didn't argue the point, merely told them he was too poor to go to a psychiatrist.

"Daddy," she addressed him. He could see the little table, the huge floppy black dress–out of season in the hazy sun–the dolls. The plastic tea set. Lela pouring with one hand, pushing up the shoulder of the dress with the other.

"What, Lela?" he answered.

Lela sipped her imaginary tea. "Didn't you love Mommy?" she asked.

"Why, Lela, what makes you ask that? I loved Mommy and you more than anybody in the world."

"Then why don't you kill the man that killed her?"

Frank looked in amazement at the child he loved so much. Where do these little things get their ideas? he wondered. He laid the stirring stick across the top of the paint can and glided over, in a dream, to where she sat.

He crouched down and placed his head gently on her arm. "Lela," he said, "nothing we do will bring Mommy back. If we killed him, there would be two people dead instead of one. He didn't want to kill her. He was drunk. It must be terribly hard for him to have to live with the memory that he caused someone's death."

Now, fourteen years later, the siren was screeching and he was going to her. He remembered that scene as he so often had, not only every word, but every detail of the setting, down to the pink floral pattern on the plastic tea set. And word had just gotten to Frank that the man had wiped out a young family of four on the San Diego Freeway near Carson.

He knew you couldn't just murder manslaughter convicts, but if he had, these four young people with a whole glorious life before them might have lived it. Maybe even a jail sentence would have taught him something.

Frank was climbing the mountain now, taking the curves with reckless panache. Harry had called him. He needed him, he said. Harry needed him, and Harry had the pigeon.

Day 41

30 | THE sound of the snow bending and breaking beneath Frank's feet was the sweetest sound he had ever heard, because every difficult plodding step brought him closer to his daughter. The sun was strong and friendly to the travelers: Frank on Moose's snowshoes and Harry on his long, thin, white Nordic skis, with the red and blue roosters on the tips. The sun in the sky was three quarters of the way home. It was unhindered by clouds or leaves on the trees and made the snow sparkle. Everything felt fresh and clean.

All Frank could think of, besides staying on his feet, was seeing his daughter. He knew how crucial it was to get his part of it right. Harry had impressed him with the danger and risks. Harry was pulling a new plastic red saucer, with two brown-paper bags, the wool coat Frank brought for Lela and the telescopic rifle. It was this big, round saucer they hoped to bring Lela out with. Frank felt secure in Harry's strong presence, but soon he would be alone, and for Lela's sake he could not misstep.

Harry had been waiting for him and, after he satisfied himself Frank came alone, they set out immediately. Harry wanted to catch the daylight. The setting sun would act as a spotlight on the front porch of the cabin and perhaps momentarily blind Whistler. And there would be no moon after dark. Whistler could disappear into the woods with Lela and in their famished condition they would probably both die of exposure. Harry had thought of everything, Frank said to himself. Frank's respect for Harry had quickly moved from grudging to groveling. Harry was getting the pigeon.

Harry gave Frank the plan while they were en route. They were going down the clearing in the trees that served as the road. Before the road turned to wind up the hill to the cabin, they would have to take as much cover as they could get from the bare trees so as not to spoil the timing of the plan. Whistler must be, Harry said, presented with a *fait accompli.*

Harry noticed Frank was breathing hard. "Frank, baby, you're in rotten shape. Too many years driving a desk."

Frank smiled his thin, tight smile. "Can't argue that. But you're looking at a guy who has only seen snow twice in his life. You expect an Olympic champion? I've never even seen snowshoes before, let alone tried to stay up on them."

"Worry about that later. Let's just get to the cabin before we analyze how hard the trip was."

"But I gotta have a rest, Harry. I'm sorry. I...I, geez, I can hardly lift my feet."

"Come on, it isn't too far. We gotta have that sun."

Breathing heavily, Frank came to a full stop and sat on a fallen tree, leaning his body back against the trunk, then bending forward, his head at his legs, to avoid fainting.

Harry looked at him with that disapproving look. "Hey, Frank boy, we can't be quitters."

"Just give me a minute, will you, Harry?" he pleaded. "I'll make it, I just need a minute." Frank drew in huge gobs of the cold air. It made him light-headed. "Oh, man," he said, his breathing deeper and slower, "the last time I've even *seen* snow was about eighteen years ago. After Ellen died I brought Lela up here for a weekend and we made a snowman and had snowball wars. We even built a snow fort. I mean, you might look like the Abominable Snowman, but I never was much of an athlete. Maybe you got the wrong guy for this job," he said in an afterthought.

"I got the right guy. Now let's go."

"Okay, okay," Frank stood up. "Just let me ask you one more thing before we go."

"What's that?" It was clear to Frank that Harry wasn't interested in talk.

"If this doesn't turn out to be exactly what we both hope...I mean," Frank continued with great difficulty, "I mean, if Lela..." He looked at Harry, who showed he understood. "I hope he didn't touch her, Harry, but I guess that's not a realistic hope."

Harry tensed. He felt the little box with the ring bulging in his pocket. He considered showing it to Frank, but decided he couldn't explain it.

Harry saw the tears forming in Frank's eyes.

"Think of what she's been through," Frank was pleading with a calm sorrow now.

Harry considered the unspoken horror.

"Harry, you're not answering me," Frank said. "I gotta have your promise, Harry. If I don't come out of this alive, I've got to have your promise you'll be good to her. You'll look out for her. If you can't marry her, you'll have to promise to be a father to her until she's out of danger. You yourself would do anything to survive. God knows all the laws you broke to bring us here today, and you know I'm not complaining, Harry, I'm eternally grateful to you."

"Shut up, Frank," Harry said finally, unable to take any more. "You see me here, don't you? Now let's move it."

Frank smiled. He stepped with new hope. He watched Harry, ahead of him, pull the red saucer with the long rope and he felt, finally, secure. If anything ever happened to him, even if Harry couldn't marry an unchaste girl, he would look out for her. Frank would go to his grave, if he had to, with a clear conscience that he had seen to his duty to the last.

For the rest of the journey Frank rehearsed his part, in the hope that if he didn't let Harry down, Harry would not let him down.

Before long, they turned off the road and into the shelter of the trees, and the going slowed. The trip on snowshoes took considerably longer than it took Harry to ski, and the sun was sinking in the western sky, but still, mercifully, a little above the treetops.

When they finally reached their destination, fifty yards from the house and diagonally in front of it, Harry handed Frank one of the bags from the red plastic saucer and squeezed his upper arm.

"Go get 'em, Frank. Any questions?"

Frank shook his head. He didn't trust himself to say anything more. He turned and made his way out on the road to find cover behind the parked, buried car.

Harry moved into his position, where he could see the back and side of the house. Frank could see the front and other side from his position.

"Whistler!" Frank called out.

The sun drenched the front porch, like a proscenium arch in a myriad of spotlights. The snow under the trees was crusty and firm. The sun sparkled on the snow on the buried driveway, dancing here and there and melting a few unique unshaded flakes into ordinary droplets.

"Whistler," Frank yelled louder. "Come on out, Whistler, it's Frank Eberhart. You're safe with me, Whistler. Come on out."

He thought he saw some movement inside the house, but nothing happened. Perhaps they went out the back, as Harry thought they might, but Harry was covering the back and he heard nothing.

"Whistler. It's Frank Eberhart," he shouted again. "I brought you some food."

The front door flew open, making a cracking sound as it bounced off the wall like a ricocheting bullet. Frank swallowed a startled cry at the sight of his daughter being dragged in front of the undernourished Frankenstein figure, her feet stumbling and unsteady under her weak legs. He almost didn't recognize her with her hair dyed and now disheveled and the unfamiliar gabardine suit and strange smudged make-up. Lela never wore makeup. Was it really she, or had he killed her already and found a dummy substitute?

Harry moved up to where he could get a clear shot of the front porch. He raised the rifle and looked through the telescopic sight and settled the cross hairs on Whistler's forehead.

Whistler was holding the pistol to Lela's temple, and Harry realized again a shot would not be possible without the chance of the pistol going off and a bullet tearing through Lela's brain.

Whistler was heaving his breath as if he were in the first stages of an epileptic fit. The sun was in his eyes. "Where are you?" he screeched. "I don't see you."

"Down here, Whistler. Behind the car. I'm not armed."

"What do you want?"

"I brought you some food."

"What for? You a friend of mine? Where my boys? Where my Bull and Moose?"

"They're safe, Whistler, they're alive. This is me, Whistler, Frank. I'm a book man, Whistler. You're not talking to Harry now."

"Where's Harry?" Whistler yelled, tightening his grip on Lela in a reflex to his mentioning the name.

"Harry's not in this. Your boys got hungry. It was easy to lure them away. I suppose you know about that, Whistler."

"What's that?"

"You know about the power you can get from feeding someone who's hungry. You won't be hurt, Whistler, but the game is up. You can't run anywhere. The nearest food is miles from here, and you'd starve to death before you got anywhere in this snow. You sink in to your knees with every step." Frank's voice was starting to go hoarse from yelling. He began to fear he wouldn't be understood much longer. "Now leave the gun and come on down here and let me give you some food."

Whistler's eyes grew as he stared into the sunlight. His tongue

257

ran slowly across his lips. "What you got?" he asked, weakening.

"I got all your favorites, Whistler. But you come on down here, I'd like to talk to you."

Harry marveled at Frank's finesse. He did it so well. "Like to talk to you." Harry would have said, "Get down here, Whistler, I *want* to talk to you." But Frank made everyone feel important. It was as though Whistler would be doing him a favor by obliging. "Like to talk to you," just like he was talking to someone important. Requesting, not ordering.

"What you got?" Whistler repeated, as though in his ravenous state it made the slightest difference what the food was. He was buying time. Trying to make up his mind on his evaporating options.

"I got all your favorites. I got salted peanuts, I got potato chips. Hot dogs. Coke. I got vanilla ice cream, an' bacon."

"Lemme see it," Whistler said, keeping the pistol to Lela's temple. Lela's eyes were barely open; Frank couldn't be sure she was still alive. He picked up the bag and opened it, taking out the can of Planter's peanuts, then the ice cream, and with a slow, deliberate routine brought out every item, as if to convince Whistler he had nothing to fear from a man who moved so slowly.

Whistler had one more question: "Where's Harry?"

"Whistler, you got nothing to fear from Harry. I'm here, I don't even know where Harry is now. You want me to go look for him, I will, but I'm taking the food or the girl with me. You decide."

Whistler licked his lips again, then looked at the semiconscious girl. All of a sudden he started laughing like a sick hyena, a burst of high-pitched lascivious laughter, followed by desperate gasps for air.

"You give Harry my message, man?"

"Sure, Whistler, I'll tell Harry anything you want me to when I see him. But Harry's not here. He knows he couldn't handle you. You're too much for Harry."

Harry had a clearer shot now. He might be able to do it. Whistler did not seem to be concentrating on his pistol as much.

The thin animal on the proscenium bathed in spotlights was giving his command performance. A one-man show with only incidental props to assist him in his triumph.

"You tell Harry," he began, his voice crackling like a discordant trumpet rising to the shrillest high notes, sourly out of tune but fortissimo, "tell Harry I fucked her!" The sounds came back down the scale in a crackling, air-sucking giggle while he shook the rag doll of a girl as though he were conducting some ghostly orchestra.

Harry tensed on the trigger. The gun in Whistler's hand was no longer pointed at Lela's temple but hanging ineffectually at his side. Whistler was jumping so nervously that he was afraid Lela would be pulled in the path of the bullet, and he didn't shoot.

Frank swallowed hard at the news and pinched his eyes for a moment, then, to control himself, took a deep breath of the chilly air.

The sun was sinking. The apparition on the porch was still performing. He shook Lela again. "You tell Harry his girl was a virgin, but she ain't no more!"

Whistler looked at Lela, his chest heaving with exhaustion. "Weren't no good though," he said, shaking her savagely then dropping her at his feet and bounding down the steps and sinking in to his knees in the snow, the pistol held high.

Harry turned the rifle, the cross hairs on Whistler's ear. Deny it, Lela, he shouted to himself. Deny it. Say it isn't true. Lela said nothing. An easy shot, Harry thought. An easy explanation. He has a pistol in his hand, he was going to shoot Frank. I picked him off just in time. Harry's life's ambition: to put Whistler to rest. A true service to mankind. Surely the worst creature that ever lived. He'll never be punished commensurate with what he did to Lela. It was the same man who defiled his girl that had fingered the death of his best friend.

But Harry couldn't do it. Whistler was sunk in the snow, weakened. His pistol wasn't pointed at anyone. Give the courts a chance at him first. That was the law. It was some new, invisible force talking to Harry now. The dim, distant echo of the ghost of Lela past, saying, "You mustn't be God, Harry. Do your duty and let God do his." His love for Lela had consumed and softened him.

His eyes focused on the motionless lump on the porch now. He thought of all the police manuals that said the safety of the victim was paramount. It was a regulation brought home to Harry with chilling conviction now as he abandoned his friend and partner, Frank, to steal around the back of the cabin, where he took off his skis and went through the door Whistler had left unlocked for quick escape, in through the tidy kitchen, untouched since Moose left, and through the living room, carrying under his arm the bag and the overcoat.

Outside, Frank was telling Whistler, in that fatherly tone of his, that he would have to drop the pistol.

"I'm unarmed, Whistler, and you know police regulations as well as I do. It is absolutely forbidden to send an unarmed man to negotiate the release of a hostage unless the place is surrounded with armed cops."

Whistler looked up from his buried legs as though he hadn't thought of that.

Frank went on gently. "So come and get the food and I'll take you in like I promised. I'm not armed," he said, wondering at his sudden ability to lie in the face of another human being, something he could never do before. "You'll get a fair trial, Whistler. I wouldn't doubt some of those high-powered lawyers of yours might even beat the rap. You know the good old U.S. Money talks in court, and nobody can ever accuse you of being poor, Whistler." Frank spoke from the inadequate cover of the half-buried car.

Whistler was considering. He had an easy shot at Frank from here. He'd seen the food. But if the place were surrounded, what would be the point?

"You can shoot me easy, Whistler," Frank said. "But you won't make another six inches without fifteen bullets in your body."

"I ain't giving you no gun of mine," Whistler said, begging to have the last defiant word.

Frank nodded. "That's okay, Whistler, just throw it in the snow somewhere."

Whistler looked back at Frank. Frank put both his arms in the air. Such an honest face, Whistler thought. A sincere man. Looked like a strict book man. A guy you could beat if you had an out, but if you didn't, he'd get you sure as God made little green apples. And here he was, Whistler chuckled out loud, and where was that asshole Harry? God, he was glad it was Frank he could surrender to. And with the place surrounded, Harry couldn't touch him.

He threw the gun as far as he could and it hit the snow and sank in. His nervous cackle bubbled forth again. Frank smiled and remained immobile. "Come and get your chow, man."

Harry moved stealthily to the front porch.

Whistler renewed his effort, lifting one leg at a time, the other sunken in the snow to the kneecap, until he reached Frank and tore into the bag of groceries while Frank stood off and watched him.

Harry was crouched on the porch. He huddled Lela to his arms and took her inside, where, with his strong arm cradling the back of her head, he put the thermos of soup to her wordless lips. He was surprised at how almost weightless Lela had become. She drank from the thermos gratefully not greedily.

Harry wrapped the warm coat about her thin shoulders. "I'm going to take you out of here as soon as you're ready," Harry said, "and I promise you I'll see that no harm comes to you again as long as I live."

"Oh, Harry," she murmured after she finished the soup, and sank back, releasing her weight to his arms, satisfied. So satisfied she felt. "I love you, Harry," she said simply. "I love you so. My thoughts about you kept me alive." She dropped her head sheepishly. "I didn't think you'd still love–"

"Sh," Harry said, covering her lips gently with a finger. "We won't talk about it now." Out of his pocket came the little box from Dimwidee and Seafurth. He opened it and slipped the ring on the finger where Whistler's bigger ring had once been.

"Oh, Harry." She put her weak arms around him and gave him a powerless hug. Tears formed in her eyes. "Oh, Harry," she muttered over and over. He looked at her new face and wiped the strange makeup off with his handkerchief, never wavering his glance from her pale, wan, weak, thin, innocent, beautiful, endearing smile; the words tumbling through his brain like bullets from his gun.

And then she told him she was still his. Still pure, unsullied, untouched even. But she had been ready, she said, and willing: to save her life for one more chance with Harry. He told her he loved her and they dissolved in each other's arms, oblivious of Frank and Whistler, outside, until they heard the shot.

She gave a little hiccup of a start. "Daddy," she gulped.

Harry leapt up and ran out of the house, his gun drawn.

Whistler was halfway through the half-gallon of vanilla ice cream–having demolished the peanuts, half the potato chips, two Cokes and three hot dogs–when he saw the gun hanging loosely in Frank's hand.

His first thought had been to confront him with a "Hey, man, you said you unarmed," but then he thought better of it. Better to catch the old guy off guard. They's no troops 'round here else they'd have come an' closed in on me. He hadn't even bothered to look back at the house. Lela was erased from his mind the moment he dropped her to make his way to the food.

Harry was castigating himself for leaving Frank alone. Another fallacy of the regulations, he thought: abandon your fellow officer in deference to the well-being of the victim.

He sank into the snow at the foot of the steps and found movement frustratingly restrained. He couldn't see anyone and feared Frank was face down in the snow while Whistler was safe under cover of the trees, the pistol in his hand. And here I am, a sitting duck for him.

Lela was starting down the porch. Harry yelled for her to stay back in the house. She didn't hear him or understand him. She kept coming.

Harry found him off to the side of the car, in a few feet of trees. There was a deathly smile on those thin, unruffled lips.

The gun hung limply from his right hand, beyond rejuvenation. The tall, thin black man lay face down in the snow at Frank's feet.

The words uttered were not by the old Frank Eberhart but by some new person–a startling unshackled spirit, an unfamiliar demon-saint.

All he said was, "Resisting arrest."

Harry fell on Frank and hugged him. In a moment Lela plowed her way through the snow and threw her weak arms around both of them, and the three of them held on to each other in love, loyalty and life itself.

EPILOGUE

DEAR *Ellen,*

Just a quick line to tell you this will be my last letter. I suppose if anyone knew I wrote you these letters they'd cart me off in a straitjacket, but when the going got rough and I had no one to turn to, it seemed to ease the pain. Not much different than saying "Dear Diary," I rationalized.

I have one last confession to make, Ellen. I lied when I said Whistler Wagner was resisting arrest when I shot him. I had an awful time convincing the brass that I shot Whistler. They were all dead sure Harry did it. After that, the resisting-arrest story went down easily.

I don't know what came over me, but when he stood so close to me– slopping up the junk food like an animal–and I remembered him on that porch shouting he had ruined our poor, sweet daughter, I went to pieces inside. Everything came to a head at once. Maybe it was the vanilla ice cream he was eating–made me think of the white wedding gown I'd pictured, the beautiful, unspoiled child grown into a lovely young woman. Maybe it was Lela's childhood question about why I hadn't killed the man who killed you. I just looked deep into his crazed eyes and brought my gun up and I never flinched, just pulled the trigger. He just looked at me, startled, the half-eaten box of vanilla ice cream in hand. Didn't think I could do it, I suppose. Well, until that moment, I didn't either.

And the other boy, the one who killed you, is serving some time in jail for his thoughtless murdering of a family of four with his treacherous automobile and uncontrolled drinking. Why do we give them all a second chance? Most of them seem to take it.

Well, I got my wish to live to see Lela married. She mar-

ried Harry and they are as happy as clams. Remind me a lot of you and me, Ellen. It would make you so happy.

There wasn't anyone happier at the wedding than Mrs. Maude Johnson. She sat there beaming and transfixed, her head bobbing, as if to some inner music. Even her grandson Luke came. Harry has been working with him, encouraging and financing trade school, where he is learning to be a plumber's helper. Harry is using the money that Luke's sister B.J. is sending to him monthly.

The brass knuckled to public pressure on Harry Schlacter. The press really played Harry up big–almost like a Cinderella story, Harry finding Lela when the cops couldn't. So to save that embarrassment, the department just made believe he was working undercover for them all the time and cracked the spectacular case under their guidance. Harry was so delighted to have his job back, he didn't say "boo." For a change, the public outcry helped him. I guess life has its compensations.

Though the department reconsidered and absolved Harry of any wrongdoing in the Rex Adams shooting, Adams' widow got something like three-point-two million for her "loss." They were willing to sweep the Badeye incident under the rug because, by now, the public had had a bellyful of the Whistler Wagner outrage.

Of course, the real irony is that Harry's so afraid Lela will be left a widow, he has refused all street work and is now comfortably tied to a desk in Internal Affairs. He seems to love it. He still goes after everything one hundred percent, and they are giving him a lot of cases where cops have shot citizens.

Lela is back teaching school in Watts. The children adore her, as we all do. She puts her whole heart and soul into her job. Reminds me a lot of Harry that way.

I pray she will continue to be safe there. Four LAPD cops are on trial for using too much force on a parole-violating felon who led them on a one hundred fifteen mph chase. He refused to submit to arrest and they had a devil of a time subduing him.

Someone caught part of it on videotape–and part of that has been played on television, ad nauseam. But they didn't *show the part where this con charges the cops.*

People were outraged to see cops in action. People have become experts on police procedures in front of the TV, without ever being out on the streets at three a.m. to smell the fear.

I'm getting a much different slant on police work myself, now that I've taken street duty. I can see why Harry's view was so different than the police view. I guess you really have to be there to know...

It's a tough time to be a cop.

Now that Harry's a desk jockey, he thinks the boys used excessive force. Now that I'm in the street, I don't think so. And it used to be the other way around. Life is so much a matter of perspective.

Anyway, we are all praying the verdicts won't cause a riot.

I have another bit of news, Ellen. Now that Lela is settled, I found myself a nice woman and we're going to be married tomorrow. I got tired of rattling around this old house alone, and today was my last day of loneliness. She's a wonderful woman, Ellen, I know you'd like her. She was Lela's glee club director at Pasadena City College and she took care of her mother till the dear old soul died at eighty-nine, so she's never been married. Her name is Jane Green. Isn't that a beautiful, simple name? We should have a long and happy life together if the age of her mother is any indication, but I just wanted you to understand why I won't be writing to you any more. You'll still be in my thoughts, of course, but I'll have other duties now.

Oh, by the way, Lela and Harry are expecting their first. I hope it's a girl.

Frank sat back at his small varnished desk and looked at the letter. I can't close with "all my love" any more, he thought. What can I say?

Then he pushed the letter aside. Ah, how ridiculous can you get? If anybody got an inkling of this...

He looked into the backyard and pictured the good times he had there with Ellen, the succeeding years brim full of love with the growing Lela. He thought of how Lela loved the barbecue he made on the little grill, and he had his solution.

With the key from his key ring that never left his waking person, he unlocked the top left drawer. As he pulled the drawer open, letters came bubbling out from every direction.

There were too many in there anyway, Frank assured himself. It was time. Then he emptied the mahogany box from the closet–the extra letters–and the gun. He didn't want to be reminded any longer of his father's suicide. The gun, he would wrap like garbage for the trash. Then he scooped the letters up, gathering each, not without love and respect, but without remorse. Without signing the letter on the desk, he added that to the pile in his hands, then opened the center drawer and took out a pack of matches advertising a local hotel.

He went out into the backyard, lifted the grill on the barbecue and laid the letters to rest under the olive tree. He struck a match and moved it from edge to edge of the myriad of letters, until each edge and corner received the flame. He replaced the grill.

Tomorrow he would scatter the ashes on Ellen's grave. Before the wedding.

He watched the yellow and blue flames encircling his mono-logues, his one-way outpourings of his innermost soul, freeing him from the phantom demons of the past. The flames danced like young children eating love, until there was no more.

Frank's eyes didn't waver from the flickering flame until there was nothing but restless flakes of black ash.

Then he went back into the house, a free man.